Moustache

Praise for *Moustache*

'S. Hareesh's *Moustache* (*Meesha* in the original) is a novel of epic dimensions, deeply rooted in the regional history of Kuttanad. It narrates the history of the social transition of this fertile region in Kerala during colonial times; but it also transcends that history to enter the realm of myth by creating a superhuman being whose elusive and overwhelming presence turns the narrative into a rare fable told in the unique dialect of the region that approaches poetry with its striking images. This novel creates a language within language, and can be placed easily among the most accomplished fictional works in Malayalam. Jayasree Kalathil, the translator, who obviously had a daunting task before her, has captured the nuanced native beauty of the original narrative.'

– K. Satchidanandan

Moustache

A Novel

S. Hareesh

Translated from the Malayalam
by Jayasree Kalathil

HARPERPERENNIAL

An Imprint of HarperCollins *Publishers*

HARPERPERENNIAL

First published in English in India by Harper Perennial 2020
An imprint of HarperCollins *Publishers*
4th Floor, Tower A, Building No. 10, DLF Cyber City,
DLF Phase II, Gurugram, Haryana – 122002
www.harpercollins.co.in

This edition published in India by Harper Perennial 2024

2 4 6 8 10 9 7 5 3 1

Published by arrangement with DC Books

P-ISBN: 978-93-5699-763-9
E-ISBN: 978-93-5357-603-5

Typeset in 10.5/14.3 Adobe Caslon Pro at
Manipal Technologies Limited, Manipal

Printed and bound at
Thomson Press (India) Ltd

FSC www.fsc.org MIX Paper from responsible sources FSC® C010615

This book is produced from independently certified FSC® paper to ensure responsible forest management.

For Achchan

CONTENTS

Author's Note ix

Translator's Note xv

Map of the Kuttanad Region xxi

1 Tricksters 1

2 Madness in the Story 13

3 Ravanan 23

4 Two People 39

5 Kuttathi 50

6 The Ghost Who Begs for Food 63

7 World-Famous Moustache 75

8 Seetha 86

9 Crocodile 99

10 In Search of Seetha 110

11 Birds 122

12 Thanulinga Nadar 131

13 Chella 144

14 Snakes 157

15 Keeper of the Diseased 171

16 An Unlikely Medicine Man 185

17	Ittichan	200
18	Two Other People	216
19	Brendon	231
20	Little Saheb	246
21	The Last Crocodile	260
22	Songs	272
23	A Wrestling Match	284
24	Kattapulavan	298
25	A Holiday Trip	312

AUTHOR'S NOTE

The story of *Moustache* unfolds in Kuttanad, an area that spreads across three districts in the southern state of Kerala, India. It is a delta region formed of five rivers that originate in the Western Ghats and hundreds of tributaries that flow into the longest lake in India, the Vembanad Kayal, which opens into the Arabian Sea near the port of Kochi. It is a waterscape, a region characterised by coastal backwaters, intricate networks of rivers and canals, vast stretches of paddy fields, marshlands, ponds, and oozy black soil. Human inhabitation is confined to the embankments of the fields and compounds connected to them. It is a region of below-sea-level farming, where farmland is created by dredging up the lake bed, and collectively farmed because of the extensive efforts needed. The fields, owned by different people, are formed into 'padasekharam' – collections of fields – by building outer bunds around them. Each of these collections has specific names.

It is common for this land to flood three times a year following the south-west monsoons. In the summer, saltwater from the Arabian Sea surges through the Vembanad Kayal, salinating the waterways and the fields. Farming this land, and everyday life within it, is a constant battle with natural forces. The area is abundant in aquatic flora and fauna. Migratory birds from Siberia and other places arrive here every year in vast numbers. Fishing is another important source of livelihood for the people.

The main events in the novel take place in the first half of the twentieth century. The fallout from the two world wars had an impact on Kuttanad as it did on other places. Kerala, the state where Malayalam is spoken, was then divided into three distinct regions: Malabar in the north, Kochi (Cochin) in the middle, and Thiruvithamkur (Travancore) in the south. While Malabar was ruled directly by the British, Kochi and Thiruvithamkur were ruled by princely kingdoms that accepted British supremacy and submitted to their authority. Kuttanad is at the northern end of Thiruvithamkur; the Vembanad Kayal traverses Kochi and Thiruvithamkur. The novel is set during a period when English education, missionary activities, and social reforms at the local level were causing changes in the social and cultural milieu.

As in other parts of India, the division of society into castes based on rules of pollution and purity existed in Kerala. Caste is still the primary signifier of worth, dignity, and position of people in Kerala. At the time period covered in the story, the impact of caste on everyday life was felt even more acutely. It controlled every aspect of people's lives – the jobs they did, the clothes they wore, the food they ate and who they ate with, how they socialised, who they touched, who they married or had sexual relationships with, the rituals of marriage, birth and death, what and how they worshipped, the type of housing they lived in, etc. Caste rules disallowed people of lower castes from being physically seen by people at the top of the caste hierarchy, and specified the distance people of one caste had to maintain from people of other castes. Caste rules also governed how people of one caste were to speak to those of other castes. Rules of caste required people to be addressed not by their names but by their caste names. Many castes were divided into sub-castes that also observed rules of propriety, pollution and purity. While some upper-caste men engaged in sexual liaisons with women from lower castes, the children born out of these relationships were not accepted as their progeny. Laws were instituted to ensure that the main responsibility of the rulers – the kings – was the welfare of those at the top of the caste hierarchy. Different castes were punished differently for the same crime.

Gender roles, and ideas around masculinity and femininity, were very much determined by caste rules. Caste exerted control over women's lives, especially their sexual lives. Victorian morality, introduced by the British colonists in the nineteenth and twentieth centuries, placed even further restrictions on women. Caste rules required that only Namboothiri women were allowed to cover their breasts. Rules of property inheritance consigned them to living as child brides of men from their castes who were often much older, leaving many young Namboothiri women to a life of widowhood. Nair women, meanwhile, were required to engage in relationships with men of other upper castes who, in other areas of life, did not even consider them to be fully human. Only women from the lower castes enjoyed a level of freedom in choosing their partners and shaping their own sexual lives, even as they were exploited routinely and made to toil for others like slaves.

The eponymous hero of this novel, Vavachan – Moustache – is a Pulayan converted to Christianity. The Pulayan community formed one of the largest groups in Kuttanad, and were predominantly agricultural workers, especially in paddy fields, although some were engaged in fishing. They usually lived in the paddy fields, in huts put up on embankments. Until the end of the eighteenth century, upper-caste landowners treated Pulayans like property and exchanged them along with the land. Missionary activities in Kerala resulted in many of them converting to Christianity. The revolutionary social reformer and anti-caste leader, Ayyankali, who is mentioned in the novel, was born a Pulayan.

The story also features a range of characters from other castes. There are Brahmins at the top of the caste hierarchy, such as the Namboothiris (Kerala Brahmins) who controlled the temples, customs and rituals, as well as a vast proportion of land resources, and influenced the kings and their governmental decisions; and Pattan/Pattar and Aiyer (Brahmin settlers from Tamil Nadu), who occupied most of the top-ranking government jobs to do with administration and taxation of regions and districts, such as those of the Peshkar and the Tehsildar. The royal families were non-Brahmin upper castes known as Kshatriyas, who were mostly born out of sexual relationships with Namboothiri men, and who followed a matrilineal system of inheritance. The novel has several characters belonging to the Nair caste, who were also matrilineal, and its sub-castes such as Pillah, Menon, Kuruppu, etc., who formed a large part of the population. The Nairs wielded, and continue to wield, an enormous amount of political, economic and cultural power in society. Before the British Raj, royal armies were made up of Nairs. They also engaged in farming, and worked as servants of the Brahmins.

Chovan (Ezhava) is another caste that appears prominently in the novel. This was a lower caste community with a large presence in the local population, who engaged primarily in agricultural work and in coconut toddy tapping. Sree Narayana Guru or Guruswamy, who was an important leader of the social reform movement in Kerala, was a member of this caste, and is another historical figure who makes an appearance in the novel.

Then there are the Nadars from southern Thiruvithamkur, traditionally palmyra workers, who, in the novel, assume considerable social power through proximity to the royal family. A range of characters from other castes, defined by the trades they were engaged in or were allowed to do, who formed the Kuttanadan community at the time make appearances: Marar (upper-caste people who did low-level jobs in the temples), Asari (woodworkers and carpenters), Kollan (blacksmiths and iron workers), Thattan (goldsmiths), Vaniyaan (oil makers and sellers), Velakkithala Nair (barbers of the upper caste), Vaathi (barbers of the lower caste), Velan (washermen), Parayan (agricultural workers and leather workers), Vaalan and Arayan (fisherfolk), Ulladan (nomadic people) and so on.

Another community represented in the novel is that of the Christians. Most histories trace the origin of Kerala Christians – known as Syrian Christians or Nasrani Christians – to the activities of St. Thomas the Apostle. In this novel, the characters with the caste name Mappila are Christians. Agriculture and trade were their main occupations, and there were a considerable number of landowners among them. Most took pride in the fact that they were upper-caste Hindus who had converted to Christianity.

The novel also has a key character, Ezhuthachan, who is from Malabar. Ezhuthachans were traditionally teachers, and is a caste not usually present in Kuttanad. There were also a small number of Muslims and settlers from Goa speaking the Konkani language in Kuttanad.

At the time Vavachan's story unfolds, the bulk of the paddy fields in Kuttanad belonged to the temples and the Brahmins. Syrian Christians and Nairs owned the rest. It is through paddy cultivation, it could be argued, that feudalism in Kuttanad was sustained. Tenant farming was taken up mainly by Christians and Nairs, and it was the Pulayans, and to an extent, the Chovans, who did the actual physical labour of cultivating the land. The lack of a clearly established system of wages, where labourers were paid a share, decided by the landowners or tenant farmers, of the harvest, made exploitation rampant. The period covered in the novel is a time when changes in social customs and hierarchies had begun to emerge. It was also a time when the idea of human rights began to have an impact in Kuttanad and the lives of its inhabitants.

This land, where I have lived all my life, holds a great fascination for me, and I have wanted to bring it into my fiction from the time I started writing. The character Vavachan is based on a man with a big moustache whom I had grown up seeing. He had an almost mythical existence in our neighbourhood. He was a mild-mannered man, and people behaved respectfully and with a sense of fear towards him. It was much later that I discovered that he had grown his famous moustache after acting in a play, and had decided never to shave it off afterwards. He was different from the ordinary and the familiar, and I think his story left a seed in my mind, which germinated and slowly grew over many years. It was not my intention to write his life story; the story of Vavachan is entirely fictional.

I did not set out to write a novel about caste politics, but the journeys I took to research this novel and the process of writing it have brought about deep changes in my own outlook and understanding. It was in preparing to write this novel that I learned how to listen intensely to Dalit history, their knowledge about their own history, and consequently to the history of caste politics in Kuttanad. There are many characters in this novel who speak in ways that are anti-women and anti-human. There have been protests about this, and I agree that these characters should have shown more care and behaved more responsibly. But novels are free countries, and there is very little a writer can do about what the characters get up to.

In this land of sticky mud, decaying mangroves, knotted networks of waterways, and endless collection of fields, there have been better and bigger fisherfolk who fished for stories. Writers like Kavalam Vishwanatha Kurup and Thakazhi Shivasankara Pillah have caught fat wallago, snakeheads and catfish from its waterscape. And there have been many more who have sieved these waters. I am not good at fishing. Even as a child, when my friends went fishing, my job was to follow them with a pot to collect the fish they caught. The fish in these waters are not easily overcome – they prick you and poke you even after they have been pulled out of the water. I was pricked and poked several times while writing this story.

Many people have helped in the writing of this novel. The novel became controversial when it was published in a country where caste privilege and prestige, as well as an almost pathological level of moral policing, control social life. Many people stood by me through it. My thanks are due to all of them, and to my life partner, Viveka, and my publisher, DC Books. I am very grateful to Jayasree Kalathil whose translation of this work has exceeded all my expectations, and to HarperCollins and our editor, Rahul Soni.

S. Hareesh
Neendoor

TRANSLATOR'S NOTE

In the chapter, 'Madness in the Story', the narrator of *Moustache* attends a book launch where he argues that it is the yearning for a good story that makes us want to read books or listen to our parents' and grandparents' stories. I agree, but what makes a story good? Our narrator will tell you that the idea that stories provide us with a moral compass or with a kind of edifying conclusion is a myth that we collectively believe in. That may also be true. For me, though, a good story is one that takes us into the nooks and crannies and the peaks and precipices of its geography and its characters' lives.

As a reader, I was instantly captivated by the nooks and crannies and peaks and precipices in *Meesha*, and the remarkable ease with which Hareesh navigates them. As the translator, the primary task before me was to work out how best to represent that. First, there was the setting itself. I have visited Kuttanad and looked at it with a tourist's eye. The land was 'familiar' to me as an enthusiast of Malayalam literature and cinema. But the more I travelled within the landscape of the book, the more it revealed its uniqueness, upsetting the general tendency to think of Kerala as a small geographical area uniform in culture and language. As a native speaker of upper-caste Malayalam from the hilly parts of Malabar, who writes predominantly in English, translating *Meesha* required traversing several cultural and linguistic imaginaries and politics. This is not only a question of linguistic differences at the level of specific words – for example, the tapioca that is 'kappa' in Kuttanad and 'poola' in Kottakkal, my hometown in Malabar. It is about the cadences, but also about the politics of the language.

Hareesh invokes how other people's words mark identities and politics throughout the book. From Vavachan/Moustache and Kuttathi/Mariamma – who are invented and reinvented, sometimes violently, through the songs sung in the fields and at the waterwheels – to the snakehead murrel/Paappu that rules over the waterways, and the cattle egret/kalimundi that spends its life migrating between two lands, Hareesh shows how language 'names' identities. And many of those who are named – most notably, Vavachan and Kuttathi – are often silent in the face of other people's words. Rendering these cadences and politics into English without erasing them entirely was a particular challenge. It required a level of immersion not just in the story but in the specificity of its many languages and silences.

As a translator, I am often asked how I ensure that readers unfamiliar with the language and culture of the original book understand the complex, multilayered situatedness of it. It is a difficult question to answer, and I tend to answer it in terms of what I *don't* do. At the level of language, I don't try to invent an approximation – a patois of sorts – in English that purports to convey the original language's musicality. Over the course of many drafts, a language evolves, one that the characters seem to be comfortable speaking. With *Meesha*, there are several languages. In the chapters set in the 'present', for example the chapters where the narrator and his son are in conversation, Hareesh's language has a different texture to other chapters. There is the mesmerising poetry of the language Hareesh uses to describe the floods, the ecology, and the physical landscape. Then again, a chapter made up almost entirely of songs of the fields and the waterwheels. All of this demands a different engagement from the translator.

Translation is a subjective process, exhilarating and anxiety-inducing in equal measure. And while all translators hope for a seamless translation that reads as though the book was originally written in the target language, it can, as Miranda France reminds us, rarely be both perfectly faithful and perfectly readable. In rendering *Meesha* into *Moustache*, I can only hope I have found the right timbre.

There is no other single marker of a virulent kind of Kerala Malayali masculinity, one that is steeped in caste privilege, than a 'meesha' – a moustache. The novel is an intimate portrayal as much of the land and its people as of this masculine physicality. It has characters that say and do the most atrocious things. It has a rich sociocultural history as well as a mythology that courses through it as naturally as blood. Hareesh's storytelling demands that we look closer, pay attention, to the almost-mythical waterscape that he has created – one that is at once mesmerising and menacing.

And so, while preparing to translate the book, I read reports on the below-sea-level farming system of Kuttanad and on the land's ecology. I read articles about the mechanics of building agricultural land from the bottom of a lake and of waterwheels, and about agrarian caste and gender relations. I pored over maps of the area, running my finger over the places through which Vavachan's meandering journey took him, and over pictures of birds, snakes, crocodiles, fish, grass, trees, and waterweeds. I then came rushing back to the novel to inhabit its landscape.

In telling the story of Vavachan, Hareesh tells us a large number of stories. Indeed, in the preface to the Malayalam edition, he says what he has done is to make a cocktail out of the stories gifted by others. Local myths and characters from the folklore and spiritual life of the place, like Muthan and Perumaadan, make an appearance, as well as figures from its history like Sree Narayana Guru, Ayyankali, N.N. Pillah, Pallithanam Luca Mathai, kings, and colonial masters – the Sahebs – like the Baker family. Historical events such as the Punnapra-Vayalar uprising, the world wars, the temple-entry movement, and sociocultural changes marked deeply by caste and gender in Thiruvithamkur at the turn of the twentieth century are alluded to in the story. Allusions to the *Ramayanam* are throughout the book. But Hareesh's touch is light, and in his hands, these are reflections on the richness of the place and time in the novel. I have chosen to keep that lightness of touch, retaining these layers in the story without slipping into overt explanations or annotations that derail the narration.

The novel is as much a story of Vavachan/Moustache and the other inhabitants of this area as it is of its environment and biodiversity, its water, fish, birds, snakes, crocodiles, paddy, coconut, banana and tapioca. Hareesh's use of magic realism reflects the land itself, and the lives built and rebuilt on the land. For the Malayali, this is bountiful land. But Hareesh takes us to its underbelly, where hunger pervades, where oppression, both of the humans and of the land and its biodiversity, rages. It is also a land where rebellion against that oppression renews and rebuilds like the land itself after the floods. As Vavachan and his pursuers navigate its intricate waterscape, what emerges forcefully in this tale of magic, myth and metaphor is how the story of human beings' relationship with land has been fundamentally defined in terms of caste and gender.

I am enormously grateful to Hareesh for trusting me with this translation, for reading and commenting on each chapter, and for responding to all of my queries. I am also grateful to Rahul Soni, our editor at HarperCollins, for inviting me to translate this book and for his careful and gentle editorial eye, and to my 'first readers' – Adley Siddiqi, Shefali Jha and Akriti Mehta – for their insightful feedback.

Jayasree Kalathil
London

MOUSTACHE

MAP OF THE KUTTANAD REGION

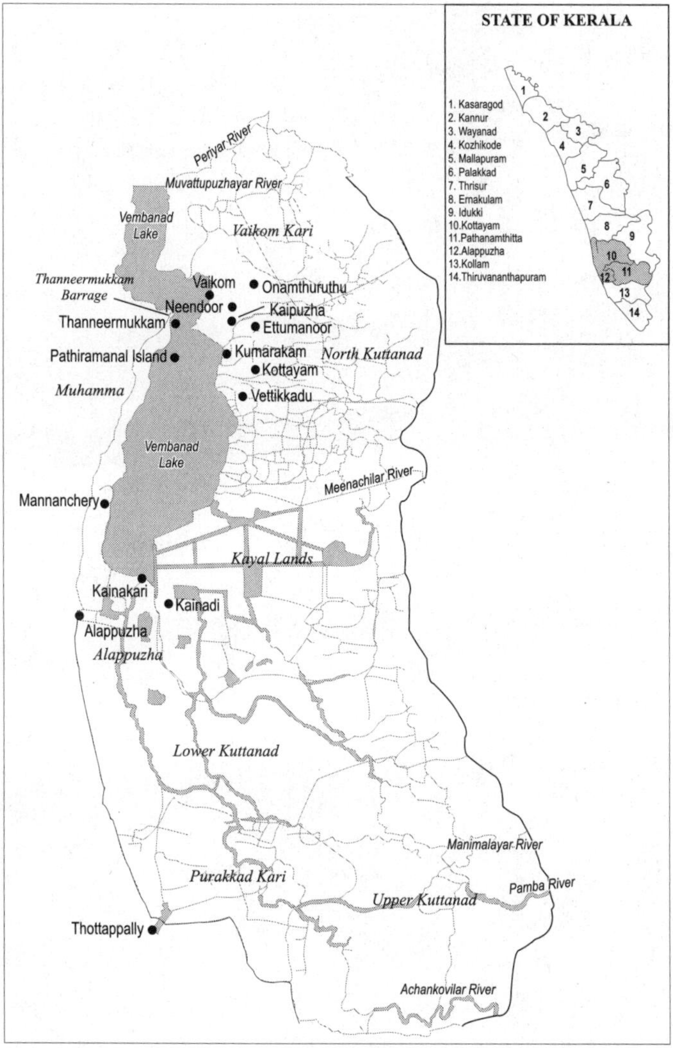

1
TRICKSTERS

Most people believe that eenampechi – the animal also known as alunku or pangolin – is a divine creature like the stork or the owl, and that the spirits of dead children appear in its form. But Paviyan, who lived on the embankment of the Chozhiyappara fields, knew for a fact that they were also somewhat stupid. In the months of Makaram and Kumbham, very early in the mornings, Paviyan would walk east to the mango tree near the dwellings of the Vaniyaan folk to collect the mangoes, small enough to be held in one hand and be squeezed over a bowl of kanji, that would have fallen to the ground overnight. This task was made stupidly easy by an industrious eenampechi who would have done the work of gathering them up through the night. Greedy for mangoes, the eenampechi would arrive as soon as the sun set, but instead of eating his fill, he would set about collecting the windfall to carry home with him, rolling each mango into a pile: one at a time … two at a time … three at a time … But it was a never-ending job as the mangoes would keep falling throughout the night, and at daybreak, having run out of time, the eenampechi would leave without having eaten a single mango. All Paviyan had to do, arriving just as the creature left, was transfer the pile of mangoes into his basket.

One night, in the month of Karkitakam, Paviyan had gone to the homes of those with overfilled grain chests and stores of paddy to ask for a handful of rice, and was walking back home, empty-handed. In the scattered light, he saw something shaped like a ball in his path. It was the eenampechi. He picked it up thinking it might amuse his children, make them forget their hunger for a while, and put it in his basket. He walked fast, hurdling over fences and water ditches, and he heard a voice: 'Slow down, Paviya, slow down.'

He realised that the eenampechi was aware of who he was, and yet bore no grudge against him.

The formidable snakehead murrel – the anglers called him Paappu, but he had another name among the fish – was an entirely different type of creature. Just as His Golden Majesty was the ruler of all this land, Paappu was the king of the numerous canals and waterways around Neendoor and Kaipuzha. Gorging on frogs and grasshoppers, he had grown as big as two mudfish, and produced thousands of offspring. Now, at his full size, disdaining fishing traps and bamboo baskets, he ruled over all fish. In the afternoons, he came up to the surface of the water to sunbathe in all his glory. On one such afternoon, Paviyan came along the canal in his narrow boat. His attention was elsewhere, and he did not see the fish. His boat, with years of experience navigating these waters, darted out of the way of the fish. Paviyan did not understand why his boat rocked suddenly. And he did not realise that, at that precise moment, something had been set in motion, and that he and his son – Vavachan – would soon be tricked and sent astray in the world of the water for the first time in their lives.

To the north of where their house stood like an untidy heap of paddy, partly sliding into the canal and partly covering the embankment, Vavachan leaned over a sluice, and gazed into the water. He spat into the canal hoping to attract spit-eating rasboras and glittering danios. He picked up the pieces of coal that surfaced when the dirt used to reinforce the field edges dried, put them into the water, and watched them float away. His mother Chella collected them and sold them to a Christian Mappila from Athirampuzha. The Mappila sold them on to blacksmiths who, in turn, lit the fires in their forges with them to make hoes, spades and plough bits that ended up back in the fields.

Vavachan did not look up when Paviyan's boat drew close, his long-oar leading it through carpets of waterweeds that kept the water cool. Paviyan's presence was natural and expected, like the shadow of a coconut tree in the slanting evening light or a stand of scutch grass nibbled by a calf. It felt as though he was always around whether he was physically there or not. Vavachan and his mother Chella found it hard to answer when people asked where Paviyan was, even though they would have watched his boat disappear down the canal. Did he go east or west? Or was he still here? It was only when, in the full morning light, he went to the open ground to defecate that Paviyan did anything that was even a little out of the ordinary. He would sit among the weeds and create an imaginary screen of coconut fronds around him, and have a long conversation with himself. Anyone else in the vicinity doing their business would feel that he was having a serious discussion with someone.

Paviyan looked at Vavachan, silently asking him to get into the boat, but Vavachan did not realise that it was an invitation until his father gestured with his hand. He scrambled up, disbelievingly, and jumped into the boat, almost toppling over into the water and frantically wheeling his arms to keep his balance. The boat, empty except for two sickles with worn blades and a small bundle of sackcloth, rocked, and Paviyan cursed. It was not aimed at Vavachan; Paviyan cursed whenever something went wrong or threatened to go wrong. Last time, when the paddy seeds sowed in the Kuttankari field did not germinate even after twenty days, Paviyan had walked along the dykes swearing loudly at the seeds rotting in the mud. It is said that if a person falls inside a boat and survives, it is better to beat them to death as they would not be of any use to anyone afterwards.

Vavachan sat on the plank, proud that he had been allowed into his father's boat, suppressing the urge to lean sideways and run his fingers in the water. Except for giving them a good thrashing with a length of coconut leafstalk a couple of times a year, Paviyan paid very little attention to his six children – he would be hard pressed to recognise his own daughters – and it was the first time one of them had set foot in his grass boat with a leaky bottom through which water seeped in and had to be bailed out every now and then.

It was noon. Pied paddy skimmers and black-tipped ground skimmers flitted in the still heat. Paviyan, a Pulayan born to work the land, moved his boat forward pushing aside the densely floating water hyacinths with his long-oar. All around him, vast fields, drained and freshly sowed, lay like upturned dirty dishes, the seedlings yet to show their green tips. Womenfolk working the fields were nowhere to be seen. Stout snakeheads lay alert, barely moving a fin in the clear water, and up in the sky an eagle soared, equally alert, barely moving its wings. Younglings of orange-and-black-marked pallathi fish went about their business, mouth-down in the mud, while mottled leaf fish hid in the darkness of the weeds by the side of the canal. Vavachan looked at an old wound on Paviyan's shin. He had slapped mud over it. It dried hard, sucking the moisture out of even the ooziest of sores and curing them.

They rowed south to the point where four canals met, and then turned west. Paviyan had, so far, only travelled up to Paivattomkarukappadam in that direction. Further ahead were Maniyanthuruthu, and the fields of Chekka and Kanyakon. The people of Kaipuzha and Neendoor cultivated the fields on both sides of the canal along these parts, and beyond that were the fields cultivated by the people of Vechoor and Perunthuruthu. When he was a child, standing at the back of his house and looking west, watching the rippling expanse of water, Vavachan used to think that all that lay beyond Chozhiyappara fields was either the lake or the sea.

Vavachan expected Paviyan to pull in at the luxuriant stands of grass along the canal, and cut them at their base, his sickle slicing through the water. But Paviyan's boat surged forward without stopping, meandering through the network of canals and waterways. He regularly delivered grass to a couple of houses that had oxen, and a Nair household with a few cows. Vavachan surmised that the last delivery may have been infested with beetles, causing diarrhoea in the cattle, and Paviyan may have been reprimanded. So now, he was on a mission to find juicy green scutch grass with fat stems and needle-sharp leaves, Vavachan guessed, and Paviyan would not be satisfied until he could throw a bundle of it in the front yard of whoever it was that had scolded him.

To the west of Makkothara, Paviyan turned the boat ashore towards a house that was visible through a cluster of banana trees. Strands cut from the outer skin of a Njalipoovan banana tree were the best to tie the grass into bundles. Dried naturally on the tree itself, they were strong enough to tether cattle.

Unaware of the role this house, newly thatched with sturdy palmyra fronds, would play in his eventful life to come, Vavachan sat in the boat, uninterested. Plaited coconut fronds supported between thick posts of flowering mallow formed the walls of the house. The door was also a plaited coconut frond. The debris of last night's wind lay scattered in the yard, and an uprooted banana tree leaned on the house. An overgrown vine climbed over the wall.

Paviyan put the banana strands in the boat, along with a small, immature bunch of Palayankodan banana. He scraped his mud-caked feet at the base of a coconut tree. Suddenly, the coconut-leaf door snatched open and, as Vavachan watched in astonishment, a woman came charging at Paviyan. It was not her but her two generous breasts that were rushing towards him in anger, Vavachan thought, breasts like none he had seen before – white, round, disdainfully looking the man straight in the eye. He imagined they had moustaches. Their nipples were small and retracted, but they looked piercingly at Paviyan in their rage, shaking their faces like sabre-toothed stone statues.

Chella, Vavachan's mother, had breasts that hung down to her belly, sucked dry by her six merciless children. They dangled on each side of her body like baya weaver nests, getting in the way as she walked or bent over her chores. Once, Vavachan had seen her toss one of those appendages with no more use over her shoulder as she went about her work. Meanwhile, his sister, bilious by nature, had a chest that protruded. Nothing sprouted on them. And the breasts of the women who jumped across the dyke behind his hut and went to work in the fields were as dark and sun-burned as their arms and legs. No one looked at them fondly. They tied them back with old rags to protect them from the razor-sharp blades of the paddy as they bent over them, and released them from their imprisonment as soon as they climbed out of the fields in the evening.

Vavachan did not see the woman's face or her features, only her breasts that changed expressions along with her words. He imagined they would burst as her anger increased, or turn into fists and beat the hell out of Paviyan.

'My bananas are not for Pulayans to come and cut down as they please,' she said.

The woman rushed towards the boat, and called Paviyan an obscene word that never should have come out of the mouth of someone her age. Sitting on the plank in the boat, Vavachan looked reverentially at the breasts looming high over him, and his heart paid obeisance as it did when he watched the light that came on in the evenings on the stone crucifix in the faraway Kaipuzha church.

'Here, take your bananas,' Paviyan said.

He threw the bunch, still oozing sap from its cut end, in front of her.

'Stuff them down your throat!'

He responded to her cursing with a string of abuse about her father, Kuttanasari, and her mother, Kavalakkathu. The daughter was even coarser than her mother, he decided, as he rowed the boat away from the embankment.

'Don't you forget that you're living on the Tharayil folk's embankment,' he said, as though he had some legitimate say in the matter.

The canal curved away to hide the house from their vision. The sun spread a cloak of silence. Vavachan decided that he had dreamt the whole thing up, sitting in the cool breeze in the boat. Paviyan continued muttering in anger.

The shortest dreams can seem as long as a whole year, or even a lifetime. One hungry evening, Vavachan had fallen asleep in the dampness under a coconut tree, and he still remembered in great detail the dream he had then. In it, he was eating something he had never eaten before, served up on an enormous banana leaf. He had recognised the pieces by touch, but when he woke up, he realised he had forgotten what they were. Still, the taste of it had lingered in his mouth and on his tongue, and he could smell the heady fragrance of curry leaves as though a bull had frolicked through a curry leaf thicket.

'You had something to eat,' his bilious sister had flared her nostrils.

'I only dreamt about it.'

'No, no. I can smell it on you,' she had insisted. 'I know – it's the smell of coconut oil.'

She could recognise the smell from the oil pots of a Vaniyaan oil-seller from Manjur who took his wares to market in a boat along the canal.

'What does coconut oil look like?' Vavachan had asked.

'I saw it once when the boat overturned. It's light green, like the weeds under water.'

Vavachan had raised his hand to his nose and inhaled deeply.

The sun was beginning to set, but Paviyan kept rowing. The altercation with the woman seemed to have made him forget his mission. Vavachan wished the boat was in the shaded part of the canal. He scooped up some water, drank it, and wiped his face with his wet hand. So far, he had not dwelled on his hunger because it was unusual for him to eat during the day. But he yearned for the tiny bunch of unripe bananas they almost had – he would have eaten them raw.

The sun sheds light but it also creates a kind of brilliance that fills one's eyes with darkness. Vavachan's eyes darkened, and through them he saw, for the first time, the endless expanse of fields around him, sown and fallow, with not a single human being in them. Where did they all disappear after turning these swamps into fields, and calling them by different names? Like a hay worker's rope, canals crossed and crossed over again, creating a snarled knot.

Paviyan would not be able to get across these fields even if he rowed until the end of his life. They had no end, like the earth itself. When the heat began to abate, he stopped the boat near a spread of grass. God alone knew why he had not stopped before, where there had been better-quality grass. He was the type of person who went after the average even when he had a chance to go for the best.

Vavachan gathered the grass Paviyan cut, tied them into bundles, and stacked them in the boat. They worked quickly, but Time played tricks on them. The cunning trickster changed what they thought, correctly, to be one minute into five or six minutes, changed each of their nazhika – twenty-four minutes – to two or three nazhika, just because he could do so, armed with the accoutrements to decide the passage of time. So when they finished their work and raised their heads, the sun had already gone off to fulfil its responsibility of bringing light to other fields in faraway lands.

Paviyan turned the boat and rowed fast, and as he came around the corner of a field, a dark shadow rushed towards them, roaring. Paviyan was confident of his ability to row in the dark, and he stood at the bow of the boat, his black body indistinguishable from the darkened sky, working hard to keep the loaded boat steady in the blowing wind. Vavachan was convinced that they were lost. 'I don't think this is the way we came,' he said.

Paviyan was angry. If they were on land, he would have slapped his son across the face. This was the first time Vavachan had been to these parts while Paviyan, his father, and his father's father knew these fields as intimately as the fields they stood watch over.

The dark shadow turned into rain, and as raindrops as big as young coconuts fell and two brilliant blades of lightning illuminated the earth, Paviyan began to think that Vavachan might be right. He could not recognise any landmarks as the darkness had rendered his surroundings monotonous. Suddenly, he remembered that he had been cutting grass where a clever chemballi fish had killed a Chovan toddy tapper.

It had happened before the time of his father's father. Early one morning, the Chovan, from Villunni, was getting ready to go to work. But his Chovathi stopped him.

'Don't go today,' she said.

They had been living together for only a week.

'Move out of my way,' he said. 'If I don't retrieve the sap-filled pot from the top of the tree, it will overflow and rot the crown. The tree will be infested with beetles.'

'Then promise me you'll come back quickly. Don't loiter. And be careful of your surroundings.'

She was aware that her Chovan had a peculiar habit. If he saw any good fish in the canal, he would stand there and watch until he worked out a plan to catch the fish.

The Chovan tried to heed his Chovathi's warning, but as soon as he had climbed down the second coconut tree of the day, he forgot all about it. There in the canal below, in a spot where the water was low, was a group of chemballi quivering in the mud. Chemballi – people also called these dark-skinned perch kallada – was a tasty fish, skinned and cooked in a curry with chillies. Even the aroma of it being fried with chilli paste in a shallow pot was a great accompaniment to a potful of kanji. The Chovan set his toddy pot down, stepped in and picked up a handful, and tucked them in the waist-fold of his towel. And then he saw another one, much bigger than the ones he had already picked up. Without thinking what he was doing, he put the one in his hand between his teeth, and bent forward to pick up the other. The fish in his mouth remembered the history of its kind and of humankind, and deciding to die valiantly, it wriggled, making the Chovan inadvertently open his mouth. It slid down his throat into his stomach. Chemballi had razor-sharp bones, far more numerous than other fish, on both sides of their bodies. Back home, the Chovathi waited in vain.

From that day on, the spirit of the unfortunate Chovan played tricks on the boats and the people who passed by the spot, making them lose all sense of time and direction.

Paviyan and his son had strayed into his trap. They rowed from canal to canal. Imagining that he recognised a collection of fields from its outer bund, Paviyan would row towards it, only to row back, realising that he had been misled. Several times he imagined that they were almost at their house. Vavachan huddled in the boat with his head bowed, his body about to collapse from hunger and cold, and bailed out the water that leaked into the boat with a piece of areca spathe. He glanced at Paviyan at the bow of the boat with amazement. He was the type of person on whom hunger seemed to have very little effect. Sometimes, he did not eat for days at a time, but if the opportunity for a meal came along, he would eat enough for two people as though preparing for the lean days ahead.

As his legs went numb in the cold water, Vavachan thought about the warm, unsalted kanji water he sometimes had. Whenever she got some paddy, Chella used it not to make kanji, but kanji water, and the children, enticed by the most pleasant aroma in the world, would drink it dry.

The boat reached a grassless spot along the canal. Vavachan shifted on the plank trying to keep his balance. The movement rocked the boat and enraged Paviyan. He raised his oar to strike his son with it, but changed his mind. The boat sat low in the water. Further ahead, Paviyan pulled up to a wheelhouse that housed a waterwheel. Pinning the boat to the shore with the long-oar, they climbed up, holding on to the thickly growing grass. It was pitch dark inside the wheelhouse, and the mud on the floor was churned as though someone had been in there during the day. There was nowhere to sit. In the flash of lightning, the waterwheel, an eighteen-leafed monster, loomed. It would have moved untold litres of water, persuaded countless fish to swim from the fields into the canals.

'No more today,' Paviyan said to himself. He turned to Vavachan: 'Why don't we stay here for the night? We can find our way in the morning.'

This was the first time Paviyan had ever asked one of his children for their opinion.

'I think we should keep going,' Vavachan said, trying to control his teeth jittering in the cold. 'Let's get home.'

Obediently, Paviyan got back into the boat.

'Water is flowing in from the east,' he said.

In the little time they had rested in the wheelhouse, the water level in the canal had risen. Further ahead, houses with pinpricks of light came into vision.

'Christian Mappila houses,' Paviyan said. 'I think we have gone all the way around, and come back to Kuttomburam.'

But he had to swallow his words immediately. A river was in front of him, larger than any canal and flowing swiftly. They inched forward sticking to the side, trying to avoid the strong currents in the middle of the river. Vavachan pushed back the branches and vines that slapped his face. They heard people calling out from the other side of the river, and Paviyan decided to cross it after all.

'Take us across,' one of the two people who had hollered to get their attention said.

The men were dressed in mundus and loose-fitting upper garments. They were thin, but seemed healthy. Vavachan had not seen a man in an upper garment until then. As they got into the boat, he noticed that their clothes were dry. It did not seem that it had rained properly in this area. The boat did not rock when they got into it, and when one of them spoke, his voice sounded as though it was coming from a hollow reed. The boat was loyal, and it never let one down regardless of the weight of the cargo in it, even when it looked like it was about to sink.

'We went out cutting grass and got late. Where would I get to if I went this way?' Paviyan asked.

'Thiruvarppu, and then into the lake. This is Kallumada. If you go west, you'll get to Olassa and Parippu. You should go back the way you came.'

The boat reached the other bank. Hearing that there was a Pulayan dwelling nearby, Paviyan set out on foot to ask for some food. Vavachan sat on a stone, keeping an eye on the boat.

The young men began to walk away, but one of them turned back.

'My name is Narayanapillah,' he said. 'And this here is Shivaramapillah.'

'Where are my masters off to?' Vavachan asked. The cold and the reverence made him huddle.

'We're going to Malaya.'

'Is this the way to Malaya?'

'This way, we'll get to Kottayam. From there, we have to travel for a few days, and then get on a ship and travel further for a couple of months.'

'Have you got people there?'

'We'll find jobs. After that, there'll be no more troubles. They pay you in British money you know, not in paddy like here.'

'So you won't come back again?'

'We'll be back. But soon there's going to be terrible hunger here, and famine. There won't be even a single grain of paddy. There's a war coming, you know, a big war.'

Vavachan understood that they were talking to him as a reward for taking them across the river.

'We might consider joining the army.'

The moon made a sudden appearance, and in its light, Vavachan watched, with a sense of disquiet, the whiteness of the men's upper garments retreating into the distance. Deciding to follow them, he had taken a couple of steps, when the boat swayed in the current, threatening to drift away. He turned back, and held on to it. He waited for Paviyan to return; he knew he would return empty-handed.

2
MADNESS IN THE STORY

My son, Ponnu, was aware that his dad had some sort of connection with stories. Every night, at bedtime, he would pester me for a story. I was quite excited in the beginning – who wouldn't be when a child begs for stories in this day and age? A good story is like an arrow from the Pandava prince Arjunan's quiver: a single arrow that becomes ten when released from the bow, and hundreds of thousands when striking the target.

But my enthusiasm did not last, and I was soon faced with a crisis. How many stories do we know that we can narrate to children in a way that captures their interest? Fifteen? Twenty? Thirty, at the most. We could keep them interested for a few days with stories from *Ramayanam* and *Mahabharatam*, but all those power struggles, pageantry and piety are for grown-ups really, not children. Besides, they have so little relevance in today's life. The great and the good in those stories are so backward compared to today's children. The most significant piece of knowledge that Vidurar, the venerated scholar before the days of Google and *Encyclopaedia Britannica*, the steam engine and the polio vaccine, held was that the earth was flat and was supported on the shoulders of seven elephants. Even a five-year-old knows so much more than that these days!

Then there are stories from the *Panchatantram*, Arabian stories, and the *Kathasaritsagaram*, stories we have all read several times over. So it surprises me that I can only remember eight or ten stories from these, which means that the rest had not really touched my heart. I could read them again and tell them to my child, but there is no guarantee that he would find them interesting. These days, he falls asleep angry at me, disappointed with the stories I try to make up on the spot, and I am saddened as I watch his interest in stories slowly wane and be replaced by computer games and cartoons that fill one's head with a void.

Then, one day, I noticed a tiny news item in a corner of the last page of the newspaper, a story TV channels had ignored completely: a NASA spaceship was set to pass above Kerala for the first time, and if the night was clear, one could catch a glimpse of it at the north-western corner of the sky around 4 a.m. The spaceship had four passengers, three Americans and a Russian, who had been living in it for the last six months doing research. The news story gave details of the money spent on the mission. I read it out to my son, showed him a picture of the spaceship that I found on the internet, and suggested that we wake up in the morning to watch it pass through the sky.

'Is it sailing through the sea in the sky?' Ponnu asked me.

'There's no sea in the sky. It's a space with nothing in it. And the ship is not like the ones we see in the sea. That's just what it is called. It's more like an aeroplane.'

'So is the sky then just lying there with weeds and grass growing in it?'

'No, no. There are no stones or soil or grass there. Not even wind. It's just space.'

How does one explain nothingness?

I set the alarm, and got up at 4 a.m., and tried to wake Ponnu up. But, snug under the covers in the cold December morning, he was fast asleep. I would not be able to go back to sleep even if I tried, so I washed my face, and went up to the roof. I couldn't remember the last time I had been up at this hour. Until recently, I had been suffering from insomnia, and could only go to bed around one or two in the morning, whiling away the night hours watching TV or reading. The problem had resolved itself now that I had taken to drinking two 120 ml shots of brandy every night, the only downside being that I was unable to get out of bed until six in the morning.

I walked barefoot on the cold floor of the terrace, looking around. No one was up, nothing moved in the darkness and patches of diffused light. I was all alone, like a man in a spaceship. No one in this universe knew I was here, and if I were to disappear, if God were to wipe me off with a damp cloth like a drawing on a blackboard, only a handful of people would remember me enough to notice my absence, and when they too were gone, no one would even know that I had existed. The vast majority of people who lived thousands, ten thousands of years ago have no names or identities. God has wiped them off the face of this earth, from people's paltry memories. Washed clothes, spread on the line to dry the night before, touched my skin. I walked to the tomatoes in the plastic grow-bags, their leaves droopy in the dewy, dark night.

It was time for the spaceship to pass by as reported in the news story. I looked up, and saw nothing special. The sky looked like a temple with all its lamps lit, some smouldering, some flickering, and others burning brightly. I could recognise some of the star clusters because, as a child, I had gone stargazing with a teacher from the Sasthra Sahithya Parishad. Looking at the sky was like watching the ocean, he had told me, what we actually see is the sky and the ocean within ourselves.

I looked towards the north-western corner of the sky. How big would the spaceship be, I wondered. As big as a bird flying high in the sky? Presently, I spotted what looked like a planet, as bright as Venus, something that should not be in that part of the sky. It was moving fast. This was it! It kept moving, and reached right above me, and I waved at it happily. If my son were here, he would have jumped up and down with joy. I resolved to make up a story that the men in the spaceship had waved back at me. Oh lucky travellers from distant lands, greetings to you from this inconsequential science buff! If I had nurtured my interest, tended its flame, I too might have joined you as you sail across the skies in your ship. But, here I am instead, in a place you would not have heard of, speaking a language unfamiliar to you. I watched intently, believing that I would miss something important if I blinked, until the bright light moved across the sky and vanished into the southern horizon.

Once it was out of sight, I began to wonder whether I had actually seen it or whether I had conjured it up in the sky of my imagination. I had to tell someone about this – it was the only way I could be sure that I had experienced this. What empty creatures we are! Our experiences and thoughts gain relevance only if endorsed by others; our lives lived only in the thoughts and memories of a handful of people who would also be dead and gone in a short period of time.

Instead of going back to bed, I decided to begin my morning walk a little early. I walked briskly, swinging my arms, along the deserted road still steeped in darkness, trying to hoodwink my body, which was built to do physical labour, and my mind into thinking that I was indeed doing physical labour. I toyed with an idea for a story to tell my son, about an unexpected meeting, on my morning walk, with a man who had died a hundred years ago. Soon, I was at the junction where I stopped to catch my breath under a streetlight that someone had forgotten to switch off. The junction and its old-fashioned shops have remained unchanged over the years. The only change from my childhood days was a few posters advertising mobile phone recharge coupons. There was a paan shop that jutted out on to the road, a rarely inhabited house with a portico, and a chai shop which looked like it was about to open for the day and had lights and movement within. It was run by the son-in-law of the man who used to run it when I was a child. I bet they even sell the same snacks, except maybe adding porotta to the selection.

At the junction, the road split into three. If I turned left, I could continue my walk along the deserted rubber plantation owned by the church. The road to the right would take me to the fish market, which would by now be crowded and noisy with fisherfolk and traders haggling over prices, throwing around obscenities and endearments in equal measure. Going straight, the road would take me to the temple where I would be able to see fair-skinned beauties fresh from their early morning baths.

Until six months ago, I used to go on these walks with a friend of mine. One day, he had asked: 'Why do you think young women bathe, make themselves pretty, and go to the temple?'

'To worship,' I had answered.

'No. Look again, carefully. Why wear their best clothes and get decked up if it's only to worship? They're subconsciously giving the signal that they are available for mating.'

'Don't talk nonsense,' I had laughed.

'If that's not the case, why do they avoid going to the temple for four or five days each month? They're letting everyone know that they are unavailable at that time. Especially the priests. As you know, they've traditionally been the experts in these things.'

Having failed to hoodwink his own body with exercise, my friend had died of a heart attack, and I have been alone on my walks ever since.

Further down the road, a bridge across a canal led to another village. On days when I felt energetic, I would stand on the bridge, breathe in the cold air, and walk on further. This morning, I walked until I came to a small cluster of shops. A movement on the veranda of the bicycle repair shop attracted my attention. He was there – the man with the big moustache. He had a towel tied around his head as usual, and was smoking a beedi. I have run into him often on this route, and sometimes exchanged a friendly 'ah' in acknowledgement. Today, however, as though he had been waiting for me, he got off the veranda, and walked up to me. Perhaps the old man – Moustache – had confused me with someone else. He looked carefully at my face as though looking for signs of deceit. Like old folks who search for hints of familiarity in the faces of unfamiliar children, he looked into my eyes trying to place my ancestors. And for the first time, I got a chance to note his remarkable features up close. His skin was wrinkled and saggy, but the muscles on his shoulders were still well-defined. The sturdy moustache covered most of his cheeks, and there was not a single strand of grey in it. The moustache gave him the appearance of a proud rooster. Still, his advancing age was evident in the way his stomach caved inwards, and in the slight dissonance in his steps.

What if, I wondered, his moustache was a magical thing like the noses in Basheer's or Gogol's stories? What if one day, confounding its owner, it grew perpetually to become one of the wonders of the world? What if it grew like a forest reclaiming land, spreading anxiety among its modern inhabitants? What if little children played with it, using it like a swing?

In the afternoon, I attended a book launch. The book was by a journalist who took his writing seriously, and I was scheduled to make a felicitation speech. A group of us aspiring writers, not yet lucky enough to have our names printed in any respectable magazines, got together in a lodge room in town once a month, where some of us would read out our stories and poems. Since there was no real hope of any of our work being published, everyone took even the most stinging criticism without complaint. Our group included a college girl and a seventy-year-old retired teacher, both equally nursing the hope that they could improve their writing and eventually have it published. The person whose book was being launched today was the most accomplished writer in our group. He had not published anything until now, but had cultivated good relationships with several editors, and we hung on to his every word as he told stories about them. I was happy to have received a place on the dais at this event as I had always felt that he thought of me as the most promising in the group.

I had been anxious about my speech, but at the event I felt that I covered some interesting things in the twenty minutes I spoke. The opportunity to speak at a book launch is a licence to say whatever one wants, and I spoke about a few things I had been mulling over in the last couple of days.

Why do we read stories and novels, I asked the audience. In order to enjoy a good story, I said, answering my own question. There was nothing else beyond that. Why did we read *Poombatta* or *Ambiliyammavan* as children, or listen to our grandmothers' stories? Just for the enjoyment of a good story. Children's stories usually ended with a moral, but that was only to deceive parents into thinking that stories were edifying. It is the same yearning that leads one to *Panchatantram* or to a novel by Pottekkad – the yearning for a good story. The idea that reading provides us with a compass for politics, philosophy, spirituality, or insight into life and all that was pure nonsense. But we don't admit this. Instead, we read Joyce's *Ulysses* with the help of guidebooks, and pretend to belong to some exclusive group who have understood the book, devour Benyamin's *Adujeevitham* in one sitting only so that we can pick it apart. As far as I was concerned, I told my audience, the best stories in the world are those in *One Thousand and One Nights*, or stories like that of the hare and the tortoise, or the crocodile who plotted to eat the sweet heart of the monkey, and that nothing else piqued my curiosity as much as these stories.

I had assumed that no one would pay much attention to my speech, but it had serious repercussions. The person who spoke next was a self-assured young man, a college student, dressed in a pair of tight jeans and an expensive shirt, whose entire body language exuded vitality. I had seen a few of his poems on social media, and they were quite good.

He began annihilating my viewpoint by quoting a section from Vailoppilli's *Kudiyozhikkal*, which talked about fools who sat on the black horses of imagination, unaware of what was happening around them in the real world. His energetic gestures and deep, masculine voice easily captivated the audience. Such was his oratory, that I found myself wanting to agree with him. I looked pathetically at myself. Writers were under attack, even being killed, and yet there were those who waxed eloquent about the literary merits of the hare and the tortoise story, he said sarcastically, at which the audience looked at me, and guffawed. It was particularly hurtful to see two pretty young women sitting in the front row covering their mouths and shaking with laughter. So cruel! I wouldn't be surprised if, consumed by their joy, they would offer themselves up to him. By the time he argued that people like me were responsible for the fascist mindset that had spread across India, everyone was looking at me with suspicion, and like a little boy being punished by the teacher and made to stand on the bench, I sat there with a foolish smile on my face until the programme ended.

Nobody paid any attention to me after the event. When I shook hands with the writer later, he gave me a smile that made his thoughts crystal clear.

Unable to stand my embarrassment, I went into a bar with a friend, Joseph, and got drunk.

'To hell with that young upstart! He's wrong and I am right,' I said, after taking out my frustration on the poor waiter who was a little slow in bringing a plate of lemon pickle to accompany our drinks. 'Speechifying is not my medium. Writing is. Even Borges has said that writing is not a faithful copy of life, and that if a Bengal tiger in a story has three legs and speaks Sanskrit, so be it.'

'I've told you before,' Joseph said. 'Either stay away from these events and sit at home, and people will think you are an intellectual. Or stop saying crazy things at these events. You're damaging your own reputation.'

'His mother's fascism!' I said, mercilessly attacking the food that had arrived in front of us. 'There is a sentence in Olassa Narayanapillah's autobiography. When the gunshot of real revolution is sounded, armchair revolutionaries will run and hide in Sabarimala. Do you see? Sabarimala! How right he was! Similarly, when there is real fascism, these idiots will grovel on the floor. You'll see, not much longer to wait now.'

'Olassa Narayanapillah? The actor and theatre personality N.N. Pillah?'

'Yes.'

'Oh, yes! Yes, what a life he lived!'

'Indeed! What a life!'

These days, however, it was not Narayanapillah's life that fascinated me. For some time now, I had been preoccupied by thoughts about the incomparable life of a local man, Vavachan. His life enticed me, much more than the lives of Papillon or Raskolnikov or Chanthrakkaran, and held my attention like the stories of the blue fox or of Gulliver.

Much later, I took a bus back home, sat on a side seat, and opened the window shutter. It was drizzling outside. The other passengers sat huddled into their seats with the shutters closed, their faces reflecting the emptiness of their minds. Why else would they not insist on sitting on the side seats and, like little children, watch the scenery outside? If a person cannot enjoy the world unfold as they travel by bus, wonder why the trees, houses and people run backwards, it means they are bored with life, and are waiting for the arrival of the man riding the buffalo – Kaalan, the God of Death.

As the bus crossed Mannanam Bridge, my excitement increased. The scenery outside was something I saw on a daily basis, but I loved watching the rain-drenched contours of my local landscape. The bus stopped at Kuttomburam, and there he was in the bus shelter: Vavachan, the man with the big moustache. He had a folded towel over his head to keep the worst of the rain away. I had never seen the old-timer travel by bus. He walked everywhere, barefoot, no matter how far he had to go. The bus started moving. I shouted for it to stop and jumped out, making my fellow passengers lift the shutters and look out. Good, at least they were alive!

I persuaded Moustache to accompany me to the nearby toddy shop. We sat across from each other at a corner table, and ordered bottles of toddy fresh from the evening's tapping, and a plate of fish gravy to lick between mouthfuls.

'Tell me about the old days,' I said.

'What to say,' Moustache said, smiling. 'If folk from my childhood were to come back to life, they'd go crazy! Girls are riding scooters. People are going to Ernakulam in the morning and coming back the very same day. Night is like day with so much light in the houses and on the roads. And no one has kanji for their morning meal. They make special snacks!'

'Indeed … Everything has changed.'

'You know the bus road by the side of the canal near your house? That used to be a skinny little ditch.' Moustache brought his hands close together. 'And the pond – it used to be thrice its size. I used to catch snakeheads in it.'

'Really!'

I had to urinate, so I stepped outside, and stood looking at the fields swallowed by darkness. The toddy shop was almost empty. A devotional song played softly in one of the rooms. It was quite late, but I did not feel like taking out my phone and checking the time. I resolved to continue talking with Moustache even if it was past midnight. By listening attentively to someone else and getting to know their experiences, we get an opportunity to live another life, to cheat the director of the play that is our life who sent us on to the stage with just one role. We get to play other roles. I let out a short howl into the darkness, and went back inside on unsteady legs. But wonders of wonders! Moustache had vanished, leaving only the empty bottles and glasses behind!

'Where's Moustache?' I asked the cook, Chandran.

'Moustache? He hasn't been in.'

'He was just here. We were drinking together.'

'Nonsense! You're quite over the limit today,' Chandran said, patting my shoulder. 'I saw you gesturing and talking to yourself, and I thought all that drinking and ganja smoking had finally caught up with you.'

'Be serious, Chandranchetta. We were right here. Look, here's the glass he drank from.'

'How's that possible? Moustache has been in the hospital for the past week. The Medical College Hospital.'

Chandran took my money, and gently persuaded me to leave.

I had a headache from having mixed my drinks, but I walked the three kilometres home enveloped in a sense of happiness. Tonight, I had an interesting story to tell my son, the story of Moustache who could simultaneously appear in different places, and disappear at will. He had a magical moustache with curved ends that touched the sky, and a spotted eagle had built a nest in it.

3

RAVANAN

Paviyan was standing in a threshing yard with its watchman, grousing about the wayward lives of harvest workers from the east, when Poovan sought him out and told him about the commotion his son, Vavachan, had created back home. Two weeks earlier, Paviyan had left home hitching a ride in a hay boat to Maniyanthuruthu. From there, he had gone to Perunthuruthu and Koduthuruthu looking for harvest work, and was now on his way back. Poovan's story made him livid, and he set off immediately.

Around a month and a half ago, two men dressed in garments covering their upper bodies had appeared in Neendoor, much to the amazement of its people. Until then, the only person they knew to own such a garment in the three miles between Mudakkalithodu and Mannanam Thodu was Tharayil Avarachan. Avarachan wore his upper garment only on the rarest of occasions, usually taking it with him, folded under the plank of his boat, on long distance journeys to Vaikom or Alappuzha. No one, including Avarachan, believed that it was an object fit to be used by a person regularly.

But now, watching the newcomers, everyone realised the respectability that the round-necked, half-sleeved, loose-fitting garments could bestow upon those who wore them. The duo walked behind a handcart loaded with what looked like a heavy iron chest, talking to each other and paying no attention to their surroundings. From Kaipuzha onwards, a string of small naked children had followed them. The few women standing in the fields and yards along the way marvelled at how the garments endowed their animal bodies with a certain delicacy, and they stared back and forth at the men and the iron chest. Many embellishments would be added to the story when they retold it later in their kitchens, and they would convince themselves that they had seen a whole group of men with garment-covered upper bodies, walking alongside a line of handcarts and bullock carts loaded with iron chests. No one would own up to the fact that there were only two men, as though a smaller number of men and chests would belittle their status as eyewitnesses.

Arriving at the market, the men in upper garments, showing no sign of unfamiliarity, entered the licensed tobacco shop owned by Chellappan Pillah. The more handsome of the two was his nephew. Chellappan Pillah invited him inside, and dusted the bench on the veranda for the other man.

'Why didn't you take the boat?' he asked.

'He's scared of boats,' Damodaran, his nephew, said, gesturing towards the other man sitting on the veranda. 'I'd loaded the chest on to a boat in Kodimatha. But he wouldn't step in. So we walked.'

Chellappan Pillah looked at the stranger on the bench in amazement. He guessed the man was at least thirty-five years old. He had several distinguishing features that were apparent at first glance: three distinct lines on the forehead, thin arms that were disproportional to his body, and long fingers. His hair lay slanted to the side like windswept grass. He had pierced ears, but wore no ear studs.

'What caste is he?' Chellappan Pillah asked.

'His name is Ramanujan. He is from the Ezhuthachan caste. We don't have them around here.'

'Is it a Brahmin caste?'

'No. It is also called Kaduppattan.'

There was a building across the road from the shop that Chellappan Pillah's uncle had constructed. Ramanujan Ezhuthachan moved into a room in its attic. Some enthusiastic volunteers carried the heavy iron chest upstairs. Damodaran went to his mother's house, where he found that the old mat he had left behind when he had gone off to Madirasi eight years ago, and the corner of the eastern veranda, protected from the spray of the rain, where he used to sleep, were still waiting for him. After the evening meal, he lay on his side on the veranda, and watched the same rain he had watched all those years ago. Turning on to his back, he noticed the rainwater leaking through the same small hole near the third rafter of the roof. He began to feel that he had never left home, never gone to Madirasi to work, never seen ships, or taken up with a Tamil woman. He had always remained here, he felt, just like his ancestors who had only ever travelled as far as Pambadi to the east, Alappuzha to the west, Kottayam to the south and Vaikom to the north. Perhaps that was enough, he mused. Why leave one's village and its intimate circles of familiarity, the people who knew one's ancestors and every moment from one's birth? Would people in Madirasi ever come to know him as the people here did, even if he lived there until his death? As his musings progressed, Damodaran began to feel that even leaving the house was unnecessary.

The day after he moved in, Ezhuthachan hung a wooden plank on the door to his room, with the inscription 'Malabar Musical Drama Troupe'. A small crowd gathered to gawk at the signboard, but Ezhuthachan ignored them, and sat in his room with the door shut. He ate the kanji Chellappan Pillah sent over twice a day. No one saw him leave the room – even to urinate. Still, in the evenings, as soon as Damodaran arrived, laughter and loud voices could be heard from the room.

Within a week, Chellappan Pillah realised that Ezhuthachan was scared not only of boats but also of water. One morning, arriving at his shop earlier than usual, he saw Ezhuthachan across the road, standing in the front yard of the building, lost in thought. He gave him a friendly smile. Ezhuthachan was dressed in a pristine mundu and upper garment, and his face was clean-shaven. When did he go to the barber, Chellappan Pillah wondered. At that moment, entirely unexpectedly, it began to drizzle. With a cry of alarm, Ezhuthachan ran back into his room. It was also raining when he came into the shop to buy chewing tobacco the next day. He waited patiently in the shop veranda until the rain stopped completely. It was evening by then. When the wind swept raindrops on to the veranda, he hastily stepped inside, looking scared. Those who watched him felt that if a drop of rain leaked through the roof and fell on to his skin, he would feel it like a drop of boiling oil.

'Does he wash his ass after he takes a shit?' Chellappan Pillah asked everyone who came into the shop, spitting on the floor.

It was disgusting to hear, but Ezhuthachan did not stink like he never washed. In the morning and in the evening, he anointed himself in strategic places with sandalwood oil brought from Mysore. He burnt fragrant herbs in a terracotta pot and stood over its fumes, fully dressed. Thus, a fragrant miasma followed in his wake, and humans and animals alike flared their nostrils.

'Where is this fragrance coming from?' Sixteen-year-old Theyyamma, who had come with her mother to have a broken ornament fixed, asked the goldsmith, Krishnan Thattan, whose shop was on the ground floor of the building where Ezhuthachan lived.

'There's a man upstairs, dressed in an upper garment,' Thattan said, poking in the pot of smouldering chaff with a blowpipe.

'I've never seen a man in an upper garment.'

Theyyamma took her mother's permission, climbed up the wooden staircase, and knocked on Ezhuthachan's door. She took the edge of his garment, and rubbed it between her fingers, acknowledging its softness.

'Is this fabric fragrant?'

'Yes. They water the cotton with attar, not ordinary water,' Ezhuthachan said.

Theyyamma had not heard the word 'attar' before. She pressed her nose to Ezhuthachan's chest and breathed in. When the pointy part of the voluptuous Theyyamma's garlic-smelling blouse caressed his chest, Ezhuthachan, who had won the hearts of countless women in Tamil Nadu, lost control of himself. But Theyyamma was not the type to reciprocate. She laughed, and ran downstairs. Despite breaking his habit and leaving his room to hang around her house for the next couple of days, and despite accosting her father in a tapioca field and giving him a bundle of beedis as a gift, he never got to set his eyes on her again.

Ezhuthachan went to take a look at a sesame field lying fallow after the harvest. There was a house in its northern corner, and he deemed the space in front of it suitable for staging their play. They took some chewing tobacco to the Christian Mappila who owned the land, asked his permission, and promised to find him a seat right in the front on all three days of the performance.

'I've never seen a play,' the Mappila said.

'You've seen Kurathiyattam at the Ettumanoor festival, haven't you?' Damodaran asked. 'It's a bit like that. There'll be songs too. The Kurathiyattam is usually performed in the fields in front of the temple, whereas here we'll construct a stage and perform on it.'

'Is the story also the same?'

'Oh, no. This story is about real people.'

But the drama *Kudiyaan*, which Ezhuthachan directed and played the protagonist in, was not an ordinary story of the people. He had spent ten years with Tamil musical drama troupes all across Madirasi Presidency, doing small roles, and helping with stage decorations and make-up. Those were stories of valiant Tamil kings and gods, and it was his life's ambition to stage such a production on his own. However, an encounter with some Congress Party members had caused a small earthquake in his mind, and changed some of his points of view. But he had no idea how to incorporate these new perspectives into his script, and his play ended up with mismatched renderings of piety, dance, princely characters and socialism floating like clumps in split buttermilk curry. He tried hard to reconcile the legend of a temple in Malabar with the story of a kudiyaan – a tenant farmer – of the temple lands, but he could neither move away from the form of the musical that was entrenched in his mind, nor keep aside the newly formed political thoughts from his writing. The result was a curious concoction. In one scene, heavenly maidens danced. In the other, the kudiyaan mouthed revolutionary thoughts. In the end, from the very first performance, no one had a good word to say about *Kudiyaan*. Those who had only seen traditional musical dramas sat perplexed, while the progressives made fun of Ezhuthachan's stupidity. Still, like all artists, he believed that his creation was a masterpiece, and that it was the audience who were not able to understand or appreciate it in the correct way. Had he been open to taking the help of someone more socially conscious, the play would have ended up being considered the first political drama, way before that honour was bestowed upon K. Damodaran's *Pattabakki*.

When, on the tenth of the month of Kumbham, a private company boat delivered three iron chests for Ezhuthachan, and volunteers carried them, unprompted, in a procession to the building where he lived, everyone was convinced that the play was definitely on. Under their watchful eyes, he wrote the date, 'Tenth of Meenam', on the wooden signboard. From that day onwards, every evening, people gathered below the building, in front of Krishnan Thattan's shop on the ground floor, but Ezhuthachan ignored them all. On his way to visit Ezhuthachan, Damodaran would chat to them a little, but he did not divulge any details, pretending that he too was in the dark.

'Are professional actors coming?' asked one.

'Maybe,' Damodaran said.

'Soon?'

'Ah...'

'I bet they come.'

One day, Krishnan Thattan declared, clearing up everyone's doubts: 'Ten actors are coming. I heard them talking.'

And he told his companion on the long walk back home across two hills in the light of a flaming torch: 'A female actor is also coming. From Kozhikode.'

From then on, private company boats arriving at the jetty were greeted by a crowd. A bunch of people sat in the shade on the coconut embankment, from morning to evening, convinced that the female actor would arrive in a special boat. They cleared a small square patch on the ground, and played pakida to kill time. Assuming that an elegant woman who got off one of the boats was the actress, they followed her, but she was a native of Poonjar on her way to the temple of Vaikkathappan, and went off in a bullock cart to Ettumanoor.

As the date of the performance drew near, there were some interesting changes in Ezhuthachan. He discarded his habitual upper garment and, wearing only a towel around his waist, began to clear the field with a hoe, digging up sesame stubs and flattening the clods, working right alongside a labourer. They constructed a stage with mangowood planks nailed across areca tree posts sunk into the ground, the roof thatched with plaited coconut fronds. The Chovathi who had plaited them had lent them for free as they would be returned after the show. Her husband helped, handing them over, hooking the end of one to the other, to Ezhuthachan, who sat on the roof laying them out on the rafters. The hot sun scorched his skin, and he was covered up to his knees in mud. Yet, Ezhuthachan did not wash himself in the evenings, and returned to work the next day with the dirt and debris still on him. The people who had breathed in the sandalwood fragrance in his wake now covered their noses as he passed by. Even in his spare time, he went around with an anxious expression on his unshaven face, deep in thought. He gave up food, smoked ganja, and stopped cleaning his teeth with chaff ash mixed with salt and black pepper. In the night, he sat sleepless in front of the building where he lived, boiling coffee husks on a fire and drinking it, unsweetened, like medicine. Some people began to doubt whether he was actually the owner of a drama troupe. His wild appearance, and the fact that he did most of the work himself, made them think he was a labourer sent to prepare everything. But the truth was that, each time *Kudiyaan* had been staged in the last four or five years, Ezhuthachan had undergone this transformation, and reverted to his old fragrant self in white garments as soon as it was over.

One day, he set out east with Damodaran in search of an arrack brewer. Along the way, he exclaimed, angrily: 'This won't do. This is not how it should be done!'

If anyone had overheard the comment, they would have assumed that Damodaran had done something unconscionable. Around two years ago, Ezhuthachan had given up on his play after it was performed in a remote village in Palakkad. No one had come to see it after the first performance. The actors, unpaid for their troubles, had called him names and left. With nowhere to cart the stage equipment, clothes and make-up, he had packed them into iron chests and left them behind a barn, protected from the rain. Then he had abandoned the respectable white clothes of a drama company owner, and returned to Coimbatore. With great difficulty, he had managed to get back into his old position in the drama company and had remained there quietly, like a newly married woman who did not want to remember her previous liaisons. When his colleagues had asked him about his play, he had behaved as though such a thing had never happened. Eventually, one day, as he sat half-asleep leaning on a pillar, glum from the scolding he had received for mucking up the make-up at a performance in Thrithala, a young man had entered his dressing room and introduced himself, thereby changing the course of his life.

'You are Ramanujan Ezhuthachan, aren't you?' the young man had asked. 'I am Damodaran. We've met before. I was there when *Kudiyaan* was staged for the first time. I thought it was an interesting experiment, although people don't take to new things quickly.'

The very next day, retrieving one of his iron chests from behind the barn, and arranging for the rest of them to be sent forth, Ezhuthachan had left with the young man.

Now, he explained the reason for his anger. The role of the policeman in the play was in jeopardy.

'Achuthan can't make it. He has gas trouble. His stomach is all bloated.'

'Let's get someone else then. I could do the role if necessary,' Damodaran said.

'That won't work. Only he can do justice to the role of the policeman.'

Back in their room, Damodaran took out the coal-black moustache made out of the fine fibre of coconut husk that was part of the policeman's costume from the iron chest and stuck it on his face. Ezhuthachan did not even glance at him.

'That moustache is suited only to Achuthan's face.'

'What if I found someone else with a face suited to this moustache?'

'I haven't seen a single face like that since I left Kochi. In fact, no one here even has a moustache. Is there some rule around here against growing moustaches?'

Ezhuthachan, who had the ability to remember even the smallest details of a person's face after just one meeting, was genuinely interested in knowing. Ever since he had come to Thiruvithamkur, other than the fine hair on the face of those who had delayed going to the barber, or the tiny embellishment some had above their upper lip in the shape of the number eleven, he had not encountered a proper moustache.

'You don't have one either,' Damodaran pointed out.

'Yes, but lots of people do where I come from. No one here does.'

'It's not banned or anything, but people here generally don't have moustaches. The maharajas of Thiruvithamkur used to have them. Marthanda Varma and Rama Varma had great big imperial moustaches. And the prime ministers – the Dalawas – like Raja Kesavadasan and Velu Thambi, also grew them. So people copied them, especially the upper caste Nairs. Then Maharaja Swathi Thirunal shaved off his moustache. Some say he did it because he was depressed from having to deal with the British. Or maybe he thought a moustache was not something that was appropriate for an artist like himself. The kings who came after also had no moustaches; the current king doesn't have one either. So now the Dalawas, other officials and the Nairs have also stopped growing them.'

'But in Madurai I met a man from Thiruvithamkur – Raman Pillah his name was – and he had a great big pointy moustache,' said Ezhuthachan.

'That must be because he was someone who wrote stories and plays about kings and other prominent people. I heard he took to the moustache after playing the role of Edgar in *King Lear*.'

When Ezhuthachan asked 'What *King Lear*,' Damodaran gave him a contemptuous look. He had great respect for artists, but the depth of their ignorance, that became apparent as soon as one scratched the surface, frustrated him.

By the end of the month of Kumbham, all the actors arrived, except the female actor from Kozhikode that Krishnan Thattan had talked about. Some came on foot and others by boat, including two blushingly beautiful young men who played female roles. They moved into the attic of the building, and spent all day sleeping on the bare floor. In the evenings, they picked jackfruits from trees which had no clear owners, cut off only the thorny outer skin, and ate the whole thing boiled. They had a trick of gouging holes in unripe jackfruits and sticking salt in them, making them ripen overnight. During rehearsals, the jackfruit expressed its innate nature in their stomachs, and made them run urgently to the clearing behind the house. This clearing would retain its name 'shit yard' long after the play and Ezhuthachan had disappeared from local memory. Within four or five days, there were no more jackfruits in the vicinity. Damodaran used his influence on the watchman of Poonjeri Thampuran's fields, and got ten para measures of paddy delivered at the building. They boiled it in the night, and laid it to dry on two mats in the hot sun the next day. Stepping out of his shop to urinate, Krishnan Thattan saw the drying paddy and felt a deep depression. He had never seen that amount of paddy in his entire life.

'There's a war going on and people don't even have kanji water to drink. He and his confounded play!' he cursed.

Thattan picked up a few grains of the paddy and chewed them. Swallowing their sweet juice, some chaff got stuck in his throat and irritated him for the rest of the day.

Ezhuthachan and Damodaran searched far and wide for a replacement for Achuthan, for a face that would suit the moustache, and for the means to feed the troupe. They heard that a banana tree with a bunch of unripe bananas had fallen over at the edge of Chellappan Pillah's field, and hurried over with a machete. They also wanted to see if the few stands of colocasia in the field had any tubers.

'The real policemen in these parts have no moustaches. So what's wrong if the policeman in the play doesn't have one?' Damodaran asked.

'It is better not to stage the play if the policeman has no moustache.'

Ezhuthachan's response made Damodaran itch to kick him into the canal below. Typical of this lot, he thought, always ready to compromise except when it comes to silly things that made them feel like great authors and artists.

By the time they got to the field, Paviyan Pulayan's third son, Vavachan, had eaten the bananas, skin and all, uncooked, leaving only the central stalk. Except for water and a wilted coconut he had found by chance, he had had nothing else for three days, and there was no prospect even for watered down kanji until Paviyan returned from the paddy harvest. His father's father had an odividya, a magic trick that he would use in the face of relentless hunger. He would shapeshift into a turtle or a dwarf snakehead, and hide in the mud and sleep until the next planting season. Vavachan took after his grandfather, Kankali, a Pulayan who was taller than average, but he did not know the shapeshifting trick to forget his hunger.

'Filthy son of a…'

Damodaran raised his hand and heaved forward, looking at Vavachan's lips and teeth sticky from the sap of the green banana.

'I'll break his jaw.'

Ezhuthachan caught hold of his waist and pulled him back.

'Wait! Wait, I think we've found our policeman.'

Damodaran suppressed his anger and, thinking about the unexpected coincidences in life, he steadied his breath and looked at Vavachan carefully. Like all men of the Pulayan caste, he was coal-black, as though he would turn the water black if he entered a river, as though if, like a dark spirit, he jumped up and touched the sky, black rain would fall. Only the skin on his face had lost some colour but, unlike other Pulayan men, a dense growth of hair covered his cheeks, chin and upper lip. Pulayan men usually did not have this kind of hair growth on their faces, and they regularly went to Pathrose Pulayan to shave off whatever they did have. Those who did not were bound to be waylaid by Pathrose Pulayan and have it forcibly shaved off with a razor sharpened on a handy stone.

'The audience will boo if we make a policeman out of a Pulayan,' Damodaran said.

'No one will think of that when they see a proper policeman. They'll be too scared.'

They marched Vavachan to Ezhuthachan's room, Damodaran leading the way and Ezhuthachan bringing up the rear. There, for the first time in his life, Vavachan ate kanji in a white enamel plate, with a mount of stewed yam in the middle like a partly submerged island. One of the actors who played female roles made everyone laugh, saying that the kanji looked whiter than usual next to Vavachan. He put his hand in Vavachan's facial hair.

'How extraordinary!' he said. 'So thick, and as strong as an elephant's hair.'

Damodaran summoned the barber Govindan. But he refused to touch Vavachan's beard.

'We are Velakkithala Nairs,' he said. 'We only serve the Nairs and the castes higher than them. If you want, there are Vaathi barbers in Athirampuzha. They cut the Pulayans' hair.'

'I'd do it,' said Ezhuthachan. 'But it has to be done properly.'

Impatient to wait until daybreak, he went off in a boat and fetched Pathrose Pulayan, who arrived pissed off that Paviyan's son had escaped his vigilance.

'Son of a whore … I'll kill you.'

Pathrose Pulayan dragged Vavachan by his ear and sat him in the yard.

'Shave only where I say,' Ezhuthachan came over brandishing a pair of scissors. Pathrose was not used to working with scissors.

'Keep the moustache as it is,' Ezhuthachan instructed Pathrose. 'Let it fan out on both cheeks. Shave the beard off completely and trim the rest of the hair.'

'I can't be making moustaches into wild boar tusks,' Pathrose refused. 'I'll just shave the lot off.'

Damodaran negotiated with him, and offered him some paddy. Finally, he agreed and sharpened his razor. Ezhuthachan sat close by with the scissors, watching his every move. But it was not an easy task. Like lichen on rock, each hair resisted Pathrose's efforts. He had never come across such resilient facial hair. When he scratched at the beard with his razor, applying only some water to it, Vavachan grunted.

'Shut up, you prick. Just wait, I'll get your father too,' said Pathrose.

A couple of times, some hair got pulled off by the root, and blood beaded on Vavachan's skin giving Pathrose a sense of satisfaction. Ezhuthachan did some trimming and, in the end, the moustache fanned out majestically. Ezhuthachan anointed it with a handful of coconut oil, shaped it to the sides, and massaged it until it glistened like the oiled back of a black bull. By then, everyone else had gone to bed. Ezhuthachan took Vavachan upstairs, sat him on a low stool, and raised the wick of the hurricane lantern. He peered at the moustache from the front and the sides, and smiled, satisfied. Damodaran, awoken from his sleep, looked at the spectacle in front of him, and felt a terror he had not experienced since the time when, during his childhood, he had found himself alone under a palmyra tree. He recalled the statue of the cruel-faced, sword-wielding doorkeeper at the temple of a demon goddess in Madirasi Presidency.

'I wasn't going to beat you,' he said to Vavachan, apologising for raising his hand at him earlier. 'Just happened in the heat of the moment…'

The policeman looked at him from top to bottom and grunted, sending Damodaran to his mat unable to sleep for the rest of the night.

The next day was the ninth of the month of Thulam. Only two days were left until the first performance.

The role of the policeman Vavachan was to perform was not as important a role in Ezhuthachan's play for him to have gone through all this trouble to find the right person. The character appeared in the second half of the play, and in only two scenes. In the first scene, he was to be present throughout but had no dialogue, and was only required to deliver a few grunts and piercing looks. In the second scene, he was to be on stage for very few minutes, but had to look at the audience and roar angrily.

The crowd that assembled to watch Ezhuthachan's play in Neendoor was much larger than any he had ever encountered. People who paid in cash, and the dignitaries who had supported in kind, sat on the wooden planks in the front. Only they could hear the dialogue clearly. Behind them, people sat or stood on the bare ground until the field was full. Except for a couple of Kakathi women who wandered from festival to festival, and an old Ulladathi, no other women were present. And no Pulayan had turned up to see Paviyan's son's performance. In fact, few in the audience knew that such a character was about to appear on stage.

The audience struggled to understand the Malabar dialect, and yet they thoroughly enjoyed the play until half-time. They exclaimed at the realistic portrayal of the temple, and the mana – the Namboothiri house – on the curtain that was the backdrop of the stage. They absolutely loved the overseer, a central character in the story, and roared with laughter at the way he dropped his shoulder cloth on the floor whenever he was overcome with anger, and picked it up and swished it, producing a 'thup' sound.

The policeman made his appearance in the first scene after the interval. The overseer threatened to have the kudiyaan's family arrested if they did not vacate the land immediately. In the split second between the threat and the policeman's appearance, an impoverished middle-aged Nair sitting in the middle of the audience shouted: 'Pulayan police.' The audience laughed even though they did not quite understand the meaning, but they were quickly stunned into silence by the sure-footed arrival of the moustached policeman, nicknamed 'Tusker'. In the heat of the moment, even the overseer curtsied, involuntarily going off script. Ezhuthachan's desperate gestures from the sidelines to bring him back to script went unnoticed, and he continued in that respectful manner for the rest of the scene. Those who sat in the front rows felt that their age-old fear of mythical, discarnate beings of darkness, such as the Rakshas and the Makkan, had finally taken physical form and appeared before them. Their terror was augmented by the enormous shadow that his body cast across the back curtain. The echo of his footfall reminded them of the local deities who wandered in the dark of night. His khaki trousers and shirt and the wide belt around his waist looked as magnificent to them as the Kaurava prince Dusshasanan's attire. His naked shins glistened like ebony wood that had been soaked in water and debarked. No one dared look at his face with its bloodshot eyes. It cast ten shadows in the confused light of the numerous lamps hung around the stage, giving him the appearance of Ravanan, the ten-headed king of Lanka. Like the kollikkoravan owl which could predict death, his grunts and grumbles sounded like roars, reaching even those at the back of the audience.

Finally, the scene was over. The audience sighed, and shook themselves out of their horror. Damodaran recognised how the play had been completely changed by this policeman with no dialogue. Ezhuthachan realised that the narrative was being derailed, and wished he had given the character a couple of lines of dialogue to clarify things. But the scariest thing was yet to come. The story proceeded as though the policeman had no further role in it, but he made another unexpected and short appearance in the penultimate scene. Just as everyone sat back expecting a solemn end to the story, he rushed on to the stage with heavy footsteps and, as though his quarry had escaped into the audience, he looked directly at them and roared: 'Da...!' The audience had a clear glimpse of his blood-red tongue and sharp teeth, and they felt that he had truly turned into the fearsome king, Ravanan. The response was beyond anything Ezhuthachan had anticipated. A wave of absolute horror washed over the audience. Those who sat in the front rows fled. The only person who remained was an elderly Brahmin, a man so old that even his eyelashes had greyed. He was the only audience member who had been sitting in a chair, blocking the view of everyone around him. Yellow old urine ran down his legs as he sat petrified, enveloped in its warm smell. In the confusion, no one waited to see the last scene, or to find out how the story ended. They ran all the way home with the sense of satisfaction of having seen the formidable pox-marked Goddess Kali in battle with the warrior Darikan in a performance of Mudiyettu.

The play was performed the next two nights, and people came, from Arpookara and from Kallara, swimming across the canals and in boats. They too were unable to sit still and witness the last scene. On the third night, as the play concluded, Ezhuthachan announced that this would be the last performance, and that they would be going back to Malabar. He thanked the audience for making it a huge success. Some people milled around the field after the play was over until the Tusker came out of the lean-to next to the stage. The sight of him made them disperse, and in the skirmish, several people were injured.

Vavachan returned to the attic room, took off his costume, and ate his kanji. Ezhuthachan told him that he would let him know of future performances through Damodaran. He removed, with loving fingers, a single grain of rice like a little crescent moon stuck in Vavachan's moustache.

The next morning, Pathrose Pulayan arrived at Paviyan's hut, his sharpened razor in hand.

'Send him out, woman,' he shouted at Chella in anger. 'I am off to Vechoor today. Won't be back for a week.'

Vavachan had gone into the fields to defecate. As he walked into the yard, Pathrose stepped back, frightened.

'How about we shave it off?' he asked, his voice shaky.

'Why? Let it be. You go away.'

There was a new maturity in Vavachan's voice that made Chella raise her head from her chore. She had not heard him return the night before, and was seeing him for the first time after the play. By the time she let out a terrified scream, Pathrose Pulayan had already crossed two fields.

4

TWO PEOPLE

Long after Ezhuthachan, his iron chests, and the drama troupe had gone back, two of the characters he had created remained, forever connected to the two local people who had enacted them in the play. One of them had discarded the character from his mind, but his countrymen did not allow him to escape from it; the other found it difficult to fully banish the character and go back to his previous life.

The former was Krishnan Thattan, the goldsmith. He had played the role of a devious goldsmith, a character Ezhuthachan had added to the script for no good reason. Watching Krishnan Thattan ply his trade, sitting in front of the smouldering pot of chaff in his shop on the ground floor of the building where he stayed, had given Ezhuthachan the crazy idea of creating such a character. Reasoned thinking was not part of his creative process, and he often added random ideas that came to him to the script. Thattan was persuaded when Ezhuthachan told him all he had to do was sit on the stage and do what he did every day, say a couple of lines of dialogue loudly, and chew some paan and spit dramatically. Thattan would have agreed anyway, eager as he was to get to know from up close the intriguing world Ezhuthachan, Damodaran and the actors created in the room upstairs, and to narrate these events with many embellishments to all and sundry.

The Thattan in the play was a devious character who not only stole bits from the gold he was entrusted to work with, but considered it to be a goldsmith's fundamental right. The overseer, who brings an ornament to be melted and remade into a new one, forbids the Thattan from stealing even a tiny shaving of the gold. The Thattan says that it is impossible to change an age-old habit. So the overseer watches the Thattan like a hawk as the gold is melted at high heat in the pot. Concerned by the vigilance, the Thattan hatches a plan.

'I give up, Master,' he tells the overseer. With you watching my every move, I can't steal anything. You've won. May I chew some paan?'

'By all means,' says the overseer, magnanimous in his victory. 'You thought you could put one over me!'

The Thattan prepares the paan with betel leaf, areca nut flakes and a lick of slaked lime paste, puts it in his mouth, and chews until his mouth is filled with the juice. Then he takes his blowpipe, and pretending to blow at the fire in his pot, sucks in a bit of the melted gold into his liquid-filled mouth. Before it can burn the inside of his mouth, he spits elaborately into the yard. The work is done, and as the overseer is about to leave with the finished ornament, the Thattan says they should weigh the final product. And lo and behold, it is a tad lighter! The overseer searches in the pot, on the floor around it, and in the folds of the Thattan's mundu but nothing is found.

'I doubted you unnecessarily,' he says to the Thattan by way of an apology. 'It must have been lost in the crafting process...'

'Lost in the craf–! See there, in the yard. There it is!' says the Thattan, proudly.

But the most interesting part of this story was yet to come. Ever since he had acted in the play, no one brought their gold to Krishnan Thattan. Those who had seen the play, and those who had heard tell of it, began to believe that Krishnan Thattan was a trickster who stole bits from the gold he was given to work with. Years passed, and Ezhuthachan and his play began to fade from people's memories, but Krishnan Thattan's name became inextricably linked with habitual thieving. Three decades later, as he lay on his deathbed, he would overhear his son speaking to the visitors who had come to see him: 'What a man he was! You must have heard about the paan chewing and the spitting…'

By then, Krishnan Thattan himself had begun to believe the story even as the memory of having acted in the play had left his mind. Around forty years after his death, the grandchildren he would never set eyes on would open a jewellery shop in Ettumanoor, and their competitors would deter customers by telling them about the ancestor who was a well-known gold thief.

Meanwhile, the policeman from Malabar, the character Vavachan had played, had left him, but he refused to shave off the moustache that was part of the costume. Two or three days after the play was performed for the last time, he resumed his habit of spending his days wandering along the edges of the fields that extended up to the horizon, looking for something – anything – to eat. Rarely did he find anything edible in this endless wandering. Even the aged mud crabs, their flesh gone bitter, scuttled sideways into the deep wetness of their hidey-holes as soon as they spotted his hungry arrival. The coconut trees refused to throw down a single, even immature, fruit. Vavachan spent an entire night crawling around in a compound where a few tapioca plants grew, their branches raised to the sky like preachers, but it was in vain as their tubers were long gone, dug out by bandicoots and humans alike. Even their tender leaves had already been picked and eaten, boiled to remove the bitterness. All he had eaten since the plate of kanji after the last performance of the play was a piece of yam. Chella had delivered grass for the cattle in a house, and they had allowed her to dig up an old coconut tree stump for firewood. She had chanced upon the yam while digging it up.

Vavachan found a rusty old knife someone had discarded. He scrubbed it for hours and sharpened it. He lay, face down, looking into the mirror-like surface of the canal reflecting the calm afternoon skies, and a terrifying stranger with a big moustache looked back at him from its depths. A school of rosy-red minnows swam through his moustache without making a single ripple in the water. Pregnant fish quietly considered the suitability of its denseness to lay their eggs, assuming that it was the tangled roots of canal-side trees. Vavachan wet his face with water, and shaved off the straggly hairs that had begun to sprout on his cheeks, trimmed a few unruly strands, and patted it into shape with wet hands.

A five-rupee-taxed boat with an orderly load of coconut husks spotted Vavachan and pulled in. Two men got out of it. They had identical reed-thin bodies, identical mundus tied around their waists, and identical sun-blackened faces.

'We've been on the lookout for you from Kaipuzha onwards,' one of them said. 'We're from Thiruvarppu. Came to Pravattom to collect husks.'

They had no difficulty recognising the moustached policeman, the character from the drama. From Arpookara onwards, they had been hearing stories about him. There was another important character in the stories they heard, but the central subject of these stories was the moustache that appeared only in two scenes. Not many who had heard the stories knew that the man with the moustache was a local.

'When is the next performance?' one of the twins asked.

'No more performances,' Moustache said. 'They've all gone back with their boxes.'

A narrow-mouthed pot was retrieved from among the coconut husks in the boat, and placed reverentially in front of Moustache. The men watched, mesmerised, as 'the policeman' drank the arrack and munched on bits of desiccated coconut. Moustache had never seen the clear liquid, brewed from toddy, before, and as the pot emptied, his cheeks and moustache quivered, and his eyes became bloodshot. He asked for a dry coconut as the men from Thiruvarppu got back into their boat and said their goodbyes.

'Do you know the way to Malaya?' he asked.

'Malaya? We've never heard of such a place,' they said, looking at each other. 'We're on our way to Thazhathangadi.'

'Do you know the way to Malabar?'

'No.'

In Vavachan's mind, the embankment turned into a stage made out of wooden planks, and the two men rowing the boat became the audience sitting in the dark. He let out an angry roar as he had in the play, and the men rowed away frantically and disappeared. They told the story of their meeting with Moustache wherever they stopped to load and unload husks, and in their own households, and in each telling, only the moustache remained the same. Sometimes he was a seven-foot tall black spirit that looked like a dried palmyra tree, and sometimes a wrestler with an enormous paunch and flabs of fat.

But the incident that would create a major commotion in Kaipuzha, Neendoor and neighbouring places was yet to occur. Intending to find Damodaran, who he felt would know the way to Malaya or, at the very least, help him get to Ezhuthachan in Malabar, Vavachan swam across the canal and set out east, crossing the Nanoottampadavu fields and a wooden bridge across Chathankari. Only older Pulayans walked along the lane beyond that was meant for bullock and buffalo carts, and that too on very rare occasions. But if he cut across the fields and compounds to the south of the lane, it would be less than half a mile to Damodaran's house. Little did Vavachan realise that this path would lead him to Kesava Pillah, a distant relative of Damodaran on his mother's side, and the owner of a hundred acres of fields, who was, at that very moment, sitting in a chair on an embankment planted with Etha bananas by the side of a Njavara rice field, drinking freshly tapped toddy. Not a single Nair or Mappila in the area stood up to him. He was known to punish all incursions with an ear-splitting slap to the side of the head. The way he dealt with a Chovathi who had dared comment on the milk-filled udders of a cow was legendary in these parts. Kesava Pillah had torn off her mundu and made her lick the cow's behind. Her kin folk had banded together to challenge him, but when they came face to face with him, they inadvertently agreed with his deeds. It was a milch cow after all, wasn't it?

Kesava Pillah drank his toddy and told his coterie a story about Njavara rice. He was an entertaining talker, and paid no attention to anything anyone said in response.

'Njavara is like some people,' he declared. 'Grows so tall and falls flat on the ground before setting grain. Then it raises it head from where it has fallen to make a tiny sheaf of grain. Why it can't just stand up and grow properly as it is meant to be, I don't know.'

Before his companion and the toddy tapper could laugh in agreement, a terrifying being broke the cover of the trees and passed in front of them, quick as a sheath of lightning. Pillah had travelled to Vaikom and Kottayam, but he had never seen a man with such a big moustache. He was reminded of an elephant that had gone mad and killed a bunch of people during a temple festival when he was a child. It had long tusks that extended to the sides. It too had a black body and bloodshot eyes, and had run amok. Before he could compose himself, the old fear made him rise from his chair with a sense of anxiety and reverence. The apparent transformation of their usually fearless master confused his companion and the toddy tapper.

Damodaran's younger sister was in the pounding house, a structure with four posts and a roof but no walls, trying to persuade her three-year-old child to eat a morsel of tapioca mixed with grated coconut. As soon as the sour-tasting, day-old tapioca touched his mouth, the child spat it out.

'Stop spitting or the Makkan will come get you,' she admonished, pointing to the yard.

The child's eyes followed his mother's finger. So far, he had only a vague idea of the Makkan, something invisible that hid in the darkness among the trees, something cruel-faced that hated disobedient children, but now there he was, materialising out of the greenery and walking up to them. The terrified child's breathless screams made the mother look up, and she grabbed the child and ran into the main house screaming right along with it.

Moustache realised that Damodaran was not at home and left. He walked aimlessly through yards and compounds. Soon it was dark, and as he walked along a freshly hoed bit of land, he stumbled on a clod of mud, and hit his head on a palmyra tree. Its rough bark snagged his moustache. Enraged by the pain, he grabbed the tree by its sturdy trunk and gave it an almighty shake. From then on, day by day, the tree began to dry as though it had been struck by lightning. New foliage and inflorescence wilted, palm fronds dropped to the ground, and finally, the crown died entirely, and it became a refuge for brooding birds.

Vavachan hurdled over fences and across canals, reached the piece of barren land behind the junction, and looked at the road. The area was deserted. Only the lamplighter squatted on the ground sucking on a beedi, waiting to put out the street lamp before its wick started smouldering. Vavachan had never met the man before. But having watched the play on all three days it was performed, the man stood up reverentially, eyes cast down to avoid looking directly at the moustache.

'Which is the way to Malaya?' Moustache asked.

The lamplighter felt that he had swallowed his tongue and, speechless, he walked slowly backwards. Moustache repeated his question a couple of times. Irritated by the lack of response, he kicked at the coconut wood lamp post. It broke in two, and Vavachan disappeared into the dark night.

Presently, two young men, on their way back from a political gathering in Koothattukulam, came down the road. One of them was the first person from Neendoor to go to college in Kottayam. The sight of the destroyed lamp post angered them.

'This can't go on. What sort of a situation is this when even the guy who played a policeman in a drama can do as he pleases?' he asked, helping the lamplighter up. 'Did he hurt you?'

'He caught me by my legs and raised me to the sky,' said the lamplighter, his imagination working overtime. 'He wanted to crack my head open on the ground. Only put me down because he saw you coming.'

The next morning, five or six young Nair men set out westwards, sharpened lengths of green wood in hand. They did not have far to go, but it was the first time they were venturing out into the fields baking under the sun. It was not the broken lamp post, but the disgrace they had suffered indirectly through what had happened to Kesava Pillah that enraged them.

'To tell you the truth, I didn't really see him,' Kesava Pillah told the men who had come to his house very early in the morning. 'I stood up because I had to fart, not because I was scared. As if a Pulayan will have the guts to come before me.'

The men smiled, relieved, even though they could tell he was jabbering on more than usual to hide his embarrassment.

'Still, we have to teach him a lesson. The Pulayans are getting too brazen. The other day, one of their women sat down to take a piss in the middle of the paddy. I gave her a good kick right on her belly.'

He sent them off telling them to help themselves to the toddy stored in a hut along their way, and asked them to come and see him on their way back in the evening.

The young men drank the toddy and set forth. As they proceeded, they beat the living daylight out of everyone who crossed their path. Pulayans working in the fields climbed out and tried to run away, but the men chased them, and flayed their backs open with the sticks. They caught a young Pulaya woman, tore off her clothes, and drove her like a cow in front of them. They struck her buttocks and thighs until they were covered in welts, and finally kicked her into a deep hole filled with water.

No one was home when they reached Paviyan's hut. They tore it down and dug up the floor. They cut down bunches of baby coconuts off the trees, and broke the tappers' pots tied to the base of the inflorescence before they left.

Finally, as darkness settled, they walked east, and stopped to rest on a bund planted with a few coconut trees. It had been fortified recently with fresh clay. They sat in a circle in a patch where the clay had dried, and began to discuss the day's adventures. Even in the dark, their faces glowed with a sense of pride in having accomplished a valiant deed in service of their community and society, and their words reflected the confidence that their achievement would be remembered and celebrated for a long time, perhaps even by their progeny. They discussed the events gravely until two of them jumped into the canal to cool their bodies. The conversation then became jovial. They felt their anger recede, and a great burden being lifted off their shoulders. As their minds settled, they felt like dozing right there in the cool breeze. Their lives were beautiful, they felt, and they moved on to telling each other, as unmarried men were wont to, their sexual conquests, both real and imaginary.

'All she had was a God-given line down there,' said one of the young men.

He was stocky, and wore red ear studs that glittered in the dark. He had a habit of making light of things, but a way of saying even the silliest thing in a low, sombre voice, persuading those who did not know him well to consider the matter gravely. So it took them a couple of minutes to realise that he was talking about the woman they had attacked and made to walk naked earlier. They found it hilarious and erupted in laughter. Even the ones who had held back earlier now jumped into the canal and roughhoused in its cool water.

One of the men urinated into the water.

'My only regret is that we couldn't find that scoundrel,' he said. 'If we had, I'd have plucked out not just his moustache, I'd have pulled out every single hair on his body. Cut off his thing, too.'

He took off his wet mundu and wrung the water out, displaying his nakedness in the spreading moonlight.

'We should get going. Let's not linger here.'

'Why? Are you afraid?'

'Of course not. It's getting late, that's all.'

He flared his nostrils and breathed in deeply.

'Can you smell that? Like boiling tapioca? That's the smell of a cobra yawning.'

The men got out of the water, wiped their bodies and walked briskly, silent now in their hurry to get back home.

At no point during the day, as they went around wreaking havoc, had they even mentioned the name Moustache. They had attacked Paviyan's hut as though it was a duty they had taken upon themselves. It was clear from the routes they took and from their bluster that they had tried to avoid a direct confrontation with Moustache, but they did not admit this fact to each other or to themselves. They had stopped in a paddy field and made a ruckus, shouting and swearing, as though to alert Moustache and allow him time to escape in case he was at home. They had snatched the net from a hapless fisherman who happened to pass by, and thrown it up on a coconut tree.

'There's someone behind us,' the man at the back of the group said as they picked their way through the darkness.

The others paid no attention at first, but when he repeated it and tried to get in front of the group, they became alert. They stopped where grazing cattle had made a clearing in the scutch grass, and stared into the darkness behind them until they were satisfied that they were not being followed. They hurried along, but the feeling remained. Turning back once again, they saw a movement among the flowering screw pine bushes on the canal side. They picked up clods of mud and threw them in that direction. Something cried out as though a clod had connected with its thick skin. Pleased, they ran, and their hearts worked hard and loud as though they were engines controlling the movement of their legs.

They did not get too far before they saw, quite clearly in the deep darkness, a forbidding face. It was broad like a hand-fan, and was almost entirely covered in a moustache, its hairy tentacles snaking sideways like sturdy bean vines. Dark as a vetiver bush, it spanned the width of a man's outstretched arms. It stood out in a disorderly demonic beauty, undisciplined yet shapely.

But surely it was an illusion, something that their anxious minds, tired from their unaccustomed exertions of the day, had conjured up because, at that very moment, Vavachan was asleep, face down on a bund at least an hour's walk from where they were. The arrack he had drunk, the long walk and the relentless hunger had exhausted him completely. Even though he was accustomed to not having anything to eat for days, he had, unlike Paviyan, Chella or their other children, lost the ability to endure hunger, his metabolism changed by the availability of regular meals while he was with Ezhuthachan and his drama troupe. Unlike other Pulayans, he would no longer be able to live without food or draw energy from the wind or the sun. All his life, he had been in pursuit, like his father Paviyan, of an occasional plate of kanji, but now he was looking for the road to a place where he imagined kanji was plentiful and always within reach. The search had exhausted him.

Vavachan slept, immersed in a dream about a plate of kanji with a dollop of stewed yam flavoured with grated coconut in the middle. Soon he would be woken up, and make some important decisions about his life.

5

KUTTATHI

Emergency report submitted before the Honourable Tehsildar of Ettumanoor by Sankunni Menon, the Pravruthyar of Kaipuzha subdivision on the twenty-second day of the month of Meenam.

> At the time of writing Kaipuzha subdivision comprised of Kaipuzha, Arpookara and Sreekandamangalam and a section of Neendoor is an area with a significant population of Southist Nasrani Christians, Ezhavas and Nairs, and two families of Malayali Brahmins. Because the land has innumerable canals and extensive paddy fields there is also a considerable number of Vaalans who fish the canals and Pulayans and Parayans who work the fields. No serious incidents affecting law and order have been recorded in this region other than the problems that arose during the great rains of 1924 and the death of a stone mason during the harvesting of a mango tree sold in public auction. This situation has now become the opposite unfortunately. It is pointed out that this state of affairs could have a deleterious impact on the state of the land as well as the availability of food supplies. It has become evident that the cause of this grievous state of affairs is the immoral and unlawful actions of one Vavachan, son of a converted Pulayan-Christian Paviyan residing in a hut built on the eastern embankment of

the paddy fields belonging to Kalappurayil Koramappila on the southern side of the waterway in Chozhiyappara fields where the northern end of Kaipuzha subdivision joins with Onamthuruthu subdivision. It is known that contrary to the customs of the land and in a manner unsuitable to the hereditary work of Pulayans this man has established a great big moustache on his face. Personal enquiries have verified this fact and also the state of affairs that is discouraging women and children even from undertaking their daily ablutions because of this man's untimely comings and goings through public paths and compounds. On the nineteenth of last month the priest of Arpookara Subramanian temple on his way to begin the daily devotions at four in the morning carrying a vessel full of water was caused to faint near Villunni from the terror of seeing a shape that may have been the Pulayan-Christian referred to herein thereby causing displeasure to the God and distress to the people. Further a Mappila woman near Tharayil who stepped out in the middle of the night to urinate has also fainted. The priest of Kuttikkal church has expressed his wish that the traders attending the twice-monthly cattle market in Kaipuzha could continue to do so without fear. The recent information that the Pulayan-Christian named Vavachan has gone missing and that he might be hiding in the fields or in deserted areas has increased the general sense of panic and fear among the public. Farmers are afraid to go into the fields alone as it is said that the party referenced herein is known to use shapeshifting tricks, attack people and steal the bundled sheaves of paddy stored in threshing yards. It is feared that the quality of the summer crop will be seriously affected by the shoddy standards of labour provided by the Pulayans now that they are left without supervision. These facts are respectfully submitted for special and urgent consideration in the hope of immediate remedies in the form of police presence and follow-up government actions.

Pravruthyar Sankunni Menon remained seated in his chair even after Rama Kuruppu, the peon, walked in front of his door a couple of times, indicating that they were running late. Menon was not satisfied with the report he had just composed even though he had copied it on to good-quality paper a couple of times. Although his handwriting was pretty at first glance, it was illegible like a bundle of hopelessly knotted thread. The reports he sent to the Taluk courts were famous for the complex rendering, from which it was impossible to decipher their point, or the truth or untruth, fairness or unfairness of their subject matter. Senior government officials too had accepted his style as the correct pro forma for official reports, and had come to think of him as the model civil servant, a master carpenter who could fashion facts into trapdoors no one could open, thus preserving themselves from any repercussions. Around two years ago, there had been a disagreement over the ownership and harvesting rights of a one-and-half-acre piece of land next to the public canal on the eastern border of Virippukalappadam, a disagreement that could have been resolved quickly through discussions. However, Menon decided to visit the place, and wrote an elaborate report. As a result of that report, almost a hundred acres of fields in that area were not harvested that year, and those fields had not been cultivated since. The parties involved had by then resolved their differences, but the Taluk office now held a hefty file, helpfully started by Menon, containing convoluted reports that transformed an issue affecting an acre of land into one that affected the entire area. People had even given up grazing their cattle in those fields, fearing that they would be caught up in some sort of legal tangle.

Still, his report on Vavachan gave Menon no sense of satisfaction. The subject matter was different from the usual issues he dealt with as the Pravruthyar of Kaipuzha – issues relating to land, or the collection of food items for Murajapam, the six-yearly Brahmin ritual at the Sri Padmanabhaswamy temple. He was in a state of contentment until last evening when, at toddy tapper Ayyappan's house, he had been apprised of the seriousness of the matter.

Pravruthyar Menon's daily evening trip to Ayyappan's house, a routine he had followed for many years, was a widely known fact, although he liked to pretend that he was inspecting his fields. He would walk fairly fast, his white mundu tucked up, and a towel folded like a pliable piece of wood on his shoulder. As he walked, his gaze would be turned upwards, which was his natural habit. But most people assumed that he walked looking up instead of ahead like ordinary folk because he was the Pravruthyar – the person in charge of setting the property tax – and that he was taking stock of the coconut, mango and jackfruit crop in order to recalculate the taxes paid. Some tried to distract him from the world above their yards by engaging him in small talk, and called him by his nickname 'Menokki' – upward-looker – instead of Menon as soon as he was out of earshot.

Menon liked to have something to tickle his palate with his toddy or arrack, but did not eat in other households, not even in Nair households, let alone in the houses of lower-caste folk. Knowing this, his wife would give him a banana-leaf parcel of a quick but tasty chammanthi made of toasted dry prawns ground with coconut, kandari chillies and salt. As soon as Menon would sit on his special stool in a clean spot under the coconut tree behind Ayyappan's house and open his parcel, his fellow drinkers from all castes would pick it clean with their greedy fingers, lauding its taste. This obvious appreciation gladdened Menon's heart, but one day he decided to pull a prank, the idea of which came to him as he watched a couple of lumberjacks sawing the trunk of a jungle jack tree on his way back from the courts. He scooped up a fistful of the damp sawdust, brought it home, and instructed his wife to make the chammanthi with it instead of the dry prawns. Devoted wife that she was, she obliged. That day too, the chammanthi disappeared as soon as the package was opened at the evening assembly of toddy drinkers at Ayyappan's house.

'Tell me,' Menon began, drinking the toddy from the coconut shell kept aside only for his use, 'how was the chammanthi today?'

'First class!' Mathamappila, the rope merchant, responded. 'My woman makes chammanthi that tastes like bird shit.'

'It had a special taste today. Must have been white river shrimps.'

Not even sawdust would survive among these toddy guzzlers, Menon concluded.

Menon was aware that Paviyan Pulayan's son had grown a moustache, but it was only when Ayyappan's Chovathi told him the details that he acknowledged it as a matter that required his attention.

'Straighten your cloth. Don't make me vomit,' the Chovathi scolded Kuttanasari, the carpenter, who, as usual, squatted on the floor wearing a piece of cloth that did not quite go around his waist.

Then she approached Menon. 'Is Your Highness aware, I wonder...' she began. 'That Pulayan boy is going around flaunting a moustache. He scared the shit out of a bunch of children who were walking along the bund last night. And it's him that burned down the hay in the Makkothara fields.'

'Where is his father Pulayan?' Menon asked.

'Who knows!' Kuttanasari said. 'Pulayan does as Pulayan does.'

The Chovathi's scolding had made no difference to Kuttanasari, and he continued sitting there with his crotch visible through the gap in his too-small mundu. This was a sight that had exasperated the women and children in all the houses he worked in. One time, fed up of the sight, a woman near Prala had emptied a pan of water she had used to wash the grinding stone after grinding chillies into his lap.

'You know those ducks that had their necks broken near the wheelhouse? It was him that did it,' Ayyappan's Chovathi continued.

'The police will be here soon,' Kuttanasari said. 'The State Congress people have called them.'

That very night, Menon, always on alert to save his own skin, sat down with pen and paper to write a report for the powers that be.

'Let him grow his moustache or beard,' he told his wife when she called him for his evening meal, 'but I must let the Tehsildar know before the police get here.'

However, words did not flow as effortlessly as they usually did from his pen. He was adept at crafting knotty sentences that made both the offender and the defender feel that the writer was on their side, while being entirely unhelpful for all practical purposes. He could cover two whole sides of the paper with one long sentence, confounding all readers. But this time, no formal complaint had been made. The moustached offender would never read his report. And the matter was not as complicated as the property cases he usually dealt with. Regardless, rereading his own report, Menon found it ridiculous. It was too simple. Even an idiot could clearly understand it.

And yet, by afternoon, with the report carefully wrapped in paper and tucked under his arm, Menon set out for the Taluk courts accompanied by the peon Rama Kuruppu. Rama Kuruppu carried a pile of registers, recording the yearly calculations of tax, bound together with jute thread. Climbing down the field edges from Villunni, they would cross Kuttomburam and Mannanam ferries, walk along the deserted slopes of Nalpathi Hill to reach Ettumanoor. Miffed that he had missed his lunch, Kuruppu walked behind Menon, spitting and muttering in a low voice. On occasions when he was forced to be in Kuruppu's company, Menon was careful to maintain a safe distance between them so that onlookers would not think they were companions. The local people were scornful of Kuruppu. Like termites on wood, he was said to feed on the essence of everyone who got too close to him. That, and his appearance that had an uncanny resemblance to a termite – thin, with the protruding belly and the colouring of an insect that lived underground – gave him the everlasting nickname, Termite Kuruppu. Later, five or six years after his retirement, on his way back from scamming some unsuspecting soul, he would come across an elephant. He would not realise that the mahout of this calm and obedient creature had gone to fetch water, and that he had left the elephant unchained, simply leaning his long stick against its ear. His innate urge to torment all creatures would rise within Kuruppu. He would take out a banana and offer it to the elephant, and as soon as the elephant extended its trunk to receive it, he would pull it back. After repeating this several times, Kuruppu would look straight into the elephant's eyes, peel and eat the banana, and throw the skin away. The elephant, pissed off for the first time since being with humans, would pin him against a fence and score him with its tusk. Kuruppu would make a narrow escape, and from then on, he would come to be known also as 'Elephant-poked Kuruppu' and 'Elephant-teaser Kuruppu'.

So it was not surprising that Menon wanted to keep a careful distance from Kuruppu. But little did he know that he would soon have to deal with specimens of humanity much more repulsive than Kuruppu, types he had never met in his life before, and do some things that would make him loath himself.

It was evening and way past regular court hours when Menon finally got to meet with the Tehsildar, Subrahmaniaiyer, the executive magistrate and tax officer for the area. The Peshkar, the official who was responsible for the governance of all of North Thiruvithamkur, and the Tehsildar's superior, had made an extremely rare and unexpected visit, which had plunged the courts into chaos. As soon as he arrived at the courts, Menon noticed clerks and peons running hither and thither with files and reports, and revenue inspectors shivering in the corners. No one seemed to remain in their seats. A fair-skinned young man, a recent recruit, wept openly on the veranda, while a policeman stood by with a perplexed expression on his face. Stern voices and the sound of files being thrown about emanated from the Tehsildar's room. The intermittent ringing of a bell was heard, as if in a funeral procession, which sent a peon hurtling into the room and out again to summon a hapless clerk inside, who was then interrogated. Some had their service books produced, and salaries mercilessly cut down on the spot.

The first thing the Peshkar, Sahasranamaiyer, examined when he arrived was the framed portrait of the Maharaja on the wall, and he noticed the nest of a mud dauber wasp in a corner of the frame, which sent him into a fury. He fired, on the spot, an unlucky peon who happened to be around, and rained abuse on the Tehsildar who came to tell him about the arrangements for lunch. Like animals caught in front of flames, the bewildered faces of prominent officials, who had, up until that point, believed that the way to earn respect is not by kindness and humility, but by cruelty and rage, were a sight to behold. They looked longingly, hoping for some respite, at the lowly employees and random members of the public who passed through, the very people they routinely treated with scorn. They felt a hitherto unknown sense of respect for the peon who serviced the interrogation room, thinking of him as Chithraguptan, the servant of Yamadharman, the God of Death, whose job it was to call out the names in the registry of death.

'He's not Sahasranaman, the one with thousand names. He's Sahasrabhagan, the one with a thousand phalluses,' a revenue inspector, who had lost his salary increment following the interrogation, told Menon. 'He's harking after something else. Won't leave until he gets it!'

The matter was simple. The Peshkar had come to know that the Tehsildar had remarried after the death of his wife. His new wife was a young Brahmin woman, and stories about her beauty had preceded her arrival. A peon on night duty, whose job it was to carry files to and from the Tehsildar's home on the eastern side of the temple, had the good fortune of seeing her with his own eyes. Early one morning, as he went to retrieve the files, she was in the yard, enjoying the fragrance of a gardenia, having finished laying the decorative kolam at the entrance to the house.

'It was like looking into the sanctum of the Goddess of Kumaranellur,' he told all and sundry. 'Skin the colour of new paddy. Such a lovely way of tying the sari.'

Like every other person who had set eyes on her for the first time, he too had been stunned by her beauty and lost his mental acumen. Although inexperienced in the ways of the world, she was someone who showed genuine interest and affection for her fellow beings, and had smiled at him and asked him something in Tamil. And perhaps she had said something in his favour; the Tehsildar also began to behave amicably with him since then.

The Peshkar's penchant for women was well-known not only in his homeland of Neyyattinkara, but also in his previous workplaces of Thovalai, Suchindram and Nagercoil, and he was perverse enough to spread the stories of his conquests himself. He took a particular pleasure in making the husbands wait outside while he slept with their wives, and believed that this was conducive to an exceptionally proficient performance in bed. Once, having spent the night with the wife of an excise officer, he emerged in the morning, content, and saw the husband nodding off in a corner of the veranda.

'Hey,' he shouted. 'Get up. The sun is shining on your ass.'

When the bewildered husband stood up, the Peshkar asked him: 'Have you ever seen your wife naked in the daylight?'

'No, Your Highness,' said the man.

'Well, go in then. Go and have a look.'

The man went in obediently.

Presently, a servant boy arrived, bringing the tobacco and betel leaves for his paan. The Peshkar summoned him.

'You, boy, have you seen a husband look at the naked body of his wife after she's spent the night with another man?'

'No, Master,' said the boy, perplexed that a prominent man such as this would even speak to him.

'Then go in quickly and have a look,' commanded the Peshkar.

At the Devaswam inn, where the Peshkar was spending the night, the Tehsildar accosted Menon in the lean-to. Kuruppu followed them.

'Either I'll lose my job, or I'll lose my wife,' the Tehsildar told Menon.

They had been friends for a long time, a friendship that had traversed the boundaries of social position and caste. Tehsildar Subrahmaniaiyer's father, Ramayyan, had come to Ettumanoor during the rule of Maharaja Moolam Thirunal, and had retired as the Tehsildar. Sankunni Menon's uncle, Sankaran Raman, who was the Pravruthyar then, had started the custom of delivering a bullock-cart-load of paddy for the retired Tehsildar every year in the month of Chingam, a custom Menon followed diligently even now. On his visits to Neendoor, Subrahmaniaiyer would not eat anywhere else, and looked forward to the tasty home-cooked meals prepared by Menon's wife, even breaking his strict vegetarianism to secretly partake of the prawn theeyal cooked with cashew nuts.

'If Your Highness won't be angry, I have a plan,' Termite Kuruppu said, addressing the Tehsildar directly.

His presumptuousness irritated Menon, but looking at the Tehsildar's hopeful face, he did not say anything. Who knew, even a crow flying by might be of assistance in these situations.

'Tell him that Her Highness is indisposed, that it is her time of the month. Then there'll be nothing to worry about for the next week or so.'

Kuruppu was a crook, but Menon and the Tehsildar felt that there was some merit in his idea. They went to the Daffedar, a civil sergeant, who had accompanied the Peshkar, and respectfully presented the case. He agreed to inform the Peshkar, as diplomatically as possible, but when he came back from his mission, he acted as though a calamity was about to ensue.

'Swamy is enraged,' he said, his crafty eyes glittering with scorn. 'He won't be mollified that easily. Find some other solution. Otherwise, I don't know what all fuss will happen tomorrow.'

In his white shorts and shirt, and the red sash across his chest, the Daffedar embodied the Peshkar's authority.

Menon took the Tehsildar aside. 'Vaniyaan Narayanan, who takes the herd bull around to impregnate cows, is better than him.'

'We'll find a way,' said Kuruppu, interfering again.

With the Tehsildar's silent consent, Menon and Kuruppu set out for Kanakkari. They were going in search of Kuttathi.

From the front of the temple, they crossed Koyippadam, and walked towards Kanakkari. By the time they felt their way along a boundary ditch steeped in darkness, carefully avoiding falling into a quarry on one side, and reached the house, Kuttathi and her husband were deep into their the evening prayers, standing on their knees. Loud calls to Jesus were punctuated with sobs, and Menon felt certain that she would pull Him down from the heavens. The prayers continued, seemingly never to end. Kuruppu coughed to attract their attention, and the husband came out limping on his ruined leg, called out a swearword, and went back inside. The volume of the prayers increased.

'He's not really her husband, you know,' Kuruppu said. 'They only got together last year.'

Two harvests ago, Kuttathi had come over from Marangattupally to help an old woman in Pulikkuttisseri. Her fair skin and sensuous body deterred everyone from putting her to work in the blazing sun for too long, and so she had sat on the field edges and still received her wages, until she abandoned the old woman and went off with a man with a limp who had come that way in a paddy boat.

Their business had a peculiar set-up. Customers could approach them day or night as long as they had a coin or a measure of paddy to pay with, although Kuttathi preferred paddy. The customer was to hand it over to the husband who sat on the veranda with a pile of pebbles in front of him. He could then go into the one-room hut with Kuttathi, and pull the plaited coconut palm that served as the door shut. The husband would, very slowly, throw out one pebble at a time from his pile, and when fifty pebbles were thrown out, he would scratch on the door as a warning. Ten more stones and the time was up, and if the customer did not come out immediately, he would start making a ruckus, and call out obscenities.

When Kuruppu explained that she was to walk all the way to Ettumanoor and make an overnight call, and that the customer was a man even more distinguished than the Pravruthyar who had accompanied him, Kuttathi demanded a whole para measure of paddy as payment. Kuruppu volunteered to walk across the Vedagiri hills into Neendoor, and personally fetch the paddy by night.

'Be careful, there'll be jackals and snakes on the way,' Menon said.

Still, he was convinced that no jackal, not even a leopard, would want to take a bite out of Kuruppu. Even if it took a bite by mistake, it would spit it out immediately.

Kuruppu left, leaving Menon and Kuttathi's husband alone in the front yard.

'She'll be right out,' the husband said.

He tended to the flame lit in the half-shell of a marotti fruit. Polio had withered his legs. He had the protruding tummy and the puffy face of a habitual drinker.

Pravruthyar Menon took in the floor of the veranda, its surface pitted without the regular application of cow-dung, and the mounts of soil in the yard that bandicoots had dug out from under the foundation. The dirty yard seemed equally neglected. The roof was thatched with palm fronds but the edges had not been trimmed and stuck out at different lengths.

'Tell her to take a bath,' Menon said.

Kuttathi refused, but when they finally reached the inn, she changed her mind. Menon pointed her to the pond behind the inn.

'Make yourself useful. Scrub my back,' she said.

The Tehsildar's wife had sent over oil, lentil flour and the crushed bark of incha to scrub her skin, and sandalwood paste to apply after the bath.

'You all trying to turn me into a Brahmin lady?' Kuttathi asked.

Menon, who normally would not even glance towards women's private spaces, stepped into the water, and began scrubbing her back.

With her Christian-Mappila smell replaced with the fragrance of incha, a sandalwood mark on her forehead, and dressed in a sari tied in the Tamil way with the help of an old woman, Kuttathi was transformed into a proper Tamil Brahmin young woman. The Tehsildar's wife loaned her a necklace made of two-pavan-worth of gold after making her promise to return it in the morning.

The Tehsildar led the decked up Kuttathi to the Peshkar's room, where he was resting after an elaborate meal of rice with ghee and various vegetable preparations including kaalan, erisseri and olan, and buttermilk, followed by the sweet payasam from the temple. Not a trace of the day's anger and belligerence remained on his face. Kuttathi had never seen a man of this size before in her entire life. Soft new fuzz covered the head which had been recently tonsured at some temple, big elephant ears with tufts of hair held sprigs of tulasi, and three wide lines of sandalwood paste decorated the broad chest. Kuttathi found the girth of his waist particularly commendable. He was only about fifty years of age, but struggled to walk on legs too small to support such an elaborate body. The room smelled of sandalwood, and its occupant exuded the fragrance of the food offered at the temple.

'Take a seat, Subrahmanian,' the Peshkar pointed to the chair.

But the Tehsildar remained standing, quickly discussed some important issues, and escaped, pulling the door to the room shut behind him with a long sigh. He went off to discuss the morning's meal with the Daffedar.

The Peshkar was impressed by Kuttathi's performance. He had never met a woman quite like her before. By midnight, he was exhausted matching up to her demands and, contrary to his usual manner, he talked with her, realising, with an element of surprise, that she was not intimidated by him. The unfamiliar feeling made him open his heart up to her, and jabber on about all kinds of things almost like a confession. At one point, he began talking about his wife, and came close to tears.

'I'm like God himself to her,' he said, burying his face in her breasts like a hungry child. 'She's so good at preparing sweet dishes. This is my first time with a Christian woman. Women from different castes are different types, you know. A Nair woman is not like a Sharasyar. And Tamil women are totally different.'

But all men are the same, Kuttathi told him. Their lives are crazed journeys constantly searching for the hearts of the opposite sex. He covered her with kisses and tried to make all kinds of promises.

'The man who brought me. He said something to Your Highness about a moustached fellow. What was that about?' Kuttathi asked.

'Ah, yes. There's a young Pulayan man going around with a big moustache.'

'A big moustache?'

'Yes. He's scaring people. And he's been doing some other mischief too.'

'I'd like to see him. I've never seen a man with a moustache.'

'Well, it's an untidy thing to have, don't you think?'

'Not at all. I think, with a moustache, a man becomes a lion.'

Then, running her fingers through the fuzz on his head, she asked, 'How many children does Your Highness have?'

'I don't have any. I've not been blessed in that way.'

'Your Highness should eat black gram and chickpeas every day,' she advised. 'Soak them in water overnight and eat the sprouts next morning. There's a little bit of weakness and this will cure it.'

The Peshkar woke up very early the next morning, bathed and went to the temple, and left without waiting for breakfast or conducting further examinations in the Taluk courts. Kuttathi left too, packing up the paddy she was given, and conveniently forgetting to return the loaned gold necklace to the Tehsildar's wife.

6

THE GHOST WHO BEGS FOR FOOD

'It wasn't like this in those days. It was dark as soon as the sun set, as dark as the tar on the road.'

I put my arm around Ponnu and began the story. He turned his face away, trying to avoid the reek of alcohol on my breath.

'And when it was midnight, local goddesses would set out to faraway temples to visit their friends and husbands and parents who were stuck in their own temples as idols. There was one goddess who would walk all the way across these fields and the lake to Arthunkal beach every night to visit Veluthachan, the white-skinned saint at the church. And there were others who went as far as Vaikom and Chottanikkara. But there was no need to be scared of any of them. They always take the same route, so we just have to be careful to avoid them.'

'So what's the problem then? Just get a flashlight and go by other routes.'

'There were no flashlights then. No electricity, no street lights. The problem was there were other beings who took whichever route they pleased – Chathan, Marutha, Yakshi, Yakshan … Remember the hill where our car stalled the other day? To the west of that, there's a cremation ground. That place is full of ghosts and spirits.'

'What about when there is moonlight?'

'In those days, there were so many trees and bushes and vines. Barely any moonlight got through all that. Also, moonlit nights are when ghosts come out. Behind every banana leaf that we think is moving in the wind, there's actually a ghost. Then there are ghosts that are not at all scared of light and, in fact, walk about with a burning torch.'

'Now you're just making things up,' Ponnu protested. 'There's no such thing as ghosts. My class teacher told us.'

I couldn't believe the kind of nonsense his class teacher was telling him. Don't they realise how dangerous it is to fill the minds of small children with rationalism? Rationalism is the most problematic philosophy in the world, one that completely kills a person's imagination and instincts. It might explain the functioning of machines, but can it explain human beings? Could a rationalist ever write a story or a poem, or experience the intensity of the endless quest for love? Wouldn't a rationalist, on hearing the story of the fly and the cat that cooked kanji, argue that they would be unable to wash the rice properly since they don't have hands, and that they wouldn't know the use of fire? One can only hope that rationalism doesn't interfere in his bedroom as he lies with his wife. There was a rationalist in Kerala who had proclaimed that if he were ever able to build the rationalist nation he imagined, only men and women in full health would be allowed to procreate, so that there would be a generation of perfect human beings. I don't see much of a difference between him and Hitler.

'Teachers are an ignorant class of people,' I told Ponnu. 'I have seen ghosts with my own two eyes.'

In those days, the spiritual being that captured the imagination of the locals was an old man with a small package of paan. This spirit appeared in the broad light of day and not in the cover of darkness, unlike spirits in most other places. He favoured deserted fields and bunds. As soon as he saw young women of marriageable age, he would smear his hands with dirt from the field, and beckon to them with an innocent expression.

'Moley, my child, look, my hands are so dirty. Would you get my paan from my mundu and put it in my mouth?'

The well-meaning young woman would pull out the corner of his mundu tucked into the waist-fold only to run, horrified, at the sight of his monstrous member that would slither out, leaving the old man roaring with laughter in her wake. When young women refused marriage proposals for no apparent reason, their aunts would ask them: 'Did you by any chance come across an old man with paan?'

The story of this paan-chewing old man ghost scared only the most gullible young women. For everyone else, this was a funny story to be told to each other, and they assumed an expression of gravity only if there were any sexually inexperienced women present. There was also talk that this was not a ghost but an actual lecherous old man, presumed to be one prominent personage or another according to people's imaginations. Even a gown-wearing Christian priest had been accused of the mischief.

But the ghost that woke Vavachan up from his exhausted sleep on the bund was not someone to be made fun of. People saw it as the terrifying personification of the myriad fears of the present and anxieties about the future that they carried within them. They did not discuss it with each other, pretended it did not exist, even as their every waking thought was preoccupied by it. Each person imagined that it was pursuing them specifically, and that it would eventually find them, and possess their bodies. They hoped, fervently, that they could avoid having to confront it, and that something magical would happen and it would disappear forever.

Vavachan had not heard of spirits of the dead, nor was he the type of person who was scared of them. Paviyan and Chella were not the kind of parents who had the time to entertain their children with stories of ghosts and spirits, or thought of such stories as important or incredible enough to narrate. Once, near Thamarachal, in the month of Thulam, Paviyan had seen a boat moving across the water without an oarsman. It was not simply floating in the water, but cutting across the currents as though it was in a rush to reach somewhere or to escape from someone. Still, he had not felt the need to share that story with anyone – not even with Chella. He would recall the incident if he had occasion to go that way, that was all. Chella, meanwhile, was the type of person who witnessed extraordinary sights within the small area of the two or three fields she traversed in the course of her daily work. A Paravan coconut picker slithering down a coconut tree upside down, paddy stalks fallen over in the rain raising their heads to see if someone was coming – she witnessed such wonders on a daily basis.

Sometimes, on blazing sunny days, the sky sheds a few drops of water on to the earth for no other reason than to make one wonder whether it was the rain, or a bird, wet from a pond, flying by. Dawn was still a good way away when Vavachan was woken up by some such drops. He sat up and wiped away a drop from his moustache, and that was when he saw a ghost peel away from an othalam tree leaning into the canal, laden with green, unripe fruit. It had the poisonous fruit in both its hands, half-eaten. It swayed in the wind like the stalk of a decaying coconut leaf, its neck limp as a wilted flower bunch. Like a hollow stem held against the wind, a whistling sound came from it as it walked.

It approached Vavachan, bent down and asked: 'Would you give me some kanji water?'

Almost simultaneously, the same ghost appeared to Pothan Mappila who was lying on the wooden plank of a boat moored in the canal near Thazhathekkuzhi, hoping for some respite from the boiling heat, and asked him the same question. But here it had a different intent.

The double-doored paddy chest in Pothan Mappila's house, made of teak wood cut in Mutholi and floated down through the streams and canals, was one that never emptied. He filled it openly by day with the paddy he cultivated in his own fields, and secretly by night from the fields where he was the watchman. He made a show of sending a couple of bullock-cart-loads of paddy to Athirampuzha, and then lamented his empty reserves and imminent starvation. Trusting no one, he spent the nights next to the chest, suffering the heat emanating from the paddy. Those who came looking for his paddy – the rats and the travelling mendicants – were his sworn enemies. He caught the rats in traps baited with dried sardine heads, and drove the mendicants away by swearing at them. He drowned the rats, trap and all, in the canal, singing:

You bastards from Kochi
Were the sardine heads salty?

He had gotten rid of all his daughters by marrying them off cunningly, giving only a couple of copper pots in dowry. Every morning, he would open the chest and measure out enough paddy for the day, and hand it to his wife: two meals with fish curry for himself, a plate of kanji with salted mango for his son, and the water from the boiled rice for his wife. He beat his wife if she so much as touched a grain that had fallen on the ground. She was also beaten if he caught diarrhoea from the palm toddy he imbibed, accusing her of casting her greedy eyes over his meals and upsetting his tummy.

Apart from rice and fish curry, Pothan Mappila's other culinary passion was buffalo meat. Even as he stood watch on the field edges, Mappila's eyes would be on the buffalo tied to the plough, his mouth salivating at the thought of the tender meat between its forelegs, just below the spine. As he passed the muddy pools of water where the buffaloes wallowed, he smelled the fragrance of gently simmering beef. If there was a buffalo slaughter in the neighbourhood, he would lend a hand, and afterwards, he would bring his share of the meat wrapped in a banana leaf, and hand it over to his wife to wash and cut into pieces which he would carefully count. He would get rid of his son by sending him on a visit to his sister's marital home. And as the meat cooked, flavoured with ground coriander, cumin and fennel seeds, he would sit right beside the pot, tending the fire and sampling it as soon as the meat began to release its juices. The son, back from the enforced visit, would be given the cooking pot to lick.

The previous year, in the month of Medam, Pothan Mappila finally managed to accomplish one of his long-standing dreams. He was in the habit of visiting the early morning cattle market on Mondays and Thursdays before going to church. At the market, buffaloes, bulls and cows stood calmly in the light of numerous hurricane lanterns, ignoring those who haggled over them. Lean-figured merchants talked in unfamiliar languages, efficiently checking their tails and jowls, while those who had settled on prices made a careful last minute inspection of the hooves of the animals they were about to buy. Even the coffee and beedi seller in the corner had a crowd gathered around him. On one such day, Pothan Mappila haggled over the price of two buffaloes he had no intention of buying, and fell out with the owners who were from Mannanam. The negotiations ended with calling each other names, and he was about to leave for the church when he saw ploughman Raman standing in a corner. Raman looked dejected; he had not managed to sell his buffaloes for two consecutive market days. Pothan Mappila approached him, and inspected the animals. Having found no ploughing jobs in the last season, Raman had lost weight, while his buffaloes, with plenty of feed and not much work, had grown plump. The buyers were ruthless, arguing that the buffaloes were too fat and no good for the plough, while a desperate Raman brought the price down steadily as the image of his starving child back home loomed in his mind.

Pothan Mappila went to Raman and pulled him close, concerned that some eavesdropper would scupper his plans.

'Listen, Raman,' he whispered in his ear, 'I'll bring you the money later. You take it to my place and tie it to the ambarella tree behind the kitchen.'

That day, Mappila ditched church and spent all day with his newly acquired buffalo, caressing its back and head, and giving it plenty of water and feed. In the night, he summoned two Parayans to slaughter it for him. They took the skin and innards away. The bones were put in the waterhole to decay. Some of the meat was set aside to be cooked into curries over the next couple of weeks, some to make pickle with, and some to be cooked with tapioca. The rest of the meat was sorted into three lots according to quality, and chopped into pieces. Then, he loaded it into a handcart and took it to the compound where the paddy was dried. For the next four days, Mappila sat up, sleepless, vigilant against dogs, eagles and crows, until the meat was dried.

The five months from Edavam to Thulam was a long celebration for Mappila. His wife was fed up, constantly looking for different ways to cook and serve the meat. In between meals, Mappila took to chewing a dried piece of meat as though he was chewing tobacco. He looked for ways to consume the meat as quickly as possible, fearing that his wife and son might be helping themselves to it secretly. He ate meat chammanthi with kanji, crushed meat with steamed pieces of tapioca, and finally commanded his wife to make puttu, replacing the grated coconut layer between the layers of rice flour with liberal fillings of shredded meat instead.

By the time the thunderous rains in Thulam ended, the meat-filled vessels were finally empty. The warm months of Kumbham and Meenam rolled in, and Mappila began to experience a burning sensation all over his body. He drew cold water from the well and poured it over his body three times a day, but this did nothing to assuage the heat he felt. In the nights, his wife fanned him with a piece of wet areca spathe, and yet he rolled on his mat tearing away his clothes. He considered getting into the canal and standing neck-deep, like a buffalo, in the water. It was only when he got into the boat and lay on a plank, with the cold water below him and the cool breeze from the fields enveloping him, that he was finally able to doze off.

But on the very second day after he found this reprieve, the ghost of a Nair who had died of starvation appeared in his boat and bent over him. It asked: 'Mappila, would you give me some kanji water?'

An air bubble rose inside him and Mappila's throat closed up. From then on, he could not swallow anything solid. All he could manage was water and a little kanji made of broken rice. Even that caused him to hiccup continuously for a while after each meal.

A month later, he went to attend a wedding in a relative's house. A hind quarter of the buffalo that was slaughtered for the feast had been hung up in the marquee for the guests to admire. Mappila felt nothing looking at it. Still, he stood below it, letting the droplets of blood fall on his bald head, and wiped them away with a deep sense of nostalgia.

Vavachan, meanwhile, wondered whether he was dreaming. He touched his moustache, and was consoled to find it in place in all its youthful glory. The ghost was still by his side, its body emaciated from hunger and thirst like a wilted papaya stem. It weaved about on unsteady legs. Vavachan remembered a story he had heard Damodaran tell Ezhuthachan about a middle-aged man who lived with an old relative, and had died of hunger. His ghost was said to do two types of harm: If it appeared to a person sleeping with a full belly, they would lose interest in food. If, on the other hand, the ghost appeared to a starving person, they would never be able to find food anywhere in the vicinity, and would be destined to wander the wide world forever in search of food.

Ezhuthachan had laughed at the story.

'You wait and see. Soon there'll be no more ghosts and spirits. Electricity has reached as far as Thrissur. When the nights become as bright as day, there'll be no more ghosts.'

Damodaran had been offended by Ezhuthachan's snide remarks.

'So what do you think will happen to the spirits of the dissatisfied and despondent dead? Are they not even allowed to wander as spirits? No freedom even in death?'

It was not dissatisfaction or despondency that had killed the Nair whose ghost had appeared before Vavachan. He had died of hunger. When he was alive, all he could talk about, whether in the temple yard or in front of the chai shop, was food. All day, he would go from house to house, trying to wheedle a meal out of them by pretending to do some work, or by flattery. In the temple yard, he would pay attention to the chatter of other Nairs with the means to eat at least two full meals a day, and make a note of any upcoming feasts – funerals, weddings, sixtieth birthdays. He would stand up reverentially at the sight of even minor cooks, and voluntarily spread stories about their culinary talents.

Upon hearing about a feast, he would set out a day in advance with a basket in hand. On his way, he would go into well-to-do households and ask for food. His stomach had the ability to digest these unforeseen meals even if it had been empty for days before that. During Edavappathy, the southwest monsoon, when food was scarce and he could find no handouts, he would curl up on his mat for days like a tortoise that had buried itself in the mud, but could rise, at a moment's notice, and eat a whole para measure of rice, with not even salt to flavour it, silently and steadily, much to the amazement of onlookers.

He would reach the location of a feast before the cooks arrived, and start the preparations. Some of them would call him names and try to chase him away, but he would hang on, helping out with the chores – fetching large stones for the temporary hearths, carrying firewood, and tending the fires. He would take on the late night task of finely chopping young jackfruits for the thoran, a distinguished task that took several hours of careful concentration. The next day, as soon as the feast began, he would find a place in front of one of the long rows of banana leaves on which it was served, twice or thrice if he could manage it, before filling his basket with leftovers from the cooking vessels and going back home.

His last feast, in Nattassery, was a special one, in which new items, unheard of in those parts, appeared on the banana leaves on which the feast was served. Instead of the usual erisseri, they served sambhar, and for the sweet finale, they served payasam prepared not with rice, but with roasted lentils. To everyone's utter amazement, they were served two pappadam and a Poovan banana. In the heaving crowd, he pushed an old man out of the way and found a seat for the first round. Later, when the crowd thinned, he had a second meal, after which he went around to the back of the house. He took in the well-looked after coconuts and banana trees laden with fruits, and sat under a mango tree, chewing paan and resting. That was when he heard the commotion at the edge of the compound where the used banana leaves were discarded in a heap. A group of Ulladan tribal folk – old people, naked young children, and women – were eating the leftovers, and filling containers made of areca spathe with the rest. A few stray dogs waited patiently for their turn. The sight enraged him. He picked up a stone and ran towards the group. Shouting, he chucked the stone at the back of a young woman with a baby on her waist. She cried out and, quickly grabbing a couple of leaves, ran behind the fence, out of reach. The dogs scattered.

As he washed his face and mouth, he felt like having one more turn before leaving. He managed to find a place in the last sitting where the relatives and the cooks were served. Olan, kichadi, and other side dishes were served. He had mixed the rice with the seasoned coconut oil, and was about to place the first morsel into his mouth when an elder, an enormous man, squatted in front of him, and asked: 'Where are you from?'

'I'm from Neendoor,' he said obligingly, mixing a little of the jackfruit thoran with the rice.

'Listen up, everyone,' the elder stood up and said loudly. 'Our fellow from Neendoor. This is the third time he is eating.'

Everyone looked at him and laughed. Those at the back of the crowd fought their way to the front to have a look. The women came out of the house.

'Actually, that's less than usual,' said one of the cooks. 'I've seen him eat five times at a funeral feast in Varissery.'

'Oh, we must honour him then,' the elder said. 'Fetch the nadaswaram players.'

The musicians were fetched. They stood on either side of him, and played an energetic ditty on the nadaswaram and the thakil. Deeply embarrassed, he tried to get up, but the elder slapped him across his face.

'Sit down,' he said. 'Don't get up until you've satisfied your craving.'

Afterwards, as he left, basket on head, they followed him until the banks of Meenachilar, booing and shouting, with the musicians beating out a raucous rhythm. Utterly humiliated, he got back home, never to leave and barely eating until, sixty days later, he was dead.

Leaving the ghost of the man who had died from the humiliation of hunger behind, Vavachan set out for home with a stomach burning with renewed hunger. He swam across the big canals and jumped over the small ones. The blush of morning was just beginning to show in the eastern sky. Birds and beasts were already scrambling for the day's food. Kingfishers and egrets rushed towards the faintest movements in water, anxious about the day ahead. Kites and kestrels woke up earlier than usual, and patrolled the land below from up above. Unmindful of the need to mate, dogs and cats scratched at holes and crevasses looking for something to eat.

Vavachan stood perplexed in front of the ruin that was once the hut Paviyan had built. The kanji pot, destined to be used only when Paviyan was home, lay upturned in the mud. Vavachan's siblings had already dispersed in search of food after a week of hunger. Chella too must have gone in search of a place to sleep.

In his confusion, Vavachan scrambled through the compounds to the east. The stems and leaves of the itchy silver colocasia had disappeared, as had the tubers and even the new shoots of tapioca. Nettle leaves, banana stems, mango kernels – everything had been eaten by desperate people as though they were the choicest morsels. They had cut down palm trees, pounded the innards, and eaten them boiled with tamarind. Not even a wilted windfall coconut was to be seen.

In the early morning light, Vavachan saw a group of men and women from lands to the west coming across the lake and the fields. On the sandy beaches that were their home, not even grass sprouted and, finding nothing to eat, they had set out to beg, going from house to house, looking for a bowl of kanji water or a piece of tapioca. They would walk all the way east, as far as Pambadi and Ayarkunnam.

By the time the sun rose properly, Vavachan had completed a circuit of all the yards and compounds in the vicinity, and returned to the ruined hut. There would be nothing in this land for him now – not a grain of rice, not even cattle feed. He stood still at the point where the earth divided into solid land and watery fields dredged up from the lake, the Vembanad Kayal, and looked eastwards and westwards. To the east, the land undulated with small hills and dark mountains in the distance. He could cut across the compounds and the lanes, travel through unfamiliar lands and fields, and eventually reach the forests. Or he could go west, to the endless stretch of untidy squares, silent, deserted, waterlogged, criss-crossed with bunds and canals, baked by the sun and smothered by the wind. For hundreds of years, in every season of hunger, people have been adding to it, building bunds to claim arable land from the swamps and the lake, creating a featureless, indistinguishable expanse of fields that turned out to be traps they could not escape. An expanse that only had a beginning, and no end.

Vavachan saw a boat with two policemen in pointy hats approaching the hut. A large crowd followed them along the canal paths. This was the first time since the beginning of time itself that the police had come to the area. The unruly colonies of ducks quietened, toddy tappers sat frozen on top of the palm trees, and Vavachan leapt westwards into the land of silence his ancestors had created.

Before they went back empty-handed, one of the policemen remarked loudly for all to hear: 'Catching a Pulayan in the fields is like looking for a needle in a haystack.'

7

WORLD-FAMOUS MOUSTACHE

'The moonlight was quite bright. I saw his face this close.'

The young man was one of those who had spent all day raising hell in the fields, beating up even the children. He had been separated from his friends as they returned home in a panic, frightened by a face looming in the dark. His friends had searched for him all night, and had finally come upon him lying unconscious among the itchy colocasia by a dried up canal. They had carried him to Kesava Pillah's veranda and poured a pot of cold water over his head. Regaining consciousness, he had sobbed calling out for his mother, and jabbered on meaninglessly. Finally, he was beginning to make sense.

'He was as tall as that banana tree over there,' he continued. 'And his moustache – ho! It was this long. And it had blood in it. Must have eaten something raw...'

'You've caught a fright,' Kesava Pillah said, irritated. 'I've seen him myself. He is dark and stocky. Have you ever seen a Pulayan over five feet tall?'

'You think I'm making this up? He lifted me by my feet and held me upside down. Then, he slapped me on the ground. He left only because he thought I was dead.'

'No man can pick up another by the feet and slap him on the ground. Only elephants can do that,' said the old man treating his wounds.

The old man was a weird looking creature, dressed in a mundu that dragged on the ground and a towel folded over his shoulder. He had a stick-thin body, a concave stomach, bow legs, and an intermittent grin that exposed his teeth. He examined the wounded man, shook his feet and all twenty of his digits, felt his shoulder joints, and turned him over and tapped on his lower back as though checking the ripeness of a coconut. Finally, he stood up, raised both his arms, took hold of the rafter of the veranda roof, and inhaled deeply. All those who suffered from asthma were like this, Kesava Pillah thought, hanging from any old structure like bats, struggling to take a breath as the moon waxed and waned.

'He'll live,' the old man said, detaching himself from the rafter, and trying to regulate his breath. 'Just shook up from running helter-skelter across woods and canals, that's all. There'll be some pain for a few days. His joints have swollen.'

'You all sound like people who stand on the banks and find fault with those swimming in the water,' the young man with the red ear stud said.

He could not make a joke of it as usual, and was angry that their story was not being taken seriously.

'We all saw him. He actually has the strength of an elephant. That palmyra tree in Arppil – he shook it and now it has dried completely. And didn't he kick the lamp post and snap it in two?'

Dismiss this as a small matter at the risk of something more serious happening in the future, the young man with the red ear stud cautioned them, and reminded them of what happens if a sapling of the deadly poisonous cheru is left to grow into a tree. Kesava Pillah felt that there was some merit in his cautions.

'You've seen Paviyan, his father,' Pillah addressed the old man. 'Looks like a pangolin, but so strong!'

The old man agreed, especially as he remembered what had happened to Machathil Luca Mappila.

Almost eight years ago, during the planting season of Thiruvathira Njaattuvela, when it had rained non-stop for over a week, Luca Mappila was sitting on the veranda watching the water levels carefully. His wife had set a pot of boiled tapioca left over from the previous night beside him, and he snacked on it, shaking off the moisture from each piece and dipping it in a paste of kandari chillies. His stores may run out of paddy but never of tapioca, and Luca Mappila and his wife have lived through many rainy seasons on snacks made of tapioca flour or stewed tapioca. Luca Mappila seemed to enjoy the spicy chilli condiment more than the tapioca itself.

'Stop eating the chillies, or you'll have trouble shitting tomorrow,' his wife said, taking the sliver of banana leaf with the chilli paste away from him.

At that moment, Paviyan appeared in the yard, holding a large colocasia leaf over his head against the rain.

'Master, if you please…' Paviyan entreated. 'Some paddy or tapioca … The children are crying of hunger. It's been days since we've been able to step out.'

He lowered the leaf and stood under the fringe of the thatched roof. It was Chella who had plaited the coconut palm fronds for the thatch, but they still let the rainwater through and drenched Paviyan.

Luca Mappila, who liked a laugh, decided to play a prank.

'We have nothing left, Paviya,' he said. 'Just the tapioca in this pot. I'll also have to go hungry from evening. Do one thing. There's the big bronze vessel on the western veranda. You can have it, but only if you can take it away by yourself. You can't ask anyone to help you lift it.'

Luca Mappila picked up his pot of tapioca and went inside the house.

The big bronze vessel at the Machathil house was famous. Christian and Nair households in the neighbourhood borrowed it whenever there was occasion to cook large quantities of rice. It was so heavy that one or two people could not move it, and usually required at least eight people to carry it away, suspended on bamboo poles inserted through the round handles on each side.

In a little while, as the rain subsided, Luca Mappila's wife stepped out into the yard. Looking to the west, she saw a man walking along the field edge, carrying their big bronze vessel upside down on his head. She shouted for her husband. Paviyan had taken Luca Mappila's challenge seriously, and had managed to carry the vessel away. Luca Mappila ran after him and begged him to return the vessel, pacifying him with a half-sack of tapioca and a measure of paddy. 'I was just joking,' he said. 'What would a Pulayan do with such a big vessel?'

At Kesava Pillah's house, the old man made the injured young man walk about slowly in the yard.

'I knew Paviyan's father too,' he said. 'I was a mere child then. He didn't have a moustache, but his face was as scary as if it had one, like that of a tomcat. He was a healer, skilled at fixing broken legs and twisted arms.'

The old man made the patient sit on the floor and examined the foot he was dragging.

'But he dabbled in magic,' he continued. 'Could make himself small, or shapeshift into a crow or a cat. It's all done in secret, in the cover of darkness, before a fire built on a deserted bund or a field. Not that he did much harm to anyone. But masters better be fair when measuring out his share of the paddy, or suffer the consequences. He liked to play pranks on women when they went out in the night to do their business. They'd hear a strange call and run away without finishing. Once, near Pulickal, they caught him and tied him up to a jackfruit tree, but in the morning there was nothing but the rope he was tied up with under the tree. I saw it with my own eyes. A thick rope, like the one used on elephants. No ordinary human could have untied those knots.'

'See, like I said, this is no laughing matter,' the young man with the red ear stud said. 'He got four out of the six of us. Me and Shivan escaped only because we ran away.'

'I really did see him,' said the wounded young man. 'At first it looked like a big black tomcat, and I was scared it was going to attack me. That's when I saw his terrible moustache.'

Finally, the old man and the young lads left. Kesava Pillah had his kanji and rested for a while. When it was full dark, he set out to his wife's house in Onamthuruthu. He did not bother taking a lighted torch with him. There were snakes and jackals along the road ahead. At one time, there had been leopards. Once, around fifty or even a hundred years ago, Pillah's mother's uncle was on his way, a basket and a winnow in hand, to harvest sesame when a leopard jumped across the path. The uncle, who was proficient in the martial dance, Velakali, confronted the leopard, stepping up in rhythm and waving the basket and the winnow. The confused leopard, never having come across humans such as the one in front of him, simply moved out of his way. The incident made the uncle famous, and caused a great deal of embarrassment for leopards in general, their reputation damaged by being compared to the crows that picked at the drying paddy and were easily shooed away with a winnow.

There were two reasons why Kesava Pillah did not take a torch with him to light his way on this treacherous path. One, his wife would consider it a sign of his bravery and be proud of him. And two, he could, if all went well, secretly visit a Vaniyaathi, a forty-something woman who knew how to entertain, along the way. Her hut, in a yard below, was visible from the path above. Kesava Pillah stepped on the stone by the fence, slid down the slope to a jackfruit tree, and landed silently behind the hut. Only the bull tethered in the yard witnessed his arrival and gave a short snort of recognition. He walked around the hut a couple of times, scratched on the door, and coughed surreptitiously, but no one acknowledged his presence even though there was a dim light inside the hut. Losing his patience, Pillah inserted a finger into the plaited palm frond that served as the door, and peeped in through the hole. He truly believed what he thought he saw. A black-skinned man with a great big moustache detached himself from the Vaniyaathi, and came rushing at him with bloodshot eyes and holding out a rough palm. The sides of his moustache seemed like two winnows coated with cow dung and polished into a smooth finish. Pillah did not wait around to consider whether the apparition was real or a combined effect of the flickering lamp and the shadows it cast. In an almighty leap, he ascended the high sides of the yard, scraping the skin on his chest against the rough earth, hurdled over the fence, and ran tumbling over the exposed roots of trees along the path where his ancestor had faced off with the leopard. He did not stop until he was safely inside his wife's house.

His wife tended to his wounded chest, wiped the beaded blood with a soft white cloth, while her older sister boiled some water. It was the older sister Pillah had married initially. But he had ended that relationship and married the younger sister. Even now, when the younger sister sat aside when it was her time of the month, it was the older sister who took care of his needs.

'I think you should grow a moustache. It would really suit your face,' his wife said, stroking his cheek as he began to doze calmly, without his usual vigorous overtures on her body. 'A small pointy moustache.'

Her soundless laughter irritated him, and he pushed her away.

Next morning, he woke up before sunrise and took another route home. He did not eat or drink at his wife's house, not even a glass of water, as her family was beneath his in status, and usually returned home before the morning meal. Walking across the step-bridge from the ferry to Prala, he ran into a group of Christian Mappilas. They were in an angry mood, swearing loudly and profusely with their mundus hitched up. Beef cattle about to be slaughtered must have escaped, Pillah mused, or someone must have kicked over the arrack still, or the church must have caught fire. Something drastic must have occurred for such a large, angry crowd to assemble.

Pillah's enquiries were greeted with respect, and they took him to Pulingayil Matha's house. Like him, Matha was also a farmer of some standing, and regularly cultivated the fields not just in Neendoor and Kaipuzha, but in Vechoor, Thalayazham and Arpookara. He had ten boats and several heads of cattle, and owned a whole collection of farm equipment including ploughs, harrows and waterwheels.

Matha seemed happy enough to see Kesava Pillah, but his face was overcast with anger and embarrassment.

'I kicked her in her guts,' he said. 'Gave her a good thrashing with the stick I use to kill snakes. I've sent word to her people. Let them take her away. We don't want her here.'

He caught sight of his mother who had wandered into the front yard brushing her teeth, and barked at her, sending her scurrying into the backyard.

'The old woman thought the world of her. Now see…'

Matha told Kesava Pillah the incident that had caused such extreme loss of face for him and his family. Under the weight of his embarrassment, he struggled to complete the story.

Matha Mappila's deceased older brother had a son who had reached the ripe age of twenty-five without managing to find a bride. The problem was that he behaved like a child even at that age, and went around pushing a young coconut on a stick like a cart, with long ribbons of drool hanging off his mouth. He threw stones at mangoes, jumped into the canal butt-naked, and ate constantly, no matter how well or how often he was fed. So even though he was from a family of some standing, no one in the neighbouring places wanted to give their daughters in marriage to him. Finally, they found a girl, around thirteen or fourteen years of age, from faraway Kannankara. She did not quite drool like the boy, but had the habit of smiling vacantly at all and sundry. She could do some odd jobs around the house, such as sweeping the yard, but was of no use in the kitchen. Once, when asked to make a chammanthi, she had ground it up adding the bitter leaves of the neem tree instead of curry leaves.

'Nothing to worry,' Kesava Pillah said. 'Our boy is also a bit less than wholesome, no?'

The marriage had taken place six months ago, but they had not been allowed to sleep together. The girl spent the night with Matha's mother instead, and all was well, until now. The previous evening, the girl went missing. They looked everywhere – in the storerooms, the attic, the paddy chests, the barns … They searched all over the compound, but the girl was nowhere to be found. Did she fall into a pond and drown? What would they say to her people in Kannankara? The neighbours got together and searched through the night in the light of burning torches, poking in the canal with sticks, looking in the abandoned wells, and going from house to house. Finally, around daybreak, someone told them that they had seen a young girl walking across the fields, and they found her sitting on the Puthankari bund with a goofy grin on her face.

'Listen to this, Pillecha,' Matha said. 'She says, in front of all those people, that she'd gone to see Moustache. Can you think of anything more embarrassing than that? The daughter-in-law of Pulingayil house has gone to see the moustache of a Pulayan boy! I told her I'll show her another place with a moustache, and gave her a good kick.'

In the afternoon, Kesava Pillah, Matha Mappila, and a few other Christians met at the rectory. Pillah and the priest, Father Thadathimaakkal, a man as fair-skinned as white men, sat on chairs, while others sat on the sun-drenched seats built into the veranda.

'It's all very well to say we should capture him, Father,' Pillah said. 'But the fields are endless to the west. If he hides somewhere in there, how do we catch him? There'll be not a soul in Kattukari and Kanyakon after the harvest. I think we should just leave him there. He'll come sidling back when he's almost dead from starvation.'

'That won't work, Pillecha,' Father Thadathimaakkal said in a placating voice, careful not to upset Pillah. 'We can do this if we all work together. We can't just let him be. We have to do something. Just this morning some duck herders came to see me. They say there was not a single egg in the enclosures this morning. Have you ever heard of such a thing happening before?'

'Father is right, Pillecha. How can we, in good faith, leave the harvested paddy in the fields now? Already there's so much theft these days, and with this, there's no telling what would happen.'

'But even the police couldn't do anything,' Pillah said.

'So now we should try,' a young man in the group piped up. 'As it is, these Chovans and Pulayans are getting out of control.'

'They better not get ahead of themselves. They'll only starve to death.' Father Thadathimaakkal laughed.

'But we have to be very careful,' Matha warned them. 'He's been seen in different places at the same time. Bet he knows some magic and tricks. He's a Pulayan after all.'

Matha Mappila reminded them that, until very recently, the Pulayans had regularly practised animal sacrifice, cutting the throat of a cockerel on a stone placed on the Chathankari bund.

'All that is in the past,' the priest said. 'Don't try to scare me. I spend the nights within the walls of this cemetery.'

'Did Moustache really have magic powers?' Ponnu asked in wonder, lying snuggly within the circle of my arm. 'Like Chhota Bheem and Spiderman? Could he become invisible? Could he fly?'

'Of course! He could disappear in an instant, like smoke,' I said. 'Sometimes he would become a falcon or a kingfisher and fly away. Or he would shapeshift into a frog or a tadpole or a minnow or a tortoise. When I was a child, I've seen him walk into a banana tree, climb right up into its most tender leaf on top, and disappear into thin air.'

'Lies! You need a wand to do magic.'

'If that's so, how come Spiderman doesn't have a magic wand?'

'Because he has a magic dress.'

'And Moustache has a magic moustache. No one else has such a big moustache, bigger than the man himself. Sometimes, it would be as small as my hand, but at other times it would be as tall as that coconut tree, or as big as a whole forest.'

'But if it is a forest, won't there be elephants and tigers?'

'Yes. Birds made their nests in Moustache's moustache. Snakes hid in it. One time, when he went into the canal to have a bath, the moustache stopped the water like a dam. The fish and the frogs thought it was the mangrove roots, and laid eggs in it. Moustache could not come out of the canal. If he did, the eggs would be destroyed, wouldn't they? So he waited for a couple of weeks until all the eggs hatched, and the baby fish and tadpoles swam away.'

'Ayyo! Such big lies! He'd be dead if he sat in the water for so long!'

'Not at all. He was like the tortoise; he could breathe on land and in water. He would dive in one canal and surface far away in another, and if anyone was watching, they would wonder how a man could emerge from the water like that.'

'But what's the point of such a big moustache?'

'What's the point? Ha! One day, Moustache was walking along. He loved to walk all over the land. When he got to a deserted place, he heard someone cry: "Ayyo! Help us … Help us…" Moustache looked all around but he couldn't see anyone. But it sounded like some children were in trouble. Moustache looked up at the sky – there was no one there. He looked at the ground and there was a hole, one that was made by a crab. Small, but so deep that it went all the way to the underworld. The mama crab had been eaten by a dog, leaving her hundreds of children stranded in the hole. They couldn't get out on their own. Moustache felt sorry for them. He rolled his moustache into a thin long point, and stuck it down the hole. And the crab babies held on to it, and climbed out of the hole. Some ran away happily, and the others lived on in the moustache.'

By the time I was halfway through the story, Ponnu was fast asleep. I got up slowly, and stepped out into the yard. There was a soothing breeze from the fields about a kilometre away. Twenty years ago, standing at this same spot, it would have felt as though the houses and the trees would topple over in the wind. Now, the fields have been pushed back, the land filled with soil, and embankments planted with coconut trees. There, at the very spot where Paviyan's hut had been, where Vavachan had started his journey, is where northern Kuttanad begins. To the west, north and south of that point, there is only thousands and thousands of fields, and waterways like a pile of hopelessly tangled thread. It extends, like a tattered map, to the Vembanad Kayal at its westernmost edge; to Meenachil, Manimala and Pamba rivers, and to Onattukara and beyond in the south; and to Vaikom and beyond in the north. I have read somewhere that deserts are traps built by God. This is a man-made trap, built by people who came down from the forests in the throes of hunger, who, over centuries, dug up the lake and marshes, and built bunds to stop the water. A place that overwhelms one with illusions of land and water, like the magical palace built by Mayasuran for the Pandavas in

Indraprastham. A place that beguiles one with trapdoors and labyrinths like the fortress of Ravanan, the king of Lanka. Countless souls have toiled and perished here, with nothing to commemorate their lives. This is a place with no history, or with a history that no one remembers, a place that was built for hard labour, and had to be vacated once the labour was done. It was to this vast expanse that Vavachan escaped, almost three quarters of a century ago. He could have lived here, like Paviyan and his father, and his father's father, if only he had taken off all of the costume he had put on for the play. Why did he run away with a policeman's moustache? Where did he hope to get to, navigating this boundless trap?

8

SEETHA

Like all days in the month of Meenam, the day ended abruptly and made way for another hot night. Light evaporated in the heat and rose to the sky, leaving behind sweltering evenings, steamy and expectant of rains. Wearing a thin mundu and a rough piece of cloth across her breasts, Seetha stepped into the yard and looked around. In the intense heat, she took off the cloth and fanned her breasts. Concerned that her body was sticky and smelling of sweat, even though she had bathed just a few hours earlier, she stepped into the canal and washed her face and armpits. The moon and the clouds rollicked in the water. The air hung heavy, dead. Fish stayed in the deeper pools of water, not bothering to look for food. Only a young papaya tree moved a single leaf, joyfully, standing by the path made by the footfall of the women who had worked the harvest that ended last week. They had picked clean even the tiniest of the fruits that had set at the base of its leaves. The women were gone now, so was the noise and bustle of the harvest. Only a few wonky planks of the frames put up for the threshers to hold on to remained in the yards. The bunds had been cut open, the water let in to drench the fields. All around Seetha's house, water lay heavy, unmoving. She would be alone now in this silent world, until the ploughmen arrived in the next season after the monsoon. Seetha looked doubtfully at the sky. A red sky was the harbinger of rains, but if it didn't rain, there would be no more rains for the rest of the month. Slivers of dim lightning flashed in the south-eastern corner.

Not content with wetting her face and armpits, Seetha removed her mundu, left it on a stone, and stepped into the water. She bathed again, scrubbing her body with her bare hands. By night Seetha, and by day Kuttanasari, the carpenter, bathed naked in the canal, and in all this time, the only person who had been lucky enough to catch a glimpse of her voluptuous body was a lonesome duck herder who had happened to pass by. Kuttanasari would scrub his loincloth on the stone, throw it at the wall of the house before getting into the water, and walk back home after his bath, naked as the day he was born. During the growing season, the women working in the fields, fed up of having to witness his nakedness, would call him names, but he was undaunted. He would retrieve his loincloth, dried and stuck to the wall, only following his evening bath after returning from work. He had never understood the need for undergarments when he was at work.

Seetha got out of the canal, dried herself, shook off her mundu, and tied it back around her waist. She looked east. Kuttanasari's arrival would be marked by the flickering flame of his torch as it followed the bends and turns of the embankment. But there was no sign of him today. Sometimes he did not come home, and would fall asleep somewhere after drinking too much toddy.

Something caught her attention. Behind the hut, near the cooking platform, there was a commotion. Annoyed, she ran over to investigate.

It was five days after the death of the Ulladathi Kathu – or Kavalakkathu as she was known, because she had lived at the kavala, the junction where three roads met – that Kuttanasari had arrived with Seetha. He asked the Tharayil family for permission to put up a hut on the southern embankment of Makkothara fields. The landowner did not quite understand why a carpenter would want to set up house on a field embankment, but he could not refuse Kuttanasari, the skilled carpenter who had built the most attractive cattle frame out of jungle jack wood for his barn.

Kuttanasari had met Kathu for the first time in the palm leaf enclosure she had put up by the side of one of the roads at the junction. She had lived there with the Ulladan who was the father of her five children, until, one day, she had called him names and run him off. Their children had, by then, gone their separate ways. Some months, they lived off what they made by begging across the villages, and in other months, they went off to catch wild rabbits and rats. Every compound with a healthy crop of tapioca had, around its edges, a private kingdom of rats half as big as cats. At first glance, only a single burrow would be visible in the grass, but rats were ferocious rulers and built an entire empire of lanes and by-lanes, as though laying out escape routes, that housed several rats and opened up at various points. Kathu would find one burrow, set a fire beside it, and fan the smoke into it with a piece of areca spathe. In a while, tendrils of smoke would rise from the various outlets across the compound, which she would close using stones and banana litter, before fanning more smoke into the first burrow. Soon, rats would jump out of the burrows straight into her sacks.

It was when she came back from a months-long trip to the festival at Edathua church that Kathu brought Seetha with her. Seetha looked no more than twelve or thirteen years of age. She was not as dark, and her curly hair, the colour of copper from lack of regular oiling, was tied back with a thread. Her legs were skinny and she was yet to sprout breasts, but she had wide eyes and a rosy, flushed face.

'She's my youngest,' Kathu told those who asked. 'She's always been around. You all never paid attention.'

Sometimes, she told people that Seetha was the daughter of a sort-of brother of hers. And at other times, when the toddy got to her head, she would even say that she had bought her paying good money.

Early one morning, Kuttanasari cleaned his teeth by chewing on a mango leaf and brushing with a crushed coconut flower stalk, and relieved himself beside a bamboo clump behind the house. He refused the kanji his wife served, took his tools, and set out to work to Kottamuri, where he was building the frame for a Varrier's house. On the way, he stopped by a palm tree with lush bunches of flower stalks hanging heavily from its top, looked up and begged like a little child for a taste of the fresh toddy that was being tapped. He embraced the trunk as though it was his own mother. Giving in to his pleading, Shivan, the toddy tapper, climbed down the ladder tied to the tree with the pot. Kuttanasari drank his fill and, as some people are wont to do when the toddy hits their stomachs, ran to the side of the canal, where he defecated explosively. He washed his behind, and came back for another taste, before walking up the sloping lane that joined the main road to Ettumanoor. Strands of glistening sunlight descended from the sky, and by the time Kuttanasari got to the road, a hazy rain started falling. He was unconcerned at first, but when the rain gathered strength, he took shelter in a hut by the side of the road. The hut, not even the size of a cattle shed, had a floor of loose mud. Chest-high posts of flowering mallow had been sunk into the earth, and supporting walls of palm leaves lashed to sticks were tied across the posts. The mallow had taken root, and new leaves sprouted from the top. The roof was dry palm fronds piled one on top of the other, but not a drop of rain fell through.

The rain continued, and Kuttanasari sat inside the enclosure, lazily listening to its music. The next day too, by the time he drank his pleaded-for toddy and came up to the road, it rained, and he took shelter in the hut. On the third day, it did not rain, but he sat indolently inside the hut. From then on, on his way to work, he stopped at the hut, and chewed paan in the company of Kathu. Unlike all the other women he came across, Kathu and Seetha did not curse him out and nag him to straighten his mundu and cover his nakedness. Instead, when he ignored his work altogether and sat there lazily, Kathu bought him toddy and paan.

One day, Kuttanasari's wife came to the hut with their two children. She shouted at Kathu. 'Why the hell would you want to keep this dried up old man here?'

From that day on, Kuttanasari stopped going back to his own home.

He was a sickly man with a bent body, lazy to boot, avoiding work for at least twenty days a month. Still, people came from all over looking for his services. His skill in building the roofs and frames for houses was well-known, and he was a highly entertaining man. When called to divine the best location for a house or a well, he would regale people with talk of water tables, spatial geometry, wind direction and so on, creating, in equal measure, anxiety and wonderment in his listeners. He was scornful of all other carpenters in the world. One time, Kuttanasari's father had calculated the correct spot for constructing a new house, and had hammered the staff marking the spot into the earth. The people of the household wanted to recheck the calculations, and called in Kuttanasari. But they did not divulge the fact that the carpenter whose work they wanted him to verify was his own father.

Kuttanasari examined the spot chosen by his father, and asked a question that would become famous all across the land: 'Which motherfucker banged his rod here?'

His last job was in the house of a Northist Christian in Athirampuzha, and Kuttanasari, who was very fond of his food, had created an entertaining scene there. When he was given lunch at his workplace, he focused more on the accompaniments, eating up the jackfruit seed curry or the fish curry faster than the rice itself. 'Rice and kanji we can have at home,' he would advise his fellow workers, 'so we should eat as much curry as we can.'

Being aware of Kuttanasari's habit, the elderly woman of the house told him, as she laid the banana leaf and served the rice and curry: 'Do watch the fish as you eat.'

So Kuttanasari skewered the pieces of fish on a stick, rammed it into the ground, and ate his food while watching it.

In preparation to live on the embankment of the Makkothara field, Kuttanasari expanded its width, and reinforced the bunds by planting four coconut trees along the edges. When the mud dried, he cut stones from a piece of weed-grown land near Thonnamkuzhi and ferried them back in a boat.

'What's this? Going to build a bungalow on the embankment, are you?' asked a Mappila who saw the boat-load of stones.

Kuttanasari used the stones to lay the foundation, and built pillars for the walls that were coconut fronds. He intended to reinforce them with wooden planks eventually. Most carpenters flout their own rules when building their houses, but Kuttanasari's house turned out to be proportionate and graceful. At the back of the house, he built a lean-to to cook in, with a thatched roof and a stone hearth. Cooking pots could be left there without fear of foraging cats or dogs, as the house was surrounded by fields. Pigeons and parakeets did not bother with rice, baffled by the way humans treated paddy, boiling it twice in water, drying it in the sun, and then boiling it again to eat. Seetha took care of the inside of the house, coating the floors with a paste of cow dung and charcoal, and buffing them until they shone. When he came home on all fours after a session with the toddy pot, Kuttanasari would lie down, pressing his face on the bare floor, breathing in its fresh new aroma, the smell of the firm dung of a cow that had fed on ripe new scutch grass. The new house gave him immense pleasure. No one would come all this way and persuade him back to work when he was in one of his lazy moods.

What he found most attractive was the location of his house, the endless fields and canals all around it. He suffered from rectal haemorrhoids and had to defecate at least ten times a day. This had been difficult to accomplish in the house he had lived in with his wife and children, which sat on a five-cent plot of land, and he had been forced to do his business in his neighbour Itty Mappila's property. In the daytime, when he squatted surreptitiously in a corner, Itty Mappila's children would boo and make fun of him. He would have his revenge when, at dusk, as he came home swaying on drunken legs, he would sing, louder than the sound of the evening prayers emanating from Mappila's house:

Jackfruit eating Itty Mappila's woman
See, she's shitting raggedy ribbon.

In his new place, there was no one to make fun of him, and he shat to his heart's content, sitting wherever he pleased. By the summer, the southern embankment of Makkothara fields was shrouded in the smell of dry shit. Recently, he had witnessed an astonishing sight when he went to build a teak bedstead for a Christian butcher near Kallara. This Mappila had constructed a palm leaf enclosure in a corner of his property, so that his wife and daughters could do their business in private.

'Shameless sods! Shitting on top of their own shit,' Kuttanasari said and spat on the ground in disgust.

The transformation Seetha underwent after moving into the new house was spectacular. Her skin took on a honey hue in the clear sunlight, her lips and cheeks turned rosy. Her shoulders and neck became soft and shiny; the nurturing wind put flesh on her skinny legs and rounded up her behind. Her breasts surged forward with nipples that gazed at the sky, challenging the masculinity of onlookers and tempting them with the promise of a safe place to rest their heads. The coppery colour of her curly hair gave way to a roaring blackness, as though pampered with a daily application of coconut oil infused with henna and kayyonni. Her sweat lost its acrid smell and sweetened like ripe jungle jackfruit, and her unpierced ears and nose shone with a misty layer of sweat.

The women who worked the fields were jealous of Seetha. The fecund fields were only two steps away, but she did not participate in the chores of transplanting the paddy, weeding, or harvesting. Her heels, scrubbed clean on the stone, did not darken from the pasty mud, her breasts and stomach were not slashed by the sharp blades of the paddy, and her palms did not turn pale and wrinkled from being constantly immersed in water.

'Ulladathi whore.'

The women, Chovathi and Pulayan alike, called her names as they weeded or sat in a circle on the bund and drank their kanji water. They accused her of keeping the same old man that her mother had kept.

'One has to be blessed to eat seeds and roots.'

'But that Kuttanasari can barely stand up straight,' said Kunheppu, the overseer of over fifty acres of fields in Makkothara and Nedumchal. 'God won't give a stick to one who can throw stones.'

'You mean he's got no stick?' The women roared with laughter. 'As if! He can hoist a frame to the roof of a house. He's quite capable.'

'Guess some things are better with age.'

Kunheppu's innuendo made them laugh again.

As she grew up, stories about the young Ulladathi woman spread far and wide. In one story, a rough ploughman, losing control at the sight of her full breasts and shapely midriff, dragged her off to a screw pine thicket and had his way with her. The girl, the story went, besotted by what had happened, invited him home the next night, but unable to match her vigour, he ran away and never brought his boat anywhere near her house again.

'Ho! She's uncontrollable,' people said, attributing the sentiment to something the ploughman, who remained unidentifiable, had told someone. As for the duck herder mentioned earlier, he was apparently herding his ducks with his narrow boat late one evening after the moon was out, getting them out of the water and on to the land, when he saw the girl standing waist-high in water, unaware of her surroundings.

'Be careful. A catfish might get in there,' he called out, overcome by a sudden joy.

The girl jumped out of the water, and completely disregarding her nudity, pelted him with mud clods, calling out the foulest words. The boat toppled, but the duck herder swam ashore and escaped somehow.

As she ran to the back of the house to investigate the commotion, Seetha saw a light approaching from the west. It was a single boat with three or four flaming torches, but the horizon and the fields lit up as though it was morning. Large shadows fell on the water-filled fields. Boats ferrying coconuts, ash or paddy did not usually bother with lights, while some boatmen hung a small lamp at the bow, the light of which made shrimps dance in the water. The torches in the approaching boat waved crazily around, but did not light up any fish or night birds. The roosting day birds were disturbed, but they stayed out of the light and flapped their wings in fright.

The boat, which usually carried ten people, had around thirty people crowded into it, and most of them were standing as if to attend to some urgent matter. Damodaran sat on the middle plank, apathetic. He had joined them voluntarily, angry at Moustache for frightening his sister and her baby, but he was hurt by the barbed comments made by people who blamed him for bringing the play that created Moustache in the first place. His long absences while he was in Madirasi meant that he did not know anyone in the boat well, and he was now contemplating how to get out of the boat and escape. A couple of times he had tried to get out when the boat neared an embankment, but the men did not let him. Their uncouth nature and distasteful behaviour annoyed him, and he sat silent and unhappy as they roared with laughter at noxious jokes. He had seen many lands and met with many types of people, but the actions of his fellow countrymen confused him. He simply did not understand why they toppled over a clay-digger boat, or let the ducks out of their enclosures. They had been rowing the boat since daybreak, searching the fields in Thandattupara, Puthanchal, Punnaveli and Nadukkari, and yet there was no sign of their quarry. By then, their early enthusiasm had waned, and they wilted in the heat. The sun had reached its zenith, and the fields around them began to display magical sights. Some began to see fields planted with paddy instead of being water-filled after the harvest, and groups of womenfolk on the bunds. The heat hit them in waves. They tried to cool themselves by pouring the water from the canal over their heads and washing their faces. And when their heads cooled, they saw the man they were after standing next to the wheelhouse on the western side of the Njavalupunja field.

Against the slope of the cloudless blue sky, Vavachan stood stroking his moustache that was a rain-bearing cloud. Behind him, nut sedge and creeping cradle grew rampant in the field that had been lying fallow for the past two seasons, and in the still canal in front of him, water sedges stood waist-deep, splaying their leaves like fingers. Like an unmoving coconut tree or a cormorant, he was part of the landscape, and invisible at first glance.

'There, over there.'

Damodaran was the only one to notice him, and directed the oarsman to the wheelhouse. Although they had shared a few days at Chellappan Pillah's building when the play was being staged, he had not had a proper conversation with Vavachan, but now he felt that they had been in a close enough relationship that he could give him a friendly wave, get him in the boat, and get his moustache shaved.

'Pull over here.'

Damodaran directed the oarsman to a fence protruding into the water. But the oarsman, terrified by the sight of the moustache that filled the space between two coconut trees, banged the water and the planks of the boat with his oar, attracting the attention of the other men. They began making buffalo-herding noises and swearing. Only one or two of them had seen Moustache before, even if only in the play.

'Sit down, you stinkers!'

The oarsman at the stern shouted when all of them stood up at once, threatening to capsize the boat. Some of them had forgotten why they had set out in the morning and started rowing in the opposite direction, and with some rowing east, some to the west, and others to the side, the boat turned in circles and began drifting towards a clump of screw pine. Those who had fallen into the water in the commotion grabbed hold of the sides and tilted the boat.

By the time the commotion ended and they managed to control the boat, there was no one around the wheelhouse. Some of the men jumped on to the bund and searched around, while others carefully and fearfully took apart the palm leaf enclosure of the wheelhouse and looked inside.

'He's gone.'

There was not even a shadow around. Damodaran sighed. Others, disbelieving he could escape just like that, continued searching among the creepers and couch grass on the embankment, and chucked mud clods into the water in the fields and into the water lilies. Yet others decided that what they had seen was a mirage in the noonday sun and got back into the boat.

Before evening, there were two more sightings of Moustache. One was quite indistinct, and might have been a flock of birds two fields away, flying in the shape of a crescent moon. And the second time, some of them ran after a shadowy figure on the overgrown embankment of the Pullukurichi field, only to return to the boat, dejected.

Investigating the commotion behind the house, Seetha thought, in the semi-darkness, that it was a dog or a swamp cat that had its head in her cooking pot. Nothing in this world scared her. She was even known to step forward and pet the flank of a charging bull. It was she who looked after the baby goat that Kuttanasari brought home once, and reared it to a full-sized billy, feeding it groundnut pumice, raw eggs and fish oil. Smelling its animal fragrance carried by the wind through the neighbourhood, she-goats trembled in sexual frenzy, and when they were brought over the next morning, it was Seetha who sat their owners on a stool in the yard and released the billy goat. Once Kunheppu brought a she-goat, which ran wildly around the post it was tied to without letting the billy goat come near it. Seetha consoled him as he worriedly scratched his head.

'Don't worry, it's her first time, isn't it? That's why.'

She tied the she-goat on a short leash to the papaya tree.

'Let her get through it once. She'll be more willing after that.'

Seetha picked up a length of firewood, and swearing at the top of her voice, she ran towards the beast that was polishing off the contents of her cooking pot. But she hesitated before striking, as she realised that there was no dog or swamp cat that stood this tall or looked this strong. The figure put the pot down and stood up, knocking his head on the slanting roof of the lean-to. His shoulders were like a vast piece of fallow land, and his chest a patch of overgrown wild grass. Not an ounce of excess fat remained around his stomach and waist, and his arms hung halfway down his thighs. His body filled an entire side of the lean-to which was open on three sides, shutting out wind and light. Seetha saw, clearly, the shiny, shapely, impossibly thick moustache with its ends tapering to a point, and the grains of good-quality Kochathikkurali rice stuck in it along with droplets of rice water. She would go hungry this evening, Seetha realised, and raised the stick angrily.

'Do you know if this is the way to Malaya?' the moustached man asked in a humble voice.

He wiped his moustache clean with the back of his hand.

'You Pulayan scoundrel…!'

Her reply to his question was an almighty smack to the side of his head. His ear buzzed as though a bumble bee was inside it. Blocking the next smack, his hand made contact with her generous breasts, warm and firm like the nest of a brooding bird. The third whack lodged on his back, and before she could land a fourth, he held her firmly against the palm-leaf wall and tried to pry the stick out of her hand. As the shapely stomach and reckless breasts fought earnestly with him, he marvelled at how small female bodies were and how they gained in stature only in the gaze of the male. Her head barely came up to his chest, and her shoulders, chest and waist were way below. Seetha was disarmed, but she fought ferociously, scratching his chest and biting wherever possible, her entire body working like a sharp, spinning vegetable knife. She kicked at his knees and grabbed his crotch.

'Filthy scamp … I'll stamp your balls out!'

The combined odour of canal water and sweat rose from her armpits and neck. Her thick hair smelled of the steam rising from boiling paddy. His nose, built only to smell sour tapioca and stale kanji water, inhaled these heady fragrances for the first time. As his belly was full, his senses were sharp, his skin, tongue and hair on alert. His lips tasted saltiness.

As a slap landed on her cheek and she fell to the floor, the single piece of cloth around her waist came untied. The moustached man jumped on top of her and bit her neck, smelled her hair and armpits, dived into the bottomless pool between her breasts and raised his arms to be rescued from it, before drowning in it again. The woman struggled, kicking and pushing until another dizzying slap made her pliant. The moustached man grunted into her, and attacked her like he had attacked the palmyra tree that had snagged his moustache and hurt him.

When the boat with the search party reached the moorings in front of Kuttanasari's house, one of the men threw the torch which had burned almost to a stump into the water. He listened to its dying sizzle and sang a ditty in an insinuating voice:

Panikathi lassie, hey, here's your Panikan
Hey, spread the mat, hey, fry the snacks,
Hey, boil the yam…

He got off the boat and walked to the back of the house, looking for coconut leaves to make a new torch. His friend lit the way with another torch which was also about to die out. And they saw, in the cooking lean-to, two shapes, their nakedness barely covered, joined in exhausted sleep. They withdrew quietly and went back to the boat.

'Come quickly. Let's beat him to death right here.'

Roaring as one, the gang of men rushed forward with whatever they could use as a weapon. Some of them went into the house, while a few slashed at the banana trees and coconut fronds with their machetes. But by the time they got to the lean-to, the moustached man had disappeared like a sliver of lightning. All they could see was the shape of an otter swimming away through the decaying bits of grass in the water-filled fields, only its head visible above the water. Even the man who had seen the sleeping figures wondered whether what he had seen was in fact an otter. Otters too had moustaches, great big moustaches.

Ignoring her struggles and screams, they tied up the naked woman and carried her all the way to Virippukala, where they deposited her behind a haystack, and took turns in ones and twos. Before daybreak, they tied a scrap of cloth around her waist and put her on top of the sacks of areca nuts in a covered boat that came that way. Its long-oarsmen watched her with interest as they rowed. A little later, when they reached a place deserted even by the birds, they tied the boat to a post. One of them moved towards her.

9

CROCODILE

With the basket of paddy balanced on his head, Paviyan had walked without stopping anywhere. By the time he reached the sluice in the outer bund of the Ayyanadan Puthankari fields, it was full dark. He had not been able to cut across the fields as they had been drenched in water after the harvest. The long walk along the outer bunds of Poovathikari and Kolamburathukari made him cough. Still, he was determined to keep up the pace. He had to walk across Mattam, Maniyanthuruthu and Kanyakon to the western embankment of Chozhiyappara to finally reach home. The summer's cultivation was over, the paddy harvested and threshed. The whole area was deserted; not even a wandering animal or a bird was to be seen. Only the wind remained, scampering noisily across the land. Paviyan watched bits of hay, desiccated in the day's heat, spinning and rising in the wind like tops. The evenings had become hotter, he realised, as it was a sight usually seen only in the high heat of the afternoon sun. He had placed a couple of pieces of areca palm spathes on top of the basket to be cut into hand-fans for the sweltering nights to come.

As night fell, the fields came alive. In the crevasses of silence, things scuttled across water and land. Man-high swarms of tiny insects rose into the air. Decaying stubs of hay exhaled their last breaths in the water. The frogs were mostly quiet, dejected in the stagnant water pumped up from canals starved of rain and life. Paviyan understood that the lonesome bull frog that croaked from the termite-infested palm fronds of the wheelhouse had seen him. 'Be careful, mind the paddy,' that's what it said.

Paviyan would not risk losing the paddy in the basket on his head, not on his life. He had left most of the paddy he had received in wages in the Valiyavelicham field covered, and the boundaries marked with burnt hay. Those who stole another person's share of paddy left covered thus would not live to see the next harvest. But what was one to do about the duck herders who would let the water in and submerge the fields without compunction? Who would one complain to? He was determined not to let that happen, and to come back and collect the rest of it the very next day.

On reaching Mattam, Paviyan looked to the south. There was not even a sliver of moonlight. Darkness congealed into squares and canal shapes. The wind had stopped. He set the basket down, and sat on the stump of a coconut tree, looking into the small canal in front of him, thinking. A couple of bubbles floated on to the bank. He stubbed them with his toes, and let his foot remain in the water, but pulled it back quickly. He had to swim across five canals, including this one, with the basket balanced on his head. The darkness of this particular night did not give him a sense of courage. The low water levels had increased the saltiness of the canal, and he did not want to swim in it. Besides, if he were to step into a ditch where the clay had been dug up, or into squishy mud, the basket would topple over. Or he might stumble over a support frame stuck into the canal floor to stop the dykes from bursting.

Wasting no more time, Paviyan walked back the way he came. There was a bridge, a long piece of a coconut tree trunk, across the canal in Koduthuruthu that was put in place for the harvest workers to walk across. He stepped on to it, and as he reached the middle, the tree groaned as though about to break. A startled water snake went splashing into the weeds. Worried that the paddy was lost, Paviyan exclaimed: 'Ayyo!' The coconut tree recognised him by his voice as the son of Kankali, who used to live on the embankment of Thazhathekkuzhi.

It relaxed its back, took a deep breath and lay still, trying not to break. Almost sixty years ago, on a night as dark as this one, Kankali had stolen twenty seed coconuts just setting sprouts that were to be planted on the Kollamkari bund. He had carried them to the Vilanguchira bund, sat down and eaten nineteen of them, tearing the husks off each coconut with his teeth. The juice from the spongy sweet sprouts inside had dripped down his arms into the water, sending spit-eating rasboras into frenzy. Belching, he had examined the twentieth coconut. If those nineteen coconuts had been planted, there would have been nineteen new coconut trees to produce fruits and toddy, leaves to make the walls and roofs of several houses, flower stalks to whiten the teeth of several people. They would have offered nineteen more coconut crowns for chembanchelli palm weevils to feast on.

The twentieth coconut had not interested Kankali. It was too light, its sprout had not yet broken through the husk. Besides, his teeth and gums were aching from ripping off the husks. So he had chucked it into the canal. Over the next two days, it had bobbed along in the currents until it had settled on the embankment of Kelakkari, sprouted, put roots, and grown to produce coconuts for over forty years. In that time, Chella had once sat under it to cut grass, and the tree had selected a good coconut and dropped it down for her. As time passed, its productivity had decreased, and one day, a Mappila from Vechoor had cut it down, transported a length of it to the Koduthuruthu canal, and set it across it as a bridge.

It would be another two days before someone else would set foot on the bridge – a man from Vechoor, carrying a bundle of straw. The bridge would break, merciless this time, and send him tumbling into the water, soaking his straw. 'Sodding bridge,' he would curse as he pulled himself out of the water and went on his way.

Beyond the fields, the land rose steeply to Perunthuruthu. Paviyan walked, inhaling the aroma of ripe jackfruit, and by the time he got to the top, the moon was high in the night sky. The terraced land had a few houses, asleep under the moonlight, some with pinpricks of light in their compounds. Having lit lamps to appease the invisible powers residing there, the humans had run back and hid in the safety of their homes. A lone man remained in a blacksmith's hut, noisily attacking iron with iron. The blacksmith was on the lookout for a spirit who frequented the area, and came out of the hut waving a pair of red-hot tongs. The tongs made contact with the spirit and sizzled as though immersed in water.

Past another expanse of fields and a canal, as Paviyan began to walk up the next rise, a kollikkoravan owl flew over his head, shouting like a person. Its wings stirred the air around his face. Paviyan had never seen the rooster-sized owl chasing its prey this close. Its cry was the harbinger of death.

A steep decline, more fields, and a further rise brought Paviyan into a parcel of land, ploughed and ready to be planted with vegetables, waiting for summer rains. Further ahead, coming up to Mudakkali canal, Paviyan stopped. The canal, almost one and a half times broader than most canals, had burst its banks; murky water flowed into the fields on both sides. Paviyan had never seen a canal with so much water at a time when almost all other waterways had run dry. The turbulent water, Paviyan guessed, was rushing in from the east. He would have to wait until morning and cross when the water levels subsided, or wait for a boat to come along.

Was there a place in the east with so much rain that all this water flowed west, even in high, dry summer? Paviyan had never thought about this. As it came downhill from Pala, the Kavanaar River split into streams and canals and, eventually, into tiny capillaries, like a tangled web of roots to bring water to the fields. No one fully realised that these met again to form small, and then large, canals, finally transforming, as it reached Kaipuzha, into the Kaipuzha River that flowed further west. Moving further and further away along the water into the distance as they cut grass, people did not recognise it as a river, only a large canal, because the vast fields that extended as far as the lake had mellowed its nature, and it flowed with the barest ripple of currents beneath its surface. The numerous waterways that joined the river along the way brought water lilies and hyacinths, pallathi and blackfish, and ducks, and converted it into an ordinary canal.

Paviyan left the Mudakkali canal and retraced his steps. He stopped at a house with a lean-to that was a dried fish shop during the day. He inhaled deeply the aroma of salted fish, and lay down below the counter with his head resting on a low stool. The lean-to was imbued with the permanent scent of countless soles, sea bass, ponies, rays, and stony-headed snappers that had climbed out from the sea to release their moisture in the fine, sparkling sand on the beaches, and huddle in salt to be savoured with kanji. There was no other smell in this world quite like that of salted and dried fish. Around five years ago, at the Vechoor church festival, Chella had managed to buy a piece of the tail of a spotted eagle ray for a bargain. She had used every last shred of it until she was left with the inedible parts. She had cut them into small bits, and put them in the fire on evenings when there was no more fish to eat. Its enticing smell had drawn the children and Paviyan, dispersed on their various concerns, to the fire, and the wind had carried the smell, stronger than the fragrance of the flowering pala, across the fields and canals, making even those who lived far away look wistfully at their fireless hearths, yearning for a pot of kanji. Stepping outside to urinate in the middle of one such night, Chella had seen two otters prowling around the hearth stones. One of them had came up to the ashes and crinkled its nose. And in the morning, there had been several birds on the branches of the flowering mallow tree, staring intently at the hearth.

Lying below the dried fish counter, Paviyan fell asleep instantly. He rarely dreamed, but when he did, they always came true. He was dreaming now, and in his dream was an unclear image of a creature with a thick outer shell.

On the counter, there was a woven palm-leaf basket packed thickly with salted, dried sardines. The chaakara season that followed the monsoon, when the waters became rich in nutrients, had brought an abundance of fish to frolic and feed at Andhakaranazhi. The fishing was plentiful, but there had not been enough buyers, and the surplus had been dried and layered in salt. These would now be scattered under coconut trees before the rains began. The salt and the smell of the sea would convince the coconut trees that they were at the coast, and they would grow in joyous abandon, and set copious fruit without allowing a single one to be snatched by the wind.

A sardine in the basket, overcome with a sense of guilt and memories of the sea, moved slightly. He had come with a vast school of sardines, and as the chaakara came to an end, he was on his way back to the deep sea with his mates when the sunlight streaming through the clear water had enticed him gleefully to the surface. The school, with many pregnant females with bellies swollen with eggs, had followed him, and the fishermen, watching the sea turn silver, had rushed over and cast their nets in a circle.

When the fish moved, a hunk of salt fell on the sleeping body below. He had been dozing only for a few minutes, but Paviyan sprang up, steeped in an anxiety that he had been asleep for a long time, and that several harvest seasons had passed meanwhile. He imagined that he could see redness spreading across the eastern sky, and hear the wise early birds setting out to catch worms. He hoisted his basket on to his head, and walked quickly to the canal bank. Ancestral spirits hiding in the compounds and holes in the fences looked askance at him, wondering what possessed him. Without the ability to speak, all they could do was watch and wonder at the behaviour of their descendants. If only they could issue fair warnings! Still, unable to bear it, an ancestor of Paviyan's father's father shouted: 'Go back to sleep, you wretch!'

But all Paviyan heard was the noisy scamper of a bandicoot in the undergrowth.

He waited, back at the Mudakkali canal. It was not light yet. The redness in the eastern sky disappeared into darkness again.

There was no sign of the boats that usually set out early for the Kuruppanthara market. Paviyan stared at both horizons, wondering whether he had lost his way. Presently, he heard the sound of a long-oar cutting through water, and a boat packed with coconut husks came along. There were two people in it, and they looked identical. Even their body shapes, mere shadows in the dark, seemed similar. Their boat held a steady pace as they rowed, silently, their oars cutting through water in symphony, and they stood at either end of the boat as though they were a single man split in two. Paviyan hollered: 'Please… take me across.'

The men stopped rowing, looked at each other, and broke into profanities. Their experiences had taught them that no ordinary human would be in this location at this time of night, and the best way to confront devious spirits was good, old-fashioned profanity. Paviyan hollered again, and the intensity of the profanities and the speed of the rowing increased, and within seconds the boat disappeared as though it had never been there in the first place.

Paviyan decided not to wait any longer, and hoping to swim across the canal at its narrowest part, he walked east along its bank. At a spot where the yearly reinforcement with clay had turned the walkway into an embankment, and considerably narrowed the width of the canal, he lowered his burden, and got ready to swim across. Something moved in the bushes. Goats that ate the bitter tapioca leaves unable to resist the taste, and human beings who intentionally consumed the poisonous fruit of the othalam tree, were known to thrash around in the undergrowth in agony. But this sound was more like the intermittent splashing of a fish caught in a basket trap. Paviyan withdrew his wet legs, and walked towards a buckthorn bush that had spread downwards from the embankment. Buckthorn was a monster with a hundred prickly hands that tightened their grasp as whatever was caught in them tried to shake itself off. It seemed this time that it was something with uncanny strength, and it shook the whole bush as though trying to uproot it. Like a snake coiled around a mongoose, it was difficult to tell whether it was the animal or the bush itself that was trying to break free.

Carefully, Paviyan approached the bush and stared into it in the negligible light. He stepped back – in anger or fear – quickly. Lifting the basket on to his head, he was about to step back into the water when the animal cried out to him.

'Stay there and die,' Paviyan told the creature. 'Or wait until morning. Someone will come along and beat you to death.'

It cried loudly. Paviyan understood that it was begging for his help.

'You can fuck right off! You think anyone would put their hand knowingly into a snake's hole?'

The creature begged, again.

'Right!' Paviyan made an obscene gesture. 'You and your kind have killed and eaten at least forty of my people.'

The animal continued crying, and Paviyan understood it was trying to tell him that it had ten eggs in its belly. He took out his sickle, its blade worn almost to nothing over the many harvests, and began hacking at the bush. The severed twigs caught hold of his legs in anger. The animal, now quiet, waited for Paviyan to finish his work.

Free, finally, from the prickly hold of the buckthorn, the creature placed its legs firmly on the ground, swished its tail, and came towards him. Paviyan saw, quite clearly, the barnacles on its ancient back.

The twins in the boat carrying coconut husks stopped at a moonlit spot along the canal. One of them peered into the water and, seeing a million stars in it, wondered whether he was looking at the sky. He looked up, and the sky rippled as though it was the canal. The men blamed each other for setting out at this godforsaken hour. One man sat on the edge of the boat, intending to defecate into the water, and scrambled up immediately, screaming. He held on to the oar, trying not to fall into the water, and pointed to the middle of the canal. Paviyan Pulayan went sweeping past them, sitting on the back of a crocodile. It seemed that the animal was riding the current, and Paviyan sat on its back holding on for dear life.

'I came across one of your kind about fifteen years ago in the Maniyaaparambu canal,' Paviyan told the crocodile. 'It was the month of Thulam. Pulayans working the Onpathinayiram fields saw something floating in the water. Looked like a thick log. We went over to have a look. We saw it only when we were close – there was a hole in its left leg.'

'It was shot,' said the crocodile.

Paviyan watched the sun come up, lighting up the cottonwood and flowering mallow trees, and the silver colocasia on the embankment. Cobwebs glittered in the grass, and leaves were wet with dew. From the surface of the water, he could also see, just below, the secret gardens the greenery leaning into the water had created for the fish and the water insects. A ripple of nervousness spread across this world as the crocodile approached. The fish hid their eggs. Even the tadpoles hung back, cautious, and Paappu, the snakehead murrel that ruled the waters, was nowhere to be seen. Kingfishers took off without a destination, their beaks pointed towards the sky.

'A white man has set out with a gun.'

The crocodile looked wonderingly at the fearless white heron which stood its ground on the embankment. The heron was not afraid of anything. A long time ago, it was the heron that used to come to the aid of the crocodiles when they got bones stuck in their throats. It would keep their mouths open with a stick, and climb in to clean their throats.

'What white man?' Paviyan asked.

'A saheb,' said the crocodile. 'He patrols the canals with his gun.'

They should have been near his home by now. Paviyan wondered why he could not spot his house, and why the sun seemed not to come out properly into the sky. Time stood still, and the embankment seemed to go on endlessly.

'Isn't that a good thing?' he asked. 'People should be able to get into the canals and rivers without fear.'

'Why do they want to get into the canals and rivers?'

'Don't we have to wash and bathe?'

'Why do you need to wash?'

Paviyan saw a jungle fig tree, almost all of its branches leaning into the water, creating a tricky spot for the boats passing by. Its trunk was covered in tasteless fruits with bitter, red seeds. He wondered who had started the rumour that these fruits were sweet. A monkey sat on one of its branches. Paviyan had never seen a monkey in these parts. Its body was covered in white and grey hair, and it opened its mouth at a passing fly.

'Hey there, friend,' the crocodile called out.

The monkey ignored him.

'My father's father had his own crocodile,' Paviyan said.

His father's father would go to the canal bank and say, 'Come out, kid,' and the crocodile would come out of the water. And when he said, 'Go on, boy,' it would go back into the water. One time, it lay below the washing stone near the canal with its mouth open, and an infant, crawling along the bund out of sight of its mother, climbed straight in and back out.

As he rode on the crocodile, lotus stems nicked Paviyan's legs. The crocodile moved through the water without creating a single ripple. The eagle does not create ripples in the sky either, Paviyan thought.

A distant noise arose from the canal on the far side of a field.

'Did you hear that?' the crocodile cocked its ears. 'It's the noise of the crowd that has set out to capture your son.'

They could see the vague shape of two groups, one wielding sticks and picks, and another in a boat armed with anything they could use as a weapon. There were at least fifty people. Shading his eyes with his hand, Paviyan tried to see if he could recognise anyone. They had set fire to the hay stumps to ward off the cold or, perhaps, for no reason at all, and they would spread and continue to smoke in the dew for days until it rained. Paviyan could see the towels tied around people's heads.

'Christian Mappilas, I wonder...'

'All castes,' said the crocodile.

'What did that good-for-nothing do now?'

Anger took hold of him when he thought that it was him and his wife and children who would suffer the consequences of his son's actions.

'He grew a moustache.'

'His sodding moustache! I'll burn him until he's hairless.'

Dropping Paviyan off at a discreet corner of the Vishakhamthara field, the crocodile climbed out of the water and lay under a coconut tree. It was a good spot to catch the sun. His mouth, meant for herons to clean and infants to crawl in, was wide open. Trying not to attract attention, Paviyan jumped across the water channels of two wheelhouses and ran home. He was determined to drag Vavachan out, assuming he was home, hang him upside down, and beat the living daylights out of him. He swore as he ran, holding his basket snugly against his left shoulder. If Vavachan was not home, his rage would explode on Chella and the other children.

But he was detected by a man cutting screw pine leaves, and he hollered to attract the attention of the crowd. Soon, Paviyan was being chased across the fields, and as soon as he was captured, Kunjappa Chovan slapped him across the face.

'Pulayan son of a whore! I'll cut your nuts off,' he said, warding off others who surged forward wanting to take a shot at Paviyan.

They piled him on to the boat that had set out to capture Vavachan, and rowed westwards.

'I'll burn him myself,' Paviyan said, standing at the bow of the boat. 'I'll even burn the moustache between his legs!'

By the time the sun was high in the sky, a large crowd flocked to the spot where the crocodile had brought Paviyan. Even women and children from the grand houses, who had never set eyes on the fields that produced their paddy, came to see the sight. None of them had seen a crocodile before. Those who were left behind when the boat had gone away with Paviyan had come back and hacked it to death with hatchets.

'So lucky!' they exclaimed, repeatedly. 'Ho! Otherwise … Those ten eggs would have hatched, and there would have been ten more crocodiles, and they would also have laid eggs and created hundreds more. Imagine!'

But what really intrigued them was the tapping knife they found in its stomach. Had anyone gone missing lately?

'Ho! Look at this,' a man poked at the knife with a stick and turned it over. 'It's been partially digested. Told you, didn't I? Even iron breaks down in a crocodile's stomach.'

10

IN SEARCH OF SEETHA

On a couch grass covered bund in the Pathinettoram field, a black turtle and a white turtle met with each other. They had been meeting in this exact same spot for over a hundred years, even before the Pathinettoram field or the Punnaveli field existed, when there was only an expanse of foot-sucking swamp of water and mud.

Like all animals in stories, they discussed the past, the present and the future. The black turtle looked at the grey pansy butterflies that had been sitting still for hours on the marsh babel plants with annoyance.

'Why can't these things piss off somewhere and do something?' it asked.

'In that case, why can't that man among the reeds get up and piss off?' the white turtle asked.

A forest of reeds, almost as high as two men, grew densely by the side of the bund, holding within it thousands of baya weavers, their nests and their whispers. Every now and then, a hundred of them would fly quietly into the sky while another hundred would come down and surreptitiously enter its depths.

'He's hiding there. He's scared of people,' the white turtle continued.

'And they are scared of him,' said the black turtle. 'I don't understand these human beings.'

'They're mad, the lot of them. Never at peace. I don't understand why they can't eat and drink and be happy with these canals and fields like the rest of us. Instead they rush about all over the place. Haven't you seen them talking to themselves when they think no one is looking?'

'They think the earth is round!' The black turtle struggled to control its laughter.

'They don't believe what they see, or what they don't see for that matter. It's funny the way they go around with that piece of cloth around their waists. The other day, one fellow took it off, made sure no one was around, and looked intently at the organ inside it for such a long time … As though he couldn't believe his eyes!'

'You know, they follow this rule of one man, one woman.'

'Yes. The pearlspot has that rule too. No wonder, it's the stupidest of all fish. If someone pokes a young coconut leaf into the water, it sees the creamy white colour and immediately sticks its head in the mud. And they can just walk into the water and pick it right up.'

'Idiots.'

'I wonder why this idiot is hiding in there with a moustache on his face.'

'And I wonder why the others are after him.'

'Did you notice where he is sitting? Right where someone beat his father's father to death and buried his body. And he has no clue! In any case, with these people, the murderer's son could later become the best friend of the victim's son. They're busy remembering things, but nothing important sticks in their memory.'

'Why doesn't he get up? I'm beginning to think he's going to stay put forever. See, the reeds have started growing through his black moustache now. Soon there will be termites and ants in them, and birds and snakes will come to eat them. His moustache will get entangled in the reeds, and keep on growing.'

'I doubt that. His mind has been obsessed with thoughts of a woman, and I think he's going to wander around looking for her.'

'Ho! These people can do nothing right.'

It was when, in the morning light of a day soon after, he saw hair-of-the-water growing in the canal that Moustache shook himself out of his stupor. The canal had, until then, remained perfectly still by day and by night, with not even the fish moving in its depths. Overnight, the plant that had been growing quietly had flowered, turning the canal red as far as the eye could see – thousands of tiny little red flowers blooming to turn the water into one enormous red flower. He thought of Seetha, as he had been for all these days. Her dense hair had the smell of boiling paddy, and all that remained in his memory of the time he had spent with her was that smell. The scabs on the scratch marks she had left on his chest had fallen off, and the wounds had healed.

A long time had passed since he had been sitting among the reeds, watching days and nights go by. For a few days in the beginning, he could hear the commotion of the people and boats searching for him. He had seen Paviyan too, a couple of times, once at the bow of a boat, and at another time, he and five or six Pulayans of his age had settled down in a patch of shade near the reeds to rest.

'I wonder if he's inside this,' Pathrose Pulayan had bent down and looked into the darkness of the thicket. 'Is that his moustache I see?'

Moustache, sitting in the dark, had been able to see everything outside clearly. He had looked intently at Paviyan, who was kneading his chest as he sat there cooling his body. He had seemed, at the same time, angry enough to beat the life out of Vavachan, and thoughtful as though looking at a field overrun by wild rice.

'No point in searching for him now,' the older of the group had said, chewing on a sprig of grass. 'Remember that buffalo calf you lost? Just think of it like that.'

'But that creature never bothered anyone,' Paviyan had responded.

Before they left, Paviyan had set fire to the edges of the reed thicket. It had smouldered for a while, and when finally it caught fire, water snakes crawled out of it and the baya weavers flew into the sky. Vavachan had remembered how his father would jerk his arms up with an annoyed expression as he stood waist-deep in water to cut grass. Small water snakes would bite his arms and hang from them, and

Paviyan would shake them off and pluck at the ones that would not dislodge. When they had gone, Vavachan had put the fire out with his moustache drenched in dew.

In the full dark, he swam across the canal and reached Kuttanasari's house. Its yard was dirty and weed-ridden in its abandonment, its palm-leaf walls powdery from termites. There were no pots and pans or firewood at the back of the house. The wind picked up, breaking off a few hands of the banana trees and shaking an entire bush of screw pine, and Vavachan wondered whether it was the beginning of a storm that would lead him astray, like the storm that had come the day he had gone with his father to cut grass. He wondered who it was that had tricked them on that day – the Chovan who had swallowed the chemballi fish, or Seetha who had cursed at them for cutting down her banana bunch.

And just like on that day, Vavachan began to feel an acute hunger. It was followed by an uncontrollable sexual desire. He entered Kuttanasari's house and searched every nook and cranny, and in a dazed rage, broke through the wall planks. He rushed off westwards, and lost his bearings in the endless fields. He swam across canals, saw moths and mating frogs like stacked pebbles. The wind stilled and the night cooled.

He opened his eyes and realised that he had been asleep, lying snugly below a screw pine shrub, which made him wonder whether he had been dreaming or whether he had, in fact, been wandering, lost. One of the screw pines had neat bunches of fruit hanging off it and another was in flower, but they were all bald; someone had cut off all the leaves. He tried to remember the woman he had overpowered in the dark, and the woman who had stood by the side of the canal and thrown obscenities at him and his father. He could not recall anything other than the warmth of her breasts and the smell of her hair. Afraid that these memories too would dissipate in a few days, he focused his mind on those sensations. But, every day, new things entered the mind, crowding out old memories until they disappeared without a trace. What is left if there is nothing to remember? Who could say the whiskered catfish was in the clear water once it had passed through?

The man in the boat had set out very early so that he could finish the day's clay digging before it was too hot. The unexpected sighting of Moustache made him scream, and in his panic, his long-oar broke and the boat tilted, throwing him into the canal. Terrified, he forgot how to swim and splashed around, swallowing the muddy water, unable to gain the far bank and too scared to climb up the near. Finally, with no other option, he caught hold of something and pulled himself out of the water. It was a hair from the moustache, and terror engulfed him once again when he discovered its rope-like strength.

'Which field is this?' Vavachan asked him, smoothing the wayward hair back into his moustache.

The man gestured wildly.

'That's the Pottaparichakari field, and this is Aanachamkuzhi. Over there is Thottuvelikkari, and that there is the field of the Mamballi folk.'

Moustache snatched the penknife off his waistband, pulled the boat closer, and ate the boiled tapioca in it. The man watched with trepidation as each piece of tapioca disappeared into the moustache. The darkness congealed in the moustache made him shiver.

'Did you come across a woman?' Moustache stopped eating, parted his moustache and asked. 'She might have been captured by some people. A beautiful woman, fair-skinned.'

The man thought for a while. 'I did,' he said eventually.

The man had black skin, except on his palms and the underside of his feet which were bleached white from being immersed relentlessly in water. His skin was wrinkled, and his eyes were red from peering constantly into water. Standing on planks laid under water and lifting blocks of clay into the boat had made his shoulders strong and well-defined.

He had heard a woman cry, he said, from a covered boat that was travelling quite fast. When she saw him, she had plucked out a hair and put it in the water, and told him quietly to hand it over to the one who would come looking for her. Vavachan took the hair, and as he raised it to his nose to breathe in its aroma, the dry strand caught hold of the moustache and entwined itself in its hairs. The clay digger watched the ends of the moustache quivering as though overcome by a great sadness.

Vavachan walked in the direction the man had pointed out, past the outer bunds planted with coconut and banana, and into the empty fields beyond. The walkways tamped down by the paddy workers' feet lay dry and dusty in the scorching sun. He took his bearings from the position of the sun, and walked across Kalathode, the Kannukalam field and Muthirakkala. In the sweltering heat without even a bamboo reed to provide a snippet of shade, he walked until his eyes dimmed with hunger and thirst. He stopped by the side of a canal and drank from it, sprawled on all fours like cattle. In the split second before his face touched the water, he saw his moustache clearly, against the reflection of the sky in the canal.

It had grown bigger and bushier. If he wanted, Vavachan could hide in it for a whole lifetime. Astonished, he looked again. He would not need to trim it or shape it any more as it had taken on its own grooming, sometimes remaining tidily shaped, and at other times lazily defying order, standing unruly with a straight back. The hair on his chin had stopped growing, and sucking up the surplus energy, the moustache grew, taking on life like a human being – sentient, irate, decorous. Vavachan considered shaving it off with the penknife sharpened on a stone, but the thought filled him with fear.

When his thirst was quenched, hunger rose roaring inside him. He stepped into the canal, plucked water lilies and, discarding their petals, ate their hearts. Smeared with their oil, his moustache shone brighter than before. On hungry days, Chella used to cook the tender leaves of the water lilies with nothing but salt and water.

Wandering away from the canal, he lost his bearings again. The sun was obscured by a cloud shaped like an elephant's mouth. Stillness prevailed, not even the flicker of dragonflies or birds. Past Venthakari and the Thattamparambu fields, he saw an approaching group of women chatting among themselves on their way to cut cockspur grass, and hid behind a swamp apple tree. Some of the women had bundles of cockspur balanced on their heads, fodder for their calves, with their sickles lodged in them. They had emaciated breasts. Hoping that they would have seen her, he held his breath and listened.

'She was screaming her head off,' said a woman who looked the youngest of the group.

She set her bundle down, washed the dirt off her hands, and pressed her wet hands on her thin, long neck.

'I only heard the sound. Didn't see her.'

'Did anyone see?'

'It was just a flash, wasn't it?'

'This must be the towel from her shoulders,' another woman said, holding up the piece of cloth in her hand. 'Where else would it have come from?'

The woman went behind the swamp apple to shake her cloth and retie it, and immediately ran back releasing an ear-splitting scream. Terrified, the other women scrambled up and ran towards the canal after her.

As they swam across the canal, she said: 'He's hiding there. His moustache is so big! He had her head in his mouth.'

Vavachan picked up the cloth from among the things the women had discarded in their panic and raised it to his nose. He searched for her smell in the piece of cloth stinking of damp and dirt from being used to catch fish in flowing water. A puffer fish, coming up from the wilting hyacinths by the water's edge, was startled by Moustache. It had never seen a creature with such a big moustache before, and taking it to be a fish-hungry otter, it puffed up its belly, displaying its fear even as it tried to frighten off its enemy. It watched as water dropped from the slit-eyes above the moustache, thickening the canal water already salty from the bodies of paddy workers who got only chaff-filled paddy as payment, and bund workers who got nothing at all.

'Puffer fish, have you seen a woman?' Moustache asked. 'Her hair looks like this.'

He held up the long hair tangled in his moustache.

The puffer fish dove back into the water without responding.

As he swam across the canal, Moustache asked, 'Kottichi minnow, have you seen a woman?'

Entangled in his moustache, a large hunk of debris – weeds, water lilies and dried grass – crossed the water. His moving body slashed a deep scar on the water's surface.

'Rainbow barb, spotted minnow, have you seen a woman?'

None of the fish responded, but they watched him. Many of them had seen him before at the Chozhiyappara embankment, catching hatchlings with a wicker basket. When the cold water from the rains in the east flowed into the canals, bringing fresh tidings, the fish, eager to find mates and to lay eggs, had rushed upstream fearlessly, energised by the call of their bodies. The whiskered catfish, dazed by the sight of water flowing from the skies, had climbed up coconut trees only to sit stunned on their crowns looking at the nothingness beyond, where they had been picked off by toddy tappers. Several other fish had been caught by fishing hooks, nets and baskets, or trapped within cages paved smooth with coconut leaf spines at the entrance, hiding the prisons within. Those who caught hatchlings were reborn as fish when they died because they were cursed by the unfortunate souls who had to die without having a chance to mate. The fish that had withstood all these misfortunes had reached the easternmost ponds and canals. And they had seen Vavachan as they swam back, peacefully, into their native waters. Now they watched, with interest, the man who had been moustacheless in those days swim across the canals. He had become painfully thin and lacklustre. It was the moustache that now led him. It grew out of control, like worms inside the tummies of children destined not to survive, sucking out his essence to keep itself glorious. If a branch grows bigger than the tree, it either breaks off or topples the whole tree. His moustache had outgrown him, and it was the moustache, not Vavachan, that now paid attention to the paths and canals, and took careful stock of the wind and the rain.

To the north was a big canal, and to the south, the waterlogged fields, and it was as he walked along the wet bund between them that he noticed, in the middle of the fields, a small islet, like a guardhouse.

It had a hut, a few coconut and banana trees, and some gardenia bushes marking the fence line. Moustache jumped into the water and swam towards it. He did not hear the black-winged gulls who called out warnings – his ears were shut by the wiry hairs of his moustache.

Moustache reached the islet and hopped over the fence. Nothing moved around the hut, and its roof, neglected for many years, was skeletal like a desiccated corpse. He trampled through the mud and the raging bushes of itchy colocasia. The hut was uninhabited, yet the smell of boiling kanji and screw pine flowers called to people far away. Moustache felt that he had swum across all these canals, trundled across acres of fields because his mind and stomach had been overwhelmed by the smell of freshly boiling kanji, and he listened carefully for the sound of its roiling bubbles. He went behind the hut, and saw an old woman bent over a stone placed on a square platform made of clay. She was scrubbing a fish on the stone. Moustache looked closer – it was a butter catfish. As it came forcefully in contact with the stone, it curved its back, and raised its head and tail.

'Could I have some kanji water?' Vavachan asked.

He realised immediately that he sounded like the ghost who begged for food. The old woman looked up. The sight of the moustache did not scare her, but Vavachan noticed that the ends of his moustache had bowed and drooped downwards out of respect for her. His legs and arms trembled in anticipation of the bowl of kanji water with a thick layer of starch on its surface and a few grains of rice that would be hiding beneath it.

The old woman stopped scrubbing the fish against the stone.

'Not kanji water,' she said. 'You'll have proper kanji with fish curry. The chillies are already ground. I'll make the curry adding some coconut pumice.'

The fish wriggled in her hand.

'Here, clean this fish,' she told him. 'Let me check if the kanji is cooked.'

Butter catfish had incomparable strength. He began scrubbing the fish.

'Did you see a woman come along this way?' he asked it.

There was no sound from inside the hut. Scrubbing against the stone did not seem to get rid of the sliminess of the fish, but he persevered using the ash and soil the old woman had piled up on the floor. The slimy water pooled around, and yet the fish, still not clean, wriggled powerfully in his hand. Suddenly, the sun went down, darkness rose along with the sound of fireflies and flapping wings. Vavachan continued scrubbing. There was no sign of the old woman, but he heard the kanji boiling in the pot, and the hiss of the fire under the pot. In the morning, he saw black ants scurrying out of the hut, escaping, he thought, from the burning firewood where they had been hiding. Night came again, and day followed. He looked out through the gaps in the gardenia bushes. Water receded from the fields, and filled with fisherfolk, of both the winged and wingless varieties. Sowing, transplanting, weeding, harvesting and threshing took place, and the fields filled with water again. Seasons recurred. Many times, it rained all day, followed by thunder and lightning in the evenings.

On a sunny day, Vavachan heard a call and raised his head. A young man with very dark skin stood before him with a mouldy, dirt-coloured cloth around his waist. He had swum across; there were bits of water weeds in his hair.

'Could I have some kanji water?' he asked.

'Here, hold this fish. Let me see if the kanji is cooked.'

Vavachan handed the fish over. The smell of the kanji pulled him in through the back door of the hut. The tamped floor treated with cow dung had cracked without repairs, and on it a pot of kanji boiled over a fire lit between three stones. The old woman sat on the floor eating, her stomach and nose were so full that she seemed about to burst. Even her eyes had grains of rice stuck to them.

'Here, take this.'

She tried to pass the mud pot to Vavachan. He extended his arm to take it from her, but the memory of a woman came back to him. He refused and ran out and jumped over the fence, but only after being forced back a few steps by the smell of the kanji. Determined to escape, he swam across the waters and sped across the land. The smell of the kanji beckoned him from across two fields.

He walked, past Malikkari and Adimathrakkari, past Mundar, where he met a boatman. He did not have to scare him with his knife because the boatman pulled in and looked at Moustache in wonderment. He built a fire on the embankment, and roasted tapioca and mud perch.

'May I touch it?' the boatman asked.

He felt the moustache with his fingers.

'Were you brought here by the eastern waters?'

Moustache grunted.

'Is it true that women can't control themselves when they see you? Can you really dig a well with your bare hands in rocky, barren soil? That's what folks are saying about you.'

Moustache looked at him, wanting to know who was spreading these stories about him.

'Everyone,' the boatman said. 'Folks in Pallippuram, Muhamma, Thanneermukkam ... I was there to pick up coconuts. But forget coconuts, there's not even windfall there. Everyone is hungry. I left as soon as I could. They'd have eaten my boat if they could!'

'What's this place?' Moustache asked, pointing to the large body of water in front of them.

'This is the Ezhumam Lake. That there is the Ezhumam islet.'

Moustache did not wait around. The boatman watched him dive into the canal and swim across.

On the other side, as darkness fell, he saw a speck of light and walked towards it. The sun had not set. His moustache had obscured the sun and created the darkness. The path to the light was filled with holes and obstacles. He stumbled and scrambled up several times, and reached the light with grazed knees. He was shocked to find an old man tending a fire in the yard. He looked exactly like Paviyan, down to the toes curving to the side and the hand that massaged the chest. Only his hair was different, longer and greyer. The skin on his neck was wrinkly and hung in wattles.

'This is the Elder,' the old man said. 'Pray to him before you go. You'll be successful.'

A darkly terrifying face with a moustache was carved on an oily stone. He felt that he was looking at his own reflection in a pool of clear water.

'A man had beaten me to death and buried me,' the old man told Vavachan as he stood there, perplexed. 'I screamed lying in that hole. After a while, I found myself on top of the grave as if someone had dug me out.'

'Have you seen a woman?' he asked.

'You'll see the woman.'

'How do I get to Malaya?'

The old man closed his eyes, and stood still for a while.

'There's no such place,' he said. 'Even if there is, it is also full of hunger and poverty.'

Vavachan walked until, as the day broke, he reached a clearing with a strong wind. Further up was a terrace of othalam and ambarella trees, and beyond that the Vembanad Kayal, exhausted from relentless waves. Lights blinked dimly on the far shore of the kayal, and as he prepared to swim towards them, five pelicans, calling sorrowfully, flew low, almost touching his head. A certainty that Paviyan was dead and that he would never see him again filled Vavachan's mind. There was no one to protect him, even if he swam across the water. Tears rained from his eyes, but not a single drop fell to the ground through the moustache.

Thinking of his father, Vavachan gathered a few stones and laid them neatly in a pile. Then he walked back, leaving the lake and its shore behind.

11

BIRDS

'Moustache's favourite weapon was a catapult.'

'Why would Moustache need a weapon?' Ponnu asked. 'He has his moustache, no?'

'Moustache is not Vavachan, and Vavachan is not Moustache, although they are the same,' I babbled, stumped.

'I know what a catapult is,' Ponnu said. 'It's a slingshot, isn't it? A crow-belt.'

'Exactly,' I said. 'You tie a piece of vine to the ends of a forked stick. When you place a stone in the vine, pull it back and let go, the stone shoots out like a bullet. Moustache would collect nice round stones from the canals. Where else would he find stones? There's only mud and chunks of coal in the fields.'

Moustache's targets were not the small stony-looking teal, but the migrant geese, larger than the common native ducks, that landed in large flocks in Kallupalamkari and Malathadam fields. They would have considered Vavachan with scorn – they had come from far away, from lands he would not even have heard of. They feasted on the paddy and water creatures, gaining so much weight that their fat behinds dragged them down when they tried to fly. And before flying back to their own lands, they had to fast for a whole week, ignoring even the fish that danced right in their faces, in an effort to lose weight.

Moustache spent the days sleeping, expansively within thickets of bamboo reed, and diminutively within clumps of scutch grass. He woke up only at sundown when he would set out with his slingshot. By then, the bashful moorhens with quietly dragging steps, and the cormorants with supple necks that spend the day diving into the canals, would have left. A few human shapes might still be around, frail and weaving in the passing wind, collecting every last grain of paddy abandoned in the empty, harvested fields, to be roasted and pounded and boiled in a pot of water, its smell, and the memories of meals past, enough to slake the hunger of their children. Even the cockspur seeds growing wild on the bunds and in the dykes would be harvested to be eaten – steamed in a cloth bundle over a pot of water, or boiled with coconut pumice.

The waterfowl, terns, and sand plovers with black beaks like clay digging picks kept careful distance, as though not to be polluted, not just from the humans but from all creatures. But the stone that went shooting from Moustache's slingshot was one at release and three on impact, hitting several birds at the same time. Those hit on the wing or the underside of their bodies would try to fly away, only to fall back to the ground to lie on their sides waiting for death.

One evening, Moustache felt that the birds had become invisible in the day's sunlight. A windless silence prevailed – even the reed beds, bamboo bushes and cane stands, home to small twittering birds, were silent. Only the thin, crazed footprints of waterfowl, shrikes and herons remained in the wet mud. The thrifty, desolate land was forsaken not only by the starving humans but, he thought, by its birds, dragonflies and butterflies. There were no leaf fish dozing at the bottom of the canals. Where could they hide in these waters as clear as a child's mind? It seemed as though no living thing was left in this world. As he was about to turn back, he heard a faint rushing sound. He cocked his ears, but could not discern the origin of the sound. It was the chirping of a large flock of birds, those that had lost their lives to the stones from his slingshot, flying invisibly around him. The wind from their flapping wings assaulted his face. As the sound of the dead receded, he heard another vibrating sound. He walked across the muddy, grass-filled field, beyond which was a secret field with clear water where dark-leafed water arrowroot grew. The plants were itchy to the touch. In the middle of the field was an islet with the grass that grew on it scorched by the accumulated guano. It was a playground for young waterfowl. The islet heaved with chicks learning to fly, jostling with each other, and jumping into the water to try out their innate ability to swim. Some behaved like human beings and pushed the ones in front of them into the water. Moustache realised that this was a world no one else had witnessed yet. Waterfowl were sharp-sensed, able to discern even the slightest movement of a leaf. As slowly and carefully as a falling feather, Moustache slipped into the water. Soothed by cooling plants, and terrified of his moustache, the water did not make a single ripple.

As he closed in on the birds, melting into the surroundings like an ordinary plant, he thought of snatching up a handful and twisting their necks, but his slingshot took aim, choosing a round pebble which, when released, would floor at least ten birds. The chicks would not have time to raise an alarm and scatter. But one or two of them had spotted the hunter, and made a tiny croak. Before he could release the stone from the slingshot, he saw an astonishing sight. Three or four of the adult birds pushed themselves forward and into the path of the shot, protecting their chicks with their bodies. Were they the mothers or the fathers? Did birds have families? Did they mate for life? Something, perhaps the same instinct that had brought them all the way here, unerringly, from those faraway lands, made them confront the slingshot in order to protect their young. A memory surfaced, of Chella, his mother, and it delayed the release of the stone from the slingshot. The chicks scattered into the water and the adults took to the air. He could still have grabbed a few from the water, but instead, he swam back to the shore. He smashed his slingshot into pieces and flung it away. And then he heard another sound rising from all four directions.

Vavachan tried to outrun the rain but it was fast, and having drenched the earth all around, it soon caught up with him. The rain in the fields was different from other rains; the drops fell with the cruelty of stones.

The sky seemed determined to pelt him to death. He took shelter under a flowering mallow tree, but the stony raindrops tore apart the canopy and battered his face as though released from slingshots.

The torrential rain leached the light off the land. Still, Vavachan saw a white shape, a shelter, on the other side of a water channel. He remembered the mushroom-sprouting lightning bolt from the previous night, but it was the first time he had seen such a big mushroom on a field edge. Usually, they grew in weedy compounds, on coconut stumps or in gaps in the fence. In the early mornings after a night of thunder and lightning, Chella would set out with baskets made of areca spathes, hoping to get to the mushrooms before others who also knew the secret, and to collect them before they were fully open. The straw-like bundles of enoki and the milky button mushrooms could be cooked with salt and a sprinkle of water. Sometimes she would slice the larger ones and roast them folded in banana leaves with hot chillies.

A human body could not hide under a mushroom, no matter how large. Moustache made himself smaller than the mushroom and squeezed under it. The mushroom cooperated and spread its cap as wide as it could.

Chella was sixteen when she had given birth to her first child, a girl. The baby had resembled Paviyan's mother – the same pout to the lower lip, tiny ears and nose, and a long neck. The child had died when she was five years old, poisoned by a mushroom Chella had fed her. A childless mother's desperate longing had transformed into a poisonous mushroom and insinuated itself into a crop of good mushrooms. Chella and Paviyan did not speak of the child ever again but, for the rest of her life, Chella would anxiously examine the mushrooms she harvested, searching through them in clear daylight.

Vavachan did not know about this sibling, but it was she who had bloomed as a mushroom and stood over him, accepting the battering rain. Huddled under her shelter, Vavachan saw, for the first time in his life, pieces of ice as big as coconuts fall on the ground and shatter. He extended his hand to pick some up, but she stopped him, told him it was dangerous. These are hailstones, she told her brother.

As the rain reduced in strength and changed into a drizzle, muddy runoff carrying leaves and twigs rushed in, and soon the canals and the fields became indistinguishable. The water eddied around the mushroom and formed a whirlpool. Vavachan watched as its mouth widened and the earth sucked in all the water. He imagined sliding into it as he had slid down a coconut tree leaning into the canal as a child. She encouraged him. He sat on the rim of the whirlpool with his legs dangling into its mouth-like opening, and looked at her for courage. Then he closed his eyes and, listening to the chatter of the waterfowl, he slid in. Was it a second or a whole year before he fell, nose first, into a canal where he opened his eyes? The fields around were unplanted, and there were other fields further away and, beyond that, more fields. Not a drop of rain had fallen anywhere. Water flowed crystal clear in the canals criss-crossing the fields, exposing their secrets to the fish. Disused walkways were overgrown with scutch grass, and the fields hid their water under bulrushes, milkweed and mountain grass. Misled by the promise of soil, a coconut had sprouted, and now stood with its fronds fanned out and tiny new fruits on its inflorescence, waiting for the water to recede. Vavachan stood on the field edge for a whole year watching the coconut, and as he watched, new spills raised the water level and the coconut bobbed up to the top of the embankment.

What if he stood right there and spent the rest of his life contemplating the coconut, Vavachan thought. He remembered what Ezhuthachan had said in a conversation with Damodaran, in the attic room of the building above the shop in Neendoor, on the day he had shaped and sharpened his moustache.

'We must write another play,' Damodaran had said. 'Not like this one with songs and all. Only about what happens around us.'

'Why do we need another play?' Ezhuthachan had been genuinely confused. 'Most people only have one wife in this life, don't they? And it is kanji that we eat every day, isn't it? So why do we need more than one play? We read the same *Ramayanam* every year in the month of Karkitakam. Still no one is bored, are they?'

Ezhuthachan believed that, in the paltry existence that is human life, we could do only one thing well, and that we experienced that one thing anew each time it was repeated. He believed it was his footloose life that had resulted in the multiple relationships he had had with women. In the process, he had not been able to get to know any of them well. All he really needed was one woman, and he spent his life in the pursuit of that ideal woman. He would be happy to spend his life working on one play, finessing it with each performance, adding new dialogue and characters, sometimes, as with Krishnan Thattan's character, just for one performance. The last play he would perform before his death, he truly believed, would be the first – same yet different.

This was a lesson he had learned from his father, Ezhuthachan had explained. Towards the end of his life, his father's only interest had been a kalmannathi robin that visited their yard, and he spent several years watching the bird. He had spent five years observing the red spot under its tail, and the white mark that became visible only in flight. Its movements and feeding habits had taken several more years of dedicated observation.

'Do robins usually live that long? Who knows,' Ezhuthachan had said. 'I believe it might have lived for more years than warranted because of the attention my father gave it.'

What was the need to do many things? Why not focus only on finding Seetha? Or on finding the route to Malaya? Why wander, inexorably, endlessly, across these fields, canals and waterways? Just this one field would do; he could look for Seetha here, find the route to Malaya right here. Convinced that the two quests were one and the same, and that both could be found right where he was, Vavachan decided to stay put on the field edge. All he would have to do, he became certain, was to watch the skies by night and the expanse of fields and water around him by day, without losing the sense of wonderment.

And so Vavachan kept watch until he no longer knew the names of years, months or days, but began to be able to predict with accuracy the appearance of the faint shadow on the north-eastern sky, a black thread swaying in the wind that gradually became a spread of smoke. He knew the precise moment at which it would metamorphose into a thousand flamingos, and the fields in which they would land, gliding on their fire-red wings. He could predict when other flocks of birds would arrive as arrowheads in the sky. These fields were not their destination, so they did not land. They only wanted to fly over the man who had become isolated.

Every five or six years, a large fireball passed overhead and disappeared into the horizon, followed by sounds of wind and flapping wings. Craving a sort of madness that only the open sky could induce, he waited for the nights to roll by. No one who has lain on their backs watching the night sky could live normally after that. It renewed itself each night, never repeating the same spectacle. In his mind, Vavachan divided the sky into circles and squares, and counted the stars. But constellations changed, and his calculations faltered. They formed and re-formed themselves into a man holding a weapon, into dogs and fish, and sometimes into a bull that chased the creatures in the sky. He ignored the moon that played hide-and-seek, grew large and small, appeared and disappeared. It was trying to distract him from witnessing other, more significant spectacles.

One morning, he was startled by folk who came looking for the man who had been isolated. They lined up in the field quietly, sometimes watching him and at other times searching in the mud and water with their beaks. The exquisite beauty of the lily trotting jacanas made all other sights insignificant, and he wanted to spend eternity looking only at their iridescent wings, the flowers on their heads, and their huddled postures.

The jacanas were tricksters who confounded those who tried to steal their eggs – the eagles, Vavachan, and the otters. They hid their dark grey-and-black eggs among the grass and the water lilies. But Vavachan figured out their tricks – a bird that sat unmoving was up to something.

Those who succeeded in tricking Vavachan went back with their chicks. As soon as they left, whiskered terns, black-headed ibises and white egrets arrived, followed, one after the other, by plovers, grebes and purple herons. One night, Vavachan saw a strange bird. Unable to land with its large, unwieldy body and wings, it turned against the wind, and lowered itself safely as though on a sail made of cloth and strings. Just before that, he had seen a light moving across the sky with a roaring sound. Men were waging war using aeroplanes somewhere, he thought, just as Damodaran had told him, and he hid in the dark, watching, wondering whether it was one such man who had landed in the field. But in the morning, the creature swept through the field gobbling up fish as though it had arrived from some famine-affected land. It made loud animal cries, and had narrow, pale yellow eyes, and a pouch under its neck, and it charged at him with its pointy beak and wings held at half-mast to the sides. If he had not moved aside in the nick of time, it would have skewered him with its beak effortlessly. Vavachan pulled out a plank that had been used to repair a crack in the dyke, and brought it smashing down on its head. It fell to the ground, screeching, thrashing hard enough to cause an earthquake, and had Vavachan worried that it would get up off the ground and kill him with ease before it died. Vavachan used the plank to turn its body over.

'Oh! It's human!' he muttered.

A short, sallow-skinned man with small eyes and a tiny nose. The body had already begun to stink. Worms crawled out of its nose and mouth as though they were already inside it in anticipation of its death. Carrion flies swarmed.

Desperate to escape from its presence, Vavachan ran, leaving fields and canals behind, and yet the boundless fields lay before him. He passed the islet with the waterfowl chicks several times. Swimming across a canal, he saw Paviyan cutting grass, standing waist-deep in the water, and his son sitting in the boat, stacking the cut grass. The sickle worked magically in the water, the grass floated to the surface without realising that it had been severed from its roots. The grass cutter would not know if it sliced through their fingers. Soon, there would be rain, dark and thunderous, Vavachan thought, and the father and son would lose their way. He left them behind, crossed another field and climbed on to its edge. He saw a glossy, fattened buffalo, stout and with a short tail, its body wet. It gave him an empty look. Its back was broad enough for a person to sit astride, and its horns were long and curved. It stood aside, holding its horns out of the way, and let him pass. The buffalo was so close to where Paviyan was cutting grass. Vavachan thought it was a good thing Paviyan had not seen it because, if he had, he would have left his son and gone home with the buffalo.

Vavachan glanced back at the buffalo several times as though not wanting to leave it behind. A buffalo could stand still for long periods of time. It had just come out of the water, and its legs and rump were covered in mud. Vavachan wondered why the buffalo, which never left its watery comfort, had climbed out of the water. It must have foreseen the imminent rains that would flood the waterways. But Vavachan did not wonder about the similarity between him and the buffalo. He would not have survived if he, too, had not run away from his masters.

If there were escaped animals in these surroundings, wouldn't there be escaped human beings too? Human beings who would have run back, like domesticated animals, into the fields, into the wild? How many would have run away, right from the time human beings began forming groups? Vavachan looked around him, searching for such souls. Dark clouds took over the sky, and a cold wind picked up. A large flock of grebes and a smaller flock of jacanas flew towards the southern corner of the sky as though anxious to get away.

12
THANULINGA NADAR

Special Police Inspector Thanulinga Nadar was suspicious of everything, especially the petiole of chewing tobacco beside the betel leaf, the areca nut and the slaked lime paste on the copper tray that was placed before him. His father, Aiya Nadar, who had died before his rightful time, had a modest tobacco shop near the Tirunelveli temple, where customers would queue up waiting for their turn to chew paan with a petiole of first-class tobacco. There was a particular pleasure to be experienced from the addition of a sliver of the petiole to the paan. As the customer began to chew the paan – bits of areca nut and shredded tobacco folded in betel leaf smeared with lime paste – Aiya Nadar would hand them a piece of the petiole with a touch more of the lime paste, and it would add a depth and tautness to the paan. Tobacco petiole was a rare commodity, but in Aiya Nadar's shop there was never a scarcity. The other paan sellers gave them only to their special customers, whereas Aiya Nadar handed them out to all without exception. No one was surprised by this apparent abundance. His family's special relationship with His Golden Majesty the Maharaja, and with the capital, Thiruvananthapuram, was well known, and people assumed that he had a special route for procuring the product.

In actual fact, Nadar's tobacco petioles were the spent pedicels of Njalipoovan banana. Nadar acquired them and had them dried secretly in the sun, a job that was his wife's main responsibility other than cooking. Once they wilted in the sun, they were soaked in a tobacco solution and dried. The dried pedicels were cut into bite-sized pieces on a wooden block by his daughter, and were then enjoyed by the folks of Tirunelveli, who argued amongst themselves about its provenance, whether it was the superior Njettekettan variety or ordinary tobacco.

Thanulinga Nadar had seated himself on the throne-like chair at the inn half an hour before the emergency meeting scheduled for 9 a.m. The arms of the chair were a little lower than the reach of his elbows, and this fact irritated him. His attire exceeded the usual standards of propriety and tidiness expected of police uniforms. It was made from a rare, good-quality material, and no amount of close inspection would reveal a wrinkle or a speck of dust on it, not even at the end of a forty-eight-hour shift. The policemen in Kollam joked that a Tamilian used a flat-iron heated with burning coals to iron him after he dressed in his shirt and trousers, with the belt pulled tight around his midriff. Nadar waited impatiently as he examined the tobacco petiole, suspiciously turning it over and over with his fingers. No one in his family, including himself, had the habit of chewing tobacco. He had even refused the paan offered by His Majesty the Maharaja, telling him apologetically that he had scientific reasons for his refusal. As the time for the meeting neared, his irritation spread to the policemen standing guard at the door, and they began to feel that they had done something wrong.

The meeting began eventually after a brief telling off of the transport official who had arrived a few minutes late. In fact, the man had arrived on time, but had been standing confounded on the veranda of the inn looking for the meeting room. Fifteen people attended the meeting, including the Tehsildars of Kottayam, Ettumanoor and Ambalapuzha, and high-ranking police officials. The Kaipuzha Pravruthyar, Sankunni Menon, although much lower in the hierarchy, had also been invited, given the exceptional circumstances. Nadar sat on his armchair in the veranda of the courtyard, while the others sat on the chairs below, facing him. Pravruthyar Menon perched on the edge of the veranda, dangling his short legs. A clerk sat on the floor in front of a low stool laid out with pen and paper, taking minutes.

'Don't any of you try to avoid the issue,' Thanulinga Nadar said.

He looked at the officials sitting in front of him, some of them his superiors and others beneath him. Compared to his physique, his voice was weak, and some of his words tended to disintegrate into phlegmy whispers and bird-like squeaks, but he overcame its embarrassment with his confident body language.

'None of you, or your departments, has informed the government in a timely fashion of these developments. Don't expect to be paid unless you do your jobs properly.'

Pravruthyar Sankunni Menon wanted to challenge him. He had anticipated the problem and had written a letter to his Tehsildar, but he did not move from his perch, scared of Nadar's rage. Instead, he waited in vain, hoping that Nadar would praise his initiative at some point.

Nadar proceeded to read aloud a copy of the speech delivered by Pallithanam Luca Mathai at the Sree Moolam Praja Sabha – the Popular Assembly of the Thiruvithamkur administration made up of members who were landholders and merchants – pausing after each sentence to look piercingly at the faces of his listeners. The indifference, habitual in civil servants, on their faces irritated him, whereas they sat wondering what he expected them to do at this time.

'Do you know who Luca Mathai is?' he raised his voice.

The Tehsildar from Ambalapuzha was about rise from his seat to say something, but Nadar's eyes pushed him back into it.

'Do you know who it is that successfully farms the fields in Kainadi, Kavalam, Kainakari, and so on? Do you have any idea who it was that reclaimed land from the Vembanad Kayal, and rescued the country from penury when crops failed as far as Nanjinadu?'

Nadar looked at the policemen standing guard at the door, and the sepoy in his half-bow, as though they were smarter than the officials in front of him.

'Are you aware that Luca Mathai has unrestricted access to His Majesty?' he shouted, throwing the paper on the floor. 'Do you even know what the Sree Moolam Praja Sabha is?'

Strange noises emanated from the attic of the inn. Sankunni Menon wondered, fearfully, whether Nadar might direct his anger at the palm civets frolicking up there.

It was three years ago that Luca Mathai had addressed the Praja Sabha before this, and his concern then had been the damage caused to the newly built embankments by the passenger boats from Changanassery that zipped by too fast. As a result, boats began plying at a snail's pace as they neared his fields and added another hour to the journey time between Changanassery and Alappuzha.

The assembled officers listened to Luca Mathai's speech as Nadar read it out to them. It began with the appropriate salutations to His Majesty the Maharaja, who had not been present, and the Leader of the Praja Sabha.

'I have no opinion about the harvest in Nanjinadu,' said Luca Mathai in his speech, taking off from the previous speaker. 'I don't know what type of seeds they sow there, or how many measures of paddy they harvest. But let me tell you, don't expect too much from Kainadi, Kavalam or Kainakari this time. We used to harvest sixteen para measures of paddy, but this year we'll be lucky if we can get four. Some fields have yielded nothing as not a single seed has sprouted thanks to salination of the fields on the one hand, and the unseasonable rains on the other. We sow the kayal fields – land dredged up from the lake – and by evening it starts raining, and the seeds are washed away. We have the utmost respect for the Pravruthyar who comes to measure the harvest, but it would be good if there was some paddy to set aside for the sowing next season.'

Listening to Luca Mathai's speech being read aloud, the Tehsildar from Ambalapuzha smiled to himself. He knew that no Pravruthyar dared go to the Pallithanam fields to measure the harvest, staying, instead, in the lean-to prepared for guests in the house, feasting on rice and pearlspot cooked in a paste of deseeded chillies by the mistress of the household. Sometimes there would be additional dishes, such as chicken curry or fried beef. And they would return, accepting the calculations and the paddy that Mathai's overseer handed over. Still, it was from the Pallithanam household that the government received the highest amount of paddy in all of Kuttanad.

'The declining harvest is one thing. We could live on rice water instead of rice itself. But what will happen when we can't even do that? There was a time when we could load our boats with paddy and hay, and go about even in the middle of the night.'

Mathai's speech was a little wanting in honesty. Usually, it was he who insisted on stopping work and returning home before sunset. If the workers did not finish loading the boat before sunset, he would declare: 'Let's not travel in the night.' His decision would be final, and the workers would grumble and go to sleep on the field edges and in the boat, while Mathai would sleep in one of the temporary shelters built within walking distance of the kayal fields. Just as each hour of the night belongs to a specific spirit of darkness, the early hour of four in the morning was Mathai's time, and he would rise and poke at the bodies around the field, waking them from their slumber in the cold, and order them to row the boats to the jetty by the Pallithanam homestead before sunrise. 'Don't tarry,' he would admonish the workers expressing their displeasure in having had to spend the night out in the open by scratching their asses and picking their teeth and smelling their fingers. 'Just accept that I have good reason for saying this.'

Even though Mathai did not, as a rule, like his boats out on the waters after dark, he had not been averse, until recently, to taking a boat out all by himself even in the thickest darkness if there was an emergency. On such occasions, as he entered the fields beyond the lake, deserted except for the stars, he would not look around. The torch-bearing souls of the dead that wandered the fields were harmless and unaware of the presence of humans. One could hear them hollering at each other. Mathai, who never defaulted on praying twice a day and making the mark of the cross every day after dinner, had nothing to fear from them.

But one day, it was much later than usual when he returned, with only an oarsman for company, from overseeing the women workers applying worm mould in the fields. It was a large, covered boat. Coconuts were piled in a corner. Mathai did not feel like eating the fish the oarsman had cooked, and he sat dozing in the boat. The boat passed close to the shore near Kuttamangalam, and in the starlight, they saw a man gesturing to attract their attention.

'Pull in, Pailey,' he told the oarsman. 'Let's not make this man spend the night there.'

As the boat pulled close, something seemed amiss. The man was a stranger, and seemed as if a shadow as tall as one and a half men had come alive, and when he got into the boat, it dipped as though four people had climbed in. Mathai and the oarsman did not speak to the stranger, and he too sat silently, staring into the darkness. They rowed him across the canal. As he stepped out of the boat, they saw, shockingly, four people disembarking. And when they got home, both of them had marks on their arms, as if a cat had scratched them.

Mathai was the only person who could talk authentically about all of Kuttanad's concerns, the only member who was also part of the upper legislative council on either side of the Vembanad Kayal and could talk authoritatively about paddy cultivation.

'The Pulayans say that the fields have an innate truth. And they are right. We could leave as much paddy as we liked in the fields without the need for a guard. Even if they had to starve to death, not a single Pulayan would steal it.'

Mathai was canny, and missed no opportunity to praise Pulayans. He had once brought Ayyankali, the social reformer and the only member of the Praja Sabha from the Pulayan caste, to Pallithanam with great fanfare, accompanied by a hundred boats and burning torches. As they sat chatting in an inner room, and later when they were eating, two people had stood on either side, cooling them with hand-fans. From the next season on, paddy had danced in the fields around Venattukayal and R Block, and the Pallithanam silos had filled faster than the coffers of Mankombu Swamy.

'But things have changed now. His Golden Majesty and the respected Diwan look after us, their children, so well. Still, now if one leaves one's paddy in the fields, not a grain of it will remain. Have we ever had a situation where we've had to build platforms in the middle of the fields to guard our paddy? No one dares to take the boat out after sunset in Kuppapuram, Cherukalikayal, Chennankari, Thottuvathala, and surrounding areas, or to dig clay or catch fish. And that's not because the scary spirit of Kalliyankattu Neeli has come to Kuttanad, but because of a man with a moustache. I have no idea where he is from, or what caste he is. It is unlikely that he's from the lands so ably ruled by His Majesty. I'm concerned that there is a gang of people with him, armed with knives and guns. Or else, how would he be so brazen? I beg you to please do the needful so that we can farm without fear in this time of famine, harvest our yields and take them home.'

Thanulinga Nadar finished reading Mathai's speech. He asked the police inspectors from Ettumanoor and Vaikom to stand up and proceeded to interrogate them for the next forty-five minutes.

'What are you claiming to have done about this in all this time?' he shouted.

The inspector from Vaikom tried to explain, reverentially, that he had personally conducted a search with two officers from Vechoor checkpost, taking a boat along the canal from Pennar to Aymanam and Kareemadam. This only made Nadar angrier.

'Who the hell asked you to go traipsing over there? Are these areas in your jurisdiction? Their concerns will be looked after by people responsible for that. So where's he now? Who's he with? Who, in fact, is he? Does anyone have any answers?'

Sankunni Menon, who had been biding his time, stood up and coughed, and when everyone focused their attention on him, he began to speak, looking every now and then at the piece of paper in his hand.

'He is the son of a Pulayan-Christian named Paviyan, who lives in the Chozhiyappara fields in Kaipuzha subdivision. They say his name is Vavachan. It is not known whether he has any other names. We'd have to enquire at the Mannanam church if we want to find out, but the church is in the jurisdiction of Kudamaloor subdivision. He grew the moustache after he performed a part in a stage play. For some time now, no one has seen him in Kaipuzha subdivision or in the area between Neendoor and Kaipuzhamuttu, and there is no record of any activity.'

'Who gave permission to stage the play?' Nadar asked.

The question sent three policemen scurrying from Ettumanoor to Neendoor in search of Damodaran who had been responsible for bringing the drama troupe, and the Mappila who had allowed the stage to be constructed on his property.

'Paviyan died in the month of Thulam,' Pravruthyar continued. 'His wife is missing. Vavachan is currently around twenty-two years of age.'

'Who the hell invited this fellow to the meeting?' Nadar asked the Tehsildar, looking scornfully at Menon.

Disrespect from superior officers had become habitual, and Menon continued sitting there without feeling overly upset until the meeting ended.

Satisfied with his own performance, Nadar seemed to calm down. He took a sip of water infused with vetiver roots and chilled in a mud pot, and rose from his seat. The policemen stood up too, but he flicked his finger at them to remain seated. He took a rolled tube of paper from the table and hung it on a nail on the wall. It unrolled to reveal a map. Drawn on good-quality bond paper in black ink, the map showed the towns between Kanyakumari and Paravur in black dots, the roads in thick lines, and the rivers in squiggly lines.

'What is this place?' Nadar asked, stabbing with his finger at the northernmost point, and answered his question himself. 'Paravur. This is Alappuzha, and this here is Kollam. This is the lake.'

Nadar's finger travelled along the curvy expanse of the Vembanad Kayal, reaching all the way to the port of Kochi. Vast agricultural fields lay to the east and south of the lake.

'This is the heart of our country. It is the boats that ply this stretch that transport all our trade goods, taking mountain products from Changanassery to Alappuzha, and returning with rope, coconut, coconut oil and paddy to lands to the east, south and north. If this

'Let me tell you a secret that most people don't know. We knew there would be a flood, and that he'd retreat because of it. Still, knowing we had no control over the weather, we were prepared and had set a trap in case those Mysore folk got across the river. A trap that could only work because of the uniqueness of this place. Kuttanad is the only place in the world which is entirely made by human beings. God had only created swamp and water, but the vast paddy fields that you see today are really only around two hundred years old. I know, unbelievable, isn't it? Kuttanad is not the real rice bowl of our land. That honour goes to Nanjinadu. Rice farming only started here when famine hit and people began to die of starvation, and the maharajas and the diwanjis allowed us to build bunds and dredge up fields from the deserted swamps and canals and mangroves. Before that, only the Pulayans and the Parayans had tried to make a living here, catching fish and sowing a few seeds whenever a stitch of land became visible.'

Nadar lowered his voice. He was about to divulge another big secret.

'Those who know this land cannot be defeated here. That's why, for over four hundred years, there were outlaws and brigands here. They could easily escape capture in the numerous rivers and canals and hideouts. Tipu would've had no chance if he had come this far. This is a land that we can flood and drain as we please, and we had drained the swamp and dammed the rivers and lain in wait. If he'd crossed the Periyar, he would have had to come this way. They had high-quality horses and cannons on wheels, but their soldiers had been trained on bone-dry lands, and there was no way they'd have managed the muddy terrain. They'd have perished right here, stuck in the mud without being able to go backwards or forwards. Meanwhile, our soldiers would've easily navigated the waterways in their boats, east to the forests or west to the sea via the backwaters. We were completely invincible in the land as far south as Onattukara.'

Nadar rolled up the map and placed it back on the table.

'Now, let's get to it. It's not the mountains to the east or the Periyar to the north that protects our country, but this land right here. Trade routes and paddy cultivation are secondary.'

Nadar had forgotten developments such as the dissolution of the Nair Army and the occupation by the British. What use was this land when its people were colonised other than to grow barely enough food to stay alive?

'So we don't want anything to happen that would jeopardise this land.'

As though suddenly remembering something, he unrolled the map again, held it up to them, and pointed to the area comprising Kainakari, Kavalam and Nedumudi.

'From the information I have received, he should be in these parts. And I also know that he has no accomplices, which is a good thing in some ways ... But apprehending a group is easier than capturing someone like him who works alone from such a place.'

Nadar made the policemen and the Tehsildars stand up and express their opinions. He was displeased when the Tehsildar of Ambalapuzha said that the situation was not as dire as it was made out to be, and that much of what was being circulated were rumours and lies.

'Well, the people and the merchants are scared. Whether it is for the right reasons or not, it is a matter of concern.'

The policemen were of the opinion that more boats and personnel should be deployed, and the patrol of the area intensified. They also suggested that the boats ferrying paddy from the kayal fields should ply in convoy, and that a register of all boats to Changanassery and Alappuzha should be maintained.

'And scare the people even more in the process,' Nadar said, mocking them. 'Fear will only increase if there are more people and commotion about this matter.'

Either he should be caught, dead or alive, Nadar said, or they should create a situation whereby he would have to run away beyond Vaikom into Kochi.

'But then there'd be problems there too. Who's to say he won't go east via the Periyar?'

Nadar's response to this question was a piercing look. He did not care about what happened in Kochi. That was a different country; its king was not His Golden Majesty. Nadar declared that he would not rest until one of the two solutions became a reality.

The next day, Nadar arrived in Pallathuruthi in a covered stealth boat with five of the smartest policemen in mufti. All arrangements, including a cook, were made for them in a house with several rooms, verandas, and food stores by the bank of the canal. By day, they roamed the canals and waterways in two boats with charts and measurement tools, pretending to be researching the development of a new boat route. By night, they searched the deserted inner lands, places people avoided even in the light of day. They came very close to some criminals the police had been searching for for a long time, but Nadar was not interested in them.

'We're here to catch one fish and one fish only,' he told his companions. 'Until we do that, we should not let even the other fish suspect our purposes.'

13

CHELLA

Like most people, on the day of her death, Chella too did some extraordinary things. But in her case, there was no one to marvel at these things after her death, or to wonder whether she had foreseen her death.

On that day, Chella overslept as though in preparation for the long sleep that was to come. It was an unusually deep sleep; face down on the bare floor, the gap of her two lost teeth smiling through her partially open lips. Towards the end of her sleep, she dreamt that she had woken up late, and that women with baskets made of screw pine leaves on their heads protecting them from the rain had already entered the fields behind her hut to start the day's work. Further ahead, a man was at the waterwheel, directing water into the channels. It was Paviyan. In her dream she did not recognise him, but she did recognise that the full-grown crop behind him was wild rice. Mature wild rice had moustaches. The man left the waterwheel and stepped into the dyke. He began pulling at a piece of coconut tree trunk that was hammered into the clay. It had taken four or five men with strong muscles to hammer the post in, and Chella wondered why this man was pulling at it. In his exertion, his thighs bulged as though air was being blown into them and, when it seemed like they would burst open with the veins engorged with blood, Chella opened her eyes.

Looking around, she realised that her dream had actually come true. The fields were drenched in sunlight, and Pulayan womenfolk had already started the day's work. Chella remembered that she had not looked at Paviyan's thighs when his dead body was brought home. The skin on his thighs had indeed split open, but no one had told Chella about it. Paviyan's legs had been long and skinny, an even size from top to feet, with no flesh on them. Only the creaking knees had stood out like big bumps.

Chella stepped outside, disoriented from having woken up in full sunlight for the first time in her life. There was nowhere to move her bowels. People were everywhere – ploughmen with their teams of oxen, women transplanting paddy ... Even the sky looked as though it was full of women workers. Chella walked across a small canal and sat under the fanned cover of a vigorous cottonwood. A buffalo wallowed in the canal, immersed up to its neck in the water. On her way back, Chella did not forget to lean in from the canal side and swat it twice on its back with a green switch. She had a special hatred for buffaloes, a hatred that had begun a few days after she had married Paviyan.

After the wedding ceremonies, Paviyan and Chella had walked down the slope from Mannanam church and come home, which, in those days, was on the embankment of the Thazhathekkuzhi fields, in a canopied boat. When she woke up the next morning, Paviyan was nowhere to be seen. It was only later that she came to know that he had a relationship with an unconverted woman somewhere east, beyond Ettumanoor and Ayarkunnam. The harvest season brought large groups of seasonal workers down from the eastern hills. Long lines of hill folk – Aalans they were called – moved west, carrying pots and pans and mats, a handful of Pulayans, Christians and Chovans among them. They were like the flocks of parakeets that descended on the fields as soon as the paddy ripened. Of all earth's creatures, parakeets held an abiding grudge against humans. They waited with their families in the hollows on top of ruined coconut trees, and descended on the fields in their thousands as soon as the paddy was ripe, cut the best stalks and carried them away in their beaks. As they flew up into the sky, an unknown urge would make one of them screech, and it would drop the stalk in its beak back into the fields. The dropped stalk would make it call out in a different tone and, hearing it, all the other parakeets would also call out, dropping their stalks back to the fields in the process. They would fly back down to get another stalk and, when this was repeated a few times, there would be no paddy left in the fields for humans.

Like the parakeets, Aalans arrived only when the paddy was ready for harvest. The backbreaking toil of preparing the fields, building up the mudbanks, ploughing, sowing, watering, weeding, transplanting, and repairing the dykes was left to the local people. At harvest time, the newcomers put up temporary shelters in yards and on embankments, and travelled from field to field looking for work, and took up all the best spots by cunning or by force. Failing that, the womenfolk among them would woo the local men. They had fairer skins from living in shady forests in the hills, and lustrous bodies from a diet of jackfruits and yams. It was one such woman who had trapped Paviyan when he was the watchman of the fields in Kuttankari. She had a family back home, but the lovesick Paviyan did not care and chased away other women who entered the fields with their sickles.

'These fields are under my watch. I'll harvest them myself.'

He found her all the best spots to harvest. Her breasts, imprisoned behind her cloth, crooned with Paviyan's chest as he helped her lift the bundles of paddy on to her head to be carried to the threshing yard. As he lifted his own bundles on to his head, his waist cloth fell off, and she laughed and tied it back for him. He put the paddy she received as her wages in a boat, and rowed it east against the strong currents. He struggled to manoeuvre the boat, weighed down with the paddy shares of many of the other workers that were loaded at her behest, through a canal clogged with grass and waterweeds, and they laughed at him scornfully. When they reached Poovathumoodu, Paviyan carried the paddy on his head, loaded it into a handcart, and pushed it all the way to her home. Some people said he stayed there for a few days after that, while others said that the cunning woman had sent him packing as soon as he had done what she wanted him to do.

When Paviyan disappeared leaving his new bride at home, he was away for a whole rainy season. The hut flooded twice. No one bothered to check whether she had enough to eat, or even whether she was alive. Chella had begun to believe that the woman in the east had trapped Paviyan for good, and that he would not come back to her.

But Paviyan came back, just before the next planting season, leading a six-month-old buffalo calf by a rope. The moment she set eyes on it, some instinctive insight made Chella conclude that the dirty creature was a gift from the whore in the east, a thought that sent shivers down her arms and legs. The Paviyan who came back was not the man with gleaming shoulder muscles and shiny eyes she had married, but a pale, thin version of him with sunken eyes, and ears that seemed enormous. He looked as though a python had sucked the juices out of him and spat him out. He would have no job this season – who would give the job of guarding their fields to someone who disappeared without notice? As for the calf, it had a bloated tummy and thin flanks. From the way it looked, it was clear that it had belonged to some heartless person. Deprived of even a drop of its mother's milk, the wretched calf stood reeling on its emaciated legs, its ringworm infested skin bald in places, with not even the energy to flick its tail at the swarming insects. It did not lie down even at night, perhaps fearing that, if it did, it may not be able to get up again.

From that day on, Chella took great care in providing for Paviyan's every need, and Paviyan took great care of the buffalo. He made a paste of kokum and nutmeg, which had been collected as they came floating down in the water from the eastern forests and carefully stored, with chilli and salt, and force-fed balls of it to the buffalo. The medicine made the calf void its bowels for days until its stomach was cleared of worms. It was reluctant to move, but Paviyan pushed and prodded it into the field grass, and it began to wallow in the mud and feed until its tummy was full.

Meanwhile, Chella had forgotten the day when she had last seen a grain of paddy, and yet she tried to feed Paviyan two full meals a day. She searched far and wide for stray spreads of wild rice. She dug up banana corms, cleaned and cooked them with salt, made stir-fries out of pigweed and other wild greens. At first, Paviyan did not like her cooking, but soon came to like it so much that he could not eat food cooked by anyone else. Chella was skilled at catching prawns in baited baskets, and whenever there was a surplus, she split them in half, salted and dried them in the sun, and stored them in containers made of areca spathe. Fried with chillies, they were delightful, and Paviyan came to like them so much that he begged for them often. Soon, he was back to his normal physical shape, ready to do two people's work single-handedly. Still, in the night, when he rolled on to her mat, Chella kicked him off and anxiously stayed awake all night. Finally, one day, as she sat kneading bran to spread on a skillet and cook, Paviyan picked her up and laid her on the floor. Chella fought back, biting and scratching his shoulder.

'Get off! You stink like that animal,' she shouted.

'But you know I don't touch it. It goes off grazing and comes back on its own,' Paviyan said, assuming that the animal she was referring to was the buffalo.

From the next night on, as soon as it was dark, Chella put the fire out and spread the mat on the floor.

'Look at you!' Paviyan teased. 'You'll tear up the mat up if I am late!'

Three years passed, and by then it was widely accepted that Chella was sterile. Fearing that her gaze or touch would bring bad luck to their children, the women who used to leave them on a spread cloth behind her hut as they went into the fields to work stopped doing so.

'It's that creature's fault,' Chella said to Paviyan, angrily.

Paviyan was also angry.

'How is it the buffalo's fault if nothing will stick inside you?'

'Get yourself another woman then.'

Paviyan's silence, as though he half agreed with her, made her sad. That night, they stayed awake, watching the thunder and lightning. The sky put up a great show, pretending to open up with rain. If it were not for the prayers he called out to his dead father Kankali, their hut would have collapsed in the wind. The next morning, there were mushrooms everywhere. Chella filled two areca-spathe baskets, and regretted not having more. The mushrooms pushed out of the soil like the spirits of the dead. Back home, she took the three poisonous mushrooms she had specially hunted out, and making sure Paviyan was not around, fed them to the buffalo.

Paviyan's buffalo ate everything. The daily diet of scutch grass had hardened its hoofs, pushed out its horns, and strengthened its body. Several ploughmen had asked Paviyan for it, but he had refused.

'Seems like you're not man enough for her. Get your buffalo to do the thing. We'll know then, won't we?' Angered by his refusal, ploughman Mathan had abused him.

On the day Chella fed it for the first time, the buffalo did not come out of the field in the evening. It stayed neck-deep in the water, paying no heed to Paviyan's whistles. By the next morning, it had moved to the western embankment.

'Buffaloes don't like to leave the water. Let it be. It will come out when it's good and ready,' people told Paviyan.

The day after that, Paviyan saw it walk across the mudbank into another field, greedily grazing on the grass.

'I think there's another buffalo inside its tummy,' Paviyan joked with Chella. 'Soon he'll eat through all the fields.'

After that, it was nowhere to be seen. Paviyan searched for it far and wide, made loud clicking noises hitting the roof of his mouth with his folded tongue, hoping to attract its attention. There was not even a dark shadow to be seen.

A boatman teased him as he searched for the beast along the bank of the Kaipuzha River.

'Don't go chasing after the buffalo,' he said. 'It's not your time yet. It'll come to you, bringing the God of Death – Kaalan – riding on its back.'

Paviyan returned home and thrashed Chella for no reason.

A month after the buffalo went missing, Chella was pregnant. For the next several years, she did not have to step into the fields. As soon as one child was six months old, Paviyan caused another accident, until, one fine day, Chella looked around and was surprised to see six children. She felt like it was only yesterday that the godforsaken beast had walked across the mudbank and disappeared.

On the day of her death, Chella walked across two fields and went to Kalichovathi's hut. On the way, she thought about her five remaining children. None of them were of any use. Vavachan, at least, was affectionate, and had always been under her foot until he was fifteen, never out of her sight. She used to worry how he would get on, scared as he was to leave the confines of Chozhiyappara. She did not think about her dead daughter – she had never given birth to such a child, nor lost her to death.

Despite her advanced age, Kalichovathi squatted under a marotti tree, digging at the root of a purple yam climbing over it.

Her son returned from the evening's toddy tapping.

'You keep digging at its root every day, old woman, and it's never going to grow,' he said.

He set down the toddy pot, and the coconut shell with the black paste-like mud that he used to seal the flower stems after cutting them to release the sap.

Chella's mother used to cut grass for them. In those days, Kalichovathi's Chovan had six buffaloes and three enormous haystacks. The children used to love dragging sheaves of hay from the stacks and feeding the buffaloes. All the old woman had now was a dried-up cow who refused to be impregnated a third time.

'It's that worthless bull,' Kalichovathi told Chella. 'They leave it here, and all it does is abuse the poor cow.'

'Be quiet, old woman,' her son scolded her.

The old woman went inside and brought a piece of mango seed appam for Chella, as there was nothing else to offer. She hoarded mango seeds like a squirrel. When there was nothing to eat and the children cried from hunger, she would cut them open, take out the kernels, grind them and strain them in water. Cooked into an appam on a griddle, they were palatable although a little bitter. Her son gave Chella some mouthfuls of toddy. It was delicious, top-quality, tapped from a single tree. If one drinks milk, it should come from a single cow. And if one drinks toddy, it should come from a single tree. Milk or toddy, both lose their quality if mixed up. If one lies down with a man, it should be one man for the rest of one's life. Kalichovathi and Chella were women who believed that. Kalichovathi had steadfastly refused the offer of marriage from her brother-in-law after she lost her husband at a young age.

The cow gnawed at the dry grass around the coconut tree it was tied to, making half-moon shapes in the soil.

'It needs some fresh grass, Kaliyamma,' Chella said.

'As if anyone here has the time to cut some grass for it,' said Kalichovathi through gritted teeth, glancing towards the kitchen side of the hut. 'All they think about is stuffing their own throats.'

'Over there in the west, there is some good scutch grass. Feed the cow its roots washed in water. She'll soon be with child.'

Despite Kalichovathi's protests, Chella picked up a sickle and walked west, looking for grass. She was not satisfied with the clumps she came across on the edges of the fields. Some were too hardened, while others were too tender. Some had been mowed down by grazing animals. She saw a vigorous spread under a coconut tree and walked towards it, only to find that it was covered in bird droppings. She looked up, and found weaver bird nests swaying from the tips of the palm fronds. They reminded her of Kalichovathi's earlobes. She had been a stark-naked nine-year-old, accompanying her mother when she went to deliver a bundle of grass, when she had first seen Kalichovathi's ears. The sixteen-year-old Kali had a short mundu around her waist, breasts that stared proudly at the sky, and downy hair in her armpits and in a straight line down from her navel. She had been sitting on a bed, washing her earlobes with salted water, suffering through the sting. Chella had looked closely and noticed that her ears had been pierced, and she had bits of coconut leaf spines in them. The next time she saw Kali, these had been replaced with two small studs. Kali's Chovan had worn red studs in his small, shapely ears that made one yearn to kiss and nibble at them. Chella continued staring up at the coconut tree with its ear ornaments, slowly rubbing her own ears. There were so many coconut trees around. Why did these birds have to hang their nests on this one?

Something in the day made her keep going. She walked until she came to a bund recently repaired with wet clay that sucked her feet in. It was in the fallow land beyond it that Paviyan had seen his buffalo for the last time. She was disappointed to have arrived at that place. This was land where the sun leached the salt out of the soil, land that was no good for paddy or grass. She walked across another field and came to a small islet that was home to waterfowl. The surroundings looked as though it had rained recently. She had never come this far before, but the place seemed familiar, as though the memory of it had been passed on to her through ancestral blood. She did not notice the mushroom with its cap collapsed as it approached the end of its day, and walked straight to a spread of scutch grass. It stood waist-high and verdant, fertilised by the dung of grazing animals.

In the dank darkness underneath the grass, a creature that had never hurt anyone so far was enjoying the cool shade. Its fate had also been preordained by God. Chella attacked the grass with the vigour she had inherited from her mother, gathering sheaves of it together with her left hand and cutting at the base with her right. The sickle was worn to a splinter, but it cut sharp, right through the creature caught within the clump of grass in her left hand. And as the sickle passed through it, it opened its mouth and bit the hand that wielded it.

Chella put the cut grass aside and examined her hand. She stepped into the canal and washed her hands and feet. As she took a couple of steps, she felt faint and sat down. Sweat poured out of her body, and she lay right there on the bare earth. A snippet of cloud moved over her bringing some shade, and a cool breeze blew in. Chella lay staring at the still, mirror-like water in the canal. As she watched, a snakehead murrel surfaced, quietly, unnoticed even by the water. It was a majestic creature with a mottled tail and a plump, dark green body.

'It was a payyani viper. I won't reach home now,' Chella told the fish softly.

She looked closely at the fish. Two fins, just below its head, moved rhythmically in the water, much like ears, and she saw, very clearly, the ear studs that adorned them.

'Have you heard of Sankaracharyar?' I asked Ponnu.

'No...'

'He was a great swamy. Left home when he was very young and travelled around the world. Still, when it was time for his mother's death, he came back home. Moustache was like that too.'

'Did Moustache come home when his father died?'

I did not reply. Fathers were procreators with no real value. It has been so throughout human history, and so it will be for the rest of history. There is only a short interval when men are valued. There are far more cows in this world than bulls. In thousands of farms and houses, countless cows give birth and produce milk, while bulls are in captivity, producing sperm without even seeing their mates. The male of the species is fast becoming redundant. I wanted to tell him that it was time that we were afraid.

I don't know why I felt like telling him that Moustache did not cry when his mother died, and that, instead, he thought philosophically about the inevitability of death. Was there a point in not crying, in accepting death as destiny? Our mouths water at the sight of food because we are preparing to digest food. Our eyes should water when faced with sadness.

Moustache knew that the way we show our respect for a dead person is through rituals. He dug a large pit and laid his mother inside it. He covered the pit with his bare hands and tamped down the soil. Then he dug another pit next to it and covered it with grass and twigs. He lay down in it as though he was dead, with his eyes shut and breath slowed. At midnight, he opened his eyes and cocked his ears. There were noises in the pit next to him, quiet conversation and movement. The henchmen of Kaalan, the God of Death, had arrived. He realised there were four of them, and they were dividing his mother's body into four parts. Moustache got out quietly and peeped into the other pit. The henchmen were hard at work, unaware of their surroundings. Unlike human beings, they were incapable of focusing on more than one task at a time. He quickly snatched one of the quarters and hid back in his pit.

A little while later, the sounds became louder, the quiet conversation turned into loud noises and hollered obscenities. Moustache listened, barely breathing. The henchmen were fighting with each other over the lost portion of the body, something that had never happened before. The fight between strong opponents reverberated across the land. Soon, there was a bright light, followed by a deep silence. Carefully, Moustache peeped out of his hiding place. Kaalan had arrived to resolve the issue. He wore a crown made of strands of palm, and had a big ledger in his hand, which he kept on the floor before descending into the hole.

'A ledger?' Ponnu asked.

'Yes. You could call it a book too, but it's impossible for us to describe its size because it contains all that's there to know about everyone alive – their dates of birth and death, their actions, things that have happened and things yet to come ... All the information about all creatures, from worms to human beings, who have lived since the beginning of the world, and about those yet to be born.'

'So it would be this big.' Ponnu held his arms as wide apart as possible.

As soon as Kaalan went into the hole, Moustache snatched up the ledger and ran away.

'And how he could run! Not like ordinary people, but with such great speed.'

Kaalan realised the danger and chased after him. Moustache ran, jumping across rivers and canals and fields, Kaalan hot on his heels. Kaalan could not catch up and Moustache could not shake him off, and so they continued the chase, crossing and recrossing the Kaipuzha River five times in the process. There was no place Moustache could run to that Kaalan did not know about. Boatmen ferrying goods in the night and fishermen fishing the waterways felt a strong wind blowing, but they did not see anything.

Finally, Moustache found an abandoned house. He ran inside and bolted the door.

'Kaalan will break the door and get in,' Ponnu said.

'No, he can't do that. Kaalan cannot enter a house without being invited in. That's the rule. He can only enter without invitation if it's time for the person inside the house to die.'

Kaalan commenced knocking on the door, threatening Moustache. He could not return without the ledger but if he remained there, the world would also be at a standstill. Moustache ignored his pleas and threats, and began reading the ledger eagerly.

'But you said Moustache couldn't read,' Ponnu protested.

'True, but you don't need to know the letters to read the ledger. You only have to open it and all the information will enter your mind.'

'Did he read about me too?'

'He read about everyone.'

Hungrily, Moustache turned the pages. He read about Paviyan, and wept. He read, with astonishment and confusion, about Paviyan's parents, and their parents before them, going far back in history. By then, it was daybreak. Kaalan made himself small, and hid in the darkness under a four-leafed pennywort. Moustache read on, for a whole day and night. He learned the magic and the mantras in the ledger. He sighed deeply reading about Seetha; swore eternal hatred for all snakes reading about Chella. He read about Ezhuthachan and his drama troupe; felt sorry for Thanulinga Nadar and the destiny awaiting him. He read what was entered in the ledger about his own destiny, and the realisation that he would be all alone forever made him sob. But reading about the stories that would be written about him by someone, ridiculous stories full of mistakes, he laughed loudly. He felt they made him someone else, and he wanted to make some corrections.

'And did he?' Ponnu asked.

'No. No one, not even Kaalan himself, can change a single line in that ledger.'

'Did the ledger talk about Moustache running away with Kaalan's book?'

'Of course.'

'And that we're talking about it?'

'There's absolutely no doubt.'

When it was night again, Kaalan came out of his hiding place and knocked on the door. By then, Moustache had finished reading the ledger, and dropped it outside through the breeze gap between the walls and the ceiling. Kaalan picked it up and went away, shouting obscenities.

Slowly, Moustache came out and looked at the changed world, and at himself. His fingertips had worn down from turning the seemingly endless pages. His mouth was dry, and the hair on his moustache had bowed in reverence. His head felt heavy and his eyelids drooped. Unable to bear the weight of the knowledge he had newly acquired, he lay down on the bare earth and dozed under the moon and the stars.

14
SNAKES

Kudamurutti Hill was a nest of poisonous snakes. There were no elephants in its forests. Elephants do not venture into areas where king cobras live. They know, instinctively, that, although king cobras do not attack willy-nilly, their bites are deadly.

Forty-seven rivulets, one hundred and fourteen streams, and countless creeks originated in Kudamurutti Hill, and merged to form the rivers Meenachilar and Kavanaar. They flowed, twisting and turning, converging and diverging, to feed the fields in the lowlands. There were not many poisonous snakes in the fields, only water snakes, mud snakes and rat snakes, and the mottled eel which had the head and body of a snake and the tail of a catfish, and was often mistaken for a snake. Its taste was reminiscent of snake meat. The poisonous snakes that one came across on the rarest of occasions, in the holes along the field edges and in the grass, were those that come floating by, caught in the eastern waters. Chella's life was taken by one such. The ordinary black and albino cobras that were found in the lowlands were nothing compared to the fierce beings of Kudamurutti Hill – a king cobra could easily swallow two of these for breakfast.

Before Chella's death, Vavachan had heard of only one other snakebite related death – that of Kalichovathi's husband, Machovan. The incident had made some people laugh, some people scared, and others ponder over the nature of death. Does the snake bite us, or do we go to it looking to be bitten? Does the poison affect the body or the mind? How long could the interval between bite and death last? They had several such doubts. The incident had happened before Vavachan's birth, even before Chella and Paviyan got married, but it was impossible to have lived in these parts without hearing a hundred different versions of the story of this death. Although the story itself remained unchanged, it was embellished in each telling, and the tangents, characters and places changed.

Machovan, a handsome man with an even-toned skin and hirsute body, had been well-known for his expertise in toddy tapping as well as in maintaining clandestine relationships. In the early mornings and in the evenings, when he climbed down after making tap-tap noises on top of coconut trees, competing with the woodpeckers, young Nasrani Christian women waited for him with coconut shells in their hands, pretending to buy toddy to make appam.

'I've never eaten appam,' he told them. 'Does it look nice? Is it sweet?'

His softly spoken words, as he poured the toddy into their coconut shells, made them shy. The only snacks he had ever eaten were made of mango seed kernels, and all he ate before climbing the coconut palms in the morning was a bowl of salted, watered down, day-old rice. Still, the sight of his well-built, powerful body made some women do crazy things when no one else was around.

'I don't trust Mappilas,' he told them.

'Why not?'

'I have my reasons. Once, the king was passing through a deserted place like this when he saw a Pulaya girl. She was very beautiful, only not as fair as you lot. The king was attracted to her, and she to him. So they did the unspeakable.'

'So...?'

'Two people saw what they did. One was a toddy tapper, and the other was a Christian Mappila who was tending to the coconut trees. The king would lose face if they spoke of this, wouldn't he? So he asked them to keep it quiet, and promised them whatever they wanted. The cunning Mappila asked him for land, while the Chovan tapper asked for permission to cover the handle of his tapping knife with gold. And that's how the Mappilas came to own all this land.'

One of the women laughed, covering her mouth.

'So is your knife gold-plated? Let me see.'

'No, I won't show you.'

They struggled with each other, and ended up snuggling.

Machovan was exempt from the usual distrust shown towards tappers who came to tap the coconut trees in Nair houses, and that was because he behaved with impeccable respect and deference. Pravruthyar Sankunni Menon had a younger sister who had lived in Kottayam and done a BA degree. One morning, as she stood in the yard combing her hair, Machovan passed by with his toddy pot. She flared her nostrils and inhaled deeply.

'Do you like the smell of toddy, Mistress?' he asked.

She did not respond. But that night, she sat in front of the lamp and wrote a poem, ending with the line: 'Chovan he is, but a glorious being.'

When the houses in the neighbourhood had to be rethatched before the advent of the rainy season, it was Machovan who would take the lead. Not a drop of water fell through the roofs he worked on. And after the thatch was laid, he would trim the ends of the plaited palm fronds, creating an even, neat edge to the roof. One day, he was working his way up the roof with two others when something stung his finger.

'Ah, I think I've got a splinter...'

He held his finger up to the others. There was a drop of blood on his middle finger. A woman, a newly arrived bride of the house, came rushing forward to examine the finger, and with no qualm that people were watching, put it in her mouth and sucked it. A year later, when he returned to rethatch the roof before the rainy season, the woman had gone back to her mother's to give birth. Machovan climbed on top of the roof, dismantled the old palm fronds, and threw them down to his co-workers. They would sort through them and reuse the good ones to fill gaps in the new roof. When he reached the place where, the previous year, something had stung his finger, he saw the dead and dried body of a cobra under the thatch. It seemed he had tied it snugly with the palm fronds on to the rafter. The sight frightened him and he scrambled down. Everyone tried to calm him down, saying that it had happened over a year ago after all. But he would not calm down and, by the time he drank a bowl of water, his body and face had turned blue, and he passed away before they could take him to the poison curer.

On the seventh day after Chella's death, as though performing the last rites that had gone undone, it started raining. Kalichovathi remarked several times that the woman who had gone to cut grass had not come back even though a week had passed, but no one paid any attention. She would continue saying this until her death several years later. It was a silent rain, with no accompanying wind or thunder, a misty drizzle that gradually gathered strength and became torrential. It continued for many days until people got so used to it that they felt it had always been raining, right from the time of their birth, and that it would never stop. Those who stood under the eaves waiting for the rain to stop returned to the yards and fields wanting to get on with their work. But what work could they do? The fields flooded, and water rose above the edges to become one with the canals. New springs sprouted in the yards. The crowns of bananas and other crop began rotting, and coconut trees leaned over. Fish swam into the houses from the yards, and at night, the noise made by hordes of frogs and crickets made people think of marauding armies of bandits. Old people who had lived longer than required died and, carrying their dead bodies, their relatives wandered in the persistent rain, looking for a bit of high ground. There was not a bird in the sky or on the ground; even the egrets and the cranes had taken cover. Stuck in the mucky mix of water, droppings and mud in their cages, and unable to swim or preen themselves, the black-and-brown-plumed chemballi ducks suffered with dysentery. New buds remained petrified on plants that had stopped growing, their leaves and roots frozen in the rain.

The last time it had rained like this, Vavachan had been a tiny tyke. There had been strong winds and thunder. Even the small fields had turned into lakes, and people had to moor their boats in the large fields to the east or tie them to the trees on the hill.

On that day, Paviyan had rowed south. The only things in his boat, other than Chella and the children, were two sickles. They had pulled in at his father's sister's hut in Kaduthuruthikunnu and stayed there, all of them starving together until, fed up, he had ventured out. He had sunk four poles and put up a roof with a few palm fronds in a bit of craggy land with exposed veins of red stone. He refused to leave even after the rains stopped and the water drained away, and they had ended up staying there for two more seasons. Paviyan had gone off looking for harvesting and threshing work to Madhuraveli, Mathankari, Mannar, Erumathuruthu and Vellasseri. Chella had begun to worry that Paviyan might end up living there permanently. That was his nature. She had wanted to return before someone else set up home on the embankment of Chozhiyappara.

'Let's go back,' she had tried to persuade him. 'It's harvest time in Neduchal and Virippukalayi.'

But he had ignored her. So, the next morning, she had taken the children and gone back to Kaipuzha without telling anyone. An angry Paviyan had followed after a month.

The rain that began after Chella's death continued, relentless even after ten days. Those were days when no one ventured out, but there were those who saw Vavachan walking along the field edges in Pulikkuttisseri, Menonkari and Kalunkathra. He had spread his moustache over his head like a giant taro leaf, sheltering himself from the rain. His moustache protected him like the dry leaf protected the mud clod in the old story. He was a lucky man. He did not need to look for a place to sleep; he could just build a tent with his moustache when night fell. Perhaps these were just the hungry illusions of those stuck at home with nothing to eat. Some even said that they saw Moustache carrying a sack of rice on his head, but how could that be when there was not a grain of rice, not even oil pumice or bran, to be had? Several people died eating bitter tapioca leaves. Others ate the palm shoots that were meant to feed the ducks, or the fish, clams and mussels they could find, boiled in salted water as there was no chilli or coriander to be had. They ate through the yams and banana stems, and turned their attention to cattle feed. Some Christians and Nairs who had seed stocks of paddy meant for the next planting season hired guards armed with machetes and hatchets, and then took to sleeping on top of their seed chests, their sleep disrupted by the distrust of their own guards. And yet, people saw, through the curtain of rain, the spectre of Moustache walking along, carrying bunches of banana and tapioca. There was a rumour that he had taken to capsizing the boats ferrying paddy.

Just as the rain began to ease in the west, it became stronger in the east. The gushing currents broke both banks of the rivers, and turned the fields, canals and lake into a single expanse of water. Realising that the entire Kudamurutti Hill had been uprooted and was floating down, the people of Petta, Punjar and Kidangoor moved far away from the banks of the rivers. The only people who stayed on were those brave enough to try their luck collecting hunks of mangrove or the mysterious neelakoduveli plants that came floating by. All across Nagambadam, Kallumada, Thiruvarppu or Thazhathangadi, there was not a stitch of land visible. The Vembanad Kayal expanded beyond Vettikkadu and joined with the rivers at Kanjiram. The water began to bring carcasses into the fields. Swollen bodies of sambar and mouse deer floated into still pools, where they bobbed peacefully on the surface. The carcasses of trees – agarwood and karimaruthu – followed; the forest itself tumbled down, tree trunks somersaulting in the current and splitting through the middle. No one noticed the snakes, coiled in the branches, desperately clinging to life. Wherever the trees came to rest, they slithered away from the water. A lot of them died, unable to survive in the bright light after the deep darkness of the forest.

Moustache knew nothing of these developments as he had been lying asleep in a dry corner of a dilapidated wheelhouse, a sleep so deep that it took him all the way to the borders of death. Reading Kaalan's ledger had exhausted him completely. There was nothing more to know, nothing left to experience in life. His body wanted to wake up, but his mind dissuaded it. His breath slowed, heartbeat stilled, and his ears shut against the 'yes, yes' sound of the rain. He looked like a god lying asleep after causing the Great Flood. Finally, when the rising cold water crept up his legs, he decided to wake up. He opened his eyes, brought his breathing back to normal, and realised that the world had turned over an entire circle of life. Everything that had happened before – Ezhuthachan, the drama, Paviyan, the moustache, Seetha – had repeated itself.

Sitting up, he looked at where he had lain and discovered the crushed body of a dead snake, almost as thick as his arm. He ran his fingers over his back and found several puncture wounds where the snake had bitten him in its death struggle. If the snakehead murrel ends its reign of terror in a pond, it can only be because of the arrival of a varaal, the giant snakehead. If a cobra had lost its venom, something very significant must have happened. He stepped out of the wheelhouse.

The flood had created an unearthly, hellish, scene for him to behold. The bits of land that had not flooded were wet and muddy, and there, like worms on a decaying corpse, covering every inch, were snakes, entwined, slithering, pulsating, desperately trying to stay alive. How many varieties? He counted: banded kraits, beak-nosed blind snakes, double-headed sand boas, puffer snakes, bronzebacks, rock pythons, tree snakes, wolf snakes ... He thought of Chella. In death, she had curled into a foetal position, her head between her knees. The nails on her fingers had worn away to the quick, the cuticles torn. The scant hair on her head was tied together exposing the white of her skull. Her body did not reflect a single joyful moment in her life. Her hollow breasts lay shrivelled, while her empty stomach was invisible. The eyes that had watched over and worried about Paviyan for a whole lifetime were partially closed, their corners sticky with rheum. The endless plodding within the little circle of her life had emaciated her legs, their heels split into deep ravines.

Sorrowfully, Moustache raised his head and looked up. There were snakes on top of the coconut trees just beginning to set fruit, on the leaf fronds, on the trunks, on the inflorescence abandoned by the tappers, even on the young leafs yellowing from the incessant rain. Saw-scaled vipers, shell-striped kraits ... His face darkened with rage, and the hairs of his moustache trembled. He saw snake-catching eagles in the sky. Their mothers were also betrayed by the snakes, and they circled, vengeful, despite being rain-drenched and with no place left to roost.

'We are together now,' the eagles told him. 'We up here and you there, down below.'

Months of undercover enquiries had yielded no leads, and money and resources from the capital had begun to run dry. Water had risen up to the windows of the house they lived in, and yet Thanulinga Nadar was not prepared to call it a day. He was the kind of person who dug out the entire tap root if he was tasked with cutting down a tree. From Nanjinadu to Neyyattinkara, in all the places he had worked, Nadar was the subject of nightmares for the criminals and a character of legends for the local people. There were fables about his left-handed slap, navel-splitting kick, and grip on the jugular. Anxiously watching the rising water, the policemen with him had gone to sleep on platforms built up inside the house, and they had not expected to be woken up so early in the morning. Nadar, who had stayed awake all night, seemed full of energy, ready to issue orders.

'This is the Kavanaar River, and this here is the Koduraar,' he told them, pointing to the places he had marked with a pencil on his map. 'There's a lighthouse here which was built by Munroe Saheb. We should go in two boats. They'll be here soon with supplies – two guns, rope, kerosene, lamps and rice.'

The policemen were sceptical because, of late, the local inspectors were not as responsive to Nadar's demands as they used to be. They were busy dealing with the flood – moving people to higher ground, confiscating secreted stores of paddy, and trying to catch the thieves who stole and ate even the seedling crops.

'Now is the time to strike. The policeman's job starts when people least expect it. Something I've learned from the white man.'

Nadar laughed. A few days of cohabiting with his team had softened his usual sternness, and he had taken to joking with them.

'I'll wait in Thiruvarppu. To the east, the passages are tolled, so he won't escape that way.'

Nadar had asked for twenty personnel but, by the time the sun rose properly, only eight policemen arrived. There was only one gun and it was difficult to keep it dry. By noon, they changed out of their uniforms, tied mundus around their waists and dirty towels on their heads, and set out in two boats. All of them were armed with clay-digging picks. They could get into the water and pretend to be labourers doing repairs to the bunds while undertaking their surveillance, or use them as weapons if needed. They would row along two canals, catch up in Neelamperur, and spend the evening there, where there was already a sizeable crowd of people from Eera and Kainadi who had left their homes looking for higher ground. No one would be suspicious.

A policeman, a native of Arthunkal, began to shake with fear at the sight of the water and the currents.

'You live on the coast and you're scared of canals and fields?' Unnithan, a close associate of Nadar, asked.

He swayed the boat and the man from Arthunkal screamed. Nadar's boat was out of sight, so the policemen roared with laughter. The man continued shivering and weeping, and his movements shook the boat. They rowed for a long time, past the Pamba River, and past canals and fields, finally reaching a field with no coconuts or banana trees on its embankment. A large group of Pulayans had gathered there. It was an unusual sight. Since there was no work in the waterlogged fields, they should be in their huts, curled up in hunger with only water to drink.

'This is the Aakkanadi field,' Unnithan said.

He was more familiar with this area than his own backyard since he farmed the fields in Cherukalikayal and R Block. He knew the exact spots in the canals where, in low water seasons, the boats would scrape the bottom.

'The watchman of these fields was a Pulayan named Aakkan. This is where he died in the dyke and became a deity.'

One time, a crack had opened in the bund due to Aakkan's inattention. The water was forceful. The crack had to be repaired quickly or the field would flood. The landlord would lose his crop, and the Pulayans who had dug the clay, built the polders, planted the field and tended to it, would go hungry. Aakkan tried desperately to repair the crack with coconut leaves, clumps of water weeds and mud, but nothing worked. So the people got him out of the field, filled him with arrack and toddy, tied a red mundu around his waist, and put ixora flowers in his hair. They stuck a piece of coconut tree trunk in the channel of the bund, its top end sharpened to a point. Then, in the blink of an eye, they tossed the half-conscious Aakkan into the channel, impaling him on the pointed wood, and quickly covered the whole thing with clay, rebuilding the bund even before the water had run red from his blood. They found a stone, washed it and placed it on top of the bund. Since then, before every planting season, the Parayans have sacrificed a rooster at the stone. They believed that Aakkan was bound to be angry and had to be pacified with rooster blood. And the Pulayans prayed for his blessings before getting down into the fields to work.

'They must be doing some ritual to get the water to withdraw,' Unnithan said.

The Pulayans stepped back at the sight of the approaching boat. They had never seen fair-skinned clay diggers before.

'What's going on here? Move aside,' Unnithan said, assuming the persona of a policeman once more.

On the ground, in the middle of the crowd, were two wriggling pythons as thick as banana trunks. Their stomachs were split open. The sight enraged Unnithan. Only he had climbed off the boat.

'Are you going to eat them? You'll catch leprosy.'

'It wasn't us, Master,' said a man with an otter-bite scar on his thigh. 'There's a man with a moustache in Pazhukkanilam, to the south. It's his handiwork. He doesn't kill them because they are not poisonous. Only splits open their stomachs.'

'Whatever for? Why leave them like this? Why not kill them?'

'They won't die, the wounds will heal in a couple of days. He just takes the eggs and the fat.'

Back in his boat, Unnithan said, 'He must have at least five or six people with him. There's no way one person can do this alone.'

'Why does he take the eggs and the fat?'

The man from Arthunkal felt a new fear other than of water slowly taking hold of him.

'Python fat is good for rheumatism. And the eggs for asthma. People shell out good money for them. Ha ha ha! Guess he reckons he's a medicine man now.'

No one laughed at Unnithan's joke this time. They were silent for the rest of the journey. When they retired for the night on the veranda of a temple official's house, after a meal of roasted tapioca, the silence continued. The bitter tapioca made one of them vomit, and the others suffered from stomach pains and headaches.

The next day, before dawn, they set out in two boats, and by the time the sun was up, they were at the place where the lighthouse could be seen clearly.

'That is Pazhukkanilam,' Unnithan told them, 'where the Koduraar River meets the kayal. This is where the bodies of those who drown in Koduraar or Meenachilar come to the surface.'

In the strong current, they rowed hard, and moored the boats with great difficulty beneath a clump of screw pine, steadying them with their long-oars. They decided unanimously to discard their plan to get into the water and pretend to be clay diggers. It would be difficult to get a foothold in the current. Besides, people in the water at this time would only raise suspicions. A wind had picked up in the morning and a slanted rain fell. They decided to wait for a while. Suddenly, the man who stood at the bow of the boat jerked his arm and jumped into the water with a loud scream. They saw the white underbelly of a small snake that had detached itself from his arm float away in the water. They held out the long-oar and brought him back to the boat. Holding on to the side of the boat, he pointed upwards and shouted: 'Snake! Snake!'

Unbeknownst to them and unaware of them, countless snakes were coiled in the screw pine bushes and on the branches of the punna trees leaning over the boat. In the panicked scuffle that ensued, one of the boats overturned. Those who fell in the water did not tarry to rescue it, but scrambled on to the other boat, and they rowed east faster than they had ever before.

Rowing against the current was nightmarish. Swollen carcasses of cows, bulls and buffaloes floated into their path, each carcass covered with the writhing bodies of flesh-eating eels. Everyone covered their noses and closed their eyes, but Unnithan was unfazed. He had seen eels come out of every orifice of the dead human corpses that surfaced in the lake, and still had no qualms about eating fried eel. The boat inched forward through dead snakes and other debris. After the animal carcasses came rotting tree trunks, with a wide variety of half-dead snakes on them. The undercover policemen stood shocked, afraid that they would slither on to the oars and get into the boat.

'Let's go back,' one man said.

'Let's get to Thiruvarppu first and meet with the boss.'

With anxious men standing up, the remaining boat was also in danger of capsizing. Unnithan saw a large hunk of debris ahead – trees, climbers and undergrowth – as though an entire forest was floating towards them. If they collided with it, their bodies would only be seen in the sea.

'Turn the boat,' he said, pointing to the south, where he saw the shape of a large boat. 'Half of us can get into it.'

It did not matter whose boat it was, they had to help. They approached the boat.

'Bring it closer,' Unnithan ordered, the policeman in him rearing up again.

In the thick rain, the boat and the boatman were not clearly visible. As the boat – an eight-rupee-taxed commercial boat – came closer, the dark shape holding the long-oar at the stern turned, and they saw, clearly, the thick moustache on his face. As panic ensued again, and their boat overturned, throwing them, screaming, into the water, they saw the deathly cargo in his boat. The hull of that big boat which was usually used to ferry plough oxen to the fields was full of the bodies of dead snakes. The men swam in all directions without waiting to help each other.

Unnithan reached the dyke of a flooded field, and saw Russell's vipers and pit vipers, with conical heads and markings on their bodies, lying on the ground, unable to move. The bite of one would make every orifice in a person's body bleed, and the chronic wound from the other's bite would get infected year after year. Looking for safety, he stepped into the field and stood in the freezing water that came up to his neck. Eventually, the rain stopped. The darkening sky leached the light away as it prepared for another deluge. As Unnithan watched the sky, resigned to the floods that it would bring to the east and to the west, he saw the astonishing sight. The man pulled his boat up to the dyke, and fell upon the snakes like an enraged otter on a shoal of fish. He smashed each head with a three-pronged iron fork and threw the dead carcasses into the boat. Unnithan watched mesmerised, forgetting to take notice of the man's physique or facial features, and the next day he would remember nothing other than the fork and the snakes.

Thanulinga Nadar had lost contact with his team, but he came face to face with his nemesis on that same evening. Looking east from the lighthouse with a quarter of its steps already submerged in water, he realised that this was a day of reckoning for him and for his enemy. His grandfather had also faced such a day in his life, a day to win over his enemy or to die trying. His opponent had discarded his big boat, and gotten into a smaller boat that propelled itself through the water with lightning speed eastwards. He followed, holding the Berthier rifle with the teakwood handle. The rifle was made by the Spanish for the World War, and there were only two in the whole country. It could focus on its target from half a mile away and shoot three rounds in succession.

But his opponent was smart and moved in such a way that it was impossible to shoot. Nadar saw, with astonishment, clumps of screw pine falling into the water in the wake of his speeding enemy, creating obstacles in his path. There was no way he was doing this alone, Nadar thought. He must have accomplices on the banks, cutting the bushes and chucking them into the water. But Nadar was not one to give up.

He realised that soon the canal would reach Thalikkotta from where his opponent could easily escape into the backwaters via Kanjiram, or into the coal-rich fields to the east which was his home. Nadar had familiarised himself with the geography of this landscape. He knew this land of fields, lakes and canals, and the smallest of its dykes as well as he knew the narrow lanes of his own home, Nagercoil. He rowed past the obstacles in the water, and turned his boat with some difficulty into a creek off the canal towards the east, before turning south again. There, at a spot where three canals joined together to form a small lake, Nadar waited among a spread of elephant mallow, rifle in hand. His nemesis was bound to come this way.

15

KEEPER OF THE DISEASED

The entity known as Perumaadan was harmless enough. But if anyone thought they could ignore him when he accosted them, as they stood in desolate lanes, fields or forests, mulling over the stillness of breezeless afternoons and dreaming about daytime naps, they would have to think again.

Vavachan urinated on a wound on his leg where a catfish had pricked him, and limped along the bund of Muppathikkari. The grass on the waterlogged ground was rotted. His legs were smeared with dirt up to his knees, and a stinking infection had spread between his toes, immersed as they were in the relentless dirt. The itch, much worse than ringworm or the naikurana plant, was insufferable. It was not uncommon to see people with advanced infections willingly put their feet in burning embers. Some people tied their toes with a strand of jute, pushed the blood to the tips, and let it out by piercing with a sharp knife. Others applied the burning sap of cashew fruit, or rubbed their toes against stones until the stones wore out. It was an infection that removed all thought from one's mind other than that of the sensation of foot rubbing against stone. But Vavachan could find no stones, so he broke off a swamp apple stem and pulled it back and forth between his toes. There were no green leaves or a single edible fruit on any of the plants, and the fish seemed to have disappeared from the canals. When the breath-giving wind blows with too much force, plants and human beings alike topple over. The rushing currents had swept up the entire fish population and transferred them elsewhere. It was a forlorn catfish, separated from its friends, that had attacked Vavachan.

Vavachan extricated the swamp apple stem from his bleeding toes. Wishing for a bit of dry, hot soil in which he could scorch his itchy toes, he walked on, and suddenly there he was in front of him – Perumaadan, a being almost as tall as a coconut tree. Vavachan could go neither backwards nor forwards until he answered his questions correctly, and Perumaadan was not one to be convinced by glib responses.

'You are scared,' Perumaadan said, gleefully.

Like all spirits, Perumaadan gained an inordinate amount of satisfaction from the fear human beings felt. But, in the next moment, he understood that the human in front of him was also a distressed spirit.

'Who are you searching for?' he asked.

'A woman,' Vavachan replied, 'with very long hair. But all that comes out of her mouth are nasty words.'

'You'll see her,' Perumaadan said. 'But be warned, it will be of no use. Tell me, why do you have such long hair on your face? From afar you look like a walking forest.'

Perumaadan looked into his eyes and understood that this man had a secret he wanted to reveal, a secret so sacred that even the ink in which this is being written should not know it. He lowered his head and pressed his ear to Vavachan's mouth. As Perumaadan stepped aside, looking satisfied with what he heard, Vavachan saw the pox that had started sprouting on his body and face. It smelled like Kadali bananas. A gentle breeze took up the smell and spread it across the land.

When the water drained after the flood, the first to perish were the ducks. Duck herders drove their flocks, starved and unable to lay eggs, to every bit of land that became visible. The exposed dirt provided plenty to eat – fish larvae, tadpoles – and the ducks turned into magical, egg-producing machines. Some were mischievous and refused to be shut in a cage, but their keepers were vigilant, knowing exactly when to pick up a newly laid egg from the dirt, looking out for the quick dip and shake of their behinds. The plentiful food in the sediments washed up by the water had to be used quickly. Duck herders, a naturally surly lot, darted all across the waterways in their narrow boats, howled for no reason, and swore loudly. Usually, at this time of year, they would be searching both sides of the Kavanaar River for choice fields where the harvesting was done, promising eggs to the guards and landowners in exchange for grazing rights.

'It's good for the fields,' they would advise them. 'They'll eat up all the cockspur and watergrass. Besides, duck shit is first-class manure.'

Those who were not persuaded would find cracks in their bunds, cracks secretly created by the deft use of a long-oar, letting water into the fields. Then there would be fights and arguments, until these were pacified by the exchange of a clutch of eggs, or if it was more serious, a mallard drake with the wings and neck trussed and ready for the cooking pot.

'Ducks are great, and so are their fruits,' the pacified farmers would exclaim, eating the duck cooked with coconut milk and green pepper, 'but the duck herders – they're real bastards.'

It was a duck herder, proud that he already had a basket full of eggs, and wondering whether to move on to Avanavan Kadamba from Vaaladikkavu, who first noticed the contorting necks of a couple of ducks in his flock as they fell dead. The sight did not make any difference to his attitude. Duck herders, as a rule, were an arrogant lot. A plentiful harvest of eggs sent them straight to the houses of well-endowed women looking for days of debauchery. And when their ducks did not lay enough, they would crawl back to the same women on their hands and knees, and suffer their scorn.

The duck herder watched a boat passing by with a man and his new bride.

'Ah, a drake from Pulinkunnu and a hen from Changanassery. You'll have your work cut out,' he taunted the man.

That was enough to spoil the man's sleep for the rest of his life, and to resolve never to send his wife to work in the fields of Pulinkunnu. Meanwhile, the duck herder found several more in his flock with contorting necks, and foul, watery excreta leaking out of their pretty behinds. By next morning, most of them were dead, and the rest sat with their heads and feet tucked into their wings, scared of the water. As the wind continued to blow across the land, birds died in their hundreds. Dead cranes, egrets and herons lay scattered across fields and canals with no one to mourn them.

After the birds, the misery spread to the people. Like water draining from the dams, the bodies of children and grown-ups alike started voiding; even the most starved surrendered to the force of dysentery and vomiting. Initially, people thought it was the bitter tapioca that was making the children ill, but soon it spread from house to house carrying the strange stench of undigested effluence. Suffocating from stomachs filled with gas, and unable to venture outside to vacate their bowels, people lay half-dead within the four walls of their homes, the floors treated with cow dung and coal slippery from their effluence. The nights filled with the uncommonly frequent calls of kollikkoravan owls, harbingers of death, and dogs howled at the moon and chased it away, immersing the surroundings in darkness.

The canals and rivers developed cracks. Vavachan sat by the side of the Maran Lake, watching the water drain away. As the land rose before his eyes, he saw some heads swimming against the current. He got up, cautious. If these were otters, he should stop them from climbing out of the water. Otters were fearless in the presence of a lone man, and were known to surround and attack. There were stories about them biting the penises off men who got into the water. Vavachan picked up clods of clay and began pelting them. A couple of heads disappeared, but the remaining kept swimming towards him. As they came close, he stopped as he realised that these were human beings, their sizes diminished from the relentless dysentery. They had left their near and dear ones and, clutching their precarious lives in their hands, they had braved the water to swim to Muthan's abode. Muthan was the protector of the destitute, guardian of the enfeebled, and they would pray for his blessings and for relief from the misery of the rising water. Only one or two out of the hundreds would reach it safely, and their lives would be saved. To those who scrambled out of the water, the moustached man on the shore looked like Muthan. Who else could it be at this time of night, at a place where it was dark even in the middle of the day? Muthan dragged a couple of people out of the water. Others were lost to the currents.

Before daybreak, Vavachan left, braving the currents and swimming across the lake, past the fields of Thorkkad and Thattarkkad, past Polachaal. He was terrified of dysentery. As a child, he had been at its mercy once, when a bout of dysentery that started with the rains in the month of Kanni did not stop until two years later. Chella had tried her best to find some nutmeg and buttermilk to treat his dysentery. The nutmeg came floating down the canals and rivers from the eastern forests, but buttermilk was available only in Nair households. A single administration of a paste made of the two would cure the dysentery, but a miscalculation of the dosage would lead to constipation which would require another medicine. Paviyan brought the nutmeg, its innards of red mace showing through its cracked shell. But there was not a drop of buttermilk to be had. Chella had tucked the nutmeg in the coconut fronds of the roof beside the tender areca spathes that the girls wore when they went out.

Vavachan crossed the crocodile-infested pond in Thiruvarppu with no fear at all. He walked on, troubled by the absence of people around. The lanes and canal banks were deserted, the huts along the way empty, not even womenfolk or a sliver of smoke from the kitchens to be seen. Boats, devoid of their owners, had freed themselves from their moorings and lay catching the sun in the middle of the lake, mating, unconcerned, with other boats. Some came back, satiated after the adventure, and stayed close to their moorings once again. Looking at the fields on both sides, Vavachan felt a deep sadness. The water had risen when the paddy, ripe and golden from the sun, was ready for harvest and would have quenched the hunger of thousands of people, but now, as the water receded, it lay rotting in the fields.

The desolation of Vettikkadu, without its usual bustle and buzz, took him by surprise. He had passed through here once, in the cover of darkness, trying to hide his thick moustache. In those days, Vettikkadu was a beacon of light in the dark nights, visible from across the Vembanad Kayal to people in Muhamma, Kannankara and Aryakkara, its canals full of covered boats waiting for the lake to quell. Lightning struck like guillotines, sending raging storms into the lake. It was here that the boats waited for the sky to clear and the westerly wind to pick up so that boatmen could hold up a palm leaf mat and be propelled at top speed across the lake. While they waited, shops selling water brewed with coffee shells, palm sugar, and boiled eggs in chilli water would spring up. Boats carrying yams, dried tapioca, coconut, ginger and bunches of bananas had to wait for several days, while those returning from Alappuzha with clothes, money and dry fish tarried for at least a day. There were toddy and arrack shops for the oarsmen on the banks. It was here that the Maharaja used to come to enjoy the evening breeze, where boatmen sat in the midnight sand telling each other stories about outlaws and discussed their fears of the entity in the middle of the lake that pulled at their oars from its depth. At sunset, women would come stealthily into the boats with their pots. There was nothing else in this world that tasted as good as the fish prepared by the boatmen and the guards of the wheelhouses. Their bodies too, having not had a chance to meet women for days on end, tasted as good as their cooking, and they were sent home to their wives with their essence and their earnings depleted.

'All these days you rowed, and you didn't get even a handful of paddy?' their wives would ask them when they returned. 'And what's gotten into you? You look so tired and weak. So pale as though you've got no blood in you.'

Beeran, a man from Vettikkadu, was a hawker of clothes. He made friends with the boatmen and bribed them with the sweets and snacks his wife made, and they let him travel to Alappuzha for free in their boats to bring back rough cotton fabric and towels to sell in the eastern villages. His daughter, Khadija, showed no interest in the goings on in Vettikkadu; not even the largest of the boats that congregated there made her want to put her head out of the window to have a look. Still, one day, two Muslim Mappilas from Petta got into a fight over her, which ended with one man holding the other's head under the water in the canal. The next day, when Beeran was not around, the winner went to his house, beat up his wife Saboora, forced Khadija into his boat, and rowed her to the middle of the lake. It was only when she came back a week later, in the broad daylight, covered in a white shawl, that people recognised her for the clever woman that she was. She did not go looking for boatmen. Those who desired her came to her with their most valuable belongings to barter.

Now, the houses were deserted and the shops were shuttered. The Vembanad Kayal lay dead without boats, wind, or waves. There was not a single fisherman to be seen in the west, and in the east, stray sprigs of paddy lay rotting in the salinated fields. Vavachan went past unkempt yards and muddy compounds to Beeran's house. Listening for movement, he knocked on the wooden planks that formed its walls.

'I had come this way in the month of Kumbham a couple of years ago, looking for a woman, and you and your godforsaken mother sent me off in the wrong direction.' Vavachan told Khadija, still angry that they had sent him on a wild goose chase.

Khadija was not scared to see the big moustache on his face, just as the pus-filled boils all over her face and neck did not scare him. She had always considered men's moustaches to be pointless. And the type of oozy pestilence that she had, a variety of smallpox called muthirapparappan, usually affected only those who were scared by the sight of an infected body. With his moustache standing guard up front, Vavachan was completely fearless.

'It's her that sowed the seeds of this disease here,' Khadija said.

She hawked up phlegm and spat on the floor. Her mouth and tongue were red with sores. Khadija told him that she had arrived, just as the rains had begun, with a Tamilian in a boat carrying a load of spoiled dried fish to be used as fertiliser for the coconuts. The Tamilian had died a couple of days later. After that, she had sat in the boat and given the pestilence to everyone. Someone had cut the moorings of her boat and sent it floating into the open lake, but there were people who had seen her scattering the seeds of pestilence with both hands, sitting on the jetty made of wooden planks nailed to coconut trunks in the pale light of the night. She had walked through the sticky mud, carrying the seeds, red and shiny like the seeds of the manjaadi tree, in a basket balanced on her head, and strewed them by the handfuls in fields and compounds, even, secretly, in the wells and among the brush torches that were hung to dry. Even her hair caused pox wherever it fell. Vavachan looked at the black earth next to where her boat had been moored and saw, astonishingly, that the pestilence had sprouted on the soil.

'So where is she now?'

'Who knows! Someone must have dragged her over there.'

Khadija pointed to the vast fields across the big canal, land which a starving humanity had dug out of the water. In the centre of those fields were Chemmayikkari and Chekuthanparambu. Those affected by the pestilence and had no hope of surviving were abandoned, forgotten by parents, spouses, siblings and kinfolk, at Chemmayikkari. They would disappear, leaving them to the care of someone who was no relation to them. This person would be someone who had survived the sickness, someone who had no feelings of compassion, not even for himself. He was the Matapathi – keeper of the diseased and the abandoned, caretaker of the graveyard. The kinfolk of those left behind were expected to provide him with toddy and arrack and meat, but regardless of what was given, he made them suffer. If they were young girls, he would not let them go even if they were cured, and used them for his sexual pleasure. And the souls of those who succumbed to the disease, their bodies rotting in their skin, hung around in Chekuthanparambu. In the night, people guarding the nearby fields could hear their protests – hisses like snakes and snorts like bulls. Saboora had succumbed to the disease, but Khadija did not abandon her father Beeran, and kept him fed, passing the food spiked on a piece of wood through the window.

Not satisfied with the destruction it had caused, the rain raced back from the north before sunset. Vavachan heard its roar and watched its slanted arrival, sitting on the veranda of Beeran's house. It stopped short of Chemmayikkari. Those whose bodies were covered in sores felt a searing pain when water touched their skin. Unlike the Matapathis, unrelenting gods, or landowning masters, the rain was not averse to compromise and left Chemmayikkari alone. Not a single blade of grass or clod of soil within it got wet.

On the wall plank of the house, Beeran's broad belt hung from a nail. He had kept his money in that belt, tied around his chequered mundu that came up to his ankles. Chella had bought a cotton towel from him one time when his boat had come along the Manadi canal. She had spread it on the edge of the field, and laid a sleeping Vavachan on it as she went to catch freshwater shrimps. Chella and Beeran might not remember this even if they were alive, and Khadija did not know about it. As he stood leaning against the wall, Vavachan felt the softness of the cloth on his back and smelled its fragrance. He felt sleepy. His moustache, wider than the veranda, spread to both sides of the house and got wet in the rain.

The rain that came in a hurry took its time to finally become a drizzle, and when it did, Vavachan swam across the canal. The currents were strong and the water had risen. In the thick darkness, the grassy outer bund of M N Block was not visible. On the far bank, Vavachan got out of the water, took off his mundu and wrung it out. As he stood naked, even Ezhuthachan, his creator, would not have recognised him. Years of relentless wandering had hardened the soles of his feet, and they left footprints like horseshoes in the soil. His body had thickened in the quickening youth, and his real face was completely covered by the moustache, erasing it out of memory. Sunburn covered his back and neck. His hair was short and thick, and his stomach shrunken and concave. The possibility that Seetha was near had awakened his groin, and he pressed his hand against it, thinking about the old smells of her body which, now, would be covered in oozy sores or lying somewhere decaying. He had nothing more to lose, and he walked on along the unfamiliar route – a ditch or a river, he couldn't tell. Although occasionally blessing the unlucky with its ire, the pestilence affected humanity as a whole as though in a fury to annihilate it only once every twelve or twenty-four years. It had been around from the time people started inhabiting Kumarakam, Konjumada, Kanjiram and

Thiruvarppu to build bunds and create fields. Chemmayikkari and Chekuthanparambu had also existed since those times. No one had walked this way in times like this since then; but Vavachan, with the moustache firmly on his face, walked everywhere, unconcerned. Would he have begun to believe that, like Perumaadan who waylaid people, or Aanamarutha who extended an elephant-like trunk and asked for toddy he too had become a powerful, magical being?

As he walked along, he heard a phlegmy murmur. It could not have been the cry of a creature as, ever since the Goddess of Pestilence had arrived in a boat with a Tamilian, even the frogs and cicadas had disappeared. He squatted and searched the area. Something was rolled up in a mat, with a big stone placed over it. He unrolled the mat which was tacky with pus and ooze, and poured a handful of water into the parched throat of its inhabitant. Presently, it moved, and Vavachan hoisted the small body on to his shoulder. Further up, he found a wheelhouse. He cleared a patch on its weed-grown floor and laid it down. All he could do then was to give it some water every now and then.

By the third day, Ramakaniyan was able to sit up. His son heard the news and arrived in a boat with food, bundles of neem leaves and two pots of toddy. He moored his boat a few feet away from the wheelhouse and looked at it anxiously. The person who came to fetch the things made him shake with fear.

'Are you cold? Your hands are shaking,' the moustached man said.

'When I was a child, my mother used to tell me scary stories about you.'

After he left, two Parayans arrived with a well-built man. They rowed up to the embankment, then pushed and rolled the man into the wheelhouse.

'Matapathi, you must look after him,' they told him respectfully. 'Everything you need is in the boat – firewood, pots, pans and all.'

Moustache looked at the patient. He was one and a half times taller than normal men, solidly built, and with a paunch. His shoulders looked like planks of wood, and he had well-defined muscles on his upper arms and thighs. But his private parts were horrifying. Pustules, ready to burst open, bloomed there like flowers.

'This is the Wrestler of Ambalatt,' Ramakaniyan told Moustache. 'The pox affects the parts of one's body that are most prized. Women usually have it the worst on their tongues and eyes.'

There were two famous wrestlers in Ambalatt, and they were brothers. The older brother was greatly skilled, and was well versed in offense and defence, shapeshifting and various other tricks.

One day, a Pathani wrestler arrived in Thiruvananthapuram. He beat up the guards at the Kizhakkekotta Fort and everyone else who stood in his way. He had been travelling steadily south, defeating all the wrestlers in the northern lands. He presented himself in front of the Maharaja and, after the required courtesies, challenged anyone from the land to defeat him. The Maharaja gave him suitable accommodations, and allowed a daily ration of two para measures of rice, a goat, the milk of two cows and an equal measure of ghee, and oil for daily ablutions, before sending word to the Ambalatt brothers. The brothers argued about who should go to take up the challenge. Since childhood, the brothers had always argued with each other even though they loved each other dearly. Finally, the younger brother prevailed, and the older brother saw him off at the jetty with his bundle. He then bathed, and sat in his wet clothes in front of a betel leaf on a stool, focusing all his attention on it, forgoing sleep and food. He watched his brother's progress with teary eyes, worried that the weather might turn too hot or too rainy.

At the palace, the challenge began at the designated time. An audience, along with the king, the royal household and other dignitaries, gathered to watch. The fight was not as the Pathani had anticipated. Unlike the wrestlers he had encountered in Telugu lands or Tamil lands, this young wrestler was not easily overcome. They wrestled for hours in the flying dust. But back home, the older brother watching the match through the betel leaf could see that his little brother was beginning to tire and make mistakes in his footwork. He would not be able to hold on for too long. He got up, and called out to the north wing of the house to his mother to ensure that the house had been cleaned and purified. He then lit a lamp and stood in front of it, praying, and disappeared on the spot. Invisible kicks and blows began to assault the Pathani who could not understand what was happening. And the little brother returned home, victorious and laden with the gifts and honours the king had bestowed upon him.

'The point is, people can be fooled with trickery, but not this disease,' Ramakaniyan said.

The wrestler could not speak, but his eyes begged the Matapathi for his mercy.

'So where's the younger brother then?' Moustache asked.

'He must have run away and saved his own skin. Can't blame him, to be honest.'

The wrestler did not last the day, and no one came looking for him afterwards.

Ramakaniyan's sores began to heal. The Matapathi applied a paste of turmeric and neem leaves, and made him stand in the canal water as he scrubbed his skin with coconut husk, removing the dried scabs of pus and letting clean blood bead in the sores. The hunchbacked old man wriggled and cried out like a little child, but when he got out of the water and dressed in a clean mundu, he raised his hands to the heavens and straightened his back.

'Ho! Feels so good!'

Ramakaniyan was an astrologer. He sat in the lotus position on the bare floor of the wheelhouse, and took out his bag of cowry shells and the wooden plank to spread them on that his son had brought for him.

'Now you go have your bath,' he said to Moustache.

'I don't bathe.'

'Well, all right then. Vagabonds, hunters, and those who live in the forests – these are exempt from bathing. They say a scoundrel is like teak wood, able to lie anywhere with impunity. People like that can eat whatever they want, do as they please, sleep with any woman they want…'

Ramakaniyan spread his cowry shells and did some calculations with his fingers. He looked up at Moustache, surprised.

'Shells don't lie. My father and I have never been wrong in our predictions. It was one of our ancestors who predicted that the younger master of Thalikkotta would have an untimely death. My father has written my horoscope only up until sixty-five years and ten days of age. After that, it is to be seen, he'd said. And look, you found me rolled in that mat on the tenth day!'

'And you didn't die, did you?'

'Well ... We don't know the day or time of your birth. But let me tell you what I saw in the shells. You have God's own horoscope – Sreeraman's. The whole world will know about you, tell stories about you, and sing songs about you. But you'll spend your whole life wandering. You'll have to give up what you search for, even if you find it. Your children will turn against you. And you'll lose whatever is the most important thing to you.'

Before Ramakaniyan left, they brought a Brahmin, the Elder Thirumeni of Swamiyaar Matam. The Thirumeni ventured out only with an entourage and accompanied by drums that alerted people of the lower castes to stay out of his way. The boat with the drummer and the hand cymbalist kept a careful distance from the canopied small boat with the Thirumeni, playing their instruments only occasionally, creating more pools of silence than sound.

'We'll come every day and check,' the oarsman told the Matapathi. 'You must let us know if he doesn't make it. Can't just bury him, there are rituals to be done.'

In the thin darkness of the wheelhouse, the Thirumeni coughed and looked at the man in front of him with fear. Oozing pus had glued one of his eyes shut, but the other one had a sliver of light in it. He was dejected at having to spend his last days with a man such as this, and he refused to drink the water the Matapathi offered him.

When it was full dark, the Matapathi took the old mat, rolled the Thirumeni in it, and carried him on his shoulder to the spot where he had found Ramakaniyan. He placed a stone on the mat above the chest and left, intending to swim across the canal, but he thought he saw another moustached man come out of the canal and pass right by him. He turned and looked several times, but there was no one there, or if there was, he had been swallowed up by the darkness.

On the other side of the canal, he cut a boat off its moorings and rowed all night. In the faint early morning light, he saw, far away under a coconut tree leaning across the water to the other side, a woman broadcasting the seeds of pox by the handful. The sight slipped from his vision a couple of times, and yet he aimed his boat at the spot and rowed hard.

16

AN UNLIKELY MEDICINE MAN

A person can die only once, but they could die in one of any number of ways. An ordinary death is the most appropriate for those who have lived an ordinary life, within the confines of their modest circumstances – a death in advanced age, for example, or after a short illness such as a fever or dysentery, a death that would surprise no one. These deaths would pass by without comment, just like their lives, their own children forgetting about them before the soil above their graves dried, only to be thought of, fondly, on rare occasions. But it is possible that even those who lived an ordinary life might have an end to their lives that made them remarkable – a sudden and unexpected death, or a protracted death after a long and strange illness that inconvenienced their near and dear ones. Then there are deaths that are uncertain because the bodies are never found, like Chella's, or deaths that confound people because of their strangeness, like Machovan's. And those who have lived an extraordinary life should have an extraordinary death. A sanyasi should die as he recites the name of God, a criminal in a knife-fight, and a king in the midst of enquiring after the well-being of his subjects. Extraordinary lives might end in inconsequential deaths too, but these would still be elevated if their deaths were spoken of as extraordinary and, thus, gained stature. Chief Minister Velu Thambi Dalawa's military chief, Vaikom Padmanabha Pillah, was captured by the British at Turuveli hills. They killed him by putting him in a drum, the inside of which was studded with nails, and rolling him down the hill, but people said that he had swallowed his diamond ring and ended his life. The floods of 1924 happened months after Maharaja Sree Moolam Thirunal had passed away, and yet people still believe that he died heartbroken at the fate of his subjects as he watched the rising floodwaters.

The death of Thanulinga Nadar, a descendent of a long line of ardent patriots, was entirely unsuited for the life and fame he had built for himself. His body was found upside down with its legs sticking up into the air, at a spot near Pallam where four canals met, a place locally known as 'Appikuzhi' – Shithole. The head and the upper part of the body had been submerged in the thick alluvial soil deposited by the rushing waters of the flood. As the water receded, it left a small muddy islet in the middle of the canal, and the legs appeared as though they had sprouted from the soil. The place had acquired the name Shithole not because people sat in a line and openly defecated there, but because it was a place where bottom-feeding catfish and carp, fish that everyone believed ate shit, were abundant and where, at the sight of a fishing hook, they lined up to kill themselves. And because of its name, those who caught fish there sold them saying that their catch had come from the gill nets set in the paddy fields. But people knew where the fish came from when baskets brimmed during times when there was no small fry, thooli or ribbon fish to be had.

The soles of Nadar's feet gazed at the sky, unable to remember the paths they had trodden. This was the first time they were seeing the sky after their childhood days of diving in the canals and the Tamirabharani River. Like the buffalo or the elephant, he had been crazy about water, refusing to come out of it, swimming across the river several times for no reason. The incessant swimming had made the muscles of his shins, thighs and shoulders shapely and toned, and, without his clothes, he looked like a broad-shouldered, narrow-hipped fish. When he was a little older, he would perform the dangerous task of diving into the sea at Sangathurai to retrieve the coins and other things onlookers threw into it.

It was the time between harvests and the fields were deserted, so no one knew for certain how long the dead body had been there. Perhaps those who had seen it had decided not to say anything about it out of fear, because a slip of khaki shorts was visible and they could tell it was a policeman. But the shoeless feet would have made them conclude that it was an ordinary 'fire-stick' policeman, one who wore a hat with a red, pointy end. They were known to mash the groins of grown men with a single kick, and to frighten women, on the rare occasions they ran into them, into losing control of their bladders. So it fell upon an unfortunate Vaalathi, a fish seller, who happened to pass that way on her way back home after a day's work, whose misfortune was yet to reach its limits, to discover the body. She was lost in thoughts about her new husband who sat at home doing nothing, expecting her to provide for him by selling fish, and it must have been the anger and sorrow that she already felt that made her scream at the top of her voice at the sight, and run to the nearby Mappila and Chovan households describing the scene. They seemed unsurprised, perhaps because they had already known about the dead body. Still, in a matter of minutes, people began gathering, and by eleven, a crowd trampled on the banana saplings on the embankment, looking at the body as though expecting the hapless soul to pull his head out of the mud and walk away. By noon, they saw a boatful of policemen approaching, and the crowd dispersed, shouting 'Fire-sticks! Fire-sticks!' The few who stayed put were sent scurrying by the policemen who jumped out of the boat and thrashed them with their lathis.

Unnithan recognised the body at once. It was people's legs that he studied first when he met them. Nadar's feet were restrained from years of living within the confines of shoes, his big toes smaller than average, and he had an old scar on the heel of his left foot. Still, Unnithan found it difficult to understand three things. First, Nadar was not in uniform when they had set out in the morning. In fact, he had never seen him wear the uniform in all the time they had stayed together in the house near the canal in pursuit of Vavachan. Second, how did the inspector, who had told them that they would meet in Thiruvarppu, end up this far away in Pallam? Had he heard that they had, in fact, encountered Moustache, and that their boat had capsized in the ensuing commotion? Third, Nadar was the type of person who left no task incomplete. So where were the shoes and socks that were part of the uniform? How did he end up dead, shoeless like an ordinary policeman?

The Assistant Police Superintendent, who was in Vaikom at the time, arrived within a few hours. The Tehsildar and the Pravruthyar had already arrived. The Superintendent sat on a bench someone had carried over, and gave orders to prepare the mahassar, and for the removal of the body. Two workers built a makeshift enclosure among the coconut trees, planting a few posts and putting up a palm-leaf thatch. They made a bed out of split areca trunks. Nadar would lie on this for the rest of the time.

The Superintendent was due to retire in a couple of months. His face reflected the anxiety he was experiencing about the fact that one of the eighty-one inspectors in Thiruvithamkur police department had died under suspicious circumstances within his jurisdiction. He was even more anxious about the fact that Thanulinga Nadar and his family had a close relationship with the royal family and the palace. Who would end up answering for this disaster was yet to be seen. As far as he knew, the dead man was the only person from the Nadar caste in the entire police force that had less than three thousand officers.

As a young man, Nadar had shown no sign of maturity even when he reached the age of twenty, and held sway over the rivers and the beaches. He would go into the houses of men who were away at sea fishing, or their women would come to him as he slept on the beach under boats. One time, two women, known for their chastity, had engaged in an open altercation because of him, attacking each other across baskets of fish. The incident had led to a public brawl on the beach that lasted a day and a night. His father, Aiya Nadar, had bundled up his son's certificates and some clothes, shut his tobacco shop, and gone off to Thiruvananthapuram, returning a month later with an appointment letter from the police department. Those who knew Aiya Nadar's father Appavu Nadar and his relationship with the deceased Maharaja Uthram

Thirunal, who was the predecessor of His Majesty Ayilyam Thirunal, did not find this surprising at all.

Maharaja Uthram Thirunal Marthandavarma and his older brother Swathi Thirunal Ramavarma were mad, each in their own particular way, but the similarity ended there. Unlike the older brother, the younger one had no interest whatsoever in music or in fasting or praying, locked inside a pooja room, disregarding the responsibilities of a ruler. The older brother emptied the coffers, giving the money away to the undeserving and to the temples, and when the British demanded taxes in increasingly sterner terms, he sullenly shut himself up in his quarters. He also had an unbridled interest in beautiful women and was prone to behaving in a beggarly manner in front of them, forgetting his position as the king.

Uthram Thirunal barely glanced at the line of beauties ceremoniously lighting his way as he went to the temple of Sri Padmanabhaswamy, their lamps held at strategic heights to illuminate their shapely breasts and navels. All he would have to do was declare that he liked one of them, and her family would summon the Brahmins and prepare a feast with a hundred dishes. But his interest in women was confined to occasional intercourse with the beautiful Madhavippillakochamma of Thiruvattar Ammachi house, who was his custom-bound consort.

Swathi Thirunal felt a fear mixed with scorn for the British, and called them mlechan – unclean – at every opportunity. He could not understand why, after he had spent so much on pooja and prayers and appeasing the Brahmins, they continued to be invincible, and why they seemed healthier by the day despite their habit of consuming animal flesh. While Swathi Thirunal hid under his bed when he had to attend meetings with the Resident Saheb in charge, his younger brother, Uthram Thirunal, was the complete opposite. From the time he was a child, on the rare occasions when he would get to see white men, he had observed them with great interest. He had even hoped to contract vitiligo so that his skin would turn white. Obsessed with everything British, he studied the English language, and paced the corridors of the palace pretending to be in the company of white men, conversing in English with himself. The courtiers watched in astonishment as the young prince, dressed in trousers and coat, ate the ilayada – a sweet made from rice-flour paste, grated coconut and jaggery steamed in banana leaves – with a knife and fork. He sang the praises of meat-eating at every chance, and stopped short of eating it himself only because he was not accustomed to it.

Still, when the older brother passed away, and it was his turn to step up to the throne, the British delayed issuing the order for two months. Swathi Thirunal had behaved like a petty woman, speaking ill of others at public baths and protesting at inopportune moments. The British wanted to impress upon the incumbent that they held all the power, that they could rule the kingdom directly, and that the king was only a figurehead and was not indispensable. But they had misjudged Uthram Thirunal. Unlike all the other native rulers they had met before, he was happy to abdicate responsibilities to them, and to sit back and enjoy their rule.

With the death of Swathi Thirunal, the poets, who had made a living by penning keerthanas and poems and convincing him that he had written them himself, the musicians and the dancers moved on to look for their livelihoods elsewhere. Instead, a Catholic priest named Douglas began visiting the new king. But, contrary to his expectations, the Maharaja was not interested in reading the Bible. He wanted to hear stories of Europe, and he built a library purchasing books from abroad. He was amazed to hear that people in Europe did not walk along pitted lanes like they did in his kingdom, but on paved roads and sturdy concrete bridges across rivers. His suggestion that an expert tile maker be brought over from Coimbatore to replace the roofs of all houses with tiles came to nothing, not because the royal decree was thought to be a folly, but because people feared that the roof tiles would fall on their heads and injure them. What the Maharaja found most difficult to understand was the fact that Europeans lived as a family with wife and children, ate three meals a day, and went to bed late in the night.

It was the priest, Father Douglas, who brought Appavu Nadar, in charge of building roads in Madras Presidency, to Maharaja Uthram Thirunal. He took to Nadar, a man who went everywhere with a compass in his hand, and was a dedicated royalist, instantly. Nadar convinced the Maharaja to set up a public works department to build a concrete bridge across the Karamana River, and as it would be inauspicious for the ruler of the land to handle iron, it was with a silver hoe, presented by Nadar, that the Maharaja broke ground and inaugurated the work.

Before long, the Maharaja became obsessed with European medicine, especially allopathy, an obsession of such rigour that it took even Father Douglas by surprise. Soon, he began to believe, after poring over books on the subject, that he had become a doctor, and that he could treat people. He converted one of the rooms in the palace to a pharmacy, and scornfully disregarding local healers, equipped it with arsenic, copper sulphate and morphine brought from England, and proceeded to make royal servants drink a solution of copper sulphate as medicine. They, in turn, took this gift from their beloved Golden Majesty home, and reverentially placed it in front of a lit lamp as though it was water from the holy River Ganga. Soon, a story of how the Maharaja had cured an unspeakable malady that had afflicted the private parts of a priest at the temple spread through the land. Sedating him with a large dose of opium, the Maharaja cauterised the affliction with a red hot iron rod, and the priest's howls of pain were heard precisely at the moment when the temple's sanctum opened for the evening prayers, shaking the rafters of the temple.

The substance that most captured the imagination of the Maharaja in those days was chloroform. He maintained a correspondence for years with R.M. Glover who had discovered its use as a sedative. But it was still not in regular use. When he heard that a Scottish man named Simpson had used chloroform on a couple of his dinner guests, the Maharaja was excited, and he summoned Diwan Krishnarao to discuss its potential in army strategies. The Diwan tried to impress upon him that the country had no army any more, and that there was no reason to explore this line of thought. But his protests went unheeded, and the Maharaja ordered him to procure some chloroform. In his letter sent to Queen Victoria congratulating her on her recent motherhood, he made particular note of the use of chloroform in enabling a safe delivery.

Finally, after three years of effort, when a small bottle of chloroform arrived in the country, it was given a ceremonial welcome at the Kizhakkekotta Fort, accompanied by Panchavadyam, an ensemble of five types of ceremonial musical instruments, and torchlights. The bottle, conveyed on top of an elephant, was ritually purified by Brahmin priests, and the Royal Hands received it and presented it in front of the Royal Deity, Sri Padmanabhaswamy. It was soon removed from there, as it was known that prolonged exposure to it would corrode the idol, and stored in a carefully temperature-controlled almirah in the pharmacy. The very next day, an experiment was conducted to ascertain its potency. Although, as a result of a larger dose than advised, a continuous tremor would afflict one of the two servants who were the subjects of the experiment, it was decreed a success.

Two months after this incident, Maharaja Uthram Thirunal Marthandavarma would conduct the first surgery in the history of not only modern Thiruvithamkur but all of India. And it was the builder of the country's first concrete bridge, Appavu Nadar, who was destined to be its subject.

Nadar had come for an audience with the king to discuss a matter relating to the rebuilding of the road between Kollam and Chenkotta. He made the required royal offerings, tied his towel around his waist, and stood bowing reverentially before His Golden Majesty.

'What is it, Nadar? You look peaky,' the Maharaja said in a pleasant voice after the preliminary exchanges.

Since it was a white man, Father Douglas, who had introduced Nadar to him, the Maharaja had taken a special liking to him. Nadar told him about a persistent stomach ache that had been annoying him for over six months. He was losing blood, could not eat properly, and no medicine seemed to be working. The Maharaja ordered him to a bed and proceeded to examine him, turning him over this way and that. An astrologer was summoned to find an auspicious date for the surgery, and within a week, a room next to the pharmacy was turned into a surgical theatre. The operating tools were ritually purified by sprinkling them with holy water and cow urine. The evening before the surgery, Nadar was given a laxative made of neervilakam seeds. Reference books that the Maharaja would need to consult were placed in the surgical room.

The surgery lasted for hours and was a great success, and when, after a few anxious hours, Nadar emerged from his chloroform-induced sleep, ceremonial fireworks were sounded. The next day, the patient sat up and had a bowl of sweetened kanji. But Appavu Nadar's surgical wounds became infected, and he died on the seventh day after the surgery. His body was taken back to Tirunelveli, which was not part of the Thiruvithamkur kingdom, in a special palanquin prepared as though for a member of the royal family. It was a day of great pride for the Nadar community and the entire town. They had never seen a funeral with so many officials and dignitaries in attendance. Appavu Nadar's son, Aiya Nadar, stood boldly and proudly before the Assistant Peshkar who had come to convey his condolences. Aiya Nadar told everyone that the Maharaja had diagnosed his father's illness as soon as he had seen him, because of which he had been able to live longer than he should have. He was promised a government job which he refused on the grounds that he was not worthy of it, and was given, instead, ten acres of land in Nagercoil, and the right to gift a bundle of tobacco to the palace on the day before the finale of the temple festival. A new rule, that Nadar households who wanted to serve sweet dishes at their wedding feasts should solicit verbal permission from Aiya Nadar's family, was also instituted.

Aiya Nadar's concern that his son, Thanulingan, would bring disrepute to the job he had organised for him did not last long. His first appointment was to the palace guards, a job usually given to Nairs only, and of course there were disgruntled murmurings about it. Thanulinga Nadar was resplendent in the uniform – red leggings with golden kasavu borders, upper garment, green hat, three white slashes across the chest, red shoes and a spear – and was striking in his dark skin and strong body. The strangeness of his voice did not make him feel inferior, as even the royal consort, the Attingal Queen, requested to be escorted by the young man with the extraordinary physique. The rumour-mongers around the palace left him alone despite feeling exceeding jealousy and caste hostility. Punctual in his duties, he immersed himself fully in the exclusive, secret world of the palace halls to such an extent that he did not avail his leave to go back home. And within three years, overtaking many others in promotions, he was appointed to the police force.

It was around this time that women were allowed into the police force for the first time, and ten women were recruited. The reasons were unclear, but there was a requirement that they should not marry. One of them, a Parukkutty from Mavelikkara, became close to Head Constable Nadar despite there being several handsome and eligible assistant superintendents and inspectors. Nadar took to swimming across the canal in the nights to the house where she boarded. His senior officer was angry, but he could do nothing as the clandestine affair could not be confirmed officially. But Parukkutty did not last long in the service. Two years later, she became pregnant, and when she could no longer hide her growing belly, she was fired from the service, and Nadar was transferred to Kollam, where they rented a house and lived together openly.

Thanulinga Nadar's fame truly began to rise after he became an inspector and was transferred to Kollam. The police stations in Kollam were much smaller than the one in the capital where he had regularly interacted with dignitaries, and he began to show reluctance to sit behind desks doing the everyday, boring tasks of his job. Instead, he began to be interested in solving cases, conducting the investigations in mufti. The local people, on meeting a stranger, began to assume that the person was Nadar, and talked about old cases and behaved respectfully. The most famous among these stories was one about how a Tamilian Chettiar, who had arrived with a billy goat to set up a goat-fat medicine establishment, had solved an old knife-fight case. Another famous incident was about Nadar capturing a counterfeiter after spending several days pretending to be a coffee-seller in the cattle market. His fame got him selected for training in modern weaponry in Calcutta. As he was waiting for his train on the station platform, dressed in his full uniform, he made the acquaintance of the venerable Kunjan Panicker. Kunjan Panicker was the Sraap, the person in charge of the financial matters of the entire land.

'I'm Inspector Thanulinga Nadar,' he said respectfully, introducing himself.

The response was a loud laugh.

'Don't try to fool me, my friend,' the Sraap said. 'I'd believe you if you told me you were the Resident Saheb. But everyone knows that Inspector Nadar is always in mufti.'

Now, the formidable Thanulinga Nadar lay motionless, permanently back in his uniform, far away from his birth land and the language of his people, by the side of a narrow embankment in a land of black mud, swamp and water. As they retrieved his body and laid him on the ground, the dirt on his face reddened with blood. There was a small shallow wound just below his ear. His eyes and mouth were closed as though he had died peacefully. The policemen and the few local dignitaries who had gathered around were not aware of the legend that was Nadar, the man who had terrorised Nagercoil and Kollam, or of his contributions to the history of policing. It was he who had introduced interrogation techniques such as the intestine-splitting punch, chilli application to the eyes, the garudan thookkam – a contraption with hooks to lift a grown man up by the flesh on his back and make him fly like an eagle. He would have become famous in this land too, if only he had been successful in his goal, and people would have forgotten about Moustache and sung paddy-field ballads about Policeman Nadar instead.

As evening arrived, the number of onlookers increased. The policemen stood guard until daybreak with dimly burning torches dipped in chaulmoogra oil. Early in the morning, Inspector General Khan Bahadur Sayyid Abdul Kareem Saheb arrived in a boat, bringing with him a doctor who would conduct the post-mortem. Khan Saheb examined the body, the spot where it was found, and the vicinity carefully.

'Who saw it first?' he asked.

He questioned Unnithan in detail, but after a while, lost patience with his rambling answers.

'What I want to know is whether you saw the man you were after in these parts. I don't want to hear about the size of his moustache, or whether he killed snakes with a three-pronged farm tool.'

He moved on to visit the rest house, where the woman who had stumbled upon Nadar's dead body was kept under lock and key. All night, the policemen had eagerly taken turns to keep guard over her.

'Did you happen to see a gun?' Saheb asked her. 'On the embankment or in the canal?'

She sat silently, wrapped in a piece of sackcloth.

'Did anyone hurt you?'

Khan Saheb suspended all the policemen who had stood guard through the night immediately.

A whole day had passed since the body was discovered, and it was beginning to rot. So the policemen buried Nadar on the embankment, bestowing the corpse with all honours. The burial pit began to fill with water as soon as it was two feet deep, and by the time it was finished, the workers were standing waist-deep in water. The policemen attached weights to the body and lowered it into the grave using ropes. The air is the same all over, so is the water. So it was to the Tamirabharani River that Nadar dived, off an embankment built up with clay from the bottom of the Vembanad Kayal in northern Kuttanad. He rose with the waves, with coins picked up off the sea floor on Sangathurai beach and lay waiting in the darkness by the catamarans.

Khan Saheb camped at the rest house for the next week, and in that time, the entire police force of the Alappuzha region congregated there. From Pallathuruthi to Kodimatha, and Thiruvarppu to Thalayazham, they searched every nook and cranny of every canal, stream, embankment, field edge and bush. Huge crowds gathered at the Changanassery jetty, in Munnattumukham, Vettikkadu and Mutherimada, expecting to see at any moment the large boat arrive with a captured Moustache in iron chains with padlocks. The policemen questioned clay diggers, duck herders and pearlspot fishermen, and went after cast-net fishermen fishing the rivers. They were determined that Moustache get his comeuppance.

Khan Saheb went back only after meeting with prominent local personages such as Kavalakkan, Pallithanam Luca Mathai and Chalayi Panicker, and taking certain decisions. An inspector would visit Kuttamangalam and Eera once a week, and once a month, boats would patrol the entire backwaters. The boat that came to take the Inspector General away was the finest ever to moor at Eera jetty, one that had an upper deck where people could sit. The driver of the boat, bored from the long wait for Khan Saheb, scolded those who touched it. When he stepped out, people gathered around him.

'What a godforsaken land,' he said, casting his eyes over the water-filled fields. 'I'm so glad I won't have to come this way ever again.'

The expectant eyes of his audience released his inner storyteller.

'He was captured the next day itself. They sent a prostitute to calm him down and put him to sleep, and cut off his moustache. Then they tied him up and beat the shit out of him. That's what you'll get if you offend His Golden Majesty.'

He told them that in Kuriyamada, they made him sit on a length of sharpened, oiled areca wood, until the sharpened end came out of the crown of his head.

'But listen to this, two days later he was still alive! His eyes were rolling in their sockets. People got so scared, they ran away. Must have started decaying by now though.'

On the journey back, Khan Saheb seemed troubled. The serene scenery outside and the cool breeze did nothing to lighten his mood.

The Assistant Superintendent who was to accompany him until Kollam asked, in a respectful voice: 'What's the matter? Are you worried that he hasn't been apprehended yet?'

'That's a different matter. The main problem is that the gun has disappeared,' Khan Saheb replied. 'When he signed in the register, Nadar had not given a reason for checking it out. It will be a problem.

Nadar was a troublemaker, but he was efficient. Never set out to do anything without studying the issue inside out. The gun could be in anyone's hand. We have to be vigilant.'

'I don't know if we should worry so much. The culprit is a Pulayan. A gun is as good as a piece of softwood in his hand.'

'But there's no guarantee that he's the one who has the gun. Besides, from what I've gathered, it will be a mistake to underestimate him.'

Khan Saheb's primary worry soon became a reality, and a report about the lost gun was filed in the Hazoor Court and the police headquarters, and whenever they had to deal with the matter, the officers and clerks alike thought of the man who had brought this headache to them. Could he not have lived quietly tapping toddy or whatever? Why did he have to insinuate himself into their lives? They competed with each other to delay processing the files and added pointless entries in them. As a result, Nadar's wife had to wait a long time for the posthumous benefits she was entitled to from the government. She had been ousted from their rented house, and now she and her child lived in an outhouse on a relative's property. A policeman who was found loitering around the place and scratching at the door in the night was caught by the neighbours, an incident that gave birth to a local saying for clandestine shenanigans: 'I was only here looking for the stolen gun.'

Eventually, the patrol and guards set up by Khan Saheb to protect the crops petered out because of lack of resources. The British government insisted on collecting all revenue to be used for a war that was being fought in faraway skies and lands, or to be made available as repayment of debts. Finally, an order was passed that designated two policemen at the Vaikom station as the only personnel responsible for continuing the search for Moustache and the gun. They sat on it for a while before going to Neendoor to start the search from the beginning. They visited the embankment where Paviyan used to live, the building where the drama troupe had lived, and the field where the play had been performed. In these places, they paced with exaggerated steps and took some measurements. They went to Makkothara, where the locals had last spotted Moustache, but by then it was evening, and too late to return to Vaikom. They had resigned to finding their way back in the morning, when they saw a boat approaching at a fair clip. It had at least twenty para measures of good paddy.

'Bring it close, prick,' one of the policemen commanded.

They took the oarsman to be someone inconsequential, and as soon as he got off the boat, one of them slapped him across the cheek.

'What's your name?'

'Pachupillah.'

'Where did you get all this paddy?'

The man stammered out an answer.

'Never mind, we'll talk at the station.'

The policemen got into the boat.

'Should we go via Vechoor and through the lake or via Thalayazham and Ullala?' asked the oarsman.

'Go between someone's legs, we don't care.'

The policemen were famished.

They went past Chozhiyappara, Kattukari, Kanyakon, Chekka and Kochu Chekka, presently reaching an islet surrounded by water. This was Pandarachira. Like the people of Thiruvarppu had Chemmayikkari and Chekuthanparambu, Pandarachira was the place where the people of Perunthuruthu and Kallara discarded their diseased and the dying. Boatmen going past this place avoided looking at it. By the time the boat got to this place, it was dark.

'Are my masters hungry?' the boatman asked. 'There's a young coconut tree over there. I can pull down some tender coconuts for you.'

Pachupillah pulled the boat close to the islet, keeping to the deeper parts of the canal. The policemen jumped out, and as they looked around, Pachupillah rowed away as fast as he could. The policemen ran along the embankment after him, shouting and cursing.

On his way back, Pachupillah warned the oarsmen of every boat he came across: 'Don't go near Pandarachira. The dead are awake and are making an almighty racket.'

17

ITTICHAN

No matter how desperate the times, or how much of the crops were destroyed by cracked bunds or flocks of waterfowl, Kavalakkan, Chalayi Panicker and Mankombu Swamy had coffers that never emptied. No police, Pravruthyar or toll collectors dared stop their paddy boats rowed by strong-armed oarsmen, and their harvests remained out of the records books. Still, lawbreaking had to be done quietly, and so it was after dark and without fanfare that the two boats belonging to Chalayi, taking a load of paddy to a Mappila in Kallooppara, set out. The night was starlit and the oarsmen rowed without much care, but as they got to Muttar, where the Pullukayar River joined the Pamba River, they began to feel uneasy. They chalked it up to the tiredness of not having eaten anything even after spending hours loading the paddy into the boat. When, presently, they got to a part of the river where silt deposits on both sides had narrowed its width, two long-oars fell across the way, striking the boat and causing it to run aground. A group of men jumped aboard and shovelled away the entire load of paddy at knifepoint.

The next day, Chalayi's musclemen came to Muttar, and beat up everyone they came across, and unable to learn anything about the bandits, they set upon the oarsmen. The oarsmen had no recollection of the faces of the thieves they had encountered in the dark, and in the agony of a kick to the navel, one of them blurted out: One of the thieves had a great big moustache.

When he heard the news, Pallithanam Luca Mathai lost his cool. There was no point in lodging complaints with the Sree Moolam Praja Sabha, or waiting for the police or the army. As it was, most of the harvest had been lost to weevils and worms. What was one to do if the rest was being looted? One Saturday, as he was measuring out paddy to the field workers, he was troubled. So much of the harvest went in wages, and he had to stop the rest from being carted away by thieves. Velan, who had come to collect his payment for getting the fields rid of rice ear bugs, tried to console him. This year, the bugs had come as soon as the fields were sowed, and if he had not smoked them away with dry spathes of coconut and chanted his mantras, there would have been nothing left to harvest.

'But we have to be vigilant,' Mathai warned him. 'He has a whole gang with him.'

Velan said he would find Moustache no matter where he hid. There was not a single field in all of Kainakari, Kavalam, Pulinkunnu, Nedumudi, Mankombu, Eera, Champakulam, Edathua or Thakazhi that the old man did not know about.

On the seventh day after setting out with his bundle, the old man caught up with the man with the great big moustache. It is not clear where exactly this happened, as the old man had a habit of telling several versions of the same story. So the places changed – sometimes, it was on an islet in the Kochi backwaters; at other times, it was in an eastern forest near Peruvanthanam, or near the Madammakkulam waterfalls, or in the Thattamala hills. After all, a man who has studied mantra and tantra does not divulge the truth to anyone. All that is known for sure is that, after giving his word to Mathai and swearing to forego his meals until his mission was complete, Velan searched across the fields and bunds, going wherever his feet led him. When his way was blocked by canals and lakes, he took the help of the boats he came across, crossing and recrossing waterways, sometimes returning to where he had started. After a week, he decided to pull in to an islet in the middle of a field. As soon as he did, he realised, watching a fully grown coconut tree shivering in the still air around, that this was Perumalam, where even the dead remained hidden. Three times Velan dipped his torch in oil and tried to light it, but each time it got extinguished as though someone had blown it out. Not wanting to test his luck, he jumped across the small water channel, and the dead flame flickered back and lit the torch.

'His moustache is nothing like we imagine,' he would say for the rest of his life, as he smoked out rice ear bugs in various fields. A year later, at the parakottu drumming at the Urali Ayyappan temple, as he sang the praises of Lord Paramashivan, he would add a couple of lines about the graveyard dweller, Chudalamadan, and his moustache.

When he finally caught up with Moustache, Velan tried to persuade him to return with him.

'You can have whatever you want,' he told Moustache. 'The master of Pallithanam has so much paddy and money. Why don't you find a good place, build a bund and live on it? I'll make sure that a couple of boatloads of paddy is delivered to you. And the kayal fields have been sown. You could take over guard duty there.'

'What would I do with paddy?' Moustache asked. 'All I want is to be left alone. I'm searching for a woman, and when I find her, I'd like to go somewhere we can live without hunger. This place is no good. All it has is mud and water and horrible people.'

'Don't you lie to me. If you have no use for paddy, why did you capture Sraap Kunjan Panicker's boat at Thottappally? What did you do with the gold coins in it? Cooked and ate them, did you?'

That particular incident had happened a long time ago, perhaps even before Vavachan met Ezhuthachan. Like Chalayi Panicker who lost his paddy, Sraap too could not lodge a complaint about his loss. He had smuggled the gold coins on the back of an elephant on its way back from Thiruvattar after a procession for His Golden Majesty the Maharaja, and had hidden them in a hole under his bed. When the sack was nearly full, he had put it in his boat to take home. But the Golden Majesty in the heavens above had other plans, and the ill-gotten sack of gold coins had disappeared in the talons of an eagle.

Velan chewed a yellowed betel leaf with bits of areca nut and slaked lime paste, dusted and retied his cloth, and warmed up to his subject.

'Don't be over-confident. Mathaichan has made an offering to Karumathra Ittichan. You won't be able to range free around here for long now.'

'Ittichan? Who's that?'

Velan was astounded. Was there anyone who had not heard of Ittichan? Any place where the fame of Karumathrakkavu had not reached? Moustache was trying to trick him, he decided. Ittichan was the type of person who did not put up with tricksters. One time, Ittichan was watching the women workers in his field, and he realised that they were dragging their feet. The one leading the work song was doing it half-heartedly, purposely slowing down the work. They straightened their backs, poked at each other, laughed, as though waiting for sunset so that they could get back home. The sun was already low in the sky, and the work would not be completed at this rate. Enraged, Ittichan took out the iron writing stick from his waist pouch, and impaled the sun to the sky with it. The women, waiting for the sun to set, were flummoxed, but Ittichan did not release the sun until the day's work was completed.

'Be careful how you speak about Ittichan,' warned Velan. 'Who do you think he is? He's had the upper hand even with Kaalan, the God of Death. He took Kaalan's ledger and did not give it back until he'd finished reading it from beginning to end.'

Moustache's moustache stood out in amazement. Another person who had the same life as him? So who was it actually who had read Kaalan's ledger? Ittichan or Moustache? Had one person's life leached into the stories about the other, or was this Ittichan a confirmed liar?

'I'll see him,' Moustache said.

'Good. Mathaichan might agree to come here with the paddy,' Velan said.

'Not him. Ittichan.'

Velan guffawed, forgetting that he was in Perumalam where quietness prevailed.

'Ittichan left home almost five hundred years ago, leaving behind all his books. No one has seen him since. He must be in Kailash, the abode of gods.'

Moustache got in the boat with Velan. The old man felt proud of himself. He had successfully persuaded Moustache into his boat – like the Namboothiri Brahmin from a long time ago who had persuaded Goddess Mathurameenakshi to go with him! As they passed through the narrow canals with depleted water levels, he tried to keep the boat in the middle so that Moustache's moustache would not get tangled in the vegetation on either side, and stood up and held the branches out of the way as the boat glided through. They entered the choppy lake, and the small country boat was carried forward swiftly by the wind caught in the moustache as though it was a sail. When the boat entered the smaller canals on the other side of the lake, women catching pallathi fish, agitating the water with banana stems, looked at the moustached man with alarm. They did not see Velan or his boat. The fish that had stuck their head in the mud, befuddled by the banana stems in the agitating water, escaped as the women stood still. They resumed beating the water and scolded the fish that had disobeyed them.

'What's this?' Moustache asked.

Man-high stands of tidy plants grew on an embankment. He had, in all his travels, never come across them.

'Jute,' Velan said. 'What do you think fishing nets are made of?'

Women sat by the side of the canal, their clothes hiked up, rolling the strands of jute that had been soaked in water and crushed, into ropes on their naked thighs. They screamed and ran away on seeing the approaching figure. Until a moment before, their inner thighs had been tickled by jute strands like the hairs of a moustache.

By the time they got to the River Pamba, crowds had gathered in all the inhabited places along the way to catch a glimpse of Moustache. They recognised him immediately. There were some people who, on seeing the awe-inspiring deity Arukola face to face, were prone to say that he was not as scary as they had imagined. Even such people were terrified as they saw this character of folklore up close.

In their imagination, the moustache had been thinner, not as black or majestic, and much softer overall. Could hair be endowed with so much vitality? Hair was like the trees that grow rampant near a spring; its surroundings wet, live, ravenous. It maintained the mystery of the secret parts of the bodies of men and women. A hairless face was as devoid of mystery as clean-shaven private parts, whereas a hirsute face was an enigmatic organ, its beautiful wilderness and treacherous paths waiting to be discovered. A man with facial hair was untamed, aboriginal, allowed to eat raw meat, and chase and subdue his mate. But a man who had surrendered his hair was required to exercise self-control, to chew his food with his mouth closed, to mate only with those he could persuade to consent, to pull up the unruly hairs of the land and cultivate the soil.

As the news of Moustache's appearance in broad daylight spread across the land, people assembled armed with weapons, hollering their anxieties at each other.

When the boat reached the deep pool of water where the nun Tharamma had died, the thought of sinking the boat and killing Moustache crossed Velan's mind. But unless Tharamma pulled at his legs from the depths, he would swim away to safety.

Tharamma was born in a well-to-do family that owned fifty acres of fields in Munnattumukham and Kannadi, around twenty heads of plough oxen, and a permanent threshing yard behind the house made of tamped-down fine sand brought over in boats. Even as a nun with a shaven head, she was beautiful, with a voluptuous body and voracious eyes, emanating an extraordinary fragrance that baths, twice daily, could not mask. Her laughter pealed involuntarily, and her vivacious nature got her into trouble with the older, shrivelled nuns at the convent almost every day. Her self-control would disintegrate, like an appam in a bowl of water, when she came across the coconut picker or the milkman, and her body would exude a fragrance that twisted one's heart.

It was because of her grandfather, a man she had never met, that she had ended up in the convent. When her father was about five or six years old, the family had farmed the Pavukari field. They discovered that, despite keeping regular watch, as soon as the paddy ripened and the grains showed their golden lips, someone was helping themselves to it. At other times, a few bunches of harvested paddy would disappear from the threshing yard. One night, the grandfather lay in wait by the edge of the field, and around midnight, he caught the thief red-handed – an old Parayan woman very near the end of her life, named Kotha. The grandfather Mappila, infuriated that Kotha had the audacity to steal his first-quality paddy, pushed her to the ground and kicked her repeatedly. Not satisfied with the punishment, he and his henchmen, inebriated on a mixture of arrack and young toddy, decided to perform an age-old custom that stringent landlords had used to punish hapless Pulayans and Parayans who disobeyed them. They put her in a boat, took her to a spot in the Pamba River, and made her stand in chest-deep water. They tied a copper pot to her neck, and made her fill the pot with river water using a coconut shell. Eventually, the heavy water-filled pot dragged her under, and she drowned. The grandfather and his gang went back home, satisfied that they had successfully upheld tradition.

But when he sobered up, the grandfather could not rest as he began to be troubled by what he had done. He went to the church with his family, prayed hard, and promised the next female child born into the family to the convent to become a nun. But the next five children to be born were boys, and so it was his granddaughter, Tharamma, who ended up fulfilling the promise.

One day, Tharamma, who usually behaved, even at funerals, in a manner not appropriate for those who had taken the vows of chastity and obedience to the Lord, stopped talking or taking part in her daily chores in the kitchen or in prayers. She refused to eat, her eyes and cheeks lost their usual sparkle and liveliness. On the third day, when the senior sisters in the convent pressed her to have some kanji, she told them she would do so after a bath. As they watched her head to the river with a copper pot, alone in the dark, the senior sisters marvelled: 'Does she not have any fear? Of spirits? Or snakes?'

At the riverside, Tharamma laid down the incha she had brought to scrub her skin, stepped into the water, and walked to the middle of the river with the copper pot in hand. The Pamba River, lost in thoughts about the thousands of years before human beings came to its shore, was still, but beneath the surface, the currents were strong. Tharamma tied the heavy, narrow-mouthed pot to her neck with a long piece of cloth that she had brought along, and began to fill the pot with a coconut shell.

The body that floated up to the surface the next day had an unnaturally bloated tummy, which told everyone that Tharamma had been at least six months pregnant. The enraged parishioners went to the rectory, looking for the priest. They were aware that it was Tharamma who brought him his evening meals. They banged on his door, but he refused to show his face. Finally, the old Mother Superior faced them, leaning on her walking stick. Having spent her entire youth in the nunnery in a vow of silence, there was no way she would lie to them.

'As my Lord Jesus is my witness,' she said, 'I have seen with my own eyes a man wading across the fields behind the convent, and breaking the fence in the middle of the night. He had a great big moustache.'

She told them that, like a wild elephant, he would rub his chest and back against the walls of the rooms where the younger nuns lay on mats on the floor and, sweating in the heat of their post-menstrual days, they would lose their minds and flail their wings against the white-washed walls and windows. Only the deeply faithful, astute in their prayers, could get through the night's suffering.

The boat moved forward and, presently, the prodigious fields belonging to Luca Mathai came into view. Men worked the soil with long-handled grub hoes, snorting deeply like bulls, and others broke the clods, while women raked the roots and weeds. Fifteen teams of plough oxen stood on the field edges, gazing at the sky. In the middle of the field, where soil salination had yellowed the paddy, an old man who looked like Paviyan spread handfuls of shell lime from a basket. The returning west wind of the evening blew over the lime dust, sending it down into the soil. All along the embankment were the temporary shelters put up by seasonal workers from the eastern hills.

It was dark by the time the boat pulled into Pallithanam jetty, and yet a large number of people had gathered to see Moustache. His torso and legs, dark and sturdy, resembled aalthadi, an offering made for the goddess Valiyaveettilamma from a mixture of jaggery and rice flour folded in an areca spathe and roasted in hot sand. His back was scarred from sunburn and salty winds. As he climbed out of the boat in the light of the burning torches, they were reminded of the painted folk masks worn by Padayani dancers. The only person who had ever sported a moustache in these parts was a lime-kiln worker, a Chetty, during the time of Mathai's father, Luca. Most of the locals, except for a few boatmen, had never had the occasion to see the man, who had lived alone next to his kiln, in person, nor had they paid him much attention when they did. Besides, his had been a soft, stunted moustache which did not grow beyond a certain point. Still, one time when the elder Luca had come along in the lime boat, it had infuriated him.

'Come here, you tramp.'

As the Chetty came over, he had extended the small knife he used to chop betel buts.

'Sharpen this on a stone and shave that thing off. And don't let me ever catch your face around here again.'

The Chetty had shaved his moustache off with a shaky hand, taken out a small coin, placed it on the boat plank, then scurried off. In those days, barbers were given a quarter of an ana or a handful of paddy as payment for shaving off moustaches. The incident had caused grave embarrassment for Lucachan, and more so when, at a wedding celebration, a prominent Nair had asked him if he would shave his armpits and other parts for him.

On the veranda with its newly built parapet, Mathaichan sat, facing west, on an easy chair. Moustache sat on a wooden armchair. It was the first time he had ever been confined to a chair, and he squirmed as though being bitten by something. Those who had come to see the spectacle had dispersed, leaving Mathaichan, Moustache and Velan alone. In the south-western corner of the front yard, a fire blazed under a boiling pot. The cooking fire in the Pallithanam yard was never put out. It would have a pot of food – kanji, stew or dried tapioca – boiling on it for the workers. It served as a beacon for the boatmen who would mark their routes watching its glow from afar. The two men sitting on the chairs were silent, almost in competition with each other on how long they could keep quiet, Velan thought. This was only the second time that a man such as this, a Pulayan, had sat on the veranda of the Pallithanam house. The first time was when Mathaichan had brought Ayyankali, the social reformer and leader of the Pulayans, in a great show of pomp and splendour.

'That time a boatful of people went to welcome him. And the banana leaf for the feast was laid in there,' Velan said, pointing inside. 'Not that the Master is concerned about such things now.'

'All it will take is a note sent to Thiruvananthapuram. The entire armed police force will be here quickly,' Mathaichan said, careful not to lose his dignity.

He glared at Moustache, his face reflecting the disquiet he felt at facing a man he had only encountered in stories and songs. Moustache's face was unreadable, unlike that of someone with a clean-shaven face.

'The Master has no time for all that, nor does he want to cause unnecessary trouble,' Velan chipped in. 'All he wants is to have his fields harvested and the paddy threshed on time.'

All the while, Moustache did not say a word. His silence perplexed them. When people get together, it is the superior among them that speaks the least, while the others tend to babble on as though aware of their inferior status. As Moustache continued to sit there quietly, their fear and respect for him increased. Mathaichan began to wonder whether his behaviour and bearing were adequate for the occasion – a self-doubt that he had not experienced even when he faced the dignitaries at the Sree Moolam Praja Sabha. The truth was that Moustache had barely spoken a handful of words since the time of Ezhuthachan's play. He had not felt the need, especially because he had a moustache on his face that communicated with those he encountered without the need for words. They say it is only those who are blind that need to use their tongue for tasks other than eating. Those who can see each other should be able to say what needs to be said without using their tongues.

The silence continued until it was time to eat. Mathaichan invited Moustache inside, but he preferred to sit in the coconut storehouse to the south of the main house. The servants quickly cleaned the place and spread a grass mat. The food was served – good-quality Koora rice, buffalo milk curd, pearlspot fish curry made with deseeded, ground chillies.

The mistress of Pallithanam was not fond of pearlspot.

'They say you can feel Kaalan's presence behind you when you eat it,' she mumbled, thinking about the bones in the fish. 'It's a fish not worth putting in your mouth, pretty only on the outside. Why people want to eat it, I'll never know.'

There were other dishes – freshwater shrimps, chicken gravy, fried meat, a pickle of fried snakehead murrel, and lemons cooked with roasted, ground chillies and coconut. To drink, there was arrack, brewed in mud pots, and cooled and distilled through lotus stems. Moustache sat beside a large pile of unhusked coconuts. He was the complete opposite of Our Lord Jesus Christ, and he drank the arrack in a matter of seconds, turning it back into water. Paying no attention to the accompaniments, he laid his hand on the rice, and as though to make up for the centuries of deprivation his ancestors had experienced, he picked up the coconuts one by one in his left hand, squeezed their milk over the rice, mixed it in neatly with his right hand and ate it. It was a sight to behold. Mathaichan's respect for Moustache grew, and when the meal was over, he did not even let him pick up his used banana leaf. And when they returned to the veranda after the meal, their positions had changed, with Moustache now sitting on the easy chair and Mathaichan on the ordinary wooden chair.

'Moustache wants to meet Ittichan,' Velan said, smiling.

'Ayyo! Best leave Ittichan alone, he is too powerful,' Mathaichan said. 'He ran away with Kaalan's ledger once. There's a house with a granary by the side of the field in Karumathra where there's a stone that is worshipped as Ittichan.'

The mistress of Pallithanam, who had come out to the veranda to see Moustache, heard him.

'Who told you Ittichan took off with Kaalan's ledger?' she asked, angrily. 'He went off to become the disciple of the Holy Father, Kadamattathachan.'

Kadamattathachan – or Kadamattathu Kathanar, the priest of Kadamattom church – was well known for his magical powers. The story was, one day, Ittichan waited for Kadamattathachan to retire for his afternoon nap and took off with the book in which the priest had written down the details of all his magic tricks and sorcery. Before leaving, he entrusted the doors and the legs of the bed with the task of responding if the priest called for him. Still, after a while, the priest was suspicious. Finding him gone, he went to Ittichan's house. No amount of banging on the door or creating a ruckus helped. Ittichan did not open the door until he had copied every last word from the book.

'Who told you this nonsense?' Mathaichan countered his wife's story. 'How would you even know? You only came here after I married you. I was born here and have been hearing about Ittichan from the time I was a child.'

Soon, the disagreement escalated; the mistress and the master of Pallithanam forgot that they were husband and wife, and began quarrelling earnestly.

'You shouldn't go looking for him,' Mathaichan said to Moustache when the argument ended. 'Don't try to take him on. Treating snakebites is his main activity these days. No matter how poisonous the snake, he'll sort it out. The people of Kainadi are never bitten by snakes because the snakes here know it is pointless.'

From Onattukara in the south to Karappuram in the north, anyone bitten by a snake would be immediately put in a boat and brought to Ittichan in Karumathra. As soon as the bow of the boat would point towards Karumathra, the person would begin to recover, and when the boat moored there, they would not even need to get off it, and would be treated right there in the boat.

'Ittichan has Vishakantachoodamani in his possession,' Velan said. 'It's the root of a plant that grows only in the deep forest. No one else knows how to identify the plant. If you separate out two strands of its roots, they stick back together if it is the right plant. All you have to do is place it on the wound, and even the strongest poison is rendered ineffective.'

The stories of snakes and snakebites heightened Moustache's interest. He began to wonder whether he and Ittichan were, in fact, the same person.

Mathaichan continued to dissuade Moustache. One of his ancestors had experienced first-hand the extent of Ittichan's wrath. Once, searching for medicinal plants, Ittichan had come to the Pallithanam property. Mathaichan's ancestor was annoyed that he was looking around his property without his permission.

'Itticho,' he called out. 'Why not come every day and weed my yard for me? I might even feed you in the evening.'

Ittichan was embarrassed, and left without taking the herbs he had collected. As he left, he threw a small plant, roots and all, into the well. The next day onwards, a mysterious stomach pain began to affect everyone in the household, and within a week they were all bedridden. Finally, someone close to the family went to Ittichan and begged him to help, and he returned to Pallithanam. With the family and neighbours watching, he climbed into the well and brought out the plant. Then he asked for some jaggery. When the plant was covered in jaggery and placed in the yard, colonies of ants appeared, ate the jaggery and died.

'An ordinary looking weed it was, but so poisonous,' Mathaichan continued his story. 'He was determined to kill off the entire family. And no one would have suspected anything because it was in the well water.'

But the stories had no effect on Moustache. Nothing could stop what was bound to be. So, the next morning, with a great deal of reluctance, Mathaichan sent for a boat.

'I'm happy to go with you anywhere else, but not to Karumathra,' Velan said.

Not one person from Kainadi or Eera would get into the boat. Was there anyone who was not scared of Ittichan? Once, before Alappuzha became a big town, Ittichan was in Punnamada, looking to get across the lake. In those days, the Vembanad Kayal was four times bigger than it was now, turbulent with big waves, and fish that swam in with the surging sea water and defied ordinary nets. When the water was clear, one could see huge rays with fan-like wings prowling the bottom, tiger prawns that could bite off a man's balls, giant barramundi with spines that could pierce and kill a person, and, amidst them, shadowy, indecipherable shapes that could be fossilised tree trunks or crocodiles. Ittichan waited, but no boatmen came along. Finally, he cut off a large banana leaf, put it in the water, and began crossing the lake sitting on it. As he rowed, he raised the bamboo stick in his hand and stirred the air with it. They say that when physicians look at a body, all they see is a collection of vulnerable spots, and that a herbalist cannot defecate on open land because they look around and see plants with medicinal properties everywhere. Ittichan, a man of supernatural powers, saw spirits and forlorn ghosts all around him in the atmosphere, and he was using his stick to clear a path through them.

Finally, two boatmen agreed to row the boat to take Moustache to Ittichan. They were from Kurichi and, like Moustache, they were sceptical of Ittichan's apparent power and prowess in sorcery. They laughed openly at the stories about Ittichan saving the lives of snakebite victims.

'Must be some water snake. Or a yellow rat snake. This is like those stories about those folk in Kumarakam catching a leopard. Turned out, it was a wild cat!'

It was into an ancient time that their boat travelled. A wind, three or five hundred years old, took up, and the lake roiled. Moustache did not see any of the fields he had seen on his way here. They were made, much later, by men, but now, there was only the endless swamp and water.

They pulled in at their destination. One of the men picked up a screw pine thorn and pricked Moustache's hand with it.

'Tell him you were bitten by a screw pine cobra. Now close your eyes and lie still.'

Ittichan sat on the veranda of his house, spinning yarn with a spindle. He stopped what he was doing, secured his bundle, and called his mother.

'I have to go some place,' he told her. 'Three people will come now. Tell them we're unable to treat the bite of the screw pine cobra here. Tell them also that people from Kurichi can't be treated here.'

He split a length of green coconut leaf spine, and gave it to his mother and walked away. When the visitors' boat arrived, she did as she was told, and as they left, she tapped Moustache with the stick.

As the house disappeared from sight, the boatmen rolled with laughter. But Moustache lay still, not laughing. They checked his pulse, lay their ear against his chest and listened to his heartbeat. There was no movement, no breath, no warmth. His feet were cold like dead wood. His eyes were lustreless.

'There'll be no more trouble from him,' Velan had said, even before the boat with the men from Kurichi and Moustache had disappeared down the canal. 'The offering of unniyappam we made for Ittichan won't be in vain.'

'So that's it? Moustache died?' Ponnu asked.

Stories that end abruptly are miserable. So are the fates of heroes who die before the story is complete. In *Ramayanam*, Raman dies before he has a chance to be reunited with Seetha. Indrajit, son of Ravanan, sends Raman, Lakshmanan and the entire army of monkeys to Kaalan's world with his arrows. It was Hanuman and Jambavan, the immortal monkey warriors, who had to struggle to save them and bring them back.

'No,' I replied. 'The story is not over. It's only in the stories that the people of Kainadi tell that Moustache has died. He's still alive in the stories that others tell.'

'Does that mean Mathaichan can now ply his boats without being scared of Moustache?'

'Yes. The people of Kainadi don't have to fear Moustache any more, just as they don't fear snakes.'

Each of us is made of the stories that are told of us. If we look carefully, we can see a train of murmuring stories following each person like the royal mantle follows an advancing king. Some people are not flesh and blood, but fully made up of stories. What is there to do when such a person – Moustache, for example – is killed off in stories?

The rest of humanity, however, was still scared of Moustache because, in their stories, he did not go to Kainadi. In their stories, he was not dead.

18

TWO OTHER PEOPLE

In the memories of the people of Kumarakam and Neendoor, there was another season of rains that had caused great destruction long before the rains that caused the floods where smallpox, snakes and Moustache reigned. At that time, water had risen like never before or after, and had destroyed the fortunes of a lot of important folk even as it built up the destinies of some others. Among them were two people – Illikkalam Avarachan in Kumarakam, and Pachupillah in Neendoor, a man so poor that he did not even possess a family name. By the time the rains ended, the destinies of these two people shone as brilliantly as the sun that emerged out of the clouds.

The month of Mithunam was almost over. Chella was among the women who were beating worms out of the fifty-day-old paddy in the fields. Paviyan had gone off a month earlier to the kayal fields looking for work. Before this, Chella had beaten worms only in the Urumbath field. The rains had held back in the months of Edavam and Mithunam. Still, the paddy grew lush in the cold water that rushed in when the dykes were opened, and in the brilliant sunlight. As the women's song wound to a stop, an elderly woman in the group felt something under her feet, and it brought a cheeky puzzle to her tongue.

'Who's it that bamboozled thousands in waist-high water?'

The women laughed, a hundred different things running through their minds as they thought about bathing in the canals and drenching in the rains. Still, no one came up with the answer.

'You all have mud inside your heads,' the old woman made fun of them.

Chella held up the broom and straightened her back like an old woman.

'I know,' she said. 'It's the snakehead murrel.'

It was a fish that could survive even without water, hiding itself away in pools of mud, and confounding the fishermen who stood in waist-high water to set their traps and baskets.

'Aha! Guess we should find you a better Pulayan for a husband.'

The old woman's response made the women laugh, but they did not hear the sound of their own laughter because, precisely at that moment, in the clear blue sky – or it might have been close to the surface of the earth – there was a crack of thunder and lightning. Such thunder and lightning in the summer, where the flash is simultaneous with the sound, foretold trouble, but this particular occurrence was one that not even the oldest among them had experienced before. The sound echoed across Kuttanad, and people in the kayal fields – in Judji Araayiram, Attumukham Araayiram, Irupathinalaayiram and Kochu Kayal – heard it. It took a while for their deafened ears to recover, and then, the stench of burning meat assaulted them. The workers stepped out of the fields and looked around, but there was nothing to see. It was clear that whoever had been hit by the bolt of lightning had been destroyed beyond any trace. Presently, thick clouds covered the sky like never before, and hung there, motionless, for two more days. Finally, on the first day of Karkitakam, the rains that flooded all of Malanad began.

When the lightning struck, Pachupillah was far away from the paddy fields, on top of Vedagiri Hill, where he was communing with the two hundred and fifty banana trees he had planted in a clearing. Each tree needed tending on a daily basis – tying the dry arms back on to the trunk to protect them from the wind, kicking back the suckers threatening to grow larger than the mother plant, checking on the supports, encasing the fruit bunches so that the fruits grew plump and round. In spite of all this, he felt that the bunches were stunted and misshapen. There had been barely any rain, and this Etha variety of banana needed its base kept cool at all times, and needed watering twice daily. But there was no one else to help with the task of drawing pots of water from the quarry pond below and lugging them all the way up the steep climb to pour at the base of each of the two hundred and fifty trees. The trees had been planted in the month of Thulam to be ready for harvest in time for the Onam festival ten months later. No amount of rain in the interim kept the trees cool as the water drained away quickly in the gravelly soil on top of the hill. Pachupillah's shoulders had broadened from the constant weight of water pots, and the stony land had chipped his toe nails and cracked his heels.

He alone knew the troubles he had to go through to get even this diminished land to cultivate. He had visited every landowning Nair and Christian household around Onamthuruthu in Neendoor, and begged for a piece of land to lease. He would have been happy with any slip of land or field lying fallow after harvest, but no one had agreed. His scornful, slippery attitude put people off. He had a habit of spitting on the floor when he passed a well-to-do person. It was an unconscious habit, but those who witnessed it took it to be a statement of the deeply held scorn of one who lived hand-to-mouth towards those who were well off. Besides, no one had seen any of his ventures come to fruition, and even if they did, it was unlikely that the landowner would see even a clutch of tapioca in tenancy payments. He took over the land that he was given, and then they had to struggle to get rid of him.

Pachupillah was aware of what people thought of him, and he went, with utmost humility, to see Kesava Pillah as a last resort. It was through Mundamattam that Kesava Pillah returned in the early mornings after his nightly visits to his wife's house. After walking up the steep slope, he would stop to catch his breath before descending towards the Asari hutments in a slip of land covered with thorny canthium bushes, which is when he would, punctually and without fail, experience the call of nature. As this was a years-old custom, an Asari woman had taken to ensuring that a patch was cleared off the thorny bushes for Pillah's needs, and her daughter would bring over a pot of water to be used afterwards. In return for this service, Kesava Pillah ensured that two para measures of paddy were delivered to them every year. The usually stern-natured Kesava Pillah was at his most relaxed immediately after he had finished his business, right there in the presence of the young woman, returned the pot and stepped outside.

Pachupillah stood, bowing as low as the earth, in the lane smelling of old and drying faeces, and presented his request to Kesava Pillah. He would like to lease the field that was cultivated only once every two years, where he could plant cucumbers, Kantharipadappan and Ethapoovan tapioca in ridges, with an under-planting of beans. Water was plentiful from the dykes that never ran dry.

Kesava Pillah walked faster in an attempt to avoid him, but Pachupillah kept up, repeating his request. Finally, Kesava Pillah thought of a clever plan.

'Why do you bother with these vegetables? Plant some bananas. You can harvest by the month of Chingam. And they bring in good money.'

Kesava Pillah had been looking for an opportunity to get back at Pachupillah after an incident that had occurred almost two years ago. There was an event, a communal meal for Nairs from all sub-castes who traditionally did not eat together because of rules of pollution and purity. The event had taken place in a specially erected marquee at the Edasseri house. Kesava Pillah had been reluctant to attend, but when some young men from reputable households in Kidangoor came to see him and respectfully made the case, he had decided to go.

'I'll come,' he told them, 'as long as the food is being prepared by someone clean and proper.'

Still, when he got to the event, Kesava Pillah regretted his decision. Folks who did not even have the wherewithal for a bowl of kanji were standing around proudly, with their towels over their shoulders. He felt his ire rising when he saw Pachupillah, a Nair from a lower sub-caste with skin as black as a dark-skinned Pulayan.

'Who are these shits?' Kesava Pillah declared loudly for all to hear. 'Look at this one – it's a Karuthedam, a black-skinned Nair!'

Everyone laughed.

When the mats were laid for the feast, Kesava Pillah was in the middle of the row and Pachupillah at its right end. Consequently, every dish was served first on the banana leaf in front of Pachupillah as though offering it first to the god Ganapathi. Everyone was eating to their heart's content as this was a change from their daily diet of watered rice. After the erisseri was served, a buttermilk curry with ripe mangoes came along, and Pachupillah talked the server into giving him a juicy mango seed. He squeezed it in his hand and licked it, mixing every last bit of juice in his rice, and then, making a circle with his thumb and forefinger, he shot the seed through to the left. Like a stone that children skip across the pond, it landed on the banana leaves in front of several dignitaries before settling, with precision, on Kesava Pillah's.

In the shocked silence that followed, everyone heard the words that came out of Pachupillah's mouth, accustomed to uttering nastiness: 'There. There's the black-skinned nut. Suck it if you want.'

Although his fellow feasters gave him a thorough beating with unwashed hands, the first communal feast in Neendoor was since then known in Pachupillah's name.

'As you say, I'll plant bananas then,' Pachupillah agreed, showing a great deal of humility. 'There are some good-quality corms in the Manakkal field. I'll dig them up, give them a good soak in cow-dung water and plant them.'

'But I'm not leasing out the Manakkal field this time,' Kesava Pillah said firmly.

Pachupillah realised that it was useless arguing further as it would only result in him never being allowed to farm the land.

'Do one thing,' Kesava Pillah continued. 'Plant them on top of Vedagiri Hill. You can start preparing the ground tomorrow itself.'

Pachupillah realised that he had been well and truly tricked. Vedagiri Hill was treacherous to climb. The top was covered in scrub and brush, and underneath them, the soil was stony. Even if the thin soil was dug and planted, there would not be a drop of rain after the month of Vrischikam. In the strong winds, the banana trees would break in half before they had a chance to fruit, unless supported by bamboo poles. But he could not refuse because this was his last opportunity to cultivate anything this year.

'One more thing,' Kesava Pillah said, 'you don't have to pay me anything. I just want to see you do well. It's a shame when a healthy man's children die of hunger.' Pachupillah's second child had died of dysentery six months earlier.

The bananas that Pachupillah planted came up well, but as soon as the young spotted leaves unfurled, the wind tore them into tatters. Still, in the fertility of the untouched soil and the warmth of the sun, the trees grew squat with thick bottoms. He had to water them in the months of Vrischikam and Dhanu. In Makaram it rained, but from Kumbham, Pachupillah broke his back carting water from the quarry pond below. He started his work at four in the morning, finishing it by the time the sun got fierce enough to kill anyone toiling under it within four to five days. Halfway through watering his crop, Pachupillah would take a break and rest, leaning against the wall on the veranda of a Marar's house next to the pond. This was the first time the Marar's woman, the Marathi, had seen a man working as hard as plough oxen. Her own husband seemed to have sworn that the only work he would do was to blow the conch at the temple three times a day, and eat most of the rice he got from there by himself, leaving only a fistful for his wife. She would give the exhausted Pachupillah a jug of buttermilk or salted kanji water. When she stepped out of the house, she would put a towel across her chest, and when the cloth slipped and exposed her breasts with their retracted nipples, soft and grey like the rabbits that emerged out of the dens in Vedagiri Hill to play under the banana trees, Pachupillah felt nothing. His thoughts were taken over by the clusters of banana he would harvest eventually. Each delay in a tree unfurling its first leaves caused anxieties about an imminent catastrophe of crown rot. Even when he finished the watering and came back to the Marar's house to bathe, drawing water from their well and pouring it over his stark naked body, all he thought about was the somewhat stunted banana in the shade of the canopy of a jungle jack tree. As he walked back home in the evenings, he did not see any of the trees or crops along his way. All he saw, everywhere, were Etha bananas.

On the third day of the rains, he returned home with mixed feelings – relief that he would not have to carry water any more, and anxiety that the rains would erode the soil at the base of the trees. For the next fifteen days, he could not leave the house. The yards flooded the next day, and the day after that, water came into the house. The entire land was waterlogged. Even the palaces were flooded as the unruly water rose, impervious to the might of kings. The pleasure palaces built by white men in cool spots up in the eastern hills came floating into the backwaters and the sea. Hilltops became boat jetties. Meanwhile, Pachupillah stayed at home, raising the platform on which he sat higher and higher as the water rose, eventually sitting under the thatch with the snakes and the rats, surviving on dried tapioca, and worrying about his banana trees that would surely have broken in the wind and uprooted in the rain. Something caught in his chest and he tried hard not to think of his crop up on the hill.

By the time the water drained, all of Malanad was destroyed. Paddy fields that were about to be harvested were waterlogged; vegetable crops decimated. Sodden in the unrelenting water, humans and rodents alike died. But Pachupillah was in for a shock as he stepped out of his house. His compound was built on a bit of swamp filled in with soil carried by the headload – a slip of land surrounded by higher ground and shaded by the canopies of trees, where even wild chillies refused to grow. All that grew there was itchy colocasia, arrowroot and weeds. But now, the compound was littered with coconuts as big as human heads that had floated in with the water. He began gathering them up, and before long, almost five thousand coconuts were piled up in every inch of his leaky little house.

When, breathless, he reached the top of Vedagiri Hill, another amazing spectacle awaited him. Only two of his banana trees had fallen. The rest stood radiant in the new sunshine. The stones and boulders had stopped the soil from eroding. The banana bunches on the two fallen trees were mature enough to be stir-fried into upperi and cooked into stews. He cut them down, gave one to the Marathi, and went home with the other.

That year, the harvest festival of Onam was a festival of want. Even those who had money to spare searched far and wide for a fistful of rice and vegetables to cook with. Gods starved in the temples with no one making offerings of rice. Pachupillah sold some of the coconuts, and had the rest pressed for oil and sold it in Athirampuzha market. Traders came from afar to Vedagiri to buy his banana bunches in auction. He sold even the edible inner stems and the corms of the trees. People fought for chunks of corm to be planted in the next season. He had made a decision to leave farming altogether. When God gives a blessing, one should not wait around expecting more; one must put that blessing to good use. So he started lending money on low interest or with parcels of land as collateral.

Kesava Pillah sent someone over to request a banana bunch, but the minion had to return disappointed. When the last of his harvest was sold for the asking price, Pachupillah bought a pot of arrack and set out for Vedagiri Hill one last time. He sat beside a rock with the Marar and drank the entire pot. By evening, the Marar fell into a drunken slumber, and Pachupillah walked down and knocked on the door of his house. The Marathi opened the door in the light of a chaulmoogra oil lamp. Pachupillah put on an expression as though something drastic had happened.

'Marar has swallowed his conch,' he said, careful to retain an expression of disaster on his face and a smile on his lips.

The young woman laughed until her belly hurt. She blew out the lamp. Pachupillah would return several times to that house in the future, but he would not even glance at the hill.

When the lightning struck, Abraham John of Manayanthra bungalow, known in those parts as Illikkalam Avarachan, had fixed the cross staff at the lakeside to the west of his house, and was getting ready to make an offset reading based on two points marked by his assistant, Irulappan. He could see silver strokes of lightning across the Vembanad Kayal and the fields, as the thunder sounded in the clear sky. He pulled out the cross staff, wiped the mud from its spike, and looked up at the sky, carefully watching the storm brewing to the west and the increasing agitation of the lake's surface. He handed over the chains and other instruments to Irulappan, and walked quickly towards Appithara.

Two years ago, in the month of Thulam, he had constructed a long open shed there, a structure with a wide roof supported on areca tree posts. He had set up seven smithies in the shed and appointed fourteen blacksmiths to work them in pairs. One would heat the iron in the anvil, and the other would strike it and forge it. The people of Kumarakam were familiar with the blacksmithing process, but this was the first time they had come across an operation where several blacksmiths worked together and were paid in paddy every evening, and they wondered whether the Illikkalam folk had given up farming and taken up working on hoes and sickles instead. It would not have surprised them because, before arriving in Kumarakam in search of good agricultural land, Avarachan had been part of the famous Vallakkalil family of metal workers who had forged the entire collection of copper pots and pans in the palaces and temples.

Avarachan had a deep interest in iron. Not satisfied with the skills of local blacksmiths, he had gone back to the land of his ancestors to bring an expert blacksmith, a Kollan named Parameswaran, set him up with his wife and children in Attamangalam, and made him the chief blacksmith in his workshop. Parameswaran Kollan was the only person who could build what Avarachan conjured up from his imagination and from the books he read. People wondered what they discussed, hunched over scribbles in notebooks late into the nights, but before long, new instruments – ploughs with chisels curved further inwards than usual, and hoes that did not require their handles to be tightened with a piece of wood hammered through their eyes – came to be used in the Illikkalam fields. His invention of the long-handled blade that could be used to cut the leaf fronds and sheaths of coconut trees was readily embraced by the local people. The harvest sickle that Parameswaran built had blades that withstood usage, and were wide enough to grab and reap three clutches of paddy at a time.

The blacksmiths had stepped out of the shed, hearing the unexpected sound of thunder. Before they could go back to their work, Avarachan arrived and called Parameswaran. If he had to discuss anything urgent, he would come up behind the person, tap them on the shoulder, and walk quickly to a point away from earshot, the distance of which increased in direct proportion to the urgency and secrecy of the matter. Parameswaran understood that, this time, the matter was something particularly important because Avarachan walked further away than usual. It was to a spot they had used only once before, and on that occasion, Avarachan had produced a picture of a clock, hand-drawn on oilpaper, and showed it to Parameswaran.

'Tell me what this is…'

'It's a clock, of course,' Parameswaran had responded. 'But where's its pendulum?'

'It's inside the clock. The white sahebs call it an anniversary clock.'

'But we can't make it until we have drawings of its insides,' Parameswaran had said, thinking about iron gears and torsion levers.

The very next day, Avarachan, ignoring his wife who was about to give birth and the harvest-ready paddy in the Methrankayal fields, had gone off to Calcutta in a boat and then a coal train. When he returned three months later, he had some books and many more hand-drawn pictures. Without checking on his wife, he had sat in the workshop directing his workers. Even when he was home, he was not like the other men of Kumarakam. He created an oasis of privacy by shutting himself in a room, and read books and drafted elaborate plans. Once a week, he went all the way to the post office in Vayaskara to check if he had received any letters. There were only two people who received letters in all of the land south of Kochi – one was Illikkalam Abraham John or Avarachan, and the other was Baker Saheb – the white man they called Kariyil Saheb – who lived in a bungalow by the banks of the Kavanaar River.

This time, Avarachan walked to a punna tree and stood under it, trampling over the hill glory plants flowering underneath, and looked up at the sky again. Like a school of tank goby in clear water, dark clouds gathered in the sky.

'Better stop the work immediately,' he told Parameswaran.

He proceeded to give instructions. The workers were to go to his house and collect a month's worth of paddy, but only after the fires in the smithies were put out, and all equipment dismantled and moved to the attic of the Manayanthra bungalow. Nothing was to be left behind, not even a piece of iron or a chunk of coal. In fact, the workshop shed itself was to be taken apart; it could easily be put back together later. Parameswaran Kollan looked up at the sky and failed to see what the urgency was about. A western wind would easily disperse the clouds. Besides, sometimes when the sky darkened in the west, the rain would fall in the east.

Avarachan was adamant, and everything from the workshop was moved to the attic of the Manayanthra bungalow, followed by the books and papers and instruments from his room. He sold the cows, and set the hens and dogs free. In one corner of the attic, he had bricks laid for a cooking fire, and stores of firewood, dried fish, tapioca and rice were assembled. Finally, the preparations were over, and Avarachan helped his wife and children up into the remaining space above the storeroom of the house. His poor wife, who usually supported his unusual ways in silence, tried to protest this time, but it had no effect. Avarachan had also instructed Parameswaran to take what he needed and return to his home in Chengaram hill.

It was not the first time Avarachan had engaged in what his relatives and neighbours thought of as a kind of madness brought on by excessive intelligence, and so they did not laugh at him. They had always considered him to be caught in a mental confusion that made him immerse himself in activities that were of no use to anyone. Even as a teenager, when others in his age group from well-to-do households, with agricultural land and coconut groves, helped with the chores – ferrying plough oxen and women workers to the kayal fields, or helping germinate paddy seeds by packing them into gunny sacks and soaking them in canal water – Avarachan had attached himself to an old white man who had come to survey the properties belonging to Kariyil Saheb. He had learned to speak English within a month. When the old saheb went back, Avarachan immersed himself in the books he had given him, and taught himself the techniques of surveying. He made a crude, two-metre long wooden ruler, used it to measure his house and compound, and drew up a map of the area. Then he set out to measure the dams, groves, canals and rivers between Attamangalam and Kaipuzhamuttu with a thirty-metre long iron chain that he got made especially for the purpose. People were confounded by the sight of Avarachan and his assistant, Irulappan, dragging this chain through the shit pits and stinky ponds of decaying coconut fronds and husks. Only the otters understood. They kept a watchful eye on Irulappan as he cleared the overgrown canal sides for a straight reading, which, for centuries, had been their chosen sites for depositing their spraint in the daytime. Humans were intelligent creatures, they knew, and they had to measure everything before making decisions, and these men, one fair-skinned and the other dark-skinned, were the first signs of how they took over the best bits of land. More, of all hues, would follow these two. The otters organised guerrilla warfare against Avarachan and Irulappan in Ummacheri, Srambichira, Manchira and, once, near Vallaara, they had to abandon their chain and run away. Still, Avarachan did not give up. They trudged across the fields and kayal lands as they were being drained, and measured them under the scorching sun. Even after the whole of Kumarakam was surveyed and charted, Avarachan's passion for mathematics and geometric concepts was not sated. If a coconut tree leaning dangerously over a house had to be tethered and pulled into a different direction, he would only begin the task after calculating the right angles involved.

This time too, in the first few days of the rains, people failed to realise that Avarachan's actions were not irrational. The compounds in Kumarakam flooded routinely during full moons and high tides. This time it was rainwater that caused the floods. Women made good use of the opportunity, and filled up their water pots. Men caught spiny eels and pearlspot that swam in with the floodwater. Children spiked banana trunks together and made rafts. This was land that needed the floods. How else would the turds deposited into the canals from the branches of cottonwood and flowering mallows leaning over the water reach the salty waters of the lakes? How else would the canal water remain clean enough for the parched field workers to dip their cupped palms in and drink?

Within a week, things changed. The rivers Kaipuzhayaar, Kavanaar and Pennar burst their banks and submerged Arpookara, Aymanam and Parippu, and the Koduraar River took Pallam, Nattakam and Kodimatha. Water from the east flowed down, and the Vembanad Kayal came up to meet it in Konchumada and Kannadichaal. Like the captain who abandons his ship at the first sight of trouble, Baker Saheb evacuated with his family to the bungalow on top of the Olassa hill, from where he watched anxiously as the land his father had raised from the lakes returned to the water. No one in Kumarakam died as they all knew how to swim. Those who stayed back, expecting the water to drain quickly as usual, watched the staggering currents that uprooted coconut trees and toppled houses. From Kavanattukara to Kaipuzhamuttu, three rivers joined together to form an endless expanse of water that flowed into the lake. Some folk took their lives in their hands and swam to the clamshell mounts in the jetty, where they survived for fifteen days on rainwater. Meanwhile, up in the attic of Manayanthra bungalow, Avarachan and his family lived well. Even in the panic of the water level reaching the rafters below, his wife felt proud of her husband. Concerned that the water would reach the attic soon, she wanted to evacuate into a boat, but Avarachan took off a palm frond from the thatch, examined the sky, and assured her that there would be no need for it. He measured the strength of the current below with a coconut tied to a string, and just as he'd predicted, their cattle barn and coconut store collapsed on the day before the water began to recede.

Finally, when the floodwater drained fully and people returned to the devastation of fallen huts and canals filled with debris, they had to face another danger. It was a washerman in Ummacheri, anxiously considering the fate of the clothes that were in his possession and were now lost to the floods, who saw the leopard in the dripping greenery by the side of the canal. It was eating a dead goat, and it looked up angrily at the washerman before running away. It must have got hurt as it fought against the currents that brought it down from the eastern forests, because it was dragging one of its hind legs. The next day, there were sightings in Kunnappalli and Nalupanku, and when it took a bite off the side of a calf in Nashnanthra, people stopped walking alone, and got together in groups at night to clank pots and pans to scare off the animal. The only person with a gun, Baker Saheb, had not returned. The master of Vishakhamthara and the Mappila from Nellanikkal went to Kottayam to report the sighting to the police to no avail. The entire land was recovering from the flood. The water had only just retreated from the palace.

On the third day of the leopard sighting, Parameswaran Kollan and Avarachan took a boat towards the Nasreth church. Avarachan had a double-barrel gun in his hand. People knew he would not fail to hit the animal as they had seen him practise almost six months earlier, aiming at imaginary targets in the deserted lake near the church. They chased the limping leopard from its hiding place in the man-high grass near the Muthan temple all the way into the churchyard. It was surrounded – the lake on two sides, the canal on one side, and humans armed with stones and sticks on the fourth. The leopard surrendered, and Avarachan shot it dead.

Six boats accompanied Avarachan on his way back home. Some people took the dead leopard to Alappuzha in a boat to submit as evidence to the authorities. Months later, the Pravruthyar brought a letter sealed with a conch-shell mark to Illikkalam. The letter informed Avarachan that he had been given an award of fifty rupees for shooting dead a leopard that had terrorised the people, and he was to go to the Tehsildar's office to receive it.

Avarachan set out the very next day, planning to walk to Kottayam. He went to the church in the morning. Then, dressed in his best mundu, a folded towel on his shoulder, and another towel tied around his head with its ends fanned upwards, he picked up his gun.

'Do you really need to take the gun?' his wife asked.

She was scared of seeing or touching it, and glanced at it anxiously.

Avarachan smiled and hoisted the gun on to his shoulder. There were many in Kiliroor, Kanjiram and Illikkalam who had, thus far, not had the good fortune of seeing a gun. He would give them a chance to see it and feel the pangs of desire.

19
BRENDON

In the stories told by the people of Kumarakam, it was on the day a young man named Ouseph – some people called him Little Saheb – brought a twelve-foot shark to the market canal that Moustache first arrived there. Little Saheb was a born fisherman, one who could put his hand in a puddle and pull out a fish. His eyes rarely left the numerous canals, gullies and water channels that criss-crossed Kumarakam. When he was not in the mood to get into the water with his nets, he would stand on the banks and catch fish with sharpened wooden arrows. In the evenings, as people sat on the embankments drinking arrack and relaxing after a day's work, he would set wagers with them and retrieve objects that they threw into the water with his arrows. So confident was he of his marksmanship that, one time, in an arrack-fuelled moment of audacity, he had put a ring around the ear of one of them and sent an arrow flying through it.

The salination of the waterways after the recent floods was more widespread than usual. Saltwater had surged beyond the check-dam at Cheeppunkal. Excited, Little Saheb rowed his boat further out, beyond Thanneermukkam. When the waterways were salinated, schools of sardines, mackerels and rays would come in from the sea through the Kochi seaport. But Little Saheb was more interested in flathead mullets and pomfrets. A fat pomfret, cooked in coconut milk, was one of the tastiest things to eat, and there was a saying about not sharing it with others, not even its head, and not even with one's favourite brother-in-law. The sun was hot and, after a while, Little Saheb stopped at a coconut embankment and climbed up to rest. He was about to slip quietly into sleep when he heard a loud splash. At first, he thought it was children diving into the water. But when he took a look, what he saw was a great white shark! Accustomed to living in the sea, it was struggling to breathe in the salt-depleted water. Ouseph jumped into the water and stuck two long-oars on either side of the shark, slanting them to join at the top, thus imprisoning it. Then he tied one end of a rope to the horn-like fin protruding from its back and the other end to the boat. Calling out to Muthan of Vilakkumaram for protection, he began rowing vigorously, holding his life in his hands. He had to row straight across the lake. If the shark struggled even once, he and his boat would be destroyed. As he moved through the lake, a feeling of disquiet took hold of him. Something was not quite right. The lake was perfectly still, with not even a ripple on its surface. There were many who had died while collecting clams in the mangroves around the islet of Pathiramanal. Their spirits hung around the area; boats passing by with big catches made them jealous, and they were known to follow them. They had seen Ouseph with his shark. He turned in their direction and urinated, making sure that the stream of piss made the mark of the cross on the surface of the water. This action calmed the souls of the dead and returned the lake to its normal nature.

Moustache's journey into Kumarakam was a meandering one that took him through the uninhabited lands of Varambinakam and Kareemadam, and then Vattakayal, where he swam across the Pennar canal. The paddy fields were fallow and no one saw his progress. Further up, near Ithikayal Lake, women washing cut-up fish in its water and children angling for minnows raised their heads to look at the hero of the songs they had sung not two months ago at the harvest, but, like everyone else, they too did not see Vavachan, only his moustache. The young boys playing by the canal did not see him as they were engrossed in the jellyfish with umbrellas above their bodies – as small as their fists and as big as their heads – that had come in as the water was salinated. They slapped their slimy legs and gloopy floating limbs with sticks, and caught the little ones and put them in inky water in coconut shells. They would release their blue bodies into the canal later. Moustache knew that children always spoke the truth, and he tried to ask them about Seetha.

The market canal had shops that opened on to the waterfront selling groceries, salt and coconut. By the time Moustache approached it, a large crowd had gathered to see the great white shark tied to a coconut tree. There was a particular pleasure in gazing at the majestic tusk of an elephant, the shapely comb of a black rooster, or the horn of a shark. Men from well-to-do families and merchants on passing boats started a bidding war for the shark, and Little Saheb egged them on, showing off its size by pulling at the rope and raising it from the water.

It was a bright day, and yet a sudden sense of gloom spread across the market canal. The dark shadow of Moustache – the man in the terrifying stories that had followed the merchant boats from the mouth of the River Periyar to Thottappally, and from Alappuzha through the endless waterways to the east – scared the bidders and they fled. Their sleep had been disturbed by recurring nightmares in which he would jump upon them with a sharp knife as they rowed through the deserted waterways of Kuttanad. And now, seeing him in person in the middle of the busy market terrified them. Meanwhile, the man who was the cause of their terror turned westward from the canal bank behind a shop blocking his way. Trouble followed him.

Furious that his sale had been disrupted, Little Saheb picked up an oar, and ignoring the warnings of the traders, followed Moustache. Just as he reached the village school, Moustache was felled with a blow to the back of his head. Little Saheb was a strong man who could easily carry two sacks of rice on his back at once, a feat he was fond of displaying for the enjoyment of others. What happened next is described differently in the many stories and songs about the incident. Even the few eyewitnesses would tell the story differently later, picking and choosing details, changing them as they saw fit.

Moustache got up, swinging his left arm. It connected with Little Saheb's lower jaw. The blow broke the side of his face, and an eye protruded out of its socket. People came to his aid only when they were certain that Moustache was long gone, and they took him in a boat to a medicine man in Veloor.

That was the night Parameswaran Kollan prepared for a dangerous task. He decided to go in search of Moustache. He had taken to plying his trade from home after Illikkalam Avarachan, enraged by the baseless accusation that he and the blacksmith, in their late night sessions at the smithies, were minting counterfeit coins, had dismantled the shed in which the smithies operated. So now, people said that the cunning Avarachan had made as much money as he could, and had destroyed the evidence before he could be apprehended.

Parameswaran Kollan set out in search of Moustache in one of Avarachan's boats. Old age and arthritis had weakened one side of his body, but he rowed the boat by himself. Avarachan had also become weak, more as a result of his neighbours' suspicions than of old age. Those who want to live a life of nonconformity should have the ability to ignore the wagging tongues and malicious minds of the imbeciles around them. Avarachan did not possess this ability, and he had abandoned many of his experiments halfway through because of the thoughtless comments uttered by mean-spirited people. The final blow had been the news that the secret police were conducting enquiries about him. He lost his spirit entirely and became bedridden. The sahebs had become suspicious of his activities, and the letters he wrote to the British government and to universities in England requesting information and technical drawings about metalworking had come under scrutiny. Putting random bits from these letters together, the authorities had come to the conclusion that Avarachan was trying to build a cannon. Enquiries about his house revealed that it was situated in a strategic position – a cannon placed on the west of the house could take out the entire water transport system of Thiruvithamkur. And if he made a second one and placed it in one of the wild, uninhabited islets in Kochi Kayal, land up to the Arabian Sea would be within its range. A World War was underway, and the secret police had been sent to keep a close watch on Avarachan and his activities. It made him shut himself up in his room, abandoning his books and scribblings. A bout of fever and shivers followed, and he took to his bed, seemingly never to rise out of it again, barely eating one meal a day, and that too only if he could be enticed with his favourite side dish of colocasia leaves.

In the darkness, Parameswaran Kollan searched each and every canal side from Kannadichaal to Konchumada. Mutherimada and Pathupanku were deserted. All across Chazhivalarthukari, Ponmanthuruth and Puthuval, there was nothing in the darkness except fireflies and the sighs of jungle fowl. Finally, he entered the backwaters. On the northern end of Appukayal, beyond God's Corner where the new fields dredged up from the lake began, the waves were tumultuous enough to make anyone call out to the gods. But before he could head out in that direction, he saw a movement on an embankment without even a shadow of a coconut tree, and he rowed towards it. He found his quarry anointing his moustache with the oil from a treadwheel.

By daybreak, they were in Avarachan's room at the Manayanthra bungalow. Avarachan's wife brought tea in bell-metal glasses for the three of them. Moustache took a sip – his first ever taste of tea – and spat it out.

'Don't worry about it,' Avarachan said.

He sat up in his bed, leaning against the headboard.

Moustache looked at the strange things scattered around the room. Large chunks of magnets, shiny like bald-headed children, lay attracting iron filings. A map of Kumarakam that Avarachan had prepared was on the wall, the rivers, canals, fields, orchards, churches, temples and cemeteries marked with different symbols. In one corner was the free-standing clock he had received as a prize at an industrial exhibition in Madras. On hearing about this achievement, a man named Gandhi had sent Avarachan a letter of congratulations. The letter, which had arrived from Kottayam to the Baker bungalow in Olassa, had been delivered in a special boat by Baker Saheb himself. After this incident, Baker Saheb, riding on his horse, had begun to visit Avarachan and invite him to Easter and Christmas feasts at his house. He also had Avarachan survey and draw up the Baker family lands in the east near Melukaavil.

'All of which was pointless, I understand now,' Avarachan told Moustache.

He extended his swollen legs.

'A long time ago, when Guruswamy had come to visit, he'd made a prediction, which I think has gone completely wrong.'

Spreading his message of compassion and social equality, and tirelessly working against the caste-ridden society, Sree Narayana Guru – people fondly called him Guruswamy – had been travelling all over the land. When he had come to Kumarakam, all the Chovans had gone to pay their respects. The Pulayans and Parayans had stood aside, watching from a distance, but Guruswamy had called them to him. The Nairs and Christians had stayed away, but the drumbeats, and the hustle and bustle of boats bringing people from all over, did not escape their notice. In the morning, Guruswamy wanted a glass of cow's milk – the only food he had in the morning – and the enthusiasts who stood around had been distressed as they had not prepared for this eventuality.

'Forgive us, Guruswamy,' one of them had said fearfully. 'There are no milking cows around here. There's one in Illikkalam, but she kicks at anyone who touches her udders other than her calf.'

Laughing, Guruswamy had handed a bowl of water to him.

'Wash her udders with this,' he had instructed them. 'She won't kick. Not today, not ever.'

That evening, Avarachan, who had been a young man then, had gone to see Guruswamy.

'Were you planting coconut saplings during the day?' Guruswamy had asked him. 'Agriculture is a noble occupation. Pleases the heart. Your trees will fruit well. Name the grove Krishnavilasam. But I know your real interests lie elsewhere, which is also good.'

Guruswamy had presented Avarachan with a coin and said, looking at the crowd that surged outside: 'Thiruvarppukara is a good place, but the people are no good. Kumarakam is the opposite.'

Avarachan drank his tea and told Moustache: 'We can accept only some of the things these venerated people say. Not all of their predictions come true. There's not one coconut tree in Krishnavilasam that hasn't set fruit. And that cow has not kicked anyone after that. But the people ... They're horrible in every land. Even Guruswamy was abandoned in the end. They didn't crucify him like Jesus Christ but they did make him carry the cross.'

It was on his way back from accepting the reward for killing the leopard that had terrorised the people after the flood that Avarachan had lost his faith in humanity. As he was coming down the hill, gun in hand, head wrapped in a towel, and the prize money safely tucked in the waist-fold of his mundu, a man in uniform had stopped him.

'Take the towel off your head, you rascal,' the man had commanded.

Avarachan had removed the towel and put it on his shoulder, released the lower fold of his mundu, and lowered the gun to the ground. He was well versed in the sciences, but had no clue about the science of managing people.

'Where did you get this gun?'

'I made it myself.'

Avarachan had proceeded to explain how he had killed the leopard and received a reward for it.

'Keep the stories to yourself. Even His Majesty the Maharaja obeys the laws of the land. Do you have a license for this gun?'

Avarachan had tried to fall at the feet of the man in the uniform, but he had grabbed him by the waist and lifted him up.

'So you admit you killed a leopard, eh? Now you can spend a few days inside. How many people have you killed with this homemade gun?'

The terrified Avarachan had finally handed over the prize money to the man in the uniform, and was let go. The gun was put in the attic that day, and Avarachan had never again touched it.

'It's all very well to say that we must do good for others, but see what happens if you do,' Avarachan said. 'Kick them, and they come sidling back. But do something good and they take you for a fool.'

Moustache had remained silent all through this, which made Avarachan suspicious. One must be wary of the silent types because their minds roil like an ocean. Hollow things make the most sound – a coconut shell, drums, a conch. Those whose minds are empty jabber on in order to cover up the emptiness, whereas those who are caught up in the agony of their own thoughts speak only to themselves.

'I've been hearing about you for a long time,' Avarachan said.

He raised the lamp and looked carefully at Moustache.

'I know much of it is the figment of people's imagination. There's no point in asking why you decided to grow a moustache and wander about without home or hearth. Trying to figure out why people do what they do is futile. Besides, if lots of people do strange things, that's supposed to be all right. But if one person does something different, then everyone starts meddling. One is allowed to be crazy only if the whole land is crazy. Still, tell me, where is your native place? Is there a purpose to your wanderings? Looking at you, you don't seem that old. But the songs … They make you seem about a hundred and fifty years old.'

Finally, Moustache made a sound. He cleared his throat but did not speak, and as Avarachan and Parameswaran Kollan sat there convinced that he would never speak, he said, 'I'm looking for a woman. I lost her a long time ago. I also want to know how to get to Malaya.'

It was not a full response to his questions, but Avarachan was satisfied. Why would a person who is in search of a new life in a new land concern himself with his old life?

'I've never been sure if there's any point in pursuing women,' Avarachan looked towards the kitchen and said in a low voice. 'Never understood the appeal anyway. A fleeting bit of pleasure, that's all there's to it.'

Parameswaran Kollan nodded in agreement.

'And Malaya … Well, I bet there's as much grinding poverty and war there as here. But there, people might leave you alone, and not get on your case for growing a moustache or wearing a mundu.'

Parameswaran Kollan tried to bring the conversation back to Avarachan.

'You don't seem too ill, child. You'll be out of this bed soon.'

'Child' was how he had always addressed Avarachan.

'Well, I don't think so. This will be the end of me,' Avarachan replied.

By then, it was light outside. The lake that had swelled and surged now lay placid as though it had attended a feast at the Baker bungalow. The wild mulberry and sneezewort on the banks shook their heads even though the air was still. Skeletal figures with gill nets went about in boats. Muddy water that flowed into the canals from the fields drained for planting stained the edges of the lake.

'People, the whole lot of them, are scoundrels. Still, there's one more thing I'd like to do before I die. Some of us are born for these things, and we should do them at least for our own happiness.'

Avarachan and Parameswaran Kollan were the type of people who could turn random bits of iron into machines. But there was one machine that had confounded them so far. Avarachan had read all the books he could find on the subject, drafted several technical plans, but nothing had been fruitful. Still, he was determined to complete this job before his time on this earth was up.

'I've met with so many white people, corresponded with many more, and most of them are the respectable kind. Their only complaint about us is that we are unhygienic, that we shit in the open and wash our butts with our hands. But there's one white man who is utterly wicked, a chancer who's always looking to succeed even if it destroys the rest of us.'

George Brendon Saheb. Avarachan's animosity towards him had two origins.

The object Brendon had invented was something that Avarachan or Parameswaran Kollan should have thought up. Indeed, Avarachan believed that he should have been the first person in the entire world to come up with the idea. Waterwheel workers working the circular treadwheels set on the bunds of the fields – the large ones with twenty-four blades and the smaller ones with fourteen blades – was one of the first sights he had seen in his life. Normally, irrigating the crops was the most difficult thing in agriculture. But with paddy cultivation in Kuttanad, with the fields lying below sea level, the most difficult task was to drain the fields. The water demanded constant attention, and all through the farming season it was kept under control by redirecting it into smaller fields through drainage channels cut into the soil, and by pedalling it up with the treadwheels. Several workers would sit together on a platform set to one side of the treadwheel, pedalling according to the levels of water measured in the coconut shells in the canals, and egging each other on with songs. The incessant pedalling would make the workers believe that life itself was a giant wheel that needed constant turning, pushing each blade down with one's feet only to have another one come rising up to one's navel, sating the hunger with one meal only to have another mealtime come rolling by.

The first time Brendon Saheb came across waterwheel workers was when he had come to rescue and repair a boat that had broken down in Aamachal and lay half-submerged in water. It was his first time in Kochi as he had spent the time before the World War in South Africa, looking for gold mines with his brothers. A short while before that, the German submarine Emden had bombed and destroyed the Madirasi seaport. Brendon had expected the war to intensify in the Indian Ocean, with more ships arriving at the seaports in Bengal and Malabar in constant need of repairs and a quiet place to have their oil changed and engines refurbished. He set up a workshop in an uninhabited islet in the Kochi Lake. But the war had ended abruptly, and as many ships as he had anticipated never materialised. Still, his foresight and intelligence had impressed the engineer, Robert Bristow. He dredged up the lake beds around Brendon's islet expanding it to a sizeable island, and gave it the name Willingdon Island after the Governor of Madirasi.

Brendon left the boat in his workers' care, and went out to watch the operation of the waterwheel. He took some measurements – the height of the bund from the field, the depth of the canal, and the surface area of the water. At the beginning of the next planting season, he arrived in a large boat loaded with a kerosene engine. As the boat turned into the canal from the lake, he caught sight of the Illikkalam house and the tower clock in front of it. The crude build of the clock made Brendon, whose family owned a watchmaking business in London, laugh out loud.

'He said I'd made a clock that should've been made a hundred years ago.'

Avarachan remembered. Brendon's laughter still wounded his soul.

'He can laugh. The Brendons have mines and companies and orchards and ships all around the world. But Illikkalam Avarachan lives in a crocodile-infested swamp in Kumarakam.'

Brendon Saheb dismantled a waterwheel, and got his workers to dig a parakkuzhi – a large ditch for the water to collect. Into the parakkuzhi, he set a para, a cylindrical wooden suction duct, with a rectangular discharge duct called a petty on top. He then produced an instrument wrapped in gunny sacks. The workers were given strict instructions to remove the gunny sacks only after the instrument was submerged inside the para. This was the secret of Brendon's invention, and he would not have anyone copy it. Finally, with a great roar, the engine came alive. And people watched astounded as the water, which had terrorised the people of Kuttanad through the ages, came sidling up, and the fields emptied before their eyes, leaving the black creepers, goosefoot and other water weeds in the mud. Panicked by the sudden disappearance of their world, catfish and perch stood on their heads, and snakeheads hid in the mud. People rushed roaring into the fields to collect them with baskets, sieve nets and even their bare hands. And those fields that had been dredged up from the Vembanad Kayal and had remained unnamed until then were given the name Brendon Kayal.

'Unlike the naysayers around here, I'm usually the one who sees the good in the things the British brought over,' Avarachan said. 'Trains, for example. Don't they let everyone in? Didn't they build a road from Kottayam to the east through the deep forests as far as they could? You should see the line of bullock carts on that road now.'

He urinated loudly into the bronze spittoon that his wife fetched for him, and checked to see if he had splashed his mundu.

'But this guy, Brendon, is not the same. His charges for draining a field are exorbitant. And he won't take paddy. Insists on money. On top of that, the owner of the field has to feed the overseer and the workers who operate the engine. At first, he would only take the fish caught in the net set on the petty, but now he won't let anyone fish in the channels either. And he won't let anyone near the engine floor. Someone will copy his invention, he reckons. That would upset his monopoly, wouldn't it? So much money he makes from the fields in Kuttanad after each season.'

'It's his invention. Let him make money.'

Moustache's response angered Avarachan.

'Well, I'm not like you. I don't concede that. Some Chovan must have invented toddy tapping but that doesn't mean it's only his family and relatives who do it now, is it? And is it only Vaalans who eat fish because the fishing net must have been invented by one of them? Those fishing traps that can be opened and shut … Valadi Kuttappapanickan was the first to make them, and others made them afterwards. That's what should happen when one invents something. Not bundle it up in gunny sacks and pop it secretly under water.'

Avarachan realised, as he watched the silent Moustache, that they were men with entirely different concerns. It made no difference to Vavachan, the son of Paviyan and Chella, whether the fields were drained by engines or by waterwheels. When harvests were over, duck herders would let the water into the fields in Chozhiyappara, and soon after that, the bunds would be opened and the fields would flood, sending water snakes and kraits into Paviyan's hut on the embankment, where they would take shelter in the thatch. Having grown up with the crawlers falling on them as they slept, Vavachan and his siblings had lost their fear of snakes quite early in their lives.

Avarachan was not especially skilled at reading the human mind. Still, he thought that Moustache had other intentions. His real goal was not the woman or Malaya, but the moustache itself. He wanted to become the moustache, Avarachan supposed, leaving his life to be filled in by everyone else through the stories and songs that emerged on the banks of the lake, the rivers, the thousands of small waterways that flowed into the lake, and the deserted and desolate lands caught amongst them.

'Do me a favour if you can,' Avarachan said. 'By the first of next month, the fields in Pathupanku will be sowed. They've started draining the water from day before yesterday. It's a new engine, and four workers and an overseer have come with it. Go there tonight with Kollan. It's bound to rain tonight. You just have to make an appearance. These days, people are scared even of the shadow of a haystack, thinking it is you.'

A man from Palluruthi named Kunjikannan was the overseer of the motor in Pathupanku fields. Pathupanku – Ten Share – was land raised up from the lake and shared equally between ten people. It would take at least a week to drain the water that surged in from the lake. The dykes were overgrown with grass and sedges and waterlilies as the fields were not cultivated the year before, and the four workers had come to clear them. Three of them went to the Nellanikkal house for their evening meal, and brought back something for the overseer and the fourth worker. The overseer liked to drink stinky, sour, two-day-old toddy. As he sipped it from a coconut shell as though it was sugared water, he wondered whether he might be able to arrange some company for the night. He had been to Edathua, Muttar and Thalavadi with the engine but it was his first time in these parts. In all of these places, he had readily found companions for the night, or it had been arranged for him. He was willing to pay whatever was required, and even to go wherever he had to.

'It's not possible, maestri,' the worker said, nipping his desire in the bud. 'The women here are Chovathis with balls. They barely service their own husbands unless they want to. Also, we'll go back tomorrow, and you'll be on your own. There's not even much moonlight. Be careful. Don't let an otter bite off your thing.'

From tomorrow, the only sign of life would be the whistling ducks and the baya weavers. At the first roar of the engine, they had taken off, but had returned later.

'Say that to your...' the overseer made an obscene gesture with his finger in the light of the kerosene lamp. 'I've worked this motor even in Pandarachira. Even four days ago, on the way here, there were those robbers who got in the boat.'

The robbers had been a man and a woman. The woman's face had been marked by smallpox, and one of her eyes had closed shut before she was fully cured.

'Those with nothing to lose don't need to be scared of anything. And there was only some kerosene, the engine, a couple of lengths of wood and iron in the boat. I lifted up my mundu like this and showed them my thing. Told them they could have it.'

'You could've taken the woman.'

'Aw ... She was a devil. One of Moustache's people.'

'You saw Moustache?'

'No, but I know they were his people.'

Before he could take another sip of toddy, the overseer felt a humming silence. A dark shadow entered the engine hut. They scrambled up. The shape gestured to him, and the overseer switched off the engine, picked up the lamp, and protecting its flame from the breeze with his hand, followed him. As the water quieted, the older man with Moustache murmured something, but Moustache held up his palm and stopped him. The overseer wanted to challenge him but he cowered when Moustache turned his face towards him.

Moustache dived into the parakkuzhi and came back up.

'It's shaped like a pot. With leaves around it.'

'Just as Avarachan said – an impeller,' said Kollan. 'Do one thing. Use your hand and measure the pot and the leaves.'

Moustache dove under the water once again. The thought that if the engine was switched on now, the man in the water would be cut to pieces, went through the overseer's mind. He tried to summon up his courage thinking about Brendon Saheb and the saintly figure of Arthunkal Veluthachan, but he stood frozen in fear, holding the kerosene lamp aloft. After what seemed like years, Moustache surfaced again. But Kollan was not satisfied with the measurements he tried to convey with his hands, and when he asked for the measurements of the curve of the leaves, Moustache climbed out, and stood stark naked and irritated. He walked down the side, and as the overseer watched, he broke the shaft that connected the impeller to the engine, as easily as picking a flower. Hoisting the iron shaft, strong enough to dispel the efforts of an elephant, and the impeller on his shoulders, he walked away without glancing at the overseer. Kollan followed fearlessly behind the man who terrified everyone else.

Before the next harvest, Avarachan hired a carpenter to make the petty and para out of jungle jack wood. Kollan made the impellers. Avarachan ordered two engines from Madirasi, which were brought on a ship to Thrissur and from there in a boat to Manayanthra bungalow. The first engine was installed in the ninety-acre fields in Pallippadam, and Avarachan christened it 'Parameswaran' after the blacksmith. The second one, installed in Venattuthuruthu, was called 'Parvathi'. Parameswaran Kollan's wife was Paru, short for Parvathi. Avarachan made a third impeller out of wood, and this one was called 'Vavachan' after his great grandfather. Avarachan was not acquainted with Vavachan, son of Paviyan from Kaipuzha. He was acquainted only with Moustache.

20

LITTLE SAHEB

Sometimes it can feel as though what happens now is what is yet to happen, or what has already happened. Sitting with Avarachan, Moustache would also have felt this, and he would have thought that Parameswaran Kollan looked like Velan and Avarachan resembled Pallithanam Luca Mathai. But things did not reveal themselves with clarity, as those were incidents in another time, from another life. All that remains of lives lived and stories told are shadows.

No one, other than Avarachan, believed that it was because of his influence that Baker Saheb – the local people also called him Kariyil Saheb – took Moustache in. Avarachan had not been able to understand why someone would want to go to Malaya when there were so many other places in this world.

'Why would a person leave his land and go away?' he asked, partly to himself and partly to Moustache. 'Because he wants to live as another. When we leave our native land, we can forget our lives thus far, forget our own names even. Start over from scratch. In a way, it's an attempt to fool the Lord. To cut off halfway through the one life He gave us, and to start another one. But it should not be like the mackerel and the sole trying to swim back into the sea after wandering into the lake. We have to think of ourselves as someone else. But you … you don't have a land of your own to leave, do you? Or is it that the whole of Kuttanad is your land now? In any case, what use is it to go away unless you leave everything behind? You want to take your moustache with you, which means your name will be the same wherever you go. And then there's the woman. You say you want to take her with you. You can't have both worlds. Either you keep the woman and the moustache and live on here, or you get rid of both and go away to a place where you'll be left alone to fend for yourself, and get on with your life without people constantly hassling you to know the name of your father or your parish church.'

When it was full dark, Moustache got into the boat and picked up the oar.

'Go to Baker Saheb,' Avarachan told him. 'Tell him I sent you. No policeman will come looking for you there. They pee in their pants when they see the white men. There's no place that the Bakers don't know. He's a farmer, but his father and grandfather were preachers wanting to convert every person around. It's funny if you think about it – even our Lord Jesus Christ didn't have such a plan.'

Baker Saheb's coconut grove was so vast that it was difficult to cover it on foot. Four Paravans from Vechoor were brought over to harvest the coconuts, but the job was never-ending, and so they became permanent workers in the grove. They would start harvesting coconuts at one end of the grove, and by the time they reached the other end, it would be time to climb the first trees again. Each harvest yielded at least four ripe bunches of coconuts from a single tree. It was when Baker Saheb began coconut farming that the local people realised coconut farming was not about plonking a coconut in the soil and letting it grow. The Saheb planted his coconut trees in an orderly manner; the distance between the trees was such that the rainwater dripping down the leaves of one wouldn't gather around the base of another. Each year, before the rains, circular trenches were hoed open around the base of the trees. Before summer, these would be filled with old husks and palm fronds to retain moisture, and sprinkled over with lime followed by cow dung from the heap behind the barns on the fifteenth day. Once a year, they were treated with dried fish brought over from Alappuzha by boat. The crowns were tidied, old spathes and debris removed, and a mixture of salt and copper sulphate sprinkled. The Saheb devised a trap, setting toddy in sections of the green stalk, for the sugar-hungry rhinoceros beetles. In the mornings, workers climbed the trees, picked out the beetles in their drunken slumber, and sent them to the next world by bashing their heads in with stones. There were coconuts, farm workers and sahebs in the next world too. While the coconut trees in the compounds across Kumarakam stood stunted with yellowing leaves even fifteen years after planting, Saheb's trees bore fruit within five years. He was of the opinion that those who helped themselves to tender coconuts, or stole bunches of ripe coconuts without permission should have their hands cut off. He forbade toddy tappers from entering the grove – a single tapped inflorescence is a loss of several mature coconuts. Instead of selling his coconuts at the market, he pressed them for oil at home in a mill operated by oxen, and Konkani wholesale merchants of coconut oil from Alappuzha Mullakkal Street arrived in their boats at the bungalow on alternate days to buy it.

There was one person who did not care about his rules – fisherman Ouseph, Little Saheb. He climbed Baker Saheb's coconut trees whenever he felt like it, cut down coconuts and sold them for whatever price he wanted. He simply was not scared of Baker Saheb.

Every morning after breakfast, Baker Saheb, dressed immaculately in a pair of khaki shorts, a half-sleeved shirt with pockets, a hat and a pair of shoes that came to just below his knees, ambled on horseback around his orchard. He had a short lathi-like stick in his hand and a modest moustache with a pointy end. To the workers tending to his land, his stature as their superior was written into his white skin, and his moustache and attire underlined his position as someone much higher in status than even the police. He had an instinct for identifying those who tarried in their work, and the womenfolk marvelled at his ability to appear before them just as they were stretching their backs. But what angered him most was coming across a woman who, in order to do her work – pulling weeds, husking coconuts or chopping copra for the oil mill – would have taken off the piece of cloth or towel tied around her breasts. He would jump down from his horse and rush towards her, stick in hand. Pointing at a grazing cow with a full udder, he would ask her what difference there was between her and the cow. His father, the preacher, had been the same. It was he who had started the custom of paying the labourers in cash rather than in paddy, but there was no work on his land for any woman who came without covering her breasts. When it became difficult to find such women, his wife, the Madamma, gave them upper garments made of coarse cotton to cover their breasts, underarms and upper backs. As they went about their work, they imagined how much better they could work if they were not trapped within those coarse garments that rubbed against their skin and caused painful welts. Only when they got off the Saheb's property and removed the garments could they breathe properly.

With the arrival of Moustache, Baker Saheb's morning amble along his coconut orchard took on the grandeur of the procession on the final day of the festival at the temple of Vaikkathappan. The Saheb's small moustache had been enough to frighten his workforce, but now, with the dark shadow of the big moustache in front of the horse, they were terrorised into complete submission. A regular pattern was established, with Moustache leading the way, followed by the Saheb on the horse, and behind them, the ledger writer and the clerk who distributed the wages.

The workers guessed that Moustache lived in the room behind the stables, where the African woman Baker Saheb had brought back to look after the horses from his last trip home to England also lived. Her job was to oil and massage the horses, and feed them boiled horse gram mixed with pebbles in the evenings. Horses were inclined to gorge on the horse gram which made them lie down on the ground, and when they did, it was a difficult job to raise them again. The added pebbles kept them searching for the horse gram in the feed, and by the time they ate their fill, it would be morning. The African woman had a statuesque body, with large breasts and a magnificent behind. She showed no signs of embarrassment as she organised the mating of the horses and cattle in the narrow barn, the cows and mares restrained on short leashes, and the bulls and stallions controlled by ropes attached to her arms. With

Moustache's arrival, nighttime fishermen brought their boats close to her room, straining their ears to catch the neighs and warbles rising above the sound of the waves, and wondered to whom the loud cries that emanated from the room belonged.

It soon became clear, as they watched the Saheb teaching Moustache to shoot the gun, that he had not taken him in to scare the workers or to control the African woman. But the complexity of the gun confounded Moustache, and he broke it in his second attempt to fill its barrel with gunpowder, husks and ground glass. From the next day, his training moved on to throwing a sharpened iron spear into the crocodile-infested pond in front of the bungalow. This training too did not last long as he was already proficient in it.

'The Saheb knows how to do these things already, doesn't he?' wondered the womenfolk watching the training.

'Maybe he doesn't want the blood of his sibling on his hands.'

'Half sibling,' others clarified.

When he first arrived, Baker Saheb's father, Preacher Saheb, had operated in the east, beyond Thodupuzha, with his father and brothers. Like Saint Francis had done with the Arayan fisherfolk on the coast, they sprinkled holy water on the Arayan tribes in the hills, changed their names, and invited them into the coffee plantations they had established in the hills. But when the cold killed the coffee bushes, the Baker brothers abandoned them and came down the hills. For a long time after that, when they went alone to worship at their shrines or to work in the hills, the Arayans would imagine seeing, in the swirling mist, a white-skinned old man stroking his grey beard and staring into their souls and at their gods. Scared of the bearded white man, their gods withdrew into the darkness of the hills.

When his brother, Henry Junior, settled in Melukavu, Preacher Saheb – whose name was A.G. Baker – came to Kavanattukara, and used his savings and the money borrowed from Mannoopparamban Mappila to dredge up a part of the Vembanad Kayal to make an orchard. There, he built a two-storeyed house, its foundation laid with thick logs of teak brought over the water in barges. This idea had come to him as he watched his workers bring up unblemished pieces of thousands-of-years-old wood as they dredged up the lake's bottom. Wood submerged in the Kuttanadan mud was preserved forever, so would the foundations of the Baker bungalow. He asked for permission to convert the locals and to build a church. The Diwan granted permission, but only to convert the Chovans and the communities below them in the caste hierarchy. Preacher Saheb was pleased with the response as he was only really interested in converting those who were used to hard work and had the physical strength for it.

Preacher Saheb invited the Pulayans, and instead of serving them food in pits dug into the yard, he fed them in plates. He gave them new names. Thus, Panackal Pulayan and Chemban Pulayan became Chacko and John when they went to work in his plantations, and when they went back home in the evenings and retrieved their old names, their prayers were heard by Jesus anyway. Preacher Saheb gave the naked urchins pieces of cloth to tie around their waists, and sent them to herd cows. In the evenings, when they returned with baskets of dung laid by the cows during the day, and tied the cows safely in the barns, they were given milk in a coconut shell and a boiled egg. The Chovans, multiplying like crows between Thiruvarppu and Vechoor, came to work on his plantations, but they did not accept his faith as they had their own gods and worship groups. Some of them had money, and there were healers, astrologers and woodworkers among them. Consequently, Preacher Saheb did not like the Chovans. He thought them arrogant, prone to climbing on rooftops and proclaiming their wealth as soon as they had two coins to rub together, and to talking back. But his wife, the Madamma, only wanted Chovathis to help her in the kitchen, and they impressed their mistress with their energy and neat habits. They found her kitchen habits bizarre. No catfish – black, golden, moustached or otherwise – or murrel or snapper were cooked in it, only milk fish, barramundi or prawns. The Madamma used only the middle pieces of the milk fish and barramundi, leaving the much tastier heads and tail pieces for the kitchen help to take home. She had a borma built, and baked cakes and bread in it, and the leftover pieces became feasts in the homes of the Chovathis.

The Madamma's constant companion was a woman whose husband was a waste of space. Her jobs were to wash and iron the clothes, and dust the rooms. Her husband had no inclination to tap toddy, to catch fish or to produce children, and whiled away his time drinking arrack. In the nights, the Madamma read to her from the English Bible, explained the meaning, taught her to make the sign of the cross and to pray on her knees. She named her Theresa, and made the other servants call her 'Thresyamma' or 'Theyyamma'.

But the gospel of the good lord did not change the predisposition that Theyyamma, daughter of Karuthakutty who had died while stealing paddy, had of helping herself to a large piece of fish or a handful of kokum whenever the opportunity arose. One day, when the Madamma was away in England and the whole kitchen was in her control, she secreted a bottle of alcohol and was on her way to her husband when Preacher Saheb caught her. He was not one to follow the teachings in his own Bible and forgive people. There was a small windowless room with a dirt floor next to the room used to store dried coconut and coconut oil – the Saheb's personal jail. All infractions were punished by imprisoning the culprit in that room for a designated number of days.

Preacher Saheb loved the rich black soil of the land and the amphibious life it nurtured, but he hated the people of the land, especially the women. He considered them wretched creatures with dirt under their fingernails, crusted nostrils, and matted hair hiding lice that sauntered on to their faces from time to time. They hid away their mud-darkened bodies during their menstrual periods, using dried banana leaves to soak up the blood. They emanated a stink like duck enclosures. Their breasts were dry, backsides narrow, heels caked with mud, and their bloodless faces had a stunned look. Their rheumy eyes were half-closed, ears leaked from infections, and toes oozed from ringworm. Still, one night, when all the workers had left, Preacher Saheb imagined that the fragrance of frankincense was emanating from the room where Theyyamma was imprisoned, and when he picked up his Bible, his fingers entangled themselves in its most problematic pages.

Banished from the bungalow, Theyyamma stood on her knees with her swollen belly, and continued making the sign of the cross and praying in a language that was neither English nor Malayalam. When she heard that a boat was leaving on the day of Makam to bring Guruswamy, she calculated the days until his arrival, cut down an almost mature bunch of Poovan banana, and set it to ripen. There was to be a delay in Guruswamy's arrival, and it caused her to forget about the banana bunch which was ripening inside the little wooden box on which she sat to rest her feet swollen from the pregnancy.

Guruswamy arrived a month later than scheduled, and the lake and the canals filled with boats. People from Pambadi to Chengalam and Vaikom to Kurichi came to Choorapparamban's copra yard, neatly dressed, and bearing gifts of banana and rock sugar. A Paravan who tried to jostle his way to the front of the crowd was pushed back by the Chovans. He was a coconut picker and they decided he had a powerful body odour from climbing the trees, an odour that did not diminish even after bathing with incha and gram flour.

'Tell me,' Guruswamy asked them. 'Who smells worse? A person who goes up the coconut tree once a day or another who does that twice a day?'

The Chovans were toddy tappers who climbed the trees in the mornings and in the evenings. They hung their heads in shame, and threw their tapping knives in the canal, vowing never to use them ever again.

On his way back, instead of going straight into the lake, Guruswamy's covered boat moored at the shore. Unusually for the afternoon, the lake was unsettled, making it impossible to row westwards. Theyyamma's house stood at the point where the land ended and the lake began. The boatmen placed a chair in the yard for Guruswamy to sit on while waiting to continue his journey. Theyyamma's belly was fully extended now, the childbirth imminent, and as she stepped into the yard, she was mortified. The smell of decaying day-old prawn shells pervaded the place, and she worried that Guruswamy's olfactory senses would be offended by it.

When it was time to eat, one of the disciples said to Theyyamma: 'Would be great if you had a banana for Guruswamy.'

'You do have some, don't you?' Guruswamy asked, as Theyyamma stood worrying about where to find a banana.

She went inside the hut and opened the box in which she had stored the bunch to ripen. It was perfect. Not one fruit had decayed, there wasn't a single black mark on any of them even though a whole month had passed.

When it was time to leave, Guruswamy pointed to the manjaadi tree in the yard.

'Don't cut this tree down,' he told Theyyamma.

He stood beside it and closed his eyes for a moment, and then, to the astonishment of everyone around, he picked up the three or four stones below it where a lamp was lit every evening. These were stones where snakes hid, where the Madan dwelled.

'We don't need these here any more,' he said, and tied them in a bundle before putting it in the boat.

People believed that it was to get rid of Theyyamma's son, Ouseph, once and for all that Baker Saheb had taken on Moustache. Moustache had already defeated him once, as soon as he had arrived in Kumarakam, an event many had witnessed or had heard about. According to some eyewitness accounts, the battle between them had lasted for hours, and they had fought across the land from the market canal to Vilakkumarakayal, hurdling over compounds and swimming across canals. Ouseph too was a strong man, well built, six and a half feet tall like his father, Preacher Saheb. He had green eyes and golden hair. A good aim and a deft left swing. He could cut down a bunch of coconuts with his teeth. He looked like a saheb, except for his slightly tanned skin.

From the time he was a toddler, Theyyamma had taken him with her to work. The Madamma never again admitted her into her kitchen, but she did the less physical jobs around the backyard. Ouseph joined the cowherds, helped with collecting the coconuts and watering the plants in the yard. But he refused to accept his wages directly from Preacher Saheb in the evenings, forcing him to hand it over to Theyyamma.

When he was older, he decided to give up all other jobs in favour of the most liberating job there was to do, a job that had no one above him to control him, or anyone below him to boss over.

'Don't have to eat shit to live,' he told his mother.

He had to work only if and when he pleased. The only disciplining was done by the lake itself, and he set out into it with his boat and fishing net.

He who had been called 'Ouseph', or 'Little Saheb' by people who could not be bothered to find out his real name, was never able to fully free himself from Preacher Saheb. The colour of his skin, and the thoughts that roared in his arrack-addled mind linked him with his father forever. He wanted to believe, with all his heart, that the Chovan who was Theyyamma's husband was his real father, and that his fair skin and golden hair were the malicious handiwork of someone who wanted to create a rift between them. Every evening, he brought the best of his catch and some freshly brewed alcohol from the islets for the man he believed to be his father. He carried him in his arms to the healer when he was ill. By then, Preacher Saheb had become old, and whenever he came across him on one of his horseback rides, Ouseph picked up bits of coconut husk, mud clods or anything else he could lay his hands on, and pelted him with it. Everyone knew that he could easily summon the police or the army and have Ouseph buried in the swamp, but all Preacher Saheb did was to slowly cut down on his journeys to enquire after the well-being of his converts until, one day, he stopped completely.

After Preacher Saheb's death, Ouseph took to pelting his son, the soldierly, disciplined Baker Saheb, known also as Kariyil Saheb. The new Saheb was the complete opposite of his father. He paid no attention to missionary services, and focused on agriculture. He planted new saplings and strengthened the embankments, began farming the church fields. He had over a hundred heads of plough oxen. He lent money to his workers on the condition that they worked for him until they paid back the capital and the interest. The unruly among his workers were tied to the mango tree in the front yard of the bungalow, and lashed. The variety of that mango, which produced unusually long fruits, would later come to be known as 'rascal mango'. He built new farmlands in Kollam and Vaikom. Unlike Preacher Saheb, he showed no interest in the landscape, flora, or fauna of his land. He brought, from England, a refrigerator that ran on kerosene, and drank the water fetched daily from the hills of Olassa instead of the murky, odorous water from the Kavanaar.

Still, like his father, Kariyil Saheb too refused to respond to Ouseph's attacks. It enraged him that Ouseph got into his canals, and helped himself to the harvest when there was no fish to be had in the lakes during the lean months. Kariyil Saheb had two sworn enemies, one a human, his half-brother, and the other a water-dwelling creature. With Moustache's arrival, it was clear that one, or both, would meet their end.

It was in the section of the woods set aside as a bird sanctuary by Preacher Saheb in the western corner of the bungalow that Moustache and Ouseph saw each other for the second time. Moustache was setting traps to catch the pythons that feasted on the Saheb's poultry, while Ouseph was in the process of cutting down a bunch of coconuts from a tree that had been uprooted. Watching the scene, Moustache wondered whether the tree had laid itself down at his feet of its own accord. In the olden days, coconut trees used to bend their heads to the Chovans, and the paddy would hold dried and ready-to-pound grains for the Pulayans. They changed their habits because of human greed.

Once, a coconut tree bent its head so that a parched Chovan could take one of the tender coconuts and have a drink. The impatient Chovan scolded the tree: 'Why can't you have this cut open for me?' From then on, the coconut tree refused to comply with anyone's needs.

And a hungry Pulayan woman asked a paddy plant: 'Why can't you hold rice on your stalks instead of paddy?' From then on, the paddy held only green grains that needed to be steamed, dried and pounded before turning into rice.

This time too, the size of the moustache or the songs and stories about it did not affect Ouseph. He was not the type to be intimidated, not even by the ocean.

'Are you the one who's come to finish me off?' Ouseph asked, holding aloft the long-handled machete with its blade sharpened in sand.

Moustache did not feel the need to respond. He had not come to kill anyone. Quietly, he set about fashioning a basket trap, bending reeds made pliable with fire. Common pierrot butterflies flitted around his moustache thinking it was a plant. Snakes usually travelled a set route, one that their ancestors would have used for eons, and anything strange along it would alert them to danger. So the trap, baited with a small chicken, had to be set a little away from it.

Ouseph tried to bait the silent Moustache.

'You're with that horse now, I hear. Irupathettichar!'

Ouseph had used the obscene word – irupathettichar – because it usually enraged even the most conciliatory person. But it had no effect on Moustache because he did not know what it meant. Someone had called Paviyan this word once, and he had come home outraged and beaten Chella and the children until his anger had diminished. Karkitakam irupathettu, the twenty-eighth day of the month of Karkitakam, was the one day of a year when Pulayans, as though affected by temporary insanity brought on by hay mould, went around pretending to be upper-caste masters; the one day their masters did not dare step out of their houses. They drank toddy and walked the roads otherwise forbidden to them on that day, but the Pulayans never lost their senses, or their etiquette. The Parayans, on the other hand, made good use of the day and acted on their grudges. But the unforgiving masters had caught up with these 'irupathettichar' – twenty-eighth-day scoundrels – and cut their throats as well as the custom. Paviyan's father, Kankali, had forgotten this, and had ventured out on the twenty-eighth day of a Karkitakam, never to return home again.

'They say human beings have four lives,' Ouseph said.

He squatted next to Moustache with his machete hanging off his shoulder, pretending that he was not going to quarrel with him.

'The lives of a horse, a donkey, a dog and an owl. Right now, you're prancing around like a horse, but soon you'll be weighed down with heavy loads like a donkey. Then you'll get pelted with stones like a dog, and finally become an owl with nothing but the hmm-hmming.'

Moustache remained passive, so Ouseph continued. Perhaps he felt that he was addressing Baker Saheb himself.

'I pelted Preacher Saheb with mud, like the dog that he was. And he died humming like an old owl. The children of thieves don't end up with a full belly.'

This was said with a sense of certainty, but Ouseph was not fully convinced that good begot good and evil spawned evil. These were mindless maxims spewed by human beings to soothe themselves, so that the vulnerable could survive and the privileged could continue exploiting others. The world was full of the children of scoundrels, and they were eating well.

'You can escape if you want,' Ouseph said softly, nodding towards the lake. 'Swim away.'

Was that a smile on Moustache's face? He was not sure. Did he smile because he had already criss-crossed the lake several times over, or because only someone who was attached to a place, had roots, would fear for their safety? Still, Moustache considered his suggestion. His quests – Seetha and Malaya – were far away from here. The Saheb had come here from a land where there was plenty to eat, and was busy producing things that he did not like to eat. He would not know the way to Malaya.

There was a movement in the lake, and Moustache walked to the edge of the water. Ouseph, thinking that he had finally paid attention to what he had said, followed.

'Don't go that way,' he said, pointing to the northern corner of the Appukayal.

It was the place where Guruswamy had discarded the stones he had picked up from the houses and bottoms of trees on both sides of the lake.

'Jesus, sahebs, swamy ... They've all only just arrived. Those beings were here from way back. You watch, they'll all come back, climbing out of the water.'

The day after Guruswamy left, Theyyamma's husband developed sores on his leg that did not heal until a month later. Every year after that, at exactly the same time, the sores resurfaced like the wounds from the bite of a Russell's viper. It was the curse of those who were ousted from their seats of stones under the trees without ceremony or succour. Once, when Ouseph was a grown man, he went into the canal in front of the house to harvest fingernail clams for the evening meal. In the salinated water, in the middle of the clams sprouting like measles, was a stone that had returned from the depths of the lake, looking for its old abode. Ouseph picked it up, washed it and placed it under the manjaadi tree. His father's leg healed and the sores never came back.

Moustache watched the water as it moved and settled. He saw something shadowy, like a piece of fossilised wood, moving away as though having recognised the man watching it. Moustache jumped into the water, holding aloft the pointed iron bar he had practised with. The creature, which had existed in these parts before Paviyan and Kankali, before the sahebs, before the time of the fields, tried to escape, hoping to avoid the extinction of its kind on that day.

21

THE LAST CROCODILE

It was clear who the Last Crocodile was waiting for, as he lay quietly in a corner of the Vembanad Kayal where the water level was low. Marsh harriers, little ringed plovers and spoonbills rested on his motionless back, taking it to be a ridge of sand or a strip of sediment. The ability to remain perfectly still and endless patience were his specialties, and he was willing to wait as long as it took. He had no more interest in the fish, or in the short, black-skinned humans who entered the water. His lonesome vigil, now, was only for one person – George Alexander Baker, the man they called Kariyil Saheb. In the single-minded focus on his goal, he did not experience the isolation of not having seen any of his kind for a very long time. He had become like someone who had come to the end of their life without having married or procreated, someone who was already considered non-existent. It was accepted that he too would soon be no more, and nothing of his kind would be left.

As he followed the Last Crocodile, iron spear in hand, Moustache imagined he was Thanulinga Nadar and the Crocodile was himself, and that the lake was the Kariyil canal. Who would win this battle? Would fate stand by the vulnerable, and leave the other upside down in the mud? Like Nadar, the Crocodile and Moustache would leave no one to follow in their footsteps. To them, the salty lake was what the Tamirabharani River was to Nadar. The people around the lake feared them just as the people along the riverside had feared Nadar, and they would forget them in a very short period of time just as they had forgotten Nadar. Knowing that the Crocodile would face him head-on at a deeper spot in the lake, Moustache turned back, found a boat, and went after him in it.

In the long history of the crocodiles that went back thousands and thousands of years, human beings were the last creatures they had encountered. From the time the vast lake had formed, muggers and swamp crocodiles had lived in it alongside other creatures, and as the water was salinated, huge saltwater crocodiles had also come into the lake. They spread inland eastwards through the waterways, the five rivers and the countless canals, built dens and laid eggs, floated log-like in the Veerambuzha River and the Kaithapuzha Lake, sunbathed with their families on the sugar-sand islands of Perumpalam, Pallippuram, Pathiramanal, Vaittilathuruthu and Nediyathuruthu.

The crocodiles had ignored the black-skinned humans when they first began to appear along the ragged slivers of land that stuck out of the swamp and water, aboriginals – Pulayans and Parayans – who had put up huts and hovels. The sludge came rising up from the bottom of the lake, offering foundations for their dwellings. They sowed just enough seeds for their meals in the patches of land where the water receded, caught the abundant fish that jumped out of the water straight into their hands. The crocodiles were spoiled for choice too between the fish and the otters, and the birds that entered willingly into their open mouths as they lay sunning themselves on the banks. The taste of human meat, unfamiliar in their cultural memory, did not entice them. Legend has it that a fifteen-foot crocodile, on his travels east along the River Periyar, had pulled a young boy into the water by his legs. But it seemed as though the boy had made a pact with the crocodile, and the crocodile held him in the water long enough for him to convince his distraught mother that he should be allowed to seek the path of asceticism and renunciation before releasing him unharmed and swimming away. The boy in the legend was Sankaracharyar, Adi Sankara, the mystic philosopher.

There were even incidents, however rare, where the crocodiles had come to the aid of the humans in crucial moments. Once, a Chetty from Madurai had been forced to run away with his family when the king had focused his lecherous eyes on his wife. After wandering around for a while, they had reached the lands west of the lake, and one night they had braved the lake in a tiny boat, hoping to make some kind of living in Thazhathangadi. It was the month of Thulam, and a storm had risen up, threatening to capsize their boat. Their screams of fright and prayers had been heard by two prominent crocodiles in the Kavanaar River at the time, the brothers Chemban and Irumban. They had appeared on both sides of the boat, and although the family was terrified by the sight of the crocodiles, they had arrived safely in Olassa, with the crocodiles holding their little boat steady in the water.

It was the second encounter between the Last Crocodile and Moustache. Their first meeting was when, early one morning, arising from a sleep filled with dreams about the Crocodile, Baker Saheb had taken Moustache in his boat to Vilakkumaram Lake. Dreams seen early in the mornings came true. The Crocodile was under a mulberry tree, lying half in and half out of the water with his eyes closed, lost in the memories of the proud lineage of his people: crocodiles who had single-handedly stood up to man-eating sharks with mouthfuls of saw-like teeth; cultivated severe personas by ignoring those beneath them; attacked wild animals that came floating down the rivers; appeared majestically to accompany the vessels of the kings. There were those who had continued to disdain humans with the last flicks of their tail as they lay dying from the cruel hunting techniques of the humans. It was only six or seven generations since they had started having to battle the two-legged creatures, as their rapidly expanding tribe had come down from the hills and forests into the swampy lands that they quickly took over. The sludge stopped rising voluntarily out of the water, and they had to dig it up to make solid ground. The early Pulayan lands became Mundadithara, Pottanthara, Pavuthara, Naarakathara, and Kalathara. They dredged up the oozy mud and stomped it into fields. Mud had an innate truth – in the fields where it was wet, it held on to the moisture and let the paddy soar, and on the bunds where it was dry, it held firm and refused to let moisture in. The rightful area of the crocodiles' existence shrank rapidly, but they were not worried. How much damage could these weaklings do, they thought. They ignored the industry around them and lay on the embankments. Little did they know that the humans would attack them.

At Vilakkumaram Lake, Baker Saheb took a shot at the Last Crocodile, and the bullet hit his armour of skin, but all it did was dislodge some of the barnacles from his back and wake him up from his slumber to escape. The Saheb criticised Moustache for not making a second attempt immediately. He believed a bit of ridicule was needed to make people like Moustache become more determined.

When the son of Henry Baker Senior, A.G. Baker – the man people called Preacher Saheb – had come down from the High Range to the western lakes, all he had in his heart was Jesus Christ and love for the flora and fauna of the land. Although he was born in India, he had studied and married in England. During his student days, he had become acquainted with Grosvenor, the son-in-law of Alexander Graham Bell, who would later become the president of the National Geographic Society, and the editor of its magazine. Encountering the extraordinary variety of aquatic life and birds, and the godless people of the land, he had decided to settle by the banks of the Kavanaar River. He observed the migratory birds that arrived in the swamps of Kumarakam as he dredged up the mud to create orchards. He saw himself in them, living out their lives across two continents, flying back and forth with unerring sense of direction and only the Good Lord as their saviour. They too held on to two names and two identities. The cattle egrets of one land became kalimundi in another, yellow bitterns became manjakocha, and Alfred G. Baker became Preacher Saheb. He set aside part of his property and let it grow wild for these migrants, and night herons, openbill storks, great tits, wagtails and black-headed cuckooshrikes made it their home. The Saheb took his early morning constitutionals breathing in the funk of their droppings. By then, he had become the local correspondent for the National Geographic Magazine, and his writings about the wildlife of the waterways of Thiruvithamkur appeared in almost all of its editions.

He wrote an entertaining essay comparing *Horabagrus brachysoma*, the golden catfish of the local canals, to the bamboo sharks of the sea, both of which laid their eggs in bunches that looked like grapes, describing in great detail their life cycle, their golden-yellow colour, the black spot on their fin, and the long stripe that ran from their gills to their tail fins. He was the first person in the world to write about the common emigrant butterfly and the fragrant screw pine. Before he embarked on the study of saltwater crocodiles, a camera arrived at the Baker bungalow all the way from England. Unlike their attitude towards other humans, the crocodiles considered the Saheb with a great deal of tolerance in those days, and they posed for him willingly as he pursued them across the kayal fields deserted after the harvests, allowing him to take several pictures – a baby crocodile on its back, a mother crocodile guarding her eggs – that challenged the limits of photography at the time.

The local people had hunted crocodiles even before Preacher Saheb's arrival, but stories of their counterattacks were rare. It was easy enough for ten or fifteen armed people to batter a crocodile on land to death, but the only ones people carefully hunted were those that ate their goats and calves, or those that had become habituated to a place. The crocodiles became dangerous if they were disturbed while mating or guarding their eggs. Like tigers, they were protective of their territory, and the relentless encroachment into their land of the human species that dug up their lakes and cleared the banks of their waterways made them jittery. There were instances where humans were wounded when they entered the water in the night to see to the dykes and bunds, but none where crocodiles had eaten a man.

The downfall of the crocodiles really began only when Baker Saheb, born and brought up in Kumarakam, took over from Preacher Saheb, and they watched, unbelievingly, as this puny human embarked on a mission to wipe them off the face of the earth. Baker Saheb rationalised his actions counting the ducks and cattle lost to the crocodiles, but the real reason was that he had become obsessed with the taste of crocodile meat after having eaten it for the first time in Africa. The tough meat sometimes tasted like a combination of chicken and crab meat. The belly meat reminded him of fatless pork, and the leg meat had the taste of frogs' legs. The tail meat was his favourite. And it had other properties too – it made him perform four times better in bed. It protected against asthma, arthritis and skin diseases, and strengthened the bones.

So it came to be that as man ate crocodile, crocodile began to eat man too. Fear of being struck by lightning did not stop anyone from going out in the night. Nor did they stop lighting their hearth for fear of fire. But death from being swallowed whole by an animal was something they could not conceive of experiencing. The people of Kuttanad were used to an amphibious life, but for the first time in their lives, they began to fear water. Clay diggers and fishermen began to imagine things pulling at their legs. Crocodiles that rested peacefully on the surface of the water were replaced by those that moved fast and lashed with their tails. They came out of the water and charged at little children.

The most feared of them all was the eighteen-foot mugger, Kariyaat Crocodile. He was large enough to swallow a person whole without having to tear him into pieces first. With that, the demand for Baker Saheb and his gun spread outside his own property. Like a saint carrying the cross, he hoisted his gun on his shoulder, and shot crocodiles all over the lake. He brought their carcasses home, and posed for photographs before hanging them upside down and skinning them. He dried the meat, and preserved the skin which had several uses.

Kariyaat Crocodile was the Kariyil Saheb among crocodiles. They were both beings of the black earth of Kuttanad. Kariyaat Crocodile ate as many humans as the crocodiles killed by Kariyil Saheb. In the animal kingdom, the flesh of the female of the species had a superior taste. Sow meat did not have the smell of pig meat, and it was the same with goat or water buffalo, so Kariyaat Crocodile had a particular preference for female flesh. He was free from the ancestral inclination to roam within his own territory, so he would venture outside of Pallathuruthi, his home, to Kavalam and Kainakari, and up to Thanneermukkam before swimming back into the paddy fields and canals of Kumarakam, spreading terror in his wake. He survived for over a decade without even a scratch, despite policemen with guns and large crowds of people armed with whatever weapons they could lay their hands on chasing after him. During the time of his terrorising reign, outer bunds lay without repairs and paddy cultivation reduced in the kayal lands. Children stopped learning to swim, and washing clothes and bathing moved on to the banks of the canals rather than in the water itself.

The day the dry lightning struck, heralding the great floods, women who stepped into the Koratti fields climbed back out quickly. An unbearable smell of decay assaulted their nostrils. The water had not started rising yet; the rain screeched and screamed only on the bunds. Parayan folk did not work the Koratti fields. The presence of Parayans and menstruating women angered these fields which only tolerated Chovans and Pulayans. The awful smell led the women to a bamboo-reed thicket which, much before their arrival, had been abandoned by the nesting birds. And there, in the middle of a large circle of charred reeds, the half-burnt carcass of Kariyaat Crocodile lay on its back, majestic even in death. There was no one on this earth who could have killed him. His carcass, as though being exhibited by the sky in the desolate silence, with its belly split open, made the women faint. It was full of gold ornaments, from the expensive palakka necklace worn by the well-off to the tiny bit of metal on black thread worn by the poor. Kariyaat Crocodile was attracted to female human flesh, and the gold and metal in his belly had attracted the lightning.

The order to systematically eradicate crocodiles from the Vembanad Lake and its surroundings was passed by the government after the arrival of crocodiles that would capsize boats in Maniyaaparambu. A battalion of twenty-five policemen armed with guns were deployed with Baker Saheb as their leader. In addition, groups of young local men were organised in each area, and they were rewarded for every crocodile carcass they brought. Crocodiles toppling small transport boats and duck herders' narrow boats were unheard of in the past, but when the humans banded together, they reciprocated by travelling in groups. A deep spot near Maniyaaparambu canal was allotted to the Pulayans to build their church, and as they were raising the foundations with clay clods brought over in boats, the godless crocodiles killed ten of them.

By then, Baker Saheb had become addicted to killing crocodiles, and not just because he liked their meat and skin. Their meat had once helped him perform like never before in bed, but now, even on nights when the Madamma was feeling frisky, thoughts about crocodiles irritated his mind like grains of sand. Their death struggle, and the blood spreading into the saltwater, aroused him more than the lustful mutterings of his partner in bed, and he woke up early in the mornings and practised with his gun, shooting into the pond and studying the deflection of the bullets in the water. The workers in his orchards did as they pleased, since his attention was elsewhere. The arrival of the white man had changed many of the thousands-of-years-old traditions of the land. Perhaps he felt that it was only with the total eradication of the crocodiles, primordial dwellers of the land, that the white man's presence could be stamped indelibly on its surface.

The Saheb began to feel frustrated with the slow pace of killing crocodiles, where he had to wait for someone to alert him to the presence of a crocodile and kill them one at a time, a process that took too much time and human resources. So he devised a plan to complete the government order in fifteen days. Led by him, local enthusiasts and the policemen, who had been put up at the bungalow and at the Annie Baker School, patrolled the waterways in boats. Their main targets were the deserted islets and outer bunds where the crocodiles came ashore to bask in the noontime sun. In one day, in Pathiramanal alone, they killed and buried around fifty. On the second day, they cleaned up Pallathuruthi and Venat Lake. Enthused by this progress, local folk cleared the banks of waterways and set upon their hole nests, stuffing straw into them and setting them on fire. Within the allocated time, the Saheb finished his task southwards from Aroor and, disbanding the group, moved into Kochi Lake on his own. The Kochi government allotted two Irish sharpshooters to help him.

Finally, having completed his mission, Baker Saheb returned to farming. People continued to seek him out when there were strange movements in the rivers or the lake, and he continued to take care of the remaining isolated animals. By then, the Saheb came to hate crocodile meat, and the Pulayans of Maniyaaparambu finished the construction of their church. The saintly figure in the display box made of jungle jack in front of the church was also a white man who, just like the Saheb, sat on a white horse dressed in trousers. The creature impaled to the ground at the end of his long spear was not a dragon, but a crocodile.

The Saheb began to suffer from terrible nightmares in which he choked on tough crocodile meat. He would wake up from these dreams with acid reflux, and would step outside and stick his finger down his throat, trying to dislodge the irritation. In the darkness, he would look at the lake, motionless with no waves or tides, quiet like a household where all the children were dead. Not even a breeze flitted along the water.

Through all this, the nest of the Last Crocodile, under the spreading roots of a verungu tree, had gone undetected, and he hunkered down in it with his mate. They had no interest in human flesh, and filled their bellies on fish and birds, venturing out only in the cover of darkness. Still, his mate was angry and anxious.

'We're all that is left,' she said, sorrowfully.

'Never mind. There's no point in challenging the white man. Let's just live here quietly. We'll make babies, and they'll soon multiply, and we'll teach them how to live quietly too.'

Only two of the seven eggs his mate laid that time hatched, one of which perished soon after, while the other grew rapidly in four months. The world was full of dangers children were not able to identify.

'Now there're two of us girls,' she said, happily.

One evening, they set out leaving the young one behind in the nest. They did not have to venture far, they could fill their bellies in a single dive underwater on the plentiful otters and mullets. A toddy tapper, on his way back from the evening's tapping, set his pot down and sat by the side of the canal to urinate. He felt the soil under his feet shifting, and as he tried to scramble up, he and his pot landed in the nest. As the strong-muscled tapper thrashed about to find his balance, he found his hands gripping the throat of a baby crocodile. That night, a large group of people ransacked the whole area searching for more crocodiles.

In a different place and at a different time, more eggs formed inside the female crocodile. She had already swallowed the tapper by then.

'It's dangerous for you to be here,' her mate said. 'Go east, follow the currents. No one will expect you there.'

There were plenty of overgrown slopes where she could build new nests.

'Don't forget. Be stealthy, be quiet. Don't let them know you're there.'

When it was time for the eggs to hatch, he followed her, swimming eastwards in the cover of darkness. How many this time, he wondered. He planned to bring them back in batches, set them up in two or three different places. On the way, by the side of a canal, he came across two humans in front of a fire, cooking their evening meal. They were boatmen who could discern even the slightest ripple in the water. He was not interested in their talk, but he overheard them anyway.

'You mean they've come this far east?'

'They found a tapping knife in its belly. Must have eaten some hapless tapper. There was a whole bunch of eggs too.'

He turned back. He wallowed in the rising saltwater of the high tide, crawled on to the bank, and lay there looking back at the lake. He had become the Last Crocodile. Encouraged by the flapping tails of his ancestors in the swamp and water, he moved away quickly, wanting to reach Baker bungalow before dark.

Past the flower garden and the rascal mango tree, below the stairs by which the Saheb emerged for his early morning walk, he dug a hole and waited, motionless, with his mouth open. Morning dawned late these days. If everything had gone as planned, the first footstep the grandson of Henry Baker Senior, who had come all the way from England to Kumarakam, would have taken that morning would have been his last. But he was familiar with the odour that emanated from a crocodile's mouth, a knowledge that saved his life in the nick of time. He ran back up the stairs and fetched his gun, but the crocodile had disappeared by then. Crocodiles could not move on land as fast as they did in water, and if this one had managed to disappear so quickly, it was no ordinary crocodile. Besides, the Saheb mused, it had set a precise trap for him, something that had never happened before.

From the next day on, gun in hand, he searched every corner of the lake and the fields, set up nets in the rooms and around the bungalow. Twice he came across it, but both times it was in the water and he was on land, and it escaped, unharmed, from his bullets. He implored the government to send him help, arguing that the lake and its surroundings were being overrun by crocodiles again, but there was no response. Even his wife, the Madamma, began to feel that the Last Crocodile was a hallucination conjured up by his obsessed mind. In all these years, she had failed to understand her husband's crocodile-induced madness, especially since they had barely ever come into the farm even when there was a large population of them in the lake.

The Saheb lost his sleep, and spent the nights patrolling his vast lands in the light of burning torches and accompanied by his trusted dog, aiming his gun at every shadow the dog barked at. One night, as he stepped into the pond to wash off the mud from his shoes at the end of a patrol, the dog began to bark and block his way, running wildly around the pond. Tired and longing for his bed, he disregarded the dog's warning and tried to step into the water again, and the dog bit his leg and pulled back. He kicked it away, but before he could step in, it jumped into the water, and in a split second, the Crocodile tore it to pieces and disappeared into the darkness. That night, he sat reading the Bible and thinking about his dog. It was the next morning that he took Moustache on as his companion. He continued thinking about his dog whenever the two of them were alone, and Moustache wondered whether the Saheb hoped that he too would one day jump into the water for him.

Moustache defeated the Last Crocodile by hitting him in his eye. The eyes and the part under the throat were the most vulnerable spots in a crocodile's body. But its tail was as strong as the trunk of an elephant. Still, when they faced each other in the middle of the lake, the Last Crocodile did not try to overpower Moustache, and only made a mild attempt to defend himself. He had expected that this man too, like all humans before him, would eventually back away in fright. He recalled the story of one of his ancestors who had befriended a human. When the human said 'Come, boy,' he would go to him obediently and accept the food offered, and when he said 'Off you go now,' he would go back.

The Last Crocodile was still alive when he was tied to a boat and dragged to the bungalow. Kariyil Saheb shot him in the head. After making sure that he was well and truly dead, the Saheb took a photo with him to hang on his wall. Until his death, he would look at the photograph as if to convince himself before he stepped out of the house.

Kariyil Saheb was a master who was kind to his subjects on occasion, and granted the wishes of anyone who pleased him.

'I want to go to Malaya,' Moustache said.

'And did he finally get to Malaya?' Ponnu asked.

'I'm not sure. But something else happened first,' I replied.

One day, the Saheb took Moustache with him to hunt birds. Usually, when he set out to shoot birds, not one but a whole crowd of local folk would go with him. He would stuff the barrel of his gun with glass and shoot at the flocks of birds in the fields, killing ten or twenty of them with each shot. The Saheb and the Madamma did not like to eat bird meat, so the dead birds were anyone's to pick. One time, he missed his target and hit one of the people picking up the birds. He was distraught, and offered every possible help to the dead man's family, even increasing the wages of his wife and children.

But this time, it was only Moustache who accompanied him. His shots brought down fat gull-billed terns and garganey ducks by the dozen. As he picked up the fallen birds, Moustache felt a bullet coming for him. Darkness had begun to spread. Moustache dove into the lake and swam furiously away. A scattering of off-target bullets landed in the water behind him. Sometime later, as the distance between him and the land increased, he sensed something. There was someone swimming right behind him.

22

SONGS

The first time Moustache heard the songs that had been made up about him was in the new kayal fields. These were fields recently claimed from Vembanad Kayal and named after kings and queens. In the middle of the furious lake, two rows of coconut tree trunks were hammered ten feet apart into the bottom, and fenced with bamboo mats. The space between the two rows was paved with sand and filled with slabs of clay dug from the lake bed, and reinforced with frames of areca wood, and the whole construction fortified with mud to construct the bund. The water inside the bund was drained, and the land thus exposed turned into fields. These fields had only been cultivated for five or six seasons. Ouseph – Little Saheb – who had followed Moustache as he swam away from Baker Saheb and his bullets also heard the songs.

Here he comes, Moustache of Kaipuzha
He's a bull that defies the plough
Hopping over hills he comes, striding through yards
His moustache brushes the rainclouds
His arms fondle the earth
Behold his moustache, here he comes,
Like a swarm of birds dark against the sky

Vavachan had heard this song before, in his childhood, sung by women working the fields. But in that song, they were talking about a bull – a white bull with black spots on its chest and forehead that flew on the plough like a bird. In the song in the kayal fields, Moustache was a man from Kaipuzha, and there were other songs in which he was a man from Pulinkunnu, a boatman from the coast, or a different man from Mundar.

In the song of the Chovathi who desired to live with Moustache, he was a sharp, swarthy Chovan from Karappuram.

Full-blooded Chovathi that I am
My skin flushed with youthfulness
I'd not have to pound paddy or cook rice
And still feed my belly all day long
If only Moustache would make me his wife

Then there were songs in which he was a Vaalan from Thanneermukkam, and a Parayan living on the embankment of the Chalakkappalli field. Confused, Moustache wondered who these songs were really about.

In the last season's harvest, the fields had yielded Nenmanikyam – Golden Grain, something that occurred only on one plant in fifty years of sowing hundreds of thousands of fields; something that, even when it occurred, might often go unnoticed. Nenmanikyam was the embodiment of the virtue and grace of the landowner and the Pulayan who stood guard over the fields. The plant with the sheaf of Nenmanikyam would be harvested and taken, accompanied by ceremonial drums and musical instruments, in a boat to the house of the landowner. A skilled carpenter would be brought to detach the central beam of the roof. The sheaf with Nenmanikyam would be placed behind it, along with nine auspicious grains, turmeric, flowers, and holy water. The beam would then be replaced. It was believed that the stores of that house would never be empty. The Goddess of Plenty would sit on the paddy heaped in their fields, and the guards would hear the grains shifting in the night. One night, a guard, unable to sleep in the whisper of the shifting paddy, called out: 'Mathi, kayal! Enough, lake!' That was how the fields of Mathikayal came into being.

The appearance of Nenmanikyam in the last harvest had energised the kayal fields. Field songs were louder and more melodious than usual. People had come from all over to work the fields – from Kainadi, Kainakari, Kumarakam and Vechoor, all only a short boat ride away from each other – and all of them had songs about Moustache. Folk from Kainadi made fun of him in their songs. In their stories, he had lost to Ittichan.

Hey you, loafer roaming the land
Hey you, wimp pecked by wild fowl
Your woman is a hussy at the jetty

At the waterwheels, men taunted each other in their songs, egged each other on, as they worked the treads in rhythm. A false move on the twenty-four-leafed waterwheel would have them plummeting to certain death and a quick funeral. In some of their songs, they sang about Moustache who had fallen off the wheel and survived without a scratch.

Songs of taunts and response, songs of bravery and bravado reverberated in the fields, and yet there were people who wandered the fields, hapless, dejected. They were the ones who had toiled hard to build the bund and the polders, and yet had not been paid in full for their labour.

'The Moustache they are singing about ... Is that really you?' Ouseph asked. 'It sounds like you, but it's not quite you either. How is it possible that you figure in the songs made even before you were born? Were there others like you before you?'

All the songs about Moustache also mentioned Seetha. In many of them, she was waiting for him, and in others she was searching for him. Whereas he, the songs said, was like wind on a rock, unmoved by women's charms.

Oh I can't live with her any more
Fresh as a hill glory sprig was she

Now a handful of wilted buds (says he)
Why did you give me hope
Why do you torment me so (says she)

Still, in almost all the songs, Moustache and Seetha get together in the end against all odds.

... And he lived with his woman
Moustache the Handsome, Moustache the Playful
Three pots of toddy on his way home he drinks
With three pots of rice at home she waits

There were songs too, where Moustache is forced to leave Seetha.

Listen, my woman, my companion,
I must go on a long, long journey

Moustache is forced to leave her and go on a journey, the songs say, because his mother asks him to, and he is allowed to return only after twelve years. There were songs in which a stubborn Seetha insists on going with him, arguing with him and starving herself until he relents. What foolishness! Would she be able to traverse these endless fields, where there were killer crocodiles and ruthless robbers, where there were folks who would kidnap her, shapeshifting into harriers and owls? There was even a song about Moustache searching for a lost Seetha.

In many of these songs, the name of a man appeared often – a Pachupillah who was Moustache's companion.

'Who's this Pachupillah?' Ouseph asked.

Moustache shrugged. There was no such name in his memory. Still, Pachupillah was with him in several songs.

Marching ahead is one Pachupillah
Side by side he and Moustache fight
Chopping heads left and right
As though clearing the ground of weeds

In the planting songs sung to bring forth bountiful crops, Pachupillah was Moustache's close friend, while in the Onam harvest festival songs he was the man who taught him martial arts. In the songs of the waterwheels, Pachupillah was the only person who stuck with Moustache even when everyone else had abandoned him, and in the songs of the plough and the songs of sowing, he was the one who searched for Seetha on Moustache's behalf. Moustache did not trouble himself with wondering who this man in the songs was. He had decided that these songs had nothing to do with him.

Pachupillah was the man who had turned the surging floodwater into wealth when it had drowned the destinies of all others. After the floods, his banana harvest on top of Vedagiri Hill and the coconuts that had come floating into his compound had fetched unexpected prices, and sealed his fortune. He gave up tenant farming and set himself up as a moneylender. With wealth came unprecedented respect and status, and Pachupillah wanted more and more of it. That there is no meaning to wealth is a story made up by the wealthy to fool the poor. It is true that in death the wealthy and the poor are equal, but that is no reason not to live well until then. Romance, lust, love – the wealthy have greater access to all of this. Pachupillah had known gut-burning hunger, had no illusions about the virtues of want and penury, and he decided to make good use of the famine that followed the floods. It was a time when even the wealthy had nothing to eat. Not a grain of rice was to be found. Even those who had secreted some paddy in their stores suffered because they were not able to take it out and use it, fearful of the government who might confiscate their stores and of people desperate enough to murder and loot them. Pachupillah became the only regular, trusted visitor in households with acres of land and income from tenant farming. Looking like an ordinary labourer or a starving neighbour begging for a bowl of kanji water, he went into their houses and bought their paddy for ready cash, and took it home in several instalments, bundled up in pieces of old cloth. Even as the paddy boiled and dried in his home, Pachupillah sent his wife out begging for handfuls of rice to keep up appearances.

In those days, paddy was sold as it was. No one considered the task of boiling, drying, toasting and pounding it to make rice to cook with a chore. Even wild rice and chaff was boiled into a bitter tasting kanji. Pachupillah was the one who started trading in rice, processed and ready to cook, and it brought four or five times more profit than paddy. He chose his customers carefully, and refused to sell rice to people who were lower in status even if they had the wherewithal to buy it. He delivered the sacks of rice to his customers himself, carrying them on his head in the dead of night and early mornings to their houses in the east. Having survived on a couple of mouthfuls of boiled yam for months on end, their children stayed awake way past midnight, waiting for Pachupillah who traversed the back lanes to their homes with no fear of the ghosts and spirits who walked the dark.

One night, a uniformed policeman stopped Pachupillah. He opened the sack, took a handful of rice and smelled it.

'Where the hell did you steal this from?' he asked, enraged.

Even high-ranking officials like the Peshkar did not have access to this amount of rice.

'Please don't hurt me,' Pachupillah fell at his feet and told him the story.

'I'll give up this work as of today, if you please. I'll survive somehow, plant some yams or colocasia on the little land I have.'

'What's the price of this sack of rice?'

'Nothing at all. Please, you can have it for free.'

The policeman forced him to accept the going rate, made him carry the sack, and led the way to his home. His wife woke up the sleeping children and served them kanji for the first time in days.

Two days later, a group of policemen captured Pachupillah after a brief chase, and took him away in a boat. From then on, he became a regular visitor to the houses of police inspectors, delivering rice under the cover of darkness to those who spent their days catching rice smugglers and black marketeers. Soon, he began to trade in public.

When the famine began to ease, Pachupillah went to see a licensed rice trader, a Konkani who, despite having amassed considerable wealth, lived in a one-room house in Thazhathangadi, near the Tirumala temple. His parsimony was evident in the vegetable peelings spread out to dry in the yard for later use.

The Konkani's wife was in the yard.

'He's over there,' she told him.

She was using her spare time to make chanaka varali – flat cakes made out of a mixture of cow dung and chaff left over from pounding paddy for rice – and sticking them on the walls of the house to dry in the sun. These fetched a good price in the western lands of the lake where they used them to light their funeral pyres.

From then on, Pachupillah and his wife stopped giving even a handful of chaff free to people for using to make toothpowder, and began making chanaka varali themselves. When a Veluthedan Nair in Thonnamkuzhi died and they were about to cut down a fruit-bearing mango tree for the funeral pyre, Pachupillah took a load of chanaka varali over and organised the funeral. And so, when people in nearby lands passed away, trees escaped the axe, and Pachupillah's cow dung and chaff turned into money.

Eventually, Pachupillah hired a workforce to boil and dry the paddy, and built a fleet of trade boats to transport rice to Alappuzha, Kollam and Kayamkulam. Merchants began to arrive in Neendoor to buy his rice wholesale. When fifteen years after the floods that changed his fortune another flood submerged the land, his fortunes did not suffer even though, this time, he did not have a crop of bananas up on a hill or an opportune harvest of coconuts brought in by the water. He had, in anticipation of the rains, dried his paddy and stored it away.

When the floodwater receded, one of his boats transporting rice, and its boatman, did not come back. Other boats went as far as Vettikkadu and turned back. The only way they could cross the lake was under the protection of at least fifteen guards armed with machetes. Pachupillah asked the police to help, but they shrugged their shoulders. There was nothing they could do about the robbers holed up in the lake and in the canals, who evaded them even before they set out to apprehend them.

Pachupillah told his workers not to take any more boats out, and set out on his own in a small boat loaded with five or six sacks of rice. He rowed north-west beyond Arpookara, Pulikkuttisseri and Kareemadam, from where he turned south and then west. Finally, he reached a hut in the Theruvilpadam field where Panakkan Pulayan lived with his woman. He carried the sacks of rice into the hut and presented them with a bundle of tobacco.

Panakkan and his woman were over seventy years of age, but they were as energetic as ten-year-olds. Having never had children, they thought of themselves as children and considered the fields their playground, something God Himself had presented them with. During harvest season, they travelled far and wide, to Thiruvarppu, Kumarakam, Vechoor, Thalayazham, even to the kayal fields, and beyond to Muttar, Nedumudi and Veliyanadu. The younger harvest workers muttered as soon as they arrived because the old-timers were excellent harvesters who could sweep through a row of paddy in no time. But as soon as they entered the fields, Panakkan would make up and sing songs that restored harmony between them and the other workers. His woman was a skilled songster too. There was no song that she did not know. By the end of the season, they would leave the field with an additional share of paddy for the songs.

'You must help me,' Pachupillah told Panakkan. 'I have no other solution.'

For many years, Pachupillah had bought any paddy left over by the year end from Panakkan, and on many occasions, on his way back from Pala and Athirampuzha, he had brought mature toddy for them.

If he took on a job, Panakkan did it well. And from then on, as soon as they entered the fields for harvest and took up the songs, he would insert Pachupillah's name into them, without losing the rhythm or missing a beat.

'You can take the boats out now,' Pachupillah told his oarsmen. 'If anyone stops you, tell them the boat belongs to Pachupillah – Moustache's own man.'

Meanwhile, the name Kesava Pillah, the man who owned a hundred acres of paddy fields, had also entered the songs, without anyone having to instigate it. Field workers sang melodious songs about how he had been frightened by Moustache, how he had plied men young enough to still have their milk teeth with arrack, and how they had burned down Moustache's hut and wreaked havoc across the land, beating up even little children. The songs described the harriers and eagles that circled above his head, and the horned prawns that waited in the water to nip off his balls, making the women snigger as they reached these parts in the songs. Kesava Pillah was a snakehead whisperer. He would place medicinal herbs in their mouths and whisper his directions to them, and when they came near the fields of his enemies, they would attack and create cracks in the bunds, letting the water in and drowning the crop, thus reducing the landowner and his workers to penury. But in the songs, Kesava Pillah's fields soured from the terror of Moustache, and when the fields dried, veins of salt crystallised all over them. Eventually, the edges collapsed and the fields were overrun with couch grass and water weeds, and turned back into swamp and water.

In some songs, Moustache was Edanadan, a mongrel, the firstborn of a Nair landowner and a Paraya woman who was indentured to him. This landowner – the Kammal – wanted to farm the seven forests of an islet in Ezhumam Lake, too dense even for the black rat snakes. He set out with his handyman, Chathambulayan, to clear the forest. Chathambulayan flew as high as the egrets and cut down seven trees. But on the eighth cut, blood sprouted from the tree. Chathambulayan begged:

Let's not cultivate the seventh lake
Let's not mutilate the seven forests

But the Kammal refused and had the forests cleared, and when the harvest of Jeerakachempavu paddy came in, it was breathtaking. As women threshed the paddy, Pravruthyar Sankunni Menon and his helper, Koyil, came to measure the harvest. They measured as they pleased, fudged the calculations, took what they wanted, and the Kammal's protests were met with violence. Koyil cut off his head and kicked it like a ball.

Edanadan Moustache, spawn of the Kammal and the Paraya woman, became a ferryman rowing a boat across Ezhumam Lake, the songs said. Once, some women from Kakkatheruvu wanted to be ferried across the lake but they did not have enough money for the fare. They told him they would pay on their way back from the market. But Edanadan Moustache was not a man of mercy.

Three pots of rice are three easy mouthfuls
For Edanadan, mongrel of Nair and Parayi
I shall have double the fee, says he
Not per head, but per breast

The women, enraged at his audacity, took off their clothes, entered the lake and swam across. As they gained the far shore, they sneered at him, saying that his father had been hacked to pieces seven days ago and yet here he was doing nothing about it. Moustache's expression changed.

Red and lion-like, eyes they flashed
Chest hair, in rage it seethed
Like a tiger, his rat-tail moustache he pulled
The hair on his head, in fury it frizzed

He threw away his oar and went home to his woman. In this song, Seetha was called Thiruthevi. He told her about his father's murder and, dressed in a warrior's loincloth, sword in hand, he set out to have his revenge. On the islet of Ezhumam, arrows came at his thighs and swords swished at his neck, but he defended himself.

Fearless Moustache faced the swords
Valiant Moustache fought off the foes
Here he is now, tall and gallant
There he is now, short and steadfast

He hacked through thirty-two of his opponents, the songs said. Shocked by the damage he caused to their men, Menon and Koyil ran away. In the fight, Moustache was also injured. Thiruthevi, the woman who was also Seetha, took him home in a boat, washed his wounds and tended to him. She gave him the healing medicines that the medicine woman Nallamma Parayi made from herbs and meat oils. When he was fully healed, he set out again to have his revenge. He went to Narayanapattan's house. Narayanapattan hid in the basement, and when his wife told him lies, Moustache threatened to dig up the basement.

He bought a new boat from Narayanapattan, paying the exact price of his father's lost boat, and when the boat would not move, he made it move with Nallamma Parayi's medicine. As he paddled the boat beyond Thiruthavalavu into the Thrinayankodam Lake, a storm arose. Moustache prayed to Lord Vaikkathappan. He went to the temple and, staying within the restricted space allowed for the likes of him – the polluted, the unclean – he made offerings of sweet jaggery payasam, gold and coconut inflorescence. He traversed ponds and fields, swam across Kaduthuruthi canal, and climbed to the top of a jackfruit tree. Standing at its crown, he crowed like a rooster. On the third crow, assuming it was morning, a woman came out to sweep the yard. Moustache accosted her, and the terrified woman told him of the plans Menon and Koyil were putting in place to defend themselves against him.

Edanadan Moustache, terror of their heart
A river they've made, his efforts to thwart
To vanquish their foe in its oily black water
They're feeding Kariyaat Crocodile, the monster

They have sharpened their spears and built drawbridges, she told him. Scared of Moustache's shapeshifting abilities, Menon had taken to killing flies and ants. But what if he turned into the spathe of a coconut frond? So he cut off the spathes of all the trees. Edanadan Moustache asked the woman for some water, and when she refused, he cut off her head and put it in the well. He chopped off the heads of people like he was slashing through the undergrowth. He burned their place of worship, and sat on the ground leaning back on his elbow watching it burn. At that moment, the songs said, Edanadan Moustache looked as though he had been sculpted out of stone, as though he was stone.

Enveloped by the plentiful and diverse songs, Moustache and Ouseph sat on the bund, leaning back on their elbows. They watched the setting sun burning itself out like the temple Edanadan Moustache had set on fire. The owner of the kayal fields, Outhachan, shaded his eyes with his hand and looked carefully at the eastern sky, and told his workers to stop and go home. Rainclouds filled the south-eastern corner of the sky, and Outhachan was certain that it would rain in Ettumanoor, Kanakkari or Vayala, and the spill water would reach these fields in two or three hours. He would wait until the fields were drenched in the cold, new water before continuing the work.

'Where to now?' Ouseph asked.

Moustache did not respond. He patted his moustache, the hairs frizzy from lack of oil. He extended his other arm backwards, placed his palm firmly on the ground, and leaned on it, watching the darkness hurry towards the west. Ouseph had grown a reddish gold moustache. Moustache looked at him with hostility. He wanted to be left alone. He wanted to continue his search for Seetha and the road to Malaya on his own. Anything that needed to be done should be done alone. Too many people together can do nothing, not even kill a snake. Fearful people feel there is strength in numbers, but all they do is chatter amongst themselves in an effort to keep their fear at bay.

Moustache felt a movement under the hand that was resting on the ground. He lifted it and found a baby frog. It was half dead. The bottom half of its body had been squashed and it tried to move on its forelegs.

'Why didn't you cry out when I put my hand on you?' Moustache asked. 'I'd have to take it off immediately.'

'How could I cry?' asked the baby frog. 'Everyone talks about you, tells your stories when they are sad or in danger. It's the songs about you that keep us going, give us hope that tomorrow will be a better day. That's what my mother and her mother used to say. So who would I call to, cry out to, when you squash me under your hand?'

Further away, Moustache saw a figure – a woman – stepping on to the field edge from the northern bund and walking towards him. The lingering glow of the dead sun lit the figure from the back, displaying the voluptuousness of her body.

23

A WRESTLING MATCH

Just like Moustache, Kuttathi too had heard the songs that talked about her as she worked in the fields breaking clay clods, a sweat cloth tied around her breasts. In the songs, her thighs were compared to aalthadi, the offering made at the temple of the Goddess Valiyaveettilamma near Onpathinayiram fields. But no one else recognised that the woman in the songs was her. How would they? She had arrived in an ash boat with her husband, put up a hut on the embankment near Chithirakayal, and lived there under her real name, Mariamma. Most of the workers were from lands to the east and west of the lake, and they went back in their boats in the evenings, leaving her and her husband behind, with only the whistling wind, the cold and the slanting rain for company. The field owner Outhachan's son, Kunjachan, had recently built an office room on the bund, a small structure with stone walls and a thatched roof. On nights when there was a sliver of light in the room, Kuttathi would go there. Eventually, the key to the room came into her possession.

Aalthadi was made out of a mixture of rice flour, jaggery and coconut, rolled in areca spathe and baked in a pit made in the sand with coals on top. It smelled divine when it was cooked well without being scorched. Kuttathi's sweat and hair also had a naturally sweet smell.

'You reckon you're from some manor house to wash your body with soap?'

Women wrinkled their noses and asked, their jealousy barely contained.

It was in the ploughmen's songs and the songs of the waterwheel workers, songs not meant for women's ears, that Kuttathi usually appeared. In them, she was a young woman from Paravur with an insatiable sexual appetite who was married off at thirteen to a man from Udayanapuram. Unable to get a full night's sleep, her husband begs to be left alone:

Hey you, fair-skinned Kuttathi of Kunnumthara
When we've had our meal and it's time for bed
Give me my mat and I'll sleep over there

In another song, the Peshkar, a powerful government official, a Brahmin in grand headgear and a coat, spent a night with her in Ettumanoor, and ran away in his loincloth, scared for his life.

Brazen is she, unabashed
Does as she pleases, unashamed

It was only Moustache, with the strength of two crocodiles and pitch-dark facial hair, who could satisfy her, the songs said. In him, she found her match. In his embrace, she surrendered like a pliable bean vine.

Kuttathi walked along the field edge and came up to Moustache and Ouseph as they sat on the embankment watching the setting sun. Moustache ignored her. They had never met outside of the songs. He had never heard of her, whereas she had been hearing only about him in the fields she had worked over the past several years. Even those who had come to her for nighttime companionship had talked incessantly about him. So Kuttathi recognised him immediately. Who else had a moustache like this in the whole world?

As huge as an elephant
As tall as a jungle jack

As tough as an iron nail
Broader than a doorframe
Yet supple and smooth
Is the hair on his face

In the blowing wind, it rippled prettily like a field of Kolappala paddy. Kuttathi was confused. How could he be so young? How was he so tender, despite feet that had turned into stone and skin that had hardened from incessant wanderings in the sun? There was another man with him, Ouseph, who had a golden beard and a mature body. Kuttathi paid him no attention, and the man too looked at her with obvious dislike. She had begun to show her age, but she was still attractive, full-bodied, her skin unmarked and her hair lustrous despite the years spent in the scorching sun and salty winds. How did she manage to keep her toenails so clean? Unlike the other women who worked in the mud, her heels were not cracked, and the crinkled skin on her neck was not lined with dirt. Her mouth was a light red from the occasional paan she chewed. The mundu that she wore looked as though it had been freshly laundered by the washerman. There was a small bundle under her arm, perhaps some areca nut and chewing tobacco, or paddy to be prepared for the night's meal.

Kuttathi and Moustache spent that night in Kunjachan's office room, sheltered from the cold and the rain, while her husband and Ouseph huddled in the hut on the embankment. Ouseph thought Kuttathi's husband was the happiest man he had ever met. Dragging his polio-withered leg, the man prepared a fire and cooked kanji, all the while respectfully gazing at Ouseph, and regaling him with stories about the generosity and valour of the dignitaries he had met in his life. One of them was a landowner from Mankombu, a place where every Christian and Nair was well-off, and the Parayans and Pulayans working for them were paid well for their labour. Still, the place had one drawback – they had never had an elephant brought to their temple festivals. It was not anyone's fault. As long as elephants didn't have wings, how would they arrive in an isolated, water-locked land? But the landowner, the Master of Mankombu, was adamant, and ignoring the advice of his own mother and everyone else around him, he went off to Changanassery. He returned with an elephant, making it swim across the lake and waterways. The scared mahout came by boat. The Old Goddess of the Mankombu temple had never seen an elephant, and the sight enraged her. The creature was unnecessary for the land and there was no real need to drag it there. The elephant was safe, but the saltwater that entered the Master's ears as he swam across the lake with the elephant never dislodged, and he lost his hearing.

It was when he went to the festival at the Ettumanoor temple, accomplishing another long-held desire, that the Deaf Master of Mankombu met Kuttathi. On the final day of the festival, he enjoyed the spectacle of Ezharaponnana – seven and a half golden elephants – where the idol was paraded in a procession. When the idol was taken away for the ritual purification at the end of the festival, the Master left the temple premises and set out for Kanakkari. There, at Kuttathi's house, another festival was taking place, and people came stealthily under the cover of darkness to take part in it. That night, the Deaf Master developed a new obsession, and in the morning, he got rid of her husband and took Kuttathi back with him to Mankombu. He installed her in a compound near his house and began to worship her all by himself.

'Ho! I was really sad,' the husband told Ouseph, dipping a coconut shell in the boiled kanji and drinking it. 'I searched for her everywhere, dragging this no-good leg of mine.'

Two or three years passed, and still no one knew who it was that had taken her or where she had been taken.

'One day, I was at the festival at the Veluthachan's church in Arthunkal. There were people everywhere on the beach, enjoying the fireworks and buying salted fish. And there they were in the middle of it all, walking as though completely unaffected by the loud bangs.'

The ear-splitting sound of fireworks did not affect the Deaf Master, and his nonchalance made Kuttathi brave. They were suited to each other, and even looked like siblings.

'Well, they took me home and let me stay in a lean-to.'

The next year, at the Mullakkal temple festival, the Deaf Master was chatting with the fireworks people. They had lined up eight mortar shells and set light to them. Seven of them went off. After waiting for a while, the Master bent over the eighth one to see what was wrong, and precisely at that moment it decided to detonate.

'If only he was still around ... we wouldn't be living like this, that's for sure,' the husband said.

Ouseph felt that despite this unfortunate development, the man was deeply content, the type of person who found satisfaction even in a coconut shell of kanji.

Moustache stood gazing at the big canal, ignoring the noise Kuttathi was making while rearranging the furniture in Kunjachan's office room. Until recently, it had been a lake, but human beings had diminished its size and made it into a placid, stagnant canal. He felt a spark of sorrow inside him. Was he also being diminished? The police had stopped pursuing him. He began to feel that the long years he had spent wandering alone, hiding from people, had become pointless. Restlessly, he stroked his moustache. Had it also diminished? Had it lost its thickness? He had left his land and his people for its sake, and they had also forsaken him because of it. He had been searching for a woman and a land far away where he could live quietly with his moustache. Beyond the canal was the lake, and beyond that the heavily populated sliver of sugar-sand beach, and even beyond that was the ocean which Paviyan, Chella or Vavachan had never seen.

Moustache wondered whether, on the fateful night he met the ghost who asked for food and realised that he would not find sustenance in his native land, he should have set out east instead of west. He had, until now, banished the details of that night from his memory. Or was it that his memory, just like his future, was only a matter of his imagination? Like the Moustache in the songs, the Vavachan in his memory was only half real. But who is to say what was real? The Moustache in the songs was the one most people believed to be true, and perhaps that made him more real and true than the real one. Kuttathi and Moustache were only faint likenesses of the people named in the songs that were surely at least a hundred years old. Now, here they were, forged copies of something that had never been, on the edge of a field that people had created out of the lake. People had mistaken this land which, for thousands of years had been a lake, for fields. But it was still a lake, and Ouseph, Kunjachan, and the queens and princes after whom the fields were named were mere stories and songs. Soon, it would change back into a lake, and even the stories with their names in it would fade away and disappear.

And so they sat, Kuttathi and Moustache, in front of an unreal light in an unreal hut on an unreal embankment, embodied only in stories and songs. A wind, eternal, since the time of the lake and even before, penetrated the newly made wooden window frame, and agitated the lamp. The flame tried to break free from the wick and slanted away, momentarily detaching itself, only to come scurrying back, panicked, to stick to it. The wind seemed determined to win back, in one night, what had been taken away and rebuilt by the most inconsequential creature on earth.

Kuttathi and Moustache embraced each other on the rough mat spread on a cot that Kunjachan used to rest on during the day. They melted into each other in the lines that were only whispered in the songs, the places that went unnamed in the stories. They rummaged through each other like animals hunting for non-existent food, empty breasts and dispassionate lips competing with each other, sending tremors through destitute waists.

Is there any other creature that falls into an exhausted sleep immediately after mating? Even the baya weaver flies energetically into the bushes after mating multiple times in minutes. Sleep is preparation for the long, endless sleep to come. As though searching for something beyond the pleasure of mating in the interlude before the long sleep, the eyes of the most powerful of human beings, Kuttathi and Moustache, closed. But before they fell asleep, he submitted his face and his moustache to her breasts and sobbed. Every man who had come to Kuttathi had done so; it was a special ability she possessed. Some would recount their sorrows as though they had finally found the all-hearing, all-knowing goddess of compassion that they had been searching for.

There were mathematicians who had told her, an illiterate woman, of their failed calculations, government officials who had divulged state secrets. The weakest among all of earth's creatures was the man who thought he had just performed valiantly in bed. 'It's all right,' Kuttathi would say to these men, running her fingers through their hair tenderly. 'Let it all go.' Morning would reveal these diminished men walking around like proud roosters with their chests puffed up.

'You're the manliest of all the men I have ever come across,' Kuttathi told Moustache.

Her fingers moved effortlessly through his moustache.

'You could have any woman you want. Then how come you're wandering around looking for this one woman? In all the ploughmen's songs you two are already together.'

Kuttathi had also begun to feel that the songs told the actual truth. Listening to the songs others had made up about her, she too had begun to transform into the version of her in the songs.

'Well, don't worry. We'll find a way. There's someone who can help. I'll take you to him tomorrow.'

The next evening, Kunjachan, having heard about Moustache's arrival in his father's fields, wanted to meet with him. He was in a happy mood as though he had won a big competition or a new bride. That afternoon, too, he had gone to the fields that his father had dredged up in his Marshall boat. Two rowboats were tied behind it, filled with paddy from his stores. The Marshall led the way like a proud drake with the two paddy boats following in its wake like obedient hens. From the bow of the boat, one could see the faint greenness of Kottayam to the east. Earlier, there would have been nothing but the volatile lake between the boat and the land. But Outhachan, his father, had single-handedly accomplished what folk from Palayi, Pallithanam and Ettupara had tried to do together and failed. His father had conquered the lake and transformed it into fields that produced Nenmanikyam, the Golden Grain. The lake had surrendered completely. Man-eating crocodiles and saw-toothed sharks had disappeared. There was nothing that would not eventually surrender to the triumph-seeking, ruthless man. If his father was the king of the lake, Kunjachan felt that he was the emperor. So far, people had entered the lake and drained its water to cultivate enough food to survive. Now, stores were brimming with paddy and coffers were full. So the only way to get further ahead was to do things that had not been done so far. Kunjachan wanted to bring soil and stones in boats and build a church in the middle of Chithira Kayal. No one should be able to cross the water without seeing the cross on its steeple. Its pealing bell and the drumbeats of its festival should echo across the water to Kuttanad in the south, Kochi in the north, the hills in the east and the sea in the west, without a single wooden stick in between to block its sound.

A speeding boat overtook the Marshall. Usually, the only boats that Kunjachan came across in this part of the Vembanad Lake were the government boats taking passengers to Alappuzha and Kottayam that crawled by as though about to capsize. But this was a new boat with only five or six passengers. Its audacious speed annoyed him. He instructed his driver to go faster, but as soon as he did, the other boat sped up in response. Kunjachan pushed his driver away and took over the controls. What ensued was a ferocious race, something that had never been witnessed in the lake before. Oarsmen of narrow boats and clam diggers watched mesmerised as the two boats created huge waves, sideswiped each other, and overtook each other inch by inch. Finally, Kunjachan pulled into Chithira Kayal five or six feet ahead of the other boat. But there was not a single grain of paddy left in the two boats tied behind the Marshall. The water had taken it all. The paddy was the workers' wages for the day, their evening meal. Yet, Kunjachan was unconcerned. There was plenty of paddy at home and he would give them twice the measure the next day, and if they had to go hungry for an evening, so be it.

Kunjachan had grown up watching the workers sweep up every last grain of paddy from the fields before it was drenched, leaving nothing even for the ducks. Consequently, he had no respect for it. Pulayans marvelled at his disrespect when, as a young boy, he would walk over the seed paddy left to dry on mats in the threshing yards. As a young man, he had married a woman from a family even better off than his, one that owned vast coconut groves. A single harvest from an islet in

Pathiramanal alone yielded over one lakh coconuts. Their house was larger than that of the king or the sahebs. They had even built a church, the church of St. Raphael, which proved that they were more aristocratic than Kunjachan's family. Still, when he was alone with his new wife on their wedding night, his instinct was to brag.

'We can see as far as your house if we climb to the top of our paddy heap,' he had said.

'That's nothing,' his wife had replied. 'Your entire paddy will be washed away in the water from the coconuts we harvest.'

Kunjachan was the sort of man who insisted that all women workers take off their breast-cloth, and made even the elderly workers beg for their rightful wages. One time, a man from Kumarakam named Kuttichovan had come to Kavalam to see Outhachan. Kuttichovan was the person who had sunk the first pole to build the bund when Outhachan was draining the lake to make the fields. It was his strength that fortified the outer bunds. So Outhachan and his wife welcomed him, gave him coffee and offered him a chair. But Kuttichovan refused the chair and the coffee. For over a week, he had been going back and forth to Kunjachan's office room in the fields, begging for his wages. He had had enough. He took off his shoulder-cloth and placed it in front of Outhachan. He then took off his mundu, folded it and placed it on top.

'Here. These came from working for you. From now on, I'll live without them,' he said, and walked away wearing only his loincloth.

'Come right in, Moustache.'

Kunjachan invited Moustache into his office room and offered him a chair. He took out a strangely shaped bottle of foreign liquor, sat on the bed rumpled from the previous night, and poured it into copper glasses. Kunjachan liked to have a drink as soon as the sun set. But he did not like to drink alone and wanted a companion who listened, preferably in silence, to his chatter. He did not go to others' houses to drink because most of these sessions ended in altercations, and there would be a price to pay in the shape of paddy for any destruction caused. Here, in the middle of the lake, altercations did not end in damage to property, only to the bodies of his companions.

'This is brandy,' Kunjachan said, inhaling the aroma of the reddish liquid. 'I've had this bottle for a couple of years. I knew I'd get to meet you one day and had set it aside to open it then.'

He walked around Moustache, slapped his muscles with his open palm checking their strength, and pulled at his moustache.

'Just like in the songs…'

Moustache drained his glass quickly, but he was not interested in drinking. His nerves, acclimatised to being constantly on alert during the untold years of wandering could not be relaxed with alcohol. Alcohol was not for those who had to be vigilant, or for those whose minds were in turmoil. As he watched Kunjachan examining him, brandy glass in hand, Moustache realised he was a man who had all good things in the world come to him easily. His eyes were lustreless, and unusually for farmers, he had a sagging stomach and a pale body. His hair had started turning grey despite his youth. He had long fingers and stooped shoulders unlike others of his ancestry. Moustache realised Kunjachan was only pretending to examine him, and that he was the sort of person who could never quite see another person, or himself for that matter, clearly.

'So, you were with that Madamma, I hear,' Kunjachan said. 'Is that why the Saheb shot at you? Be careful of these madammas. Going around shooting at crocodiles and wild cats is all very well, as long as the wife is not left alone in the night. White men don't seem to understand that, otherwise land turtles and water snakes will take over their beds.'

All the stories Kunjachan had heard about Moustache described his relationships with women. In them, women came looking for the man with the moustache; the wheelhouses and reed beds in the endless fields became the locations of his sexual conquests. In them, women swam across canals and trampled over swamps to find him, unable to resist their desires. Women from well-to-do households, with the means to eat three square meals a day, were more affected, the stories went, and they offered themselves up to him in the water, in the open, in the mud.

'Do you have a magic birthmark or something?' Kunjachan asked in a raised voice.

As far as Kunjachan was concerned, the measure of a man was in the number of women he had slept with. He believed in no other marker of a man's worth. Moustache ignored him, and faced with his silence, Kunjachan began to describe his own worth.

'Nair, Namboothiri, Pulayan, Ulladathi, Asari, Konkani, Tamil Brahmin, blushingly beautiful Nasrani Mappila ... I've had them all.'

He let out a shout and voiced his personal philosophy: 'If you're faced with snakes or women, it's best to react quickly. If you wait, they'll slither away.'

He poured himself another glass of brandy, drank it, and sat on the bed with a sad expression on his face.

'I have only one more desire. I'd like to see how it is in the bedrooms of the royal household. They're all out for something ... Money, paddy ... Even the ones at home want something. We take care of them to ensure that they sleep only with us. Otherwise why would they agree to be with us?'

Kunjachan glared at Moustache trying to figure out what he could possibly have given all the women he was supposed to have been with.

With his drinking buddies, Kunjachan's generosity knew no bounds. He plied them with alcohol regardless of their caste or creed. But as soon as the alcohol got to his head, he wanted to engage in wrestling matches with them. Despite his obvious frailty, he believed himself to be strong and valiant even when he was not drunk, a belief his companions usually did not challenge. If he laid his hand on a sack of rice, there would be a story about how he single-handedly lifted a twelve-para-measure sack of paddy and put it in the boat.

Kunjachan cleared a space in the middle of the room, moving the bed, chair, mats and the lamp in the little office room to the sides. There was a pile of shell-lime powder, meant to be spread in the field, in a corner of the room. Kunjachan dusted his hands with it and, dressed only in a rarely washed pair of underpants, stepped up to Moustache.

'Ever since I heard that you'd rolled in the hay with Madathil Kalyani, I've been meaning to try a hand with you.'

Kunjachan tried to force Moustache to the floor, pushing his head and neck down, and sticking a knee under his body. Normally, his opponents conceded these impromptu wrestling matches, pretending to put up a defence as they would if they were play-fighting with little children. A victory over a rich man was futile, especially a man such as Kunjachan with vast lands that produced heaps of paddy. It was better to stoke his ego, let him believe in his superior strength and valour. Allowing a rich man to save face saved a poor man his livelihood.

His opponent was stronger than he had expected, Kunjachan realised. He stuck his arm under Moustache's armpit from the back, and kicked at his heels with his right leg. After a few tries, Moustache fell on his knees. It hurt him. He felt pain. Vavachan had never been able to stand pain. It made him lose control, just as it had, a long time ago, with Kuttanasari's foster daughter.

Moustache stood up and came towards Kunjachan. What happened then is in the songs.

Desist, you cheat, cease
Or you'll know my hand
Raging thus, Moustache drops
To the floor falls his puny foe
Moustache picks up by his feet
The son of Murikkummoottil
And slaps his body on the floor

The man with the big moustache, the one who was reduced to tears when memories of his mother surfaced, the one who could not bear physical pain, picked up the darling son of Murikkummoottil Outhachan by his feet, slapped his body on the floor, and walked away without looking back.

With no look of regret, he walked away
Steady in the wind like an ordinary boat

'Are you saying there are two Moustaches in the story?' Ponnu asked, surprised.

Ponnu's confusion was not surprising as I had been telling him only those stories of Moustache that were suitable for a little boy to hear. Perhaps differentiating between what could be told to him and what needed to be withheld from him was just foolishness on my part. No one else in this world genuinely enjoys a story as much as a young child. I had one of them in front of me, a mind filled with natural curiosity and wonderment, one that would not be preoccupied, while listening to the story, with structural inadequacies, anachronisms, or character and plot developments – a mind that listened without reservations. Flying tigers, talking monkeys, mountains that moved out of the way, magical Seethas, ethereal beings that stood guard over ponds ... They know all of these exist. They harbour no doubts about the vengefulness of snakes or the cunning of foxes or the extraordinary memory of elephants. They are unconcerned if the story does not reflect the times in which it is set. And if the story is boring, they are equally capable of disengaging from it and focusing their attention on other concerns.

'Yes, there are two Moustaches,' I said, firmly.

Moustache and Ouseph did not have to go in search of the man Kuttathi said would be able to help them. He was indebted to her, and he came to them. Some women have the power to change a man completely in just one night. Ouseph watched the man as he manoeuvred his boat to the embankment and climbed on to it with some difficulty. He was a counterfeit copy, a fancy dress version, of Moustache. He too had a moustache, an unattractive, impoverished one, and he had the pale body and thin fingers and toes of an insect that dwelled in the dark crevasses of houses. Ouseph doubted whether this imposter could help them.

'Very glad to meet you,' the man said.

He stood in front of Moustache and proudly fingered his own moustache.

'People are scared of me too, but no one has ever thought I was you. I'm happy to live in your shadow.'

The man, Narayanan, thought of himself as the descendent not of the two-bit robbers that hid in water channels and islets, but of the torch-bearing bandits who had terrorised the lake when it was as vast and turbulent as the sea. In their time, the swamp and water had not made way for paddy fields. Even the kings had feared venturing into these areas that steadfastly ignored their laws and customs. Travelling between Thanneermukkam and Pallathuruthi, one was forsaken even by gods. Only Muthan could come to one's aid.

He too had, in the darkness of a long-ago night, dragged a woman into a boat and on to an islet by force. And like everyone else who had done such a deed, he too had felt like crying, much later. 'You should grow a moustache,' Kuttathi had told him, running her fingers through his greying hair, trying to soothe him. 'A big pointy moustache.'

'You can come with me,' Narayanan told Moustache and Ouseph. 'As of now, people have only heard about Moustache. When they see you in person, this land will go back to how it was over two hundred years ago.'

Like Ouseph, Moustache too was not convinced by this aging man. He seemed to be trying to actualise, to make real, the things that he had done pretending to be Moustache, and the stories that had been told about him. Narayanan noticed their distrust. Using his long-oar to pull back the boat that had begun to drift away in the current, he said: 'To be honest, I don't know where Malaya is. I only know the land around this lake. But the woman you've been searching for … I know where she is now.'

His words tempted them. As though to prove his trustworthiness, he showed them his shoulders.

'It was a long time ago. I tried to stop the man who was taking her away.'

Narayanan had truly believed that he was Moustache when he had done it. Or, at least that he would become Moustache through this deed.

'And he tried to cut off my arms.'

Ouseph and Moustache saw the old, puckered scars on Narayanan's shoulders.

24
KATTAPULAVAN

There are two creatures that are called pulavan. One is an ordinary pulavan that is a water snake, and the other, the kattapulavan, is a mud snake. There were plenty of both these creatures all around Kuttanad. They caused no harm to anything other than frogs and small fish, and were not even worthy of being called snakes. However, when a person was described as a kattapulavan, everyone would know immediately that this person was not ordinary or harmless. There was a reason behind this.

In those days, the name kattapulavan also conjured up images of two entirely different men in people's minds. One was a middle-aged Pattar, a Tamil Brahmin from the Mankombu Swamy household, and the other was a man from Thanneermukkam who never came out of the water.

Ordinarily, Pattars, as a caste, were excellent cooks and connoisseurs of food. Despite wearing the sacred thread asserting caste privilege, and a lineage that included cunning and clever people such as Ramayyan Dalawa who was the Diwan of Thiruvithamkur during Maharaja Anizham Thirunal Marthandavarma's rule, everyone, especially the Nairs, regarded them with disdain. There was a saying among the Nair community: If there was nothing else to eat, one could survive on grass, and if there was no one else to marry, one might consider a Pattar. Still, the Mankombu Swamy household, landowners and excellent agriculturists, were held in high regard across the land. They had acres of arable land on both sides of the River Pamba, all along Pulinkunnu and Mankombu. But the Pattar of this story was different from them. As he went around inspecting the cultivation, he did not chat with the boatmen about the paddy, the rains, the weevils or the transplanting. Instead, he sat in the boat gazing into the clear water, absorbed in the magical landscape underneath, imagining forests, palaces, promenades, kings and hunters. His companions wondered whether it was a secret desire to eat roast fish that glittered in his eyes as he watched the shad and the catfish and the king crab in the water. If it was so, it was dangerous, especially at his age. There was a story about a Namboothiri Brahmin from Alappuzha who happened to eat fish by mistake and became obsessed with its taste. He began insisting on eating his rice mixed with fish curry and seasoned buttermilk – two types of food that should never be eaten together. A Portuguese cook was quietly brought to the coconut storehouse at the family household, and the Namboothiri engaged in unfamiliar culinary pleasures as enthusiastically as in clandestine affairs. However, overconsumption of this forbidden food finally caught up with him, and he passed away from an ulcerated intestine.

The Pattar was lackadaisical even in the fields, and showed very little interest in the crops. Instead, he stood gazing into waterwheel tanks and channels. In the fields that spread to the horizon, workers, confident that the master was otherwise occupied, spread handfuls of mud instead of paddy seeds, sticking their hands in the basket of seeds on their heads only on the rare occasion when he glanced absentmindedly in their direction. This was dishonest work, no doubt, but on the days when the Pattar came to oversee the work, their children slept with their bellies full of kanji made out of the sprouted seeds.

Eventually, the Pattar stopped going to the fields. It was then that the extent of his fascination with the waterways was fully revealed. He had placed two kattapulavans someone had caught for him in a stone trough, and had taken to observing them closely. It was widely assumed that the viper was the only snake that reproduced by giving birth rather than laying eggs. The Pattar believed that the kattapulavan also gave birth to its young. He was determined to be the first person to prove it scientifically through close personal observation, and have an article published in a journal in England or somewhere else equally prestigious. Soon, he had several other ponds and troughs built around the house. People who brought him specimens of kattapulavan were rewarded with a small measure of paddy. It was quite easy to catch a kattapulavan, using a coconut-leaf spine with a noose on its end, but the Pattar examined all specimens brought to him carefully and closely, and only accepted those which were in pristine condition. Overnight, the insignificant creature became a thing of great value, and in times of want, women and children took to searching for kattapulavans in running water and in sluices, standing stock-still holding their breaths with their dip nets.

The other person who came to people's minds when they heard the name 'kattapulavan' was from Thanneermukkam, the land of Vaalan fisherfolk. Further to the west, in Thaikkal, Arthunkal and Kanichukulangara, they were known as Arayans. Arayans were sea fishermen who caught seer fish, tuna, sardines and milk fish, while Vaalans caught shrimps, pearlspot, snakeheads and wallago in inland canals and lakes salinated by the same sea that surged through the port of Kochi. Lake fish was an acquired taste, but once familiar with it, people found it more nutritious and flavoursome than sea fish. The Pulayans, Chovans and Christians also got into the waters with gill nets and shrimp nets, but it was the Vaalans who were fishermen by trade. For the others, the lake provided recourse when there was no other work, and while they often left without catching anything, the Vaalans managed to catch something even when fish was scarce. It took even more skill and a great deal of cunning to get a good price for their catch. Their women carried the fish in baskets balanced on their heads to the east, and sold them from house to house, persuading the householders with their musical talk. The Vaalans were known for their silent patience as they stood for hours on end in deserted corners of the waterways, but when they left with their catch, it was as though their tongues were blessed with the gift of words by Goddess Saraswathy herself.

There was one man among them who had never caught even a spit-eating rasbora, and whose tongue was crooked. His name was Kattapulavan, and like the snake whose name he bore, he rarely left the water. He and his two younger brothers had learned to swim even before they could walk. He moved silently through the lakes and canals, observing his surroundings, only his head visible amidst the water hyacinths and swamp grass. Like the turtle and the otter that also did not like to leave the water, he could hold his breath underwater for long distances. But no water creature attacked him, and unlike the clam pickers and waterwheel workers, the cold water did not affect his virility.

One day, Kattapulavan rose to the surface of the water, and told his brothers: 'I saw a river.'

'What? There's a river under the lake?'

The youngest brother was unconvinced, but the middle one had no doubts. Like children going after a new type of dragonfly or a bee, they dived eagerly into the water. Following their older brother's directions, they rode the current and came to a river under the lake on the western edge, flowing all the way from Pallathuruthi through the Kochi port into the sea. They drank the water, and it tasted as clear as the water of the Kavanaar or the Pennar. Still, they were not surprised. They had seen so many things under the lake. Once, in a deep spot near Pallippuram, they had come across the skeleton of a creature larger than an elephant.

The lake was at its narrowest in Thanneermukkam. If one hollered while standing on the near bank, the sound would travel as far as the church of Vechoor Muthi on the opposite bank. The eastern bank was not as inaccessible as it was near Muhamma – a boat could cross over in less than two minutes. And because of it, no boat carrying goods or people could ply between Kochi and Alappuzha without the folks of Thanneermukkam knowing about it. Kattapulavan began his work, sometimes alone and, at other times, with his brothers, as soon as darkness fell. They would swim up to the boats and board them. Trying to resist them in the water was as futile as standing up to elephants in the forest. Some would hand over all their money and escape. Kattapulavan was not interested in the copra or coconut oil in the boats. It was too difficult to handle and to store. But he would throw the goods in the water if money was not handed over. Boatmen prayed for a calm passage through the lake when they had women in their boats. Kattapulavan and his brothers were known to appear beside boats caught in a storm as though to rescue them. They would leave the men to their fates, and drag the women by their hair to overgrown spots nearby. The islets of Pathiramanal and other isolated places held the suppressed screams of so many unfortunate women.

It was to Kattapulavan that Narayanan was taking Moustache and Ouseph. He chewed the greying end of his moustache that he had grown because of Kuttathi.

'After what happened in Kavarchapaadam a long time ago, no one attacked women in those parts except Kattapulavan and his brothers,' he told them.

The reddish golden hairs on Ouseph's moustache quivered untidily in the wind. Only Moustache's moustache had no one behind it. It was all there was.

Kavarchapaadam – looting fields – was an area in Kainadi where lawlessness ruled, and bandits sowed terror and harvested wealth. In those days, the lake lay exposing its watery essence, the fields around it barely cultivated. The forests on its shores were deserted, their floors unmarked with lanes. The few penurious inhabitants stayed confined to their hutments and the little patches of land they worked. The only way out was through the lake ruled by torch-bearing bandits. When there were no travellers to rob, they would come in their fast boats lit by flaming torches to the well-to-do houses on the verges of canals snaking away from the lake. They took everything – from cooking pots to paddy stores, from lamps to livestock. When they came across women in the middle of the lake, they took all their ornaments, and disregarding caste or status, they forced themselves upon them, and afterwards cut their throats.

The leader of one such gang was a man named Thumbelkuruppu. Most of the members of his gang were Parayans, and they spread fear along the banks of the Pamba River from Muttar onwards, and along the lake from Eera to Alappuzha, killing and looting for their leader. They preferred livestock and women as their share, the ornaments and money were for their leader who stayed back at home, and looked after them and gave them weapons. One time, they chanced upon a substantial loot, and came back to Thumbelkuruppu roaring victoriously with a blood-soaked bundle of banana leaf. He stepped into the water happily, washed the blood off the bundle and opened it. The contents made him dizzy. The bloody ornaments, made of beaten gold, were familiar.

'And the person … Is she alive?'

That day Thumbelkuruppu disbanded his gang, and the place where his niece was murdered by his own people came to be known was Kavarchapaadam.

'This is the first time Kattapulavan has had a woman live with him permanently,' Narayanan said.

They set out in his boat, keeping to the darkness. It was a full moon night, and the lake was soaked in silvery light. The tide rose silently, and as it submerged the greenery on the small islets, several moons rose in the lake. Moustache looked back and forth at the clear sky above and its faithful copy in the lake. Faithful copies of his own being sat at the bow and the stern of the boat, and rowed harder and more enthusiastically than him. Moustache himself was the copy of a copy. If Ezhuthachan was alive today, would he remember the character in his play, the moustached policeman to whom he had not bothered to give even a line of dialogue? He must have created the policeman as the reflection of a policeman, or several of them, he had met in his life. But there was a huge distance between the policemen in real life and the one in the play. And the moustached man who had appeared onstage was not the same man who had escaped into the paddy fields, or the one who was described in the stories and songs. There were great chasms of difference between the events described, and between the iterations of the man himself. Even if Ezhuthachan remembered the character that he had created, he might not know that the man who played it had refused to take off the costume, and had run away, creating numerous stories, more famous than his play that had failed to find success. Even if he had come across stories of Moustache, he might not remember the character he had created, or recognise him in the stories. A father and his son were fundamentally strangers, and so were faithful copies of the same thing.

The boat pulled into Pathiramanal, an islet that reinvented itself every night. The otters that lined up on it as soon as it rose from the water jumped into the lake, barking and cackling. Ouseph and Narayanan marched in through the bushes of flowering screw pine as though desperate to prove that the stories they had heard were true. In the stories and songs, Seetha was with Moustache, not Kattapulavan. Stories were made up about Moustache, and so he must now change to become the stories. Ouseph and Narayanan were like two children obsessively listening to the stories, disregarding hunger and thirst. Stories are realised through the minds of the listeners, and their minds worked, eagerly and energetically, to ensure that Moustache's story would have the ending that they desired. Narayanan knocked on the door of a house Kattapulavan used to frequent in his lustful days. A woman, her youth beginning to fade, opened the door instantly as though she had been waiting for them. She protected the flame of the lamp with her hand, sending their faces into shadow. She looked pleased. For the five or six years she had lived with Kattapulavan, she had been scared that someone might come looking for him on one of the nights he was at home. Now, in her relieved happiness, she lifted a corner of her mundu and covered her sagging breasts.

'He doesn't come here any more,' she told Narayanan, as though they had known each other for a long time. 'Must be with her.'

She knew where he had put Seetha up. There was no secret that women did not know. They just pretended not to know things.

Back in the boat, Narayanan said: 'No one can catch him in the water or the bunds, not even the police or the army.'

The police had apprehended Kattapulavan only once, a long time ago when he was not as harmful as he would become later, and that was when he had come out of the water. His brothers tended to him afterwards, healing the damage he had sustained from the encounter. They buried him neck-deep in the powdery sand. Digging another hole next to it, they burned herbs and medicines in it, and directed the smoke using hollowed-out reeds to the bruises on his body, and fed him medicines prepared with the flesh of a black cat and a goat. When he emerged from the sand, he was stronger and more energised than ever before.

The home Kattapulavan had set up for Seetha was reminiscent of the place where she had lived with Kuttanasari, except that there were no fields around it. The walls lined with wooden planks on the inside had vines clambering over them on the outside. The floor was polished cow dung, just as she liked it. Instead of the embankment, it stood on a ridge of sediment between the lake and the canals, reinforced with clay clods to stop the water rising above it. Flowering mallow poles and othalam trees with their green ear studs protected the house from the wind. It was an unassuming home; no one would look at it twice. She liked it that way – she disliked being disturbed even by the birds flying over her compound. There were no creatures to poke around, and yet she walked vigilant around the pallathi and chemballi snapper laid to dry on mats in the hot sun. Even Kattapulavan had to announce his arrival with a holler before the boat pulled up, otherwise she raged at him. She had no desire to be out in the world; she was content to safeguard her own little patch from it.

'So this Kattapulavan – is that a snake or a person?'

A five-year-old's intelligence turned into a question.

'Sometimes a snake and at other times a person.'

'But when it is a snake, won't people beat it to death?'

'Well, it's possible. People tend to beat snakes to death as soon as they set eyes on them. Even when they don't want to harm us, we go after them and kill them. God makes us do that. It's in the Bible.'

'Is Kattapulavan poisonous?'

'No. But in the water he is very powerful. He hides among the water grass and watches us, and we don't even realise he's around. We really can't touch him when he's in the water.'

'What can we do then?'

'Well, everyone and everything has a point of vulnerability no matter how strong. You know, like Samson and his hair, or Karnan and his ear ornaments. For the rhinoceros, its horn is the most vulnerable, for the eagle, its talons. And for Moustache, his moustache which is larger than any other in the whole world. Do you know what Kattapulavan's vulnerability is?'

'No.'

'His brothers. They're his strength as well as his vulnerability. His left arm and his right arm.'

'So what do we do?'

'On land, Kattapulavan is just an ordinary pulavan. Easy enough to grab by the tail and smash on the ground. So Moustache's friends hatched a plan. They befriended his youngest brother, honoured him and gave him things.'

'Gifts?'

'Yes. They asked him why his brother had taken up with a woman and made a house for her. They told him he was not interested in his brothers any more, that he didn't love them as much as he used to. After a while, the brother began to feel that this was true. That this woman was a bad influence and had come to cause a rift between them. And he agreed to get his brother out of the water.'

'And…?'

'And after he came out of the water, he and Moustache would stop Kattapulavan, while Moustache's friends would get rid of Seetha. But don't let the middle brother know of your plans, he warned them. He never questioned his older brother.'

'And what happened?'

'So the little brother told Kattapulavan that the middle brother was in danger and got him to come out of the water. In the moonlit night, he ran to rescue his brother whom he loved dearly. But suddenly his brother was right there in front of him, and he realised it was a ruse. He turned back, but a dense, dark forest had appeared behind him, with rocky outcrops of hair as strong as scrub. Such sudden darkness that he had only ever seen when rain-bearing clouds appeared from the east. But he was not scared.

'He looked sadly at his youngest brother who had betrayed him.

'"Guess you'll kill me now," he told Moustache. "But remember, this is a man who betrayed his own brother, and sure as hell he'll betray you too one day. But don't punish him for it. He's too young to realise the consequences of his actions."'

'Did Moustache kill Kattapulavan?' Ponnu asked.

'I don't know. All I know is that he defeated him as he did all other men. The stories say that he killed him, and the songs say that Kattapulavan left the land and went far away. Either way, he must have fought really hard.

'Like a termite in a mound, he hid
Flapping like a rooster, he flew
Like a jackal in the bushes, he ran.

'Whatever happened, from then on, Moustache would have to be vigilant. If Kattapulavan had died, he'd come back as a spirit. Or if he had gone away, he was sure to rise stealthily out of the water and get his revenge.'

'Does Moustache only defeat men?' Ponnu asked.

Seetha warded off all advances from Ouseph and Narayanan. Like a mother hen protecting her chicks, she scratched and screeched around her house and the islet. Narayanan tried to reason with her.

'Have you not heard the songs?' he asked. 'In all of them, you're with him. Isn't he better than all the other men?'

She ignored him. Those songs and stories – they were not about her. How dare they make them up and try to trap her in them?

Moustache did not realise it was only the third time he had actually seen her in real life. The difference between the Seetha in his mind and in the songs and the figure in front of him stunned him. On their first encounter, on the night he and Paviyan had been led astray in the canals, she had paid him no attention. Her rage had been focused only on Paviyan, and all Vavachan had seen were her breasts. Those breasts seemed the same, but she had bound them flat to her chest with a piece of cloth. After he had escaped into the fields as Moustache, she was the only living person who had stood up to him. Trying to recall the smells that had triggered his desires on that day, he walked towards her. But she stood her ground, a dancing goddess extraordinarily powerful in her abode, refusing to leave it, unaffected by conciliation or intimidation. In the light of the moon, dark scars from the pestilence stood out on her shoulders, face and neck. The left eye had closed shut when the pox healed, but her body remained voluptuous, like the undulating eastern hills visible from the fields.

Unlike anyone else before, Seetha ignored the moustache and looked Moustache straight in the eye, and when he averted his eyes, she spat on his face. Without a word, Moustache put his arms around her and carried her to the boat. She fought harder, and he parted the long vines of her hair in the middle and tied her to the seat plank with it.

By the time they reached the middle of the lake, it was morning. They rowed hard to reach their destination before the day heated up. Trade boats plying the lake moved away from their shadow.

Narayanan pointed to a boat piled with paddy and covered with hay.

'That boat belongs to someone who's your benefactor. No toll collector dares approach it.'

Moustache sat in the boat wishing, hoping, that the songs would finally come true. He wanted to be left alone with Seetha, find an islet or an embankment to set up home. He looked at Ouseph and Narayanan wondering when they would go away and leave them alone.

Narayanan pulled the boat in under a punna tree and stepped off. Leaving Ouseph to watch Seetha, he walked a little distance from the boat with Moustache.

'Untie her,' he told Moustache in an admonishing tone.

'What if she runs away?'

'She won't. But if she does, let her go,' Narayanan said.

He thought about what his life had become since he had met Kuttathi.

'You don't know how to behave with women,' he told Moustache. 'This big moustache and strong muscles aren't enough. None of that matters to them. They have to make up their own minds. They're not scared of blood. They see too much of it anyway. And they're not scared of a moustache either. They have to like it for themselves.'

'And in the end Moustache and Seetha lived as king and queen forever, didn't they?'

Ponnu's question reflected the usual rationale of stories, ones that adults concoct for children, with happy endings. They reflect the same idiocy that is contained in self-help books on how to succeed in life. Why do we feel compelled to inculcate in them the idea that life is a string of good things that lead, eventually, to a successful destination? Soon enough, they realise we have been lying to them all along. There is nothing more nonsensical in this world than stories that end in moralistic life lessons or in the triumph of good over evil. The story of the mud clod and the dry leaf, where the mud clod protects the dry leaf from the wind, and the dry leaf protects the mud clod from the rain, is actually a lesson about the tragedy and darkness that engulf marginalised lives. And yet we narrate them as though it was a comedy of errors, portraying the protagonists as stupid and unintelligent.

'Not exactly,' I replied. 'Defeating Kattapulavan increased Moustache's fame. From Kayamkulam Lake to Veerambuzha, from Onattukara to Kodungallur, no one travelled along the tributaries and waterways of Periyar, Meenachilar, Pamba and Manimalayar rivers without thinking about him and his friends. The shadows of the night took on his features. The police forces of two lands – Kochi and Thiruvithamkur – were after him. In those days, these were two separate countries. But the lake straddled both, waters flowed both ways, and the fish and the tortoise swam between them.'

'Could people also come and go between them?'

I did not answer. Instead, I said: 'But everything comes to an end. There's nothing that is constant.

'One night, as Moustache lay asleep under a covered boat, an acquaintance of Narayanan approached him as though it had been planned in advance. He stood above him, cautious, watching the surroundings, barely breathing. It was pitch dark, but Moustache saw him clearly. The man had an even skin tone and a thin body. He wore a white upper garment and a mundu that reached his ankles. He had a gravelly voice and a way of repeatedly explaining what he said, as though he was teaching.'

'What did he say? Was he a wizard?'

'That's actually an interesting story. In the western part of the Vembanad Kayal, there was a place called Cherthala, where people walked dragging their swollen feet. To the north of it, there was a small village named Vayalar surrounded by water on three sides. Apparently, all the men in this village had grown moustaches. The government and the landowners told them to shave them off but they refused. And it seemed that the army was being summoned to make them comply. But the people of Vayalar were adamant, and were preparing to take on the army with spears made of bamboo and areca.'

'I bet they won. There are lots of moustaches, no?'

What was the point of instigating the poor to grow moustaches? It was more difficult to overcome a single, determined person. A crowd, on the other hand, is easily defeated. I continued the story.

'There's no one who hasn't heard about you,' the man told Moustache. 'It's time you proved your might. They're expecting you to join them with an army of five thousand men from both sides of the lake. I don't know where this idea came from, but everyone seems to truly believe it. If you're with them, there's absolutely no doubt they'll win.'

The man looked expectantly at Ouseph and Narayanan.

'Where am I to find five thousand men?' Moustache asked him.

The man decided to use the opportunity to impart his knowledge.

'In the war in *Mahabharatam*, Lord Krishnan chose a side and look how powerful they became. Your presence is equal to that of five thousand men.'

'I've never heard such stories,' Moustache said. 'I don't want to go. I like to go where I want to go.'

'You think the army will let you be once they defeat the villagers?' the man was annoyed. 'They'll search these canals and fields with a fine-toothed comb. The army is not like our fire-stick police. They have guns.'

'It seems the villagers are making up songs about your arrival, and preparing to defeat the army,' Narayanan intervened.

Moustache smiled, his teeth gleaming whitely from behind the curtain of his moustache. They realised that it was the first time they had seen him smile.

'I haven't promised anyone anything. I'm not coming.'

Displeased, the visitor left. Ouseph and Narayanan went with him. Free at last, Moustache thought, and sighed as he watched their boat disappear into the darkness.

'And did the moustached villagers win the battle?' Ponnu asked.

'How could they? The British sahebs' army confronted them with smoking guns.'

'Do the sahebs have moustaches?'

'They have them if they want and don't have them if they don't. But, you know, when they were fighting with the villagers, there were two things that surprised them. One was that there was a man among the villagers who looked just like a saheb, with golden hair and white skin. And there was another man who had a gun in his hand when all other men fought with sharpened wooden spears. A gun that had belonged to the government and had gone missing a long time ago – a Berthier rifle.'

'Did the army come after Moustache after they defeated the villagers?' Ponnu asked.

25

A HOLIDAY TRIP

I had decided I would make Ponnu's summer holiday this year special. Children live for holidays; their time in school is only a long sleep between two holidays. Ponnu wanted a boat trip around the lake. But the houseboats, refurbished old-fashioned covered boats targeting the tourist market, were expensive and tawdry. Travelling in them, one had to endure the nonsensical descriptions and history prepared purely for the tourists by their staff, and the one-fourth Chinese, one-fourth North Indian fare that was sold as authentic local cuisine. So why not take the government boat, I thought. The Alappuzha–Kottayam service that had been suspended for years when the bridge at Kanjiram was being built had recently been reinstated, and it would suit my skinny wallet better as it charged eighteen rupees to go across the lake to Alappuzha instead of the ten thousand rupees that the houseboats demanded. I remembered that there had been no complaints when the boat service was suspended. It was not a necessity these days, as there was not a single shore left in these parts that did not have roads suitable for cars. In the past, the only way to reach Alappuzha was by boat, but now there was the Alappuzha–Changanassery road across Kuttanad and the Pamba River, and the Thanneermukkam Bund Road across the lake. Besides, there was no pressing reason to go to Alappuzha any more. The old trading capital of the state is now a ghost city; its position has been handed over to Ernakulam.

Just as I had expected, there were only a handful of people waiting for the boat in the early morning chill, most of them as elderly as the boat itself – an asthmatic old thing that travelled blindly back and forth across the most beautiful part of the whole world. The driver struggled to manoeuvre it through the densely growing water hyacinth and African payal. The Thanneermukkam Bund had stopped the salination of the lake water, but it had upset the ecosystem and created the perfect habitat for the water hyacinth which had multiplied and choked the waterways. And the African payal, brought by some plant-lover to these parts, had escaped from the aquariums into the canals and the lake itself. Once upon a time, paddy-field workers had drunk the water directly from the canals, but now it stank of dirt and decay, and caused rashes on the skin.

As soon as the boat left the jetty, the magnificent scenery that had hidden itself from the prying eyes of the town was revealed. The early morning mist shrouded the embankments. In bygone days, these embankments were regularly strengthened with clay dug up from the lake and stomped down by the Pulayans. Now they had stone walls and coconut groves to reinforce them. Cracked bunds that destroyed crops were a thing of the past. The fields themselves have changed, their endless expanse tamed into small patches of land with boundaries of coconut trees and bunds wide enough for four-wheeled vehicles. Still, the outer bunds were overgrown, fecund jungles of wild fig and kaakkapazham, and tumbling vines as high as a man. When Vavachan had escaped into these fields, it was kaakkapazham, a fruit similar to the custard apple, that had helped sustain his life. Today, it has been renamed as 'noni fruit', and several products made from it are sold in the markets. I had once attended a presentation by a direct marketing representative who had an interesting story to tell about this fruit.

The marketing representative was dressed in ironed clothes and a necktie. He had drawn a picture of the fruit on the blackboard.

'Look,' he had said, 'our elders called this kaakkapazham – the fruit that crows eat. Have you ever seen a dead crow other than the ones electrocuted on the power lines? They are known to be immortal, and that points to the medicinal properties of this fruit.'

He had gone on to claim that the fruit had properties that protected against cancer and other major illnesses, and that many of the westerners who came to Kerala had the ulterior motive of acquiring this fruit.

Gazing at the overgrown bunds, a passenger said: 'It's full of mongoose, pangolins and rat snakes.'

This was a timeless place which had once been filled with the echoes of the footfalls of field workers, the hollers of ploughmen, and the chatter of womenfolk. In harvest season, migrant workers from the east and hawkers selling duck eggs and coffee had lived on the embankments. Today, most of the fields lay fallow, weed-grown; the land raised centuries ago from swamp and water was returning to its innate nature. Now, only a few enterprising people, with an eye on government subsidies, ventured to cultivate these fields. Paddy is not a highly valued commodity any more, and very few workers enter the fields to tend to it, to build the polders, protect the edges, weed out the wild grass, and transplant the seedlings. Machines do the harvesting now, and so there is no need to build threshing yards or to measure out wages in paddy. The only workers who enter the fields these days are the daily wage migrant labourers from northern India who are sent in only when the paddy is too flattened to be harvested by machines.

Our boat reached Vettikkadu, and the driver switched off the engine. A boatman, wearing only his underclothes, got into the water to clear the weeds entangled in the propeller. This was the place where Moustache had met Khadija, the place that had been forsaken when the pestilence hit, from where he had set out to Chemmayikkari in search of Seetha. The bustle of the covered boats transporting goods from the mountains was now a long-ago memory. I don't think Moustache would have come this way after that.

As Narayanan's friend had predicted, the British army, having defeated the rebellious moustached villagers, had not given up the pursuit of Moustache. They searched every inch of the lake, the canals, the islets, and the houses all across the eastern shore of the lake for him, and for the few small-moustached villagers who had escaped capture. By then, Moustache had left the fields and the lake that had protected him for all those years, and had gone east, either up the Meenachilar River or the Periyar, into the forests with Seetha. In the stories of the first migrants to the highlands, there is mention of a moustached man who had helped their ancestors clear the forests and prepare farmlands, a man who scared everyone but was scared of a woman. The stories also mention a moustached man who was the helper of the Tamilian bulldozer operator who had come to cut a tunnel through the hills when the Kottayam–Kumali road was being modernised. It is said that both of them were plagued by nightmares about their bulldozer overturning ever since they had cut the road through the ancestral burial site of the aboriginal people of the land, the Adivasis.

The landowning class used to joke that the Pulayan, no matter how far he went or how wide he ranged, would come right back to the edges of the fields. Moustache too returned, after an absence of many long years, without Seetha. Some parakeets defy domestication no matter how gentle the owner, and some yam vines refuse to be trained no matter how hospitable the support. Those who survive smallpox do not usually get afflicted a second time because they develop immunity against the disease. But the pox erupted for a second time on Seetha's face, and a shivering fever that was common in the hills laid her low. Still, just before she took her last breath, she spat on Moustache's face.

Moustache did not want to stay on in the land of strangers where he buried her. So he came back, rowing his boat down the Meenachilar into one of its tributaries, and then into the Mudakkali canal, with only the remnants of the memories of his life with Seetha for company. By then, times had changed. Neendoor had forgotten the stories about

Moustache and the days when growing a moustache was a matter of considerable consternation. There was still some feeling that those who grew inordinately large moustaches were arrogant, but even teachers sported 'eleven' moustaches that looked like two lines above the middle of their upper lip, or the 'centipede' moustache that took up a considerable amount of time to groom. Pointy moustaches fashioned out of facial hair left to grow unchecked until it could be trimmed, oiled and shaped were still rare. When the sons of those who had met Vavachan in real life grew up and became policemen, they created these proud pointy moustaches on their faces. When they appeared on festival grounds, crowds dispersed as quickly as they had done when the policeman in Ezhuthachan's play had appeared onstage. And these new policemen vented their anger and frustrations on the moustaches of the criminals they captured.

As Vavachan's boat moved along the canals, large crowds gathered along the canal paths from Pallithazhe junction to Chozhiyappara. Most were local people, but there were a few eager boatmen from the western parts of the lake who were at Athirampuzha market at the time. Moustache was more dazzling in the stories of their lands than in those of Neendoor or Kaipuzha. In the crowds were people who had known Paviyan and Chella, and those who were acquainted with their other children. Only a handful of people could recognise Vavachan by sight. A few older Mappilas remembered the play that was staged in a sesame field for three days, and a couple had even seen it. But no one in the crowds that assembled along the canal paths had seen Vavachan after the play was over and he had refused to shave off the moustache. He had allowed himself to be seen only by a handful since then. One was Pathrose Pulayan, who had lived an extraordinarily long life, and had passed away only a couple of years before. Kesava Pillah had disappeared after being involved in property business for many years with his nephews. He had moved successfully from one property related case to another until, one day, three young men had waylaid him, destroyed the documents he had with him, and sent him into penury.

As the crowds watched, the sky and the atmosphere at the spot where Anjumana canal and Mudakkali canal met darkened. Slowly, the darkness moved south announcing Vavachan's progress down the canals, and when he came into view, they gasped at the majesty of his moustache. Women and the young ran away, panicking. The moustache was larger than anything they had conjured up in their wildest imagination. As the boat passed between two low-growing branches of the flowering mallow on each side of the canal, wide enough for ordinary people to pass through, the hairs of the moustache got entangled in them. Two brave young men swam out and disentangled them.

Another family had set up home where Paviyan's hut used to be, and the women and children living there had started crying, convinced that Moustache would tear their home apart. But Vavachan paid it no attention, not even with his memories. He looked, instead, to an embankment further ahead, where he had met the ghost who had asked him for food. He knew, with certainty, that this land had nothing to offer him, not even food. Vavachan rowed on without stopping, and the crowds watched as his boat disappeared with the dark rain-bearing clouds into the western horizon.

After the brief layover in Vettikkadu, our boat entered the lake. The roiling waves and turbulent currents of the old days were consigned to memory, but the Vembanad Lake still possessed a wild, untamed beauty.

'This is the lake,' I told Ponnu as the boat swayed. 'Your great grandfather, my grandfather, Pachupillah, was quite the businessman. He used to row his trade boats across this lake to Alappuzha and Mattancherry.'

'Oh! Wasn't he scared?'

'Of course he was, but he was quite clever.'

Pachupillah had never had the occasion to meet Moustache. Still, he managed to insinuate his name into the songs about Moustache, thus protecting himself. He would have prospered even if he had not thought of this ruse, but the journey into prosperity that he had set himself on as a way of getting back at his detractors would not have been as smooth. And now, here I am, his descendent, writing my own name into the story of Moustache.

The lake that, like humans, became volatile in the evenings lay motionless in the morning chill. All other creatures had set out on their day's work. Little birds skimmed over the surface; cormorants silently shook their necks in the water; lines of migratory birds swayed across the sky like wind-ragged threads. A middle-aged man stood by a boat steadied with a long-oar, and dove for clams. He came up shaking away the plastic entangled in his fingers. I had read recently in the newspaper that the bottom of the lake was now covered in a two-metre-thick layer of plastic instead of seed clams, rays and aquatic grass. Instead of fossilised pieces of wood and coal, it was empty bottles of alcohol that swept down the five rivers in the rain. People would laugh if they were told that, until seventy years ago, there were crocodiles and sharks in these waters; that, before the Thanneermukkam Bund was built, Kumarakam fishermen used to catch mackerel and sardine that swam into the lake with the surging seawater. According to the figures, the lake has shrunk by one-third of its size in the last one hundred years.

The boat pulled in to Chithirakkadavu although there was no one to embark or disembark. Here were fields that Outhachan had dredged up from the lake, and now they lay abandoned. The Chithira church he had built was also abandoned, with no priest to offer Holy Qurbana or parishioners to receive it. The bunds around the fallow fields had started to disintegrate and let the lake back in. I sent out a silent prayer that the lake would quickly claim back what had once belonged to it before new tourist resorts are built. It was impossible to know where the office room that was Kunjachan's playground had been, where Moustache had defeated him, where, finally, Kuttathi had helped him find one of the two things that he had spent most of his life searching for. I was suddenly overcome by a certainty that although Moustache's life had no more stories to add, stories told about him had not come to an end.

Five or six years ago, before Moustache Vavachan, the man I had met sometime in my younger days, had begun spinning stories in my mind, I was obsessed with food in all its variety. I travelled to Tamil Nadu to sample Thalappakatti biriyani, ennai kathirikai and Chettinad delicacies; tasted spicy pickles in Andhra Pradesh and potato stuffed parathas in Himachal Pradesh; searched for the best mutton kebabs made by the Muslim communities in Bangalore … I believe that no other country has the culinary diversity we do. Each village has its own cuisine. In coastal Kerala alone, there are more than a hundred ways of cooking fish. In Pune, I met a woman named Anisa Kooka who cooked some Parsi dishes for me – fragrant rice, sali murghi, and a beautiful dhansak made of tender lamb. As I rested after stuffing myself on the excellent food, I was curious to know about her name.

'Kooka! That's an unusual name…'

'Think about it,' she said, laughing. 'There's a Parsi by that name who's done something that all Indians can be proud of. If you can give me the correct answer, I'll cook you another Parsi dish.'

My mind scrambled through the general knowledge books I had read while trying to get a job, and the names of famous Indian Parsis – Tata, Dadabhai Naoroji, Pherozeshah Mehta, Feroze Gandhi … No Kooka among them. I gave up.

'Try harder,' she said. 'There's a connection with aeroplanes.'

'Bobby Kooka!' I said.

'Correct! He's my father-in-law.'

I marvelled at the history unfolding before me. The famous mascot of Air India, the Maharaja with the impressive pointy moustache, was Bobby Kooka's idea. Air India was founded by Tata, and in the year the company was taken over by the Indian government, a man named Umesh Rao had designed its mascot based on Kooka's idea.

'It's the most wonderful of all airline mascots I've seen,' I said. 'So regal … Is it an actual maharaja of Parsi descent?'

Anisa laughed.

'No, no. "We call him a maharaja for want of a better description, but his blood is not blue. He may look like royalty, but he isn't royal."

Bobby himself said this when someone objected to the symbol of affordable air travel in India being a maharaja. In fact, you'll be amazed to know that he got the idea for the mascot from your place. He had some relatives in Alappuzha who were merchants, and they told him some scary stories about a man with a big moustache. I guess those stories stayed with him.'

'In that case, I must put on record my objections about Air India not giving us Malayalees due credit,' I told Anisa. 'Sit on the Maharaja's shoulder one day and come to Kerala. I'll make some fish curry with mangoes for you.'

I got off the boat with my son, and walked along the Mullakkal lane, which was crowded as the temple festival was going on. The town of Alappuzha was built by Diwan Raja Kesavadasan, the moustached prime minister of the moustached king, Dharmaraja. Did Vavachan ever visit this town? It is unlikely that he would have shown his face in a crowded place like this during his furtive life. Still, Alappuzha is a land defined by the lake and the numerous canals sprouting from it, and it is in their stories that the lore of Moustache achieved more glory than those along the eastern lands of the lake.

We walked for a while and went into a new-style restaurant, and ordered puttu and duck curry. When he escaped into the fields, Moustache was in search of the road to Malaya. The search for Seetha came later, and he managed to find her. Even Ponnu did not ask whether he ever found his way to Malaya. My belief is that he never managed to find his way there. But recently, I read an article in a travel magazine about Singapore, which was part of the old Malaya. The author of that article was also a food enthusiast, someone who travelled the world sampling unusual flavours and wrote about them to make the rest of us drool. 'Living to Eat' – that was the title of his regular column in the magazine. He wrote about a restaurant chain that served traditional Malay food in Singapore – a land predominantly populated by people of Chinese origin. It was named 'Meesai'! Meesai is the Malay word for moustache, the origin of which must have been Tamil, for in the land of Chinese and Malay people who rarely had moustaches, where else would it have come from? The history of the restaurant chain was compelling. It was named after a man with a moustache who had lived there for a while. The current owner's father, who had started the restaurant, had taken in the man with the moustache, and the initial investment for the restaurant came from the money he made exhibiting the man's extraordinary moustache. I think this moustached man must have been a Tamilian – there was no dearth of moustaches among the Tamil – and not Vavachan, son of Paviyan. It would be too far-fetched to think that he could have travelled across the seas and ended up in Malaya. Still, I could not help thinking, there were moments and places in the story of Vavachan's life that are unclear to the rest of us.

What if, on the night he set out with his father to cut grass and got lost in the canals, something else had happened? What if the boat, in which they took Narayanapillah and Shivaramapillah across the river, had not threatened to drift away in the current? I found it interesting to imagine what would have happened if Vavachan had joined them and gone away with them to Malaya. Would Ezhuthachan have found another man to stick the moustache on and perform the role of the policeman in the play? Would that man have frightened the audience as much as Vavachan did? If it had happened, the stories about Moustache-Vavachan would never have been born. The Last Crocodile might have lived longer, and perhaps even had his revenge on Baker Saheb, the man who had annihilated his clan. The people of Kuttanad might have had to wait longer to learn the secrets of the petty and the para that turned the waterwheels and irrigated their fields.

Would Narayanapillah and Shivaramapillah have, in the rest of their lives, remembered the Pulayan boy who took them across the Kallumadayar River on the night they left their home in search of a new life? It was unlikely, as their lives turned out to be interesting and eventful, but there was an intriguing similarity between Narayanapillah and Moustache. Moustache refused to give up the costume he had put on for the play. Narayanapillah too ended up in the world of theatre, and even when he took off his costumes, people refused to accept it.

Narayanapillah and Shivaramapillah's journey to a new life landed them in the middle of a war. The eastern edge of the world was on fire. Japan had taken over Java, Malaya and Singapore, committed mass murder in China, turned women into sex slaves in Korea. Blood and fire rained over the region. Japan was considered undefeatable, and they were bound for India next, having conquered Burma along the way. The British who had ruled India for centuries were about to be defeated. The thought of a liberated India energised Narayanapillah. He joined the Indian National Army, picked up the gun, and joined the war against the British.

But the gods above had other plans, and they rolled the dice that decided destiny differently. Japanese forces and the Indian National Army reached as far as Kohima, but had to retreat. At the western front of the war, Mussolini was beaten to death by his own people, Hitler killed himself, and atom bombs were dropped on the Japanese who refused to surrender.

When, twelve years later, a penniless Narayanapillah and his friend Shivaramapillah returned to Kottayam and reached Kallumada, no grass boat wandered into their path to take them across the river. But the war experience had made them bold, and they swam across the river and went home.

Narayanapillah married the woman who had waited for him all this while, and returned to Malaya. The place was devastated by the war. Yet, those who were ready to work hard were respected there, and were able to make a decent living. For several years, he lived there experiencing the hardship of life, and eventually returned to Olassa with his wife and child. His only asset was the conviction that he could make a living anywhere. He had seen the world, come to know people of many colours, religions and languages, but now he was back in a world where people were cowards, scared even to go across a bund, and lazy, seeing idleness as a sign of nobility.

Still, his fellow beings were not to be trifled with. Narayanapillah, as an enlightened man, tried his hand at many trades in order to make an honest living. He was aware that a capitalist model of making a profit was exploitative yet legal. But his efforts came to nothing as he was scuppered at every stage by his fellow men.

His wife was an intelligent woman.

'You've got to change,' she advised him. 'Nothing can be gained here on the straight and narrow. You need to know how to put on an act. You've got to learn how to hide your intentions and act differently.'

Narayanapillah persevered until, eventually, he was completely broke. People from whom he had borrowed money chased after him, and he took to walking all the way to Kottayam each morning in an effort to avoid them. But he could not hide there either as they had their eyes everywhere.

Finally, he found a place where he could spend his day safely – the public library, a place no one would think of looking for a man who was penniless, and a place no one would chase one out of until it was time to close. Those scurrying around with the concerns of everyday life do not usually end up there. It was a place that attracted those who patiently watched life go by, slowed their pace, even their breathing, sending their eyes into a deeper contemplation. Narayanapillah realised that the library had withstood, silently and motionless, the commotion of a war on the other side of the world where fire had rained from aeroplanes. He began spending his days there pretending to read until, eventually, he started reading for real. Narayanapillah was a man of extremes, and as his reading progressed, he realised that Malaya, America, Russia and Japan were all accessible right there in the library, and he regretted having been away all those years while he could have hidden himself in the world of books.

As he began reading plays, he remembered what his wife had said to him, that he had to put on an act in order to survive in this place. Why not, he thought, and began writing plays. He needed actors to perform them, and he turned to his family and close relatives. Slowly, Narayanapillah and his theatre company began to acquire fame. The people who came to see his plays were familiar with two types of theatre – stories based on myths and legends, or stories of impossible revolutions. And they flocked to see his plays that dealt with ordinary lives and had dialogue that oozed a biting sarcasm. He was no comparison to Moustache, but his confident presence on the stage made them anxious. And there were murmurs, scandals. Onstage, his daughter was his wife, his wife was his mother, and his wife's sister was his lover!

'I just don't get it,' he said to his wife. 'When one tries to live, they want you to act. And when you act, they say that's real life…'

I wanted to ask Moustache whether he knew Narayanapillah, the actor. It would have been impossible to live out a whole life without having watched his plays and heard his magnificent dialogue delivery. Would Moustache have recognised him?

War is a peculiar thing – it destroys some things even as it builds other things up. Narayanapillah, who had joined the Japanese side in the Second World War, came back home to become the well-known playwright and actor, N.N. Pillah. Meanwhile, a soldier named Sathyanesan Nadar who had fought for the British returned home to become a police sub-inspector and, later, the film actor, Sathyan, who twice won the State Award for best actor.

After our meal, I planned to take a bus to Muhamma, and take the boat from there to Kumarakam, where the lake was at its widest. The driver of the boat was a friend of mine from college. He picked up my son, sat him on the top and showed him the sights.

'Do you think I could get an autorickshaw from the jetty to Kavanaar River?' I asked him.

'Yes, but agree on a price first. All of them are terrible brendons.'

The First World War had gifted two words to our local vocabulary. One was 'brendon', after Brendon Saheb, the man who mechanised the waterwheels of Kuttanad. It meant someone who took undue advantage of circumstances. The other was 'yemenden', our way of localising the word 'Emden'. When our people heard about the German submarine, Emden, that caused havoc at Madirasi sea port, they exclaimed: 'Ayyayyo! What yemenden!'

And the word stayed, helpfully providing a way to express our feelings of awe about anything extraordinary.

In Kumarakam, there is a field named after Brendon Saheb, the white man who had come to repair ships during the war. And the lake he drained using the petty and the para he invented is called Brendon Lake. Does anyone remember Moustache, the man who put a stop to Brendon's brendonness? When Narayanapillah came back from Malaya, Moustache's shadowlike presence was felt all across the fields, streams and canals in Olassa and Parippu. He was bound to have heard the stories about Moustache without recognising the young lad in the grass boat who had helped him across the first barrier in his long and convoluted journey.

By the banks of the Kavanaar and the lake, the land set aside by Preacher Saheb for the bird sanctuary still exists. In its dense greenery are nests of cormorants and colonies of bats. But there are very few birdwatchers. The only people who enter it are lovebirds from the city's colleges. Avoiding the watchful eyes of the guards, they climb up the watchtowers to stand naked and rub their beaks together like birds, ruing the fact that the world does not leave them in peace.

'Look, this is the Saheb's bungalow,' I told Ponnu.

Preacher Saheb's teak bungalow is now a five-star hotel.

'Shall we go in? We could look at the crocodile pond and the rascal mango tree,' Ponnu said.

'We can't. They only let rich people in.'

'Was the Saheb also like that?'

'No. You see that school there? The small tile-roofed building? That's the Annie Baker School. The Saheb built it in memory of his little sister who died, so that the children of the poor had a place to study.'

The hotel owners have given employment to local women. They walk around the cottages with long sticks in their hands. The trees that grow around the hotel compound are owned by the government, and the women's job is to quietly dislodge the newly built birds' nests from its branches. Sometimes the nests have eggs or chicks in them, and they shatter on the ground below. Bird droppings stink. The guests who pay top dollar should not have to smell it.

Moustache passed away on the last day of the holidays. I would not have heard of his passing if a friend from Pinanjirakuzhi who knew about my fascination with Moustache had not called to inform me. I sat Ponnu on my motorbike and went across the Kuttomburam Bridge. Never again did Moustache live in the land that refused him sustenance. On rare occasions, he visited the Kuttomburam toddy shop. When he came back and went past where Paviyan's hut had been, he ended up on an embankment in Arpookara where Chella's father had lived. He built himself a hut on it without bothering to take the permission of the landowner. No one challenged him. And although he lived on the embankment, he never took part in the activities in the fields. Like Ouseph, he lived doing the most liberating work in the world – fishing – and he only caught snakeheads which he sold at the junction. If other fish strayed into his nets and baskets, he let them go.

On the eastern corner of the yard of the dead man's house, a blue awning had been put up with a row of red plastic chairs under it. Fifty or so people stood under the awning and around the house. The place looked very similar to Paviyan and Chella's place on the embankment in Chozhiyappara, with the fields in the front and the canal at the back, the house sitting as though partially in the water. Calendars bearing the logo of the Co-operative Bank hung on the walls made of hollow bricks. The floor was cement. The yard was almost non-existent, and yet there were a couple of flower pots. The windows were curtained with old churidar shawls.

I entered the room with Ponnu. It was quiet, no sobs or sadly muttered reminiscences. The deceased was on a bed. A lamp burned at the head of the bed. Eyes don't always tell one the truth, so I looked, again and again. I looked at the three women sitting around him, and looked back at him again. The body on the bed was that of a stranger.

It was very thin, and left almost all of the space on the bed empty. The hands were folded near the waist. It was dressed in an unaccustomed white shirt. And the face was clean-shaven. The soles of the feet that had roamed the world endlessly were pale, as though they had never touched the ground. I was convinced that this was a stranger and that was why the women around the body were whispering to each other and laughing.

'What happened to Vavachan chettan's moustache?'

I took Kuttan, Vavachan's son, aside and asked him. The woman who had lived with Vavachan afterwards – Kuttan's mother – had passed away twenty years ago. They had had four children. The older two were also dead, leaving Kuttan and his sister. The women around the body were Kuttan's wife and distant relatives.

'Oh, that…' Kuttan said. 'You know how it is at the Kottayam Medical College wards. People come to gawk at the moustache. Even the student doctors were touching and stroking it. There's barely room to turn around, and what with all these gawkers … I got a pair of scissors and cut it off.'

'Is the funeral at the Mannanam church?'

Kuttan laughed. 'No, we converted back. Published in the gazette and all. Father has never been to church either.'

'Don't be fooled by the way he looks now. What a man he was!'

I heard someone in the crowd joke.

'Was that Moustache?' Ponnu asked as I started the bike.

'No. I was mistaken.'

'Oh … Magic?'

'Yes.'

The bike sped across the field. There are no more songs in these fields, no more stories in people's memories. Either everyone has forgotten them or they existed only in our collective imagination. The past itself is a creation. The bike picked up speed, sowing songs and stories into the fields on either side only to be forgotten again.

That night, I did not send Ponnu to bed early. Instead, we got on the bike and went to the temple of Muthan near the Vilakkumaram Lake.

At one time, it had been a field. One day, a Pulayan was hoeing the field when a person dressed in white clothes came up to him. The Pulayan did not recognise Muthan.

'I'd like some kanji water,' Muthan said.

'I don't have the time to fetch kanji water,' the Pulayan replied. 'I've got to hoe this field.'

But when the person repeated his request, the Pulayan set his hoe down, and went off and fetched some kanji water. Muthan drank it and left, satisfied. The Pulayan picked up his hoe to continue his work and saw, to his astonishment, that the entire field had been hoed neatly.

There was a 'Kolam' performance at Muthan's temple that night. Accompanied by drums, and in the light of burning torches, the Kolam danced on one leg. The other leg hung limp above the ground.

'What happened to his leg?' Ponnu asked.

I took him to the riverbank.

'In the old days, many boats used to go this way in the night. If someone was travelling alone, they would see a figure standing across the river, with one leg on each bank.

'Ho! So it must have been huge!'

'Yes. But it was harmless. When the boats neared it, it would lift one leg and let them pass. One day, Moustache came along this way. But the figure did not let him pass. He asked several times but it refused. So Moustache prayed to Muthan. Muthan was angry. He smacked the figure's leg with his broomstick, the handle of which was bound in silver. And its leg became limp and useless.'

'Is that the one who's dancing?'

'Yes, that's the one. So … what do you think of our Moustache?'

'Ho! Super!'

'No, yemenden!'

S. Hareesh is the author of two novels and three short-story collections. His novel *Meesha* won the Kerala Sahitya Akademi Award, the Vayalar Award and the Deshabhimani Award; and its English translation *Moustache* (translated by Jayasree Kalathil) won the 2020 JCB Prize for Literature. His short-story collections include *Adam*, for which received the Kerala Sahitya Akademi Award in 2016, *Rasavidyayude Charithram* and *Appan*. He is also a recipient of the Geetha Hiranyan Endowment, the Thomas Mundassery Prize and the V.P. Sivakumar Memorial Prize. Hareesh hails from Neendoor in Kottayam district, Kerala.

Jayasree Kalathil is the author of the children's book *The Sackclothman*, which has been translated into Malayalam, Telugu and Hindi. Her translations have won the JCB Prize for Literature (for S. Hareesh's *Moustache* in 2020), the Crossword Book Award (for N. Prabhakaran's *Diary of a Malayali Madman* in 2019), and the V. Abdulla Memorial Translation Award (for Sheela Tomy's *Valli* in 2023). *Valli* was also shortlisted for the 2023 National Book Award from the American Literary Translators Association, the 2022 JCB Prize for Literature, and the Atta Galatta–BLF Book Prize 2022. Jayasree lives in a small village in the New Forest, UK.

HARPERPERENNIAL

Harper Perennial presents special editions of its finest books in translation

Apradhini
Shivani
Translated from the Hindi by Ira Pande

Avasthe
U.R. Ananthamurthy
Translated from the Kannada by Narayan Hegde

Blue Is Like Blue
Vinod Kumar Shukla
Translated from the Hindi by Arvind Krishna Mehrotra and Sara Rai

Diary of a Malayali Madman
N. Prabhakaran
Translated from the Malayalam by Jayasree Kalathil

Farewell, Mahatma
Devibharathi
Translated from the Tamil by N. Kalyan Raman

The Golden Gandhi Statue from America
Subimal Misra
Translated from the Bengali by V. Ramaswamy

A Name for Every Leaf
Ashok Vajpeyi
Translated from the Hindi by Rahul Soni

Moustache
S. Hareesh
Translated from the Malayalam by Jayasree Kalathil

Seven Sixes Are Forty-Three
Kiran Nagarkar
Translated from the Marathi by Shubha Slee

Shameless
Taslima Nasreen
Translated from the Bengali by Arunava Sinha

HARPERPERENNIAL

Age of Frenzy
Mahabaleshwar Sail
Translated from the Konkani by Vidya Pai

A Life Incomplete
Nanak Singh
Translated from the Punjabi by Navdeep Suri

Mohanaswamy
Vasudhendra
Translated from the Kannada by Rashmi Terdal

The Music of Solitude
Krishna Sobti
Translated from the Hindi by Vasudha Dalmia

No Presents Please
Jayant Kaikini
Translated from the Kannada by Tejaswini Niranjana

A Preface to Man
Subhash Chandran
Translated from the Malayalam by Fathima E.V.

The Secret Garland
Andal
Translated from the Tamil by Archana Venkatesan

Shala
Milind Bokil
Translated from the Marathi by Vikrant Pande

The Weary Generations
Abdullah Hussein
Translated from the Urdu by the author

Written in Tears
Arupa Patangia Kalita
Translated from the Assamese by Ranjita Biswas

Bhima
M.T. Vasudevan Nair
Translated from the Malayalam by Gita Krishnankutty

Chemmeen
Thakazhi Sivasankara Pillai
Translated from the Malayalam by Anita Nair

Ghachar Ghochar
Vivek Shanbhag
Translated from the Kannada by Srinath Perur

Hindutva or Hind Swaraj
U.R. Ananthamurthy
Translated from the Kannada by Keerti Ramachandra and Vivek Shanbhag

The Liberation of Sita
Volga
Translated from the Telugu by T. Vijay Kumar and C. Vijayasree

A Life Misspent
Suryakant Tripathi Nirala
Translated from the Hindi by Satti Khanna

The Sea Lies Ahead
Intizar Husain
Translated from the Urdu by Rakhshanda Jalil

Selected Poems
Joy Goswami
Translated from the Bengali by Sampurna Chattarji

Wild Animals Prohibited
Subimal Misra
Translated from the Bengali by V. Ramaswamy

Wild Words
Malathi Maithri, Salma, Kutti Revathi and Sukirtharani
Translated from the Tamil by Lakshmi Holmström

HarperCollins *Publishers* India

At HarperCollins India, we believe in telling the best stories and finding the widest readership for our books in every format possible. We started publishing in 1992; a great deal has changed since then, but what has remained constant is the passion with which our authors write their books, the love with which readers receive them, and the sheer joy and excitement that we as publishers feel in being a part of the publishing process.

Over the years, we've had the pleasure of publishing some of the finest writing from the subcontinent and around the world, including several award-winning titles and some of the biggest bestsellers in India's publishing history. But nothing has meant more to us than the fact that millions of people have read the books we published, and that somewhere, a book of ours might have made a difference.

As we look to the future, we go back to that one word—a word which has been a driving force for us all these years.

Read.

Harper Collins

4th

HARPER PERENNIAL

HARPER BUSINESS

HARPER BLACK

हार्पर हिन्दी

HarperCollins *Children's Books*

HARPER DESIGN

HARPER VANTAGE

Harper Sport